A REQUIEM FOR FALLEN STARS

Cadence of the Fallen, Book One

Hazel S. Wilkes

A Requiem for Fallen Stars is a work of fiction. Names, places, and incidents either are products of the author's imagination or are used fictitiously. Any resemblance to actual events, locales, or persons, living or dead, is entirely coincidental.

For the hearts tucked away in the shadows—
The light is not lost, merely waiting.

GLOSSARY

Abdites (Ab-dye-ts): Corrupted wielders lost to the forbidden magics.

Adhara (Ahd-hara): Goddess of love and beauty.

Ahlai (Ah-lay): The Mother Goddess, mother to the Canamae.

Anatheima (An-nah-thee-mah): Capital city of Anatolé Kingdom.

Anatolé Kingdom (An-nah-tahl-lay): The Rising Sun Kingdom.

Algol (Al-goal): God of trickery and deception.

Astralis (Ah-straw-lis): God of the stars and heavens—god of justice.

Araceli (Air-rah-cell-ee): Goddess of health, fertility, and purity.

Ardoris Festival (Are-door-ris): Comet festival hosted yearly in the Anatolé Kingdom.

Bathara Academy (Bah-thaar-rah): Magical academy located in the borderless region—where wielders study to become Jurafen.

Cahlmon Orius (Kahl-mon Oh-rye-yus): Master at Bathara who teaches wielding techniques and magical theory.

Canamae (Con-uh-may): The primary gods, also known as the pillars of the mortal world.

Casimir Vivaldri (Cas-ih-meer Vih-val-dree): Son of the first-ever Rivarian King—the first Crown Prince of Rivara Kingdom.

Dyotana (Dye-oh-tan-nah): Small, translucent caterpillars that live in rock faces, composed of glowing blue bodies that appear almost crystal-like.

Draven (Dray-ven)

Endymion Mountains (En-dim-ee-uhn): Mountain range located in the northwestern region, composed of anthracite.

Erandor Kingdom (Air-en-dor): The Kingdom Between Rivers.

Gardner (Guard-ner): Said to be Ahlai's children, Gardners are similar to apothecaries, but are able to concoct more elaborate potions, tonics, and elixirs using methods only known to themselves.

Great Clamatè War (Claw-mah-tay): A great war that transpired at the dawn of the Three King System, involving gods and mortals alike.

House Dalmar (Dahl-mar): A Great House and Archblood—progenitor bloodline for dark magic.

House Fjolla (Fee-olla): A Great House and Archblood—progenitor bloodline for ice magic.

House Sulien (Suh-lee-in): A Great House and Archblood—progenitor bloodline for fire magic.

Illithious Lake (Ill-lith-ee-ous): A burning lake composed of flames.

Jurafen: (Jur-ah-fen): Physically fit, strategic, and possess high moral integrity, these are the wielding soldiers of Solaya who vow to protect society from threats of creatures, magic, and man alike—adhere to a strict ethical code and are bound to no king, answering only to the Tani.

Keziah (Keh-zee-ah): The capital city of the Rivara Kingdom.

King Alastair (Al-a-star): Presiding king over Rivara Kingdom.

King Erasmus (Ur-az-muhs): Presiding king over Erandor Kingdom.

King Yarum (Yah-rue-mm): Presiding king over Anatolé Kingdom.

Kiran (Keer-on)

Klytis Hilthrop (Kuh-lie-tis): Resident aether-wielder for King Alastair.

Laktî (lock-tee): Substance in a wielder's veins that allows them to harness the properties of magic.

Lyra Izacalli (Leer-rah Iz-uh-call-ee): Daughter of a Gardner, and night attendant for King Alastair.

Magaius (Mah-guy-is): Casimir Vivaldri's best friend, as noted in his journal, dating four-hundred and eleven years ago.

Meiji Himari (May - jee Hee-mah-ree): Healer.

Merikh (Mare-ick): God of death and ends; god of war.

Mirefiends (Meer-fee-nds): Tiny creatures located in the Bog.

Morwenna (More-wen-nah): Goddess of water, known Daughter of the Moon.

Raffir (Rah-fear): God of the harvest and prosperity.

Raima (Ray-muh): Village that House Sulien presides over.

Rivara Kingdom (Rih-var-rah): Kingdom Loved by the Gods.

Saffi (Sah-fee): Goddess of cunning and knowledge.

Solaya (Sol-aye-yah): Name of the continent that houses the Three Kingdoms—Rivara, Erandor, and Anatolé.

Tani (Tahn-nee): Highest order of magical governance. Their laws must be followed by all the Three Kingdoms, without question, as stated in the Accord of Three Kings.

Toellor (Toe-lore): Stone prison located within the Spicere Mountains where Abdites are contained.

Tuarana's River Lace (To-ah-rah-nah): A network of braided rivers located in the far northeastern corner of Solaya.

Turely Sea (Too-rel-ee): Northern sea that separates Solaya from the Silver Isle.

Tynan Dalmar (Tie-nen): Head of House Dalmar and also Supreme Commander over Erandor's formidable legion—known as the Master Strategist.

Wynn (Win): A wolf-like creature that cannot survive in sunlight, featuring exceptional strength, sharp eyesight, and superior speed and hearing. They feed off of forbidden magic.

PROLOGUE

The smell of burning flesh was impossible to ignore.

But worse than the fire, worse than the death, was the child's scream. She crumpled before the flames, knees slamming into the dirt as a wretched sob tore free from her throat. She beat the ground with her tiny fists, lost to a grief too vast for someone so small, too young to understand that loss does not listen, does not bargain.

After the man folded the scroll, he wanted to help the girl. He wanted to hold her, comfort her, soothe her—provide her any sort of protection from the guilt surrounding this horrendous fate. But the King would never allow it, and he would only make matters worse if he tried.

So he stood there silently and watched as the putrid, sickly sweet smell of burning skin wafted through the air. He listened to the hiccupped sobs and whispered apologies tumble from the girl's lips, feeling tormented by the scene blazing before his eyes, noting the strange contrast between the flames and the hazy twilight. He couldn't help but think something so beautiful should not accompany something so horrific.

Then again, the most horrifying things always wear the mask of something beautiful.

The King looked over at him, emotionless. "See to it the child gets taken back to my estate and placed with a ward. I have plans for the girl."

He dipped his chin. "Yes, Your Majesty."

The King kicked his heel into his horse's side, ready to ride back down the hill. Until, without warning, he stopped.

The sound of the child's desperate pleas crescendoed, her shrill voice cracking because her vocal cords were no longer able to withstand such violent abuse. The ground rumbled, and the air sharpened with an almost palpable electricity.

He studied the child before glancing at the King, catching the slight twitch of his brow. And so the man wondered...

Could it be that the warning the child's mother had given him all those years ago was true? Was this proof of what she claimed to have seen in the Veil? He hadn't believed her—not fully. Not because he thought her a liar, but because some things should be impossible.

But he knew impossible was a human word, and human words had no merit in the dealings of gods. Plus, he felt it. Felt the magic being pulled from his veins as easily as plucking a red spider lily from a field of white gardenias.

And so he knew.

Just as the girl's mother had warned, the Cycle had chosen.

And it had chosen her.

He had to act quickly if he wanted to prevent the child from revealing herself to the King. So, he made a decision that he would later scrutinize, questioning if he had made the right choice.

He reached down within himself, summoning the full weight of his magic before the King could become aware of what he had done. He sealed the girl's magic deep, deep within her, erasing any lingering traces of it from her veins. For she was young, and the magic was only just now awakening, and so the child could not know what power truly lurked beneath her skin.

It was a decision that had blessed him; it was a decision that would haunt him.

When he would later ask the child how she felt, she would tell him she felt inexplicably empty—like something was ripped from her, leaving her without some vital piece of herself.

He would never tell the child the feeling was not for the reasons she thought it was.

CHAPTER ONE

There are layers to winning, just as there are layers to losing, but one thing is always true—

Losing sucks.

Tonight, Eri observes me like a man who believes he's won. It's evident in the way he drags his eyes over my skin as I glide from table to table, pouring Rivara Kingdom's famed Sparkling Ecstasy into goblets.

My sheer golden pants sway with every step, and the braided metallic gold top hugging my chest leaves little to the imagination. Lilac hair cascades down my exposed back like a frosted river, thick braids woven between the strands. And of course, tonight's uniform would not be complete without the golden diadem adorned with a single, gleaming amethyst resting atop my head, catching the light as I work.

The King of Rivara says it pleases him to see the jewel that so closely resembles my eyes hovering just above my brow.

I fill the final goblet at my current table and work my way to the next. Eri tracks my movements, a smug expression glinting in his gaze.

Oh, he definitely thinks he's won.

He's certain when he approaches the king tonight, his request will be granted, and he'll be given exactly what he desires—a night with me, King Alastair's prized night attendant, adored by nobles and emissaries alike.

But what Eri doesn't know is I am the daughter of a Gardner, raised to understand the intricacies and power of every herb and plant known across the Three Kingdoms of Solaya—knowledge I have become quite adept at using to my advantage. For within these kingdoms, magic determines your value while blood determines your worth, and I have neither magic nor a reputable bloodline, so I must use every means at my disposal.

Because even though there are nights I don't mind my role—like when I stumble upon a partner who takes pleasure in giving, making the assignment almost enjoyable—there *are* other types. Those whose hunger burns differently. Who takes and devours without asking, claiming what they wish without a care in the world.

It is for those nights, and those partners, I have crafted a plan. One that relies on the herbs they so carelessly overlook. And if I am expected to entertain Eri tonight, it is a plan that will not only be useful but necessary.

Later, beneath a midnight sky shimmering with stars on the cusp of dawn, when Eri and I are locked inside the entertaining chamber the king relished in creating, I will propose a toast. And as Eri sips from his goblet, eager to slip into bed, he will also be ingesting the sleeping tonic I forged from the white soporis plant. Then, within a matter of minutes, Eri will be pleasantly unconscious, and all I'll have to do is wait a respectable amount of time before departing.

It is a plan that is as simple as it is effective, working not only for me, but for the other night attendants who, two years ago after I experienced a particularly dark night, received their own vials—each paired with a detailed anonymous note of instruction I spent hours poring over.

I finish my next table and glimpse Eri still leaning against a marble pillar, arms crossed over his chest, eyes still pinned on me. Though I know I shouldn't, I shoot him an ambiguous look. One that could be interpreted as either a look of desire or a look that politely screams *fuck off.*

Naturally, I mean the latter, but it appears Eri interpreted it as the former.

He pushes off the pillar and saunters toward me, hooking his arm around my waist and pulling me close. The smell of alcohol sits heavy on his breath.

I fight the urge to gag.

"I've been watching you all night," he purrs. "I can see why you are King Alastair's favorite toy."

Gods, I wish I didn't have to keep my tongue on such a tight leash. I've got an arsenal full of words I'd love to let roll from my tongue.

But I can't.

Eri is the right-hand general to the Supreme Commander over Erandor Kingdom's formidable forces. Which makes him someone I'd prefer not to trifle with. *Especially* not tonight.

For tonight, the Rivara Kingdom hosts the other two kingdoms within our realm, Erandor and Anatolé, as we celebrate The Founding: the day on which the Three Kingdoms were forged, carving new borders across Solaya, turning it from a unitary land ruled under one king into a harmonious Three King System, igniting the Era of Peace.

Hosted by a different kingdom each year to further broker political synergy, the King of Rivara has gone to great lengths to ensure everything is perfect for tonight's celebration. And unfortunately, I'd imagine gagging in Eri's face and turning him away in front of the other kings, their emissaries, generals, advisors, other courtiers, and all high-ranking nobles would *not* fall on the list of what he deems as acceptable behavior during such a prestigious event.

So, sometimes defiance lives in the subtleties.

"And we toys live to serve our masters," I croon, leaning away from him.

Okay, maybe my voice hadn't been as sickeningly sweet as I meant, sounding more like I swallowed bitter fruit than sweet nectar, but I doubt Eri will notice.

Eri's grip on me tightens. "Such sarcasm coming from such a pretty face is unbecoming of a servant."

Shit.

He noticed.

I guess I should have expected that. A person doesn't become the right-hand to the greatest strategist seen in centuries if they're a complete and total dimwit.

I wiggle free of his hold and dip my chin. "Apologies, my Lord."

He musses a hand through his neatly slicked-back hair, and a low hum rattles in his throat. Eri inclines his head at me, a serpent's smile curling on his lips. "You can make it up to me. I think providing me with a show should do."

A...*what?*

Feigning ignorance, I lower my eyes. "I'm sorry, my Lord, but I don't follow."

He frowns, studying me. "I suppose I shouldn't expect you to, seeing as you're just a whore and all." He curls two fingers into my thin top and tugs. "Entertain me. Entertain *us*. It is a very special celebration, after all. One worthy of your...services."

"Later," I begin. "When all hav—"

"—*Now*," he interrupts.

My heart picks up in my chest as anger floods my system. The truth of it is, the king already planned my role in the entertainment for tonight, but this vile, repulsive, *mouth-breathing—*

I clamp down on my thoughts, not allowing myself to walk down the shadowy road paved in anger and frustration.

I continue playing the role of ignorant servant instead. "Sorry?"

Eri pinches the bridge of his nose. "Really, we should cleanse the realm of such incompetence." He sighs, twirling an impatient hand. "Dance. Strip. Give us *something* worth watching."

I know I shouldn't deny his request outright. I know the punishment for offending a noble. But Eri's entitlement—his self-imposed right to *claim*—has me feeling uncharacteristically bold, and the words tumble from my mouth before I can think better of it. "Absolutely not."

His eyes flare with challenge, and he arches a brow. "Oh? You think you have a choice?" He traces a cold finger down my arm. "Let me spell this out for you: I make a request, and you grant it. That is the nature of the relationship between a Lord and a servant." He watches me closely for a reaction.

One I make sure not to give.

After a moment, he huffs an amused laugh and saunters over to a vacant seat. Eri neatly folds one leg over the knee of his other, and rests his hands in his lap. "Go on," he sings loud enough for all to hear. "*Dance.*"

The King of Rivara, Alastair, bellows his regal voice. "What is the meaning of this, Eri? Do you seek to torment my prized attendant?"

Eri rises and bows deeply at the waist. "Not in the slightest, Your Majesty. I just hoped, on this very special day, my fellow noblemen and I would experience some of the fabled entertainment we've heard so much about."

King Alastair wears a lazy grin as he rests his cheek on his fist. "And so you wish to see the girl dance?"

Eri's eyes darken as he smiles. "If His Majesty would allow."

The king laughs. "I do so love it when she does." He looks over to the King of Erandor, Erasmus, perched on a golden throne to his right, and then to the King of Anatolé, Yarum, who is slumped unenthusiastically in his throne to King Alastair's left. "What do my fellow kings think, hm?"

King Yarum speaks first. "I say do as you please, Alastair. It is your hall after all."

King Erasmus nods in agreement. "We are not so ill-mannered to refuse any treats your gracious kingdom may offer us."

King Alastair smiles with approval. "Very well, then." His eyes glide to mine as he commands, "Entertain us, girl."

The warning resting behind his gaze screams in the place of silence. *Do not embarrass me. If you do, I'll make you wish you hadn't.*

I have been defiled and belittled in many ways, but there is something about this particular moment that pricks my skin and causes me to boil deep in the pit of my stomach. The king has commanded it, and so now I have lost, and Eri has truly won.

And I am so *gods-damn* tired of losing.

Yet what can I do? After what happened with my mother, I am blood-sworn to the king, forced to serve him no matter how unnerved and tiny his demands make me feel. If I want to survive, I have no other choice but to obey.

No matter how much I want to rebel.

Words my mother once spoke to me echo through my bones. *They can take, and take, but the one thing they can never take from you is your reaction to things.*

I steel my features and force myself to swallow the stinging bitterness, accepting the cruel truth. Nothing will change this. No one is coming to my aid, and there is no room for negotiation.

Honestly, if it wasn't so demoralizing, I may have just laughed at the poetic irony of it all. For it always seems to come back to the eyes of men, expecting everything while offering nothing in return.

I glance at the king, clamping down on my jaw. His lips curl with a delighted grin as he waves a lazy hand at the instrumentalists, instructing them to resume playing. They obey, their fingers plucking their harmonic strings, filling the air with a haunting rhythm, cementing my damnation in a deceptive mask of beauty.

I resign myself to my fate and let muscle memory take over, my hips swaying as my arms move in tune to the music. As I begin to dance, I glimpse the many heavy-lidded, drunken eyes—hungry and ready to devour.

Fighting a disgusted sneer, I reach back and fiddle with the clasp of my top. Yet right as my breasts threaten exposure, a loud crack splits the air, and a cloud of total darkness clots at the glass roof. Around the banquet tables, goblets tumble, spilling liquids across the floor and in laps. All the braziers, lanterns, and candles are snuffed out, leaving the now-dark room covered in a blanket of silence.

And that sound...

The strange darkness...

It's the result of someone's magic, and unauthorized magic in the Great Hall, *especially* while the king is hosting, is an offense worthy of death. Who would be so bold not only to commit such an outrageous act in the presence of the king, but in the presence of all *three* kings.

And why?

King Alastair's voice booms, anger lacing through his words. "Terian, dispel this magic at once. Fire-wielders, reignite the braziers and the candles."

Light slowly returns to the room as Terian works, and the braziers flicker back into existence. Leaning against a pillar and flicking a finger in the direction of the oil lamps—tiny fires awakening within the glass when he does—stands a man with ruby-red hair. I catch his eye, and his head cocks ever-so-slightly to the side, an inscrutable smile tugging at the corner of his lips.

My brows twitch as I study the man. I've never entertained him, nor do I recognize him, so why is he looking at me like that? Not with lust or desire, but...intrigue, perhaps?

I follow his wandering gaze to the exposed midnight sky above, the inky cloud now receded into nothing more than a ghostly vapor. As I stare, I feel a gentle touch glide down my cheek, lingering no more than a second or two.

Normally, I would jump at the unexpected touch. Yet, for some reason, there is something disarming about it. Confused, I glance around the room, noting those within stepping distance. Finding nothing unusual, my eyes return to the pillar where the red-headed man stood, but he is already gone.

Interesting.

After a few seconds, the darkness vanishes completely, and an errand boy runs in. He takes a winded bow.

"Your Majesty."

"What is it?" King Alastair's voice is anything but patient.

"It is the stables, sir. We think an oil lamp was accidentally knocked over. They are..." He gulps. "Well, the stables are on fire."

King Alastair's stony expression is as unnerving as it is unreadable. "Then take all those in the hall who wield water magic and be done with it."

The errand boy nods before bowing. "Yes, Your Majesty." He makes for the exit.

"And boy," The King calls out, his tone wrapped in ice.

The boy stiffens before turning and again bowing at the waist. "Your Majesty?"

"Tell the stablemaster to expect a summons from me later."

The words deflate my heart and heat my blood simultaneously. I clench my teeth and ball my hands tightly, reminding myself again and again I can not speak out of turn.

I am all too aware of what a summons from the king means, and the stablemaster is a kind man who truly loves the horses he cares for. He will not deserve whatever cruel punishment the king will bestow upon him for this interruption.

The boy inclines his head, acknowledging King Alastair's request, and shuffles out of the hall with the grumbling water-wielders.

Eri returns his attention to me. "Well? What are you waiting for? Don't just stand there. Dance for us as your king commanded."

I open my mouth to speak, but King Yarum's voice fills the room, his Anatolian accent heavy on his tongue. "I extend my apologies, Lieutenant Commander Valenwood, but I've decided I want the girl to attend to only me for the rest of the evening." He turns to the King of Rivara. "Would you deny me that privilege, Alastair?"

King Alastair snorts a dry laugh. "I certainly would not." He pauses, a wry smirk twisting his features. "Though I must admit, I find myself surprised by your request. You aren't usually one to indulge in such things."

King Yarum huffs a hollow laugh, and he musters a smile I notice does not reach his eyes. "Consider me particularly captivated by your attendant."

King Alastair smiles, pleased. "Most are."

Ignoring him, the King of Anatolé directs his attention to me. "Come here, girl. I should like you by my side for the rest of the evening."

Slightly baffled but unwilling to waste the chance to escape Eri, I shoot him a pointed look then race up the dais as gracefully as possible. I stand just behind King Yarum's throne, stepping beside him when he motions for me.

When he looks at me, I'm stunned by how crystal-clear the green of his eyes is—sharp and vivid like a tourmaline stone, framed by soft smile lines. His golden-brown skin is kissed by the sun, and his dark hair is a mess of curls. There's a warmth about him. An inviting quality.

King Yarum studies me for a long moment, something unreadable passing through his eyes. Eventually, he reverts his attention to the ongoing celebration, holding out his goblet when it needs refilling. I grab the pitcher of Sparkling Ecstasy from the small gilded table and carefully pour it into his cup, clutching it to my chest, stepping back into the shadows after, hoping to remain invisible for the rest of the party.

As the guests grow drunker and their actions bolder, I let myself drift, slipping further from the noise, shutting out the debauchery around me.

Yet something lingers deep in my bones—an intuition I'm unable to place.

The feeling stays with me for the rest of the night.

CHAPTER TWO

Alone in my bedchamber after one of the king's parties…
Now, *that* is a gift.
And a rare one.

As his prized attendant, I am expected to entertain his guests for the *whole* night. He made that crystal clear four years ago when I turned seventeen and was formally transferred from the kitchens, forced into the role of night attendant—his version of poetic justice.

Though, I personally would label it as sadism.

I fall back onto my thin bed, spreading my arms out like a raven in flight. The mattress has little give, and the wooden bed frame creaks as the weight of my body falls against it. I blow air from my lips, puffing out my cheeks, and I replay the night's events in my mind.

Eri is self-righteous and entitled like many others I've served before, so I simply write him and his actions off, not deigning to give him further thought.

He isn't worth my energy.

And the dark cloud of magic was an interesting turn of events, leaving me to wonder if the display was some unspoken political commentary, or a cryptic statement directed at one of the three kings. Outbursts are rare, yes, but they do still happen. And if one was attempting to make a statement, The Founding celebration would certainly be the perfect place to do so.

Then, there is King Yarum Calliva of the Anatolé Kingdom.

Throughout the night, there had been something largely unspoken in his gaze. I could see it when I caught him glancing at me sidelong. Yet when the celebration ended and King Yarum made for his chambers—me trailing behind, expecting to fulfill my duties—he simply cupped my hand and softly instructed, "Go and get some rest. I no longer need your services."

And that had been that.

I have spent many years learning to recognize what lies behind a person's gaze. Humans are capable of great deception, but the eyes almost always betray the truth. Most of the time, motivations, actions—they are tied to a specific agenda. Sex, political advancement, favor with the king—there always seems to be something.

But with King Yarum?

I haven't the slightest clue what he was after. Why he helped me, only to dismiss me by the end of the party.

Even stranger yet, I couldn't help but notice the way King Erasmus and King Alastair sauntered off in the direction of King Alastair's council chamber once the festivities were trickling to an end, leaving King Yarum behind. Though, he seemed completely content to be without an invitation to whatever activities their after-party entailed.

Still...

Odd. It was all so odd.

A familiar rhythmic knock sounds from the other side of my chamber's door, putting an end to my contemplations.

The first true smile I've worn in hours appears on my face. "It's unlocked," I say to the door.

The all but rotted wood creaks open, and Gray walks in, looking regal and handsome.

I remove the woven diadem from my head and place it on the small table next to my bed. "Hi, Gray."

He latches the door behind him before sitting next to me on the bed. Gray sighs. "My father told me what happened in the hall. Are you okay? I heard things were...not great tonight."

I muster a weak smile. "I'm fine. It wasn't anything I'm not used to." I start unraveling the half-braid stretching across the crown of my head.

13

"The unauthorized magic certainly made for an interesting spectacle."

He chuckles, shaking his head. "Leave it to you to find such a thing amusing."

My fingers tug at the lilac strands until they are unbound and falling freely. "Well, what else would it be?"

"Oh, I don't know." He makes a show of thinking. "Alarming? Worrisome? A bad omen?"

I snort a laugh. "A bad omen? Really? And when is it you became so superstitious?"

He pouts his lip. "You wound me, Lyra. I have always been a man of the gods."

"Of course you have," I say through mocking laughter while tugging my sad excuse for a shirt up.

"Here," Gray says, leaning over and unlatching his satchel. "I brought you my most comfortable tunic." He pulls out the cream-colored shirt featuring baggy sleeves and a tie closure, placing it in my hands.

I squeeze the soft fabric, glancing down at it. "A true man of the gods after all."

Gray Nightenjoy.

Though not in blood, he is the closest thing to family I have. We first met one night when I was six. I was out far too late playing in the gardens, and while navigating the dimly lit halls, trying to return to my chambers, I somehow got turned around—finding myself in Gray's instead.

"Who are you?" he had asked me in his tiny six-year-old voice.

"I'm Lyra. Lyra Izacalli," I had answered. "Who are you?"

Through the dark, I heard a clanging sound as something metal was set down.

"I am Gray Nightenjoy," he replied, his voice softening. "Why are you in my family's chambers, Lyra Izacalli?"

It still makes me laugh when I think of the defensiveness in my voice when I replied, "*Your* family? These chambers belong to my mother and me. I should ask why you're here."

"Afraid not," Gray had said. There were padded footsteps as he walked over to an oil lantern and lit it, revealing the wing's standard living room—

same layout, same tiny kitchen, but completely different furnishings.

I remember swallowing hard when I saw a metal candlestick resting on their wooden table—Gray's weapon of choice.

The rest was history.

Gray and I became inseparable. It was a convenience that our mothers were both Gardners and were also already friendly with each other. They adored our budding friendship, and I can still recall many evenings where we would sit around a burning hearth together, my mom and Gray's parents enjoying a nice wine while Gray and I sucked on sweet fruit, giggling obnoxiously and wrestling on his family's rug.

I have many sleepless nights where I long to return to those evenings. Us all together, smiling and laughing without a care in the world. But my mother has since passed on to the Hanging Gardens—the paradise all Gardner's ascend to once life has fled their bodies—making my desire nothing more than a baseless dream woven from untieable threads.

When King Alastair demanded I be placed with a ward, Gray's family insisted it be them. They argued they were the most fitting choice, seeing as I was already familiar with them, and Gray's father had just become the king's closest advisor. From what I was told, the king reluctantly agreed, but he agreed nonetheless.

The Nightenjoys spent the next six years raising me as their own. Providing me food, giving me shelter, an education, and a proper upbringing—despite the tasks I was made to complete after my mother's passing being anything but proper. But when I turned seventeen and began to officially work as a night attendant, the king forced me out of their care, demanding I take residence in the crumbling, all-but-abandoned wing of his estate.

And it's been that way ever since.

I stand up, the tunic nestled tightly in my grip, and shuffle to the back of the room. "How did training go today?" I ask Gray as I remove the gods-awful top from my chest.

"It went...as expected."

My brows furrow at the odd note in his tone, and I steal a quick glance at him before stripping off my pants and tugging the oversized tunic over my head. The smell of cedarwood and amber wraps me in a familiar hug, its calming effect immediate.

I return to the edge of the bed, plopping myself down and folding my legs comfortably. "Why'd you say it like that?"

"Like what?"

I arch a brow and cross my arms over my chest.

Gray sighs—long and deep—and runs a hand through his brown hair, the waves flowing down his neck, grazing his shoulders. "Well, my instructor decided something today."

"Oh? Do tell."

He fidgets with his fingers, and my heart suddenly finds itself skipping at strange rhythms. "He decided that, given the way my magic has developed and progressed over this past year, I am the kind of wielder Bathara Academy looks for. He said as much to my father and my mother as well, and..." Gray exhales loudly through his nose. "Well, I am to participate in this year's entrance exam into Bathara."

I blink, equal parts stunned and overjoyed for him. "What? Gray, that's...that's amazing! And a huge compliment. Are you excited? What do you thin—"

My sentence falls short when I glimpse the grim expression lining Gray's face—notice the tension stiffening his posture.

I tug at my brows. "Why don't you look happy about this?" I drop my head to catch his lowered eyes. "If you pass the exam and gain admittance into Bathara, you get to become a Jurafen, Gray. A gods-damn Jurafen. You'll be granted respect, honor, status, comfortable wages—be celebrated as a hero. You'll get to have full control over your life." I swallow against the cruel tinge of envy the sentence makes me feel.

"I know," Gray murmurs. "It's a privilege to have someone think I'm capable of such an honor, but..." He finally lifts his eyes to me, and his expression looks pained. "I have to leave Keziah, Lyra. I have to leave *you.*"

Though I'd be lying if I said the thought didn't split my heart in two, I still manage a smile and put on a brave face. "We have time. We'll just have to make the most of—"

"—I leave in two days," Gray interrupts, his words tumbling from his mouth like they don't belong on his tongue.

"Oh," is all I can seem to find for a reply.

Gray blows out another loud sigh and drops his head into his hands. I shimmy across the bed, closing the distance between us, and I place a comforting hand on his back, rubbing in soothing circles. "I wasn't expecting to lose you so soon, but there's nothing to be done about it. This is a good thing—a good opportunity."

Without lifting his head, he mutters in a low tone, "I can't leave you."

"You must."

He finally lifts his head, only to prop his chin on his fists instead, staring off toward the other side of the room. "I can't. It'll feel like I'm leaving half my heart behind. For fifteen years, we've been at each other's side."

"I know," I mumble, well aware of how lonely—how lost—I'll feel once Gray is gone. "And believe me when I say my heart will never be whole in a life where I can't knock on your door because I finally remembered to return your shirt."

He lets out a small laugh, and my heart is happy at the sight.

"But you and I both know you can't pass up this opportunity. Plus, the realm deserves to have someone like Gray Nightenjoy protecting them." I lift my hand from his back, choosing to instead let my head fall to rest on his broad shoulder.

"How will I know you're okay? That you aren't hurt or worse..." Gray's eyes darken as he silently considers the risks of my position. "Since you possess no magic, the Ever-Know Quill isn't an option."

I intertwine my fingers through his. "Then I shall write you letters the magic-less way."

Our fingers still clasped together, Gray guides my hand to his lips and presses a kiss softly against the back of it. "Two days," he muses in a soft voice.

"Two days," I repeat through a small smile.

"What should we do with them?"

I think for a moment. "What we've always done," I finally answer. "Spend them at each other's side."

CHAPTER THREE

The following morning, I crack my swollen eyes open and find Gray—his hair a disheveled mess, an arm draped over his face—sound asleep next to me.

His mouth hangs slightly ajar, and it's comical how perfectly content and cozy he looks, even in sleep. I chuckle quietly to myself and shimmy back down under the covers. As my eyes fall shut once more, however, a hollowed out hole awakens, gnawing at the center of my heart.

There will be no more nights where Gray stays with me, making sure the night terrors keep away. No more mornings where I wake up and look over, immediately comforted by the sight of him. No more late night conversations, morning strolls, afternoon adventures—nothing.

It'll soon all disappear.

I don't let myself fully acknowledge the gravity of that. Instead, I drift back to sleep, entering a landscape where broken hearts disappear and dreams come true.

By the time my eyes flutter open again, Gray has disappeared, and there is a note where his body had once rested.

Helping my mother. Feel free to join us when you wake. We could use your unrivaled abilities.

Actually, a morning spent helping Gray's mother with her work sounds exactly like the type of thing I need.

I crawl out of bed, tend to my morning hygiene, get dressed, and head to Gray's family chambers. I knock twice at their door before creaking it open. Immediately, the fragrance of aromatic herbs and earthy warmth, paired with the faint tang of something bitter, wafts into the corridor, overtaking the air.

Gray has something green smudged on his forehead, his hair tied back neatly, and a stone pestle in his hand. Azalea, Gray's mother, works on something next to him, her graying hair pulled back into a braid that falls over her shoulder while she works.

Spotting me first, Azalea stops what she's doing and shifts her attention onto me, a kind smile pulling at her lips. "Oh, Lyra. I'm so happy you're here. You're a much better assistant than Gray."

Gray glances over at me, a wrinkle in his brow, before back at his mom. Succumbing to the undeniable truth, he simply sighs before returning to grinding whatever is in his mortar. "At least I try."

Azalea kisses his cheek. "And that's all a mother could ever ask of her son." She dusts her hands off on the hem of her dress before reaching into a cabinet and pulling out the heavy cloth apron that once belonged to my mother. She holds it out for me.

I meet her in the center of the kitchen, take the apron, and sling it over my head, tying the ends together. "So, what are we making?"

Gray shoots me a pleading look. "An aphrodisiac."

My brows rise to my hairline. Keeping my voice intentionally level, I chirp, "Oh? And who requested it this time?"

I despise the way my stomach somersaults with uncertainty. The way I'm forced to wonder if someone will try to use the aphrodisiac on me. I resent myself. I resent the king.

"A lady-in-waiting," Azalea answers while measuring out a spoonful of thick, sticky liquid. "She claims it's for her aging husband, but I heard a rumor she wishes to use it to seduce a rather handsome noble."

Relief washing through me, I chuckle. "I wouldn't be surprised. This world isn't kind to those of us who are untitled, and women will go to extreme measures to ensnare a noble in their webs."

Without looking at me, Azalea chides, "Who knows. One cannot pretend to understand a stranger's motivations." She shoots me a very pointed look.

Message received.

I should know better than to prematurely judge people and their actions—no matter how transparent they may seem.

I begin helping Azalea with her tincture when Gray blows out a breath. "The Damiana's officially all grounded. Should I fetch the divine water?"

"Please," Azalea answers. "I have fresh jars back there in the corner." She jerks her chin to the other side of the room, near the large bookcase adjacent to the hearth. Once Gray is out of earshot, Azalea drops her voice and glances over at me. "I suppose Gray told you his news."

"He did."

Azalea studies me before returning to her work. "It will be hard on him—saying goodbye to you. He cares for you deeply."

"I know," I murmur. "But like I told him last night, he must go."

She glances over her shoulder at Gray, and I follow her lead, watching him rummage around for the jars.

Though his brown hair is the same lightened shade Azalea's had once been, Gray is the spitting image of his father. He has the same tall build with the same broad shoulders, the same sharp jaw, and even a similarly sloped nose. His eyes are painted with the same colors as his fathers, too—like moss and gold, a flare of burnt copper weaving through the cracks. Gray also possesses his father's mind—incisive and filled with a shrewd intellect—and they both share a similar love for the history of our lands.

But it is Azalea's kind heart that beats in Gray's chest. Her warm smile that tugs at the corners of his lips. He effortlessly displays her unyielding patience, and he carries her love for music within him. I remember the day he told her he wanted to learn the double-flute—she was over the moon, telling anyone who would listen.

When I return my focus, I find Azalea's perceptive gaze on me. She arches a brow, silently beckoning me to speak.

I stare at the Gardner supplies, tracing a discarded woody stem. "I'm going to miss him, Azalea." My brows crinkle with thought. "I'm trying to be strong for him, pretending like everything will be okay—like *I* will be okay. But if I'm being honest..." I look up and meet Azalea's soft eyes, dropping my voice. "I'm not sure I will be. He's been there for all my hardest days, all my darkest nightmares—made me smile even on days I didn't think it possible." I pause, a weight pushing against my chest. "How does someone willingly say goodbye to a person like that?"

Azalea studies me for a long moment, something soft passing through her expression, and pulls me into her arms, kissing the top of my head.

She squeezes tightly.

When she releases me, I'm surprised to find her eyes glassy and swelling with unfallen tears. "You are so much like your mother."

My heart squeezes, and for a moment, I wonder if anyone's heart has ever exploded from feeling too many things at once before—especially while trying to avoid feeling anything at all.

She holds my eyes. "The words most worth saying are often the hardest to speak. But I have no doubt you'll find the courage to say them. At least some day."

I tug my brows together, catching an underlying implication in her tone, when Gray returns, a jar of divine water in hand.

He holds it up with a smile. "Got it."

Azalea watches me a second longer, her expression both tender and stern—a strange combination she's mastered. "Excellent," she chirps. "Set it on the counter there, and I'll finish up the tincture after a much needed rest."

Gray does as instructed.

I remove my apron, folding it with great care, and return it to its place in the cabinet. "I have to go, too. The king is hosting tonight, and I need to get ready." I scoff a sardonic laugh. "You should see the outfit he's picked out for me. It's ridiculous."

Gray tilts his head, frowning. "How much longer do you think you'll be a night attendant?"

I shrug. "Who knows. Night attendants are different from courtesans because we are in direct service to the king, so it's not like we can get bought out or anything." For the first time in quite some time—

because I find pondering this question only leads to preventable anguish and rage—I consider what Gray's asked. "I suppose I'll never be released from the king's service. He'll probably force me to fulfill my duties until my body withers, and my face is no longer desirable."

Gray's lips twitch with the makings of a sad smile. "That could never happen. Your face is too remarkable to be considered anything else."

My answering smile is soft.

His face scrunches with continued thought. "There has to be something that can be done."

How do I gently shatter his optimism and inform him there isn't? I can't just outright tell him, because that would involve explaining to him that my role, my at times demoralizing duties as a night attendant, are meant to serve as punishment. Meant to keep me from forgetting what transpired that night.

As if I could ever forget.

"It is what it is," I murmur instead, unable to meet Gray's eyes.

"It's not right. You basically have no freedom serving the king, and that's not the way it should be."

"Yet, it is the way it is."

"But it shouldn't have to be. Shouldn't—"

"—Gray." I cut him off, unable to hear anymore. "Drop it. Please."

His face falls, his wary eyes heavy with sadness. "I worry about you, Lyra. Especially now that I won't be around anymore."

My voice is more bitter than I mean it to be. But sometimes, when a wound is opened, whether intentionally or not, one must be prepared to face what leaks out. "And what does your presence change about my situation?"

Gray openly winces. "Lyra, come on. That's not fair."

I make for the door. "I need to get ready."

※≈ ≈※

My night in the Great Hall is a simple one.

Tonight, the king entertains a few traveling merchants, emissaries from Erandor Kingdom, and even some instructors from Bathara. I listen carefully as they discuss some of the young nobles rumored to be taking the upcoming entrance exams. My ears prick when I hear them mention Gray.

"I hear Sterling Nightenjoy's son is planning to take the exam," an older man with salt-and-pepper hair and a face full of stubble says to the group seated at his table.

"It's remarkable their bloodline hasn't yet been given the rank of nobility," a woman with disheveled silver hair replies. "Aside from Sterling being the king's most trusted advisor, the Nightenjoy line seems to be one of the select few bloodlines capable of producing powerful wielders with different magic types. Sterling is a Sealer, and I hear his boy wields illusionary magic. Extremely rare to see such a magical heritage in one line."

A man shoving drink down his throat halts only to respond, "I heard the king already offered Sterling noble rank—*twice*—but he refused the title."

"*Refused?*" the salt-and-pepper-haired man spits. "How does someone refuse a king? Not only that, but *why* would someone refuse the title of nobility?"

A man with long, curly white hair leisurely shrugs. "People have their reasons, Cahlmon."

I suppress the urge to interject myself into their conversation. It heats my blood listening to them discuss Sterling like gossiping girls.

Despite my annoyance, however, I do understand the root of their curiosity; the Nightenjoy bloodline *is* well-known throughout the Three Kingdoms. As a bloodline almost as old as the Sulien or Fjolla line—two of the remaining progenitor bloodlines for magic, known as the Archbloods—the Nightenjoy line has garnered the respect of many for both their enviable range of magic-types and their unrelenting virtue. To any inquiring minds, I suppose it truly is a wonder why they remain untitled.

He refused to receive the gift.

I wonder if that's true...

If it is, I also can't help but wonder why he would do such a thing.

Sterling is a man who possesses considerable foresight and bases his decisions on what he deems the most desirable outcome. So...

What benefit has he gleaned from remaining untitled that everyone else has missed?

The night ends in the monotonous drone of standard festivities one might expect from the King of Rivara, and I escort my assignment out of the hall once all is said and done. I guide her to the entertaining chamber, and I immediately pour us a "celebratory" drink, not wanting to bother with conversation or idle petting tonight.

I'm simply not in the mood—a weighted ball still sitting heavy in my stomach from my conversation with Gray.

Within a few minutes, the woman is passed out on the sheets, and I am counting down the seconds until I can exit the chamber without it being considered suspicious. I don't even reach for one of the books I have hidden under the bed, feeling too out-of-it to find my freedom in a page.

When enough time has passed, I take my leave and find myself wandering outside, strolling the grounds until I reach my favorite building. It is smaller compared to the others, but the craftsmanship is masterful—the three marble pillars at the front carved in stunning detail. Along the backside, a flimsy rope ladder hidden behind overgrown shrubbery extends from the roof down to my feet. I climb the rungs to the top, crawling up onto the flat surface.

At the roof's center, patiently awaiting my return, is a pallet of different fraying blankets and an oil lantern. Normally, I'd make straight for the set up and settle myself comfortably. But tonight, I'm not in the mood to just lay down and stare up at the sky.

So, I instead walk to the edge of the roof, propping myself up on the thin marble railing, and relish in the tiny current of electricity coursing under my skin as my feet dangle above the ground. I stare out at the picturesque scene, moved by how strikingly beautiful Rivara Kingdom's capital city, Keziah, is at night.

Channels of crystal water run through the city, flowing in through aqueducts from the westward Halmion Ocean. Buildings artfully erected from marble scatter along the edges of the channels, their ornate roofs painted in a beautiful sky-blue to complement the translucent waters. The city is softened by a warm, golden glow, and above the glowing town rests a cluster of sandy-like stars composed of purples, whites, and blues, streaking the sky in dazzling rods of light.

Of the three kingdoms, the Rivara Kingdom is the smallest, yet it is regarded as the Kingdom Loved by the Gods. There are many stories of love and war, of betrayal and heartbreak, that circulate the myth and lore of Solaya—many of which directly involve the gods and take place within our borders. Yet I believe the natural phenomena that grace our skies is what truly earned the Rivara Kingdom its title. We have the colored stars, the Great River of Light, and the unyielding silver moon which sometimes kisses our land, draping the world in a kaleidoscope of water-like shadows.

There is such astounding beauty within these borders—sights I used to love and cherish, eagerly begging my mother to go outside and observe.

But now when I sit and stare out at these lands, at displays that once fueled the hopeful flutters of a tiny, unblemished heart, I am simply reminded that no matter how lovely the cage is made to be, it is still a cage, and without freedom of choice, I will never be able to truly relish in this kingdom's beauty again.

I exhale a long sigh as I glide a hand down my face and stare out at the haze of purple streaking across the sky.

A voice sounds from behind me. "I thought I'd find you here."

A small wave of relief washes through me, even if I refuse to show it.

Without so much as glancing over my shoulder, I mutter, "It's the middle of the night. You should be in bed. "

I hear him snort a laugh. "And are you my mother now?" Gray positions himself next to me on the roof's edge and nudges his shoulder into mine. "I went to your chambers to bring you a shirt since you mentioned your outfit for tonight was ridiculous. I waited and waited, and when you never came..." He huffs a tiny breath and rubs at the back of his neck. "Well, after the initial worry went away, I realized you were probably out here."

"You found me," I murmur in a dry voice.

Through the sides of my eyes, I see Gray's brows lower. He watches me for a moment before adding, "I also went to your chamber to apologize, Lyra."

I glance at him sidelong, and the softness resting within his eyes, the sincere apology overflowing in his expression...

I sigh, conceding my silly anger. "You don't need to apologize. I know you were coming from a good place. Really, I should be apologizing. I shouldn't have snapped at you like I did—you didn't deserve it."

Gray lowers his head to catch my eyes. When I refuse to look at him, he lightly grips the bottom of my chin with his thumb and index finger, and he lifts my gaze to his. His expression is steady as he softly says, "You never need to apologize for responding to how I made you feel. Your feelings matter more to me than my pride, Lyra."

Unable to string a sentence, I swallow back the lump in my throat and nod.

"Now," he begins, his tone considerably lighter. "I hope you don't have any plans tomorrow, because if you do, I'll have to kidnap you, and I'm not keen on learning what the dungeons are like right before I leave for Bathara."

I open my mouth to reply, but before I can get a word out, Gray lifts a finger and adds, "And before you say you have to entertain, I checked with my father, and he said the king is not hosting tomorrow, so you should be free."

I arch a brow at him, the smile pulling at my lips as helpless as it is amused. "And if I object?"

Gray mocks an indifferent shrug. "Then it looks like I'll become quite familiar with the dungeons."

I scoff a laugh. "I'll be sure to visit during your incarceration."

He leans toward me, a new light burning behind his eyes. "And *I'll* be sure to pick you up from your chambers at sunrise."

CHAPTER FOUR

True to his word, Gray lets himself into my room and yanks the covers off me at first light.

I string together a creative line of unkind words and throw a pillow at him. Ultimately, however, I peel myself out of bed, attend to my needs, and dress myself. By the time I'm finished—now dressed in a thinly woven sweater and breeches, since the Rivara Kingdom currently sits in the in-between of summer and autumn—I'm fully ready for whatever it is Gray has planned.

Wearing a sand-colored tunic paired with a brown vest, gold stitching weaving down the center along the seams, Gray's brown hair is half-drawn, and he has his leather satchel strapped across his chest. He pushes off the wall outside my chamber and flashes me a grin, extending his hand, offering me a pewter cup. "For you."

The aromatic smell of citrus and cinnamon fills the air, and I immediately recognize the sweet scent as I inhale the steam.

It's my favorite tea.

My tongue salivates. "Thank you." I take the cup from his hand and blow on the scalding liquid. "So what is it you have planned for us today?"

"Oh," he lilts through a smile. "You'll find out soon enough."

I arch a brow at him as I sip on the tea.

He just smiles wider in response.

"Can I at least get a hint?"

Gray cocks his head, thinking. "Alright," he says after a moment.

"We'll need to pay a visit to the stables first."

My eyes narrow on him. "The stables? So we need horses?"

His growing smirk is his only answer.

I'm about to point out that we're not supposed to just take the horses when a memory strikes me.

Tell the stablemaster to expect a summons from me later.

I shove my cup back in Gray's hands. "Give me two more minutes."

When those minutes pass and I return from rummaging around in my room, Gray watches me with an inquisitive expression pinching his face.

He lifts a brow. "Do I even want to ask?"

I adjust the pack on my back, looking through it a final time, making sure I have everything. "You'll find out soon enough," I mutter, trailing behind Gray as we walk down the corridor.

⁂

We reach the stables, and I see the errand boy that ran in during The Founding mucking out a stall near the front.

"Hi, Thestis." Gray walks over to the stall the boy is working on and rests his hands and chin atop the thick wooden planks. "How's your training going?"

The boy halts mid scoop and slowly swivels his head in Gray's direction. His eyes brighten with excitement, and he drops the shovel as he scurries over toward Gray, propping himself atop a hay bale to be at eye level. "Is it true you're going to be a Jurafen?" He asks, his voice rattling with awe.

Gray chuckles. "It is true I'm going to try."

The boy's eyes grow round as the moon. "Wow," he breathes. "That is so cool."

Gray lifts his chin from the stalls and ruffles the boy's hair. "If you keep your training up, you might become a Jurafen someday, too."

Two expressions pass simultaneously across the boy's face. The first is one of dreams and hope, but then the second expression washes over his features like a tidal wave sweeping loose sand from a shore. His face

28

falls, and he pouts his lip. "My 'Ma told me I shouldn't hold on to such silly hopes. She said everyone knows only nobles or those from exceptional bloodlines like yours get to become Jurafen. No one like me has ever become a Jurafen before." He pauses, pulling a lone straw of hay from the bale. The boy—Thestis, Gray had called him—grumbles, "She thinks it's nice you train me in your free time, but she also thinks it's a waste of time."

Gray trains him?

I didn't even know that. Though, it at least explains how he seems to know the boy so intimately.

Gray's eyes soften. With his hand still resting atop the boy's head, he replies, "Do you know the tale of the first Rivarian King, Isaphus?"

Eyes now glued to the ground, the boy nods.

Gray's smile is kind. "Good," he says. "Then it will come as no shock to you when I say Isaphus was nothing special. He was not a noble. He did not hail from any exceptional bloodlines. He was just a simple man who was good and true, who worked hard to provide for his people."

"What's your point?" Thestis mutters.

Gray tilts the boy's head back, forcing him to meet his eyes. "My point," he muses with a gentle yet sturdy tone—one that reminds me of Azalea, "is that if Isaphus told people when he was your age he would become the first king of a newly founded kingdom, people would have laughed at him and told him there was no chance in..." Gray glances left then right, lowering his voice to a dramatic whisper. "*Hell.*"

The boy snickers, and Gray smiles.

"Though what your mother says is true about the current state of Jurafen, that is not to say you couldn't be the first to break the mold. The exams are open to everyone for a reason. And if you work hard, Thestis, I am confident you can be whatever you want to be in this world."

The boy flicks his eyes at me, and I have to force a smile to my lips.

The truth is, I can't in good conscience say I buy into what Gray is saying—even though I know he truly believes it. But I fear I am too jaded to believe in fairytales and happy endings.

The stablemaster appears from the back of the stables, limping over to us. "Well, what a pleasant sight for these old eyes." His stark-white hair is half-drawn, and his bushy white eyebrows are as overgrown as ever.

I eye his movements closely and, just as I anticipated, they are incredibly stiff and rigid.

The stablemaster, Delroy, addresses the boy. "Thestis, why don't you take that bucket there and fetch the horses some fresh drinking water."

Thestis jumps down from the hay bale, scuttling over to the bucket. "Yessir." He pauses, glancing over his shoulder at Gray. "Thank you," he murmurs.

Gray dips his chin at Thestis, his eyes warm and kind, and then Thestis scurries out of the stables to fetch water, leaving just Delroy, Gray, and myself.

"The stables seem to be in excellent condition considering there was a fire only a few days ago," I observe with a mild tone.

Delroy grunts his agreement. "It would seem hay bales were left in front of the stables, and a lantern was left atop of them, catching the straw on fire. The water-wielders were able to put it out before the flames could cause too much damage."

"How convenient," I mumble, finding that odd.

Delroy hobbles to a nearby stool and eases himself down. Taking that as my opportunity, I slide the pack off my shoulders and rummage through it, collecting what I'll need.

"Did my father make the necessary arrangements for us to take the horses?" Gray asks.

"He did," Delroy answers. "I have two horses tied up out back, saddled and ready to go for your journey."

Gray inclines his head. "Thank you, sir."

I grab the final item—a tin container—and rise. "Before we go," I say, turning to Delroy. I soften my voice, but make sure to keep my expression steady, not allowing any signs of pity to leak through. I know Delroy would hate that. He is a good man, but he is also a proud man. "Would you let me take a look at your back?"

Delroy stiffens. "Why do you ask?"

"I was in the Great Hall when Thestis ran in, and I heard the king mention summoning you." I don't bother mincing words with Delroy—he hates that, too. "You and I both know I am all too familiar with what those words imply."

Delroy releases a drawn out sigh. I glance over at Gray, who now has a wrinkle in his brow.

Gray knows about some of the nights where I received my own summons for doing something that displeased the king. But he certainly doesn't know about all of them, or about how demoralizing they could become—how painful.

It would have broken his heart. And I couldn't stand to watch someone as pure and good as Gray be broken.

"Very well," Delroy murmurs. I walk over to him, and as soon as my fingers graze the threads of his tunic, he adds in a low voice, "Please, be gentle."

Understanding settles deep in my chest, my heart squeezing with it.

"I will," I assure him.

When I lift his shirt, I have to fight against the hiss threatening to blow through my teeth. His back is...well, it is a mess, to say the least.

Sensing my reaction, Delroy supplies, "King Alastair found my inability to watch over the stables particularly disappointing, but not as disappointing as the interruption to The Founding it caused. He said I forced a great deal of embarrassment upon him, and that I was lucky to be keeping my toes."

My stomach churns with disgust. "You've watched over these stables for many years without fail. The king is cruel, and you should ignore him."

Delroy huffs an amused laugh. "Careful who you speak such words to, Lyra. Cruel he may be, but he is still a king."

I click my tongue. "This will hurt a little."

"That's alright. I may be old, but I am not frail."

The corner of my lips tugs with a smile. I first reach for the vial containing a strong antiseptic I had previously made. I pop off the top, and I douse Delroy's skin with it. He sucks in a breath through clenched teeth, but past that, Delroy remains silent. I let the solution bubble on his back before next applying a healing salve. I screw the lid off the tin container, and I swipe two fingers into the balm. As gently as I possibly can, I swipe the salve along the oozing lacerations across his back. After I finish, I dress his wounds in clean linen bandages, thankfully already infused with fresh lavender.

"He wouldn't let you see a healer?" I ask as I finish up.

Delroy shakes his head. "I was to be reminded of my incompetence so that it may not happen again."

I fight the urge to spit on the ground at the words. Instead, I reach for the dark brown glass bottle filled with a deep amber liquid. It is my own personal supply, used to help ease the pain from wounds inflicted onto me. "Hold out your tongue," I instruct Delroy.

I walk around to face him, finding his brows deeply furrowed."I know you are quite skilled like your mother was, and please know I trust you implicitly, but do you mind telling me what you are about to make me ingest?"

I huff a laugh, amused. "It is a willow bark tincture I made for myself. I'll only release a few drops onto your tongue. It'll help ease your pain."

Delroy nods and does as I ask, sticking out his tongue. I pull the dropper from the bottle, and I squeeze a few droplets from the tip. "There," I say, finished. "That should help ease some of your discomfort for a while. I'll come find you in the morning to re-dress your wounds and give you more of the tincture if you're still in pain."

Delroy's pale-blue eyes soften as a smile spreads across his face. "You take after your mother more than you know."

Tiny needles prick my heart at the words. Still, I smile in response, and collect all my supplies, placing them back in my pack.

Gray kneels down next to me and whispers, "So that's what you went back to your chambers for?"

I nod.

He places a hand on my cheek, sweeping his thumb across my skin, studying me for a brief moment before rising and turning to Delroy. "Is there anything I can help you with before we depart with the horses?"

Delroy lifts himself from the stool and waves Gray off. "I have

Thestis helping me attend to the stables today. He's a good boy, that one."

"He is," Gray agrees. "And quite talented."

Delroy nods his head slowly, as if with contemplation. After a brief passing silence, he says, "You two better get on your way. Don't worry about me. I'll be fine."

When I stand, slinging the pack over my shoulders, I face Delroy, who reaches for my hands and cups them between his own. "Thank you, my girl. You do your mother's legacy justice."

The words strike me like an arrow to my heart. I release a shaky breath and steady myself, plastering a warm smile to my lips. I squeeze Delroy's hands. "Thank you. Like I said, I'll be back to check on you tomorrow."

Delroy dips his chin. "Go," he instructs. "Best not dilly-dally any longer."

CHAPTER FIVE

The sun is high in the sky as the horses' hooves stomp on the soft cleaver grass.

"That was kind of you. What you did for Delroy," Gray says from beside me, the reigns of his horse clutched loosely in his hands.

I glance at him side-long before reverting my gaze forward. "That wasn't kindness. It was human decency."

I hear Gray huff a laugh. "Human decency, kindness, call it what you like—you still did it, and it was still an admirable thing."

Wanting to remove the attention from me, I reply, "And what about you?"

"What about me?"

"You've been training that errand boy in your spare time."

Gray is silent for so long, I steal a glance at him. His eyes seem fixed on something in the distance. "Thestis is a good kid," he finally says. "His ice magic is something special. I think even a Fjolla would find themselves impressed by it."

I snort my disagreement. "Right. Like an Archblood would deign to give a poor errand boy the time of day."

When I glance at Gray, I find him frowning at me. "Just because they're Archbloods doesn't mean they're assholes. Sure, they're a Great House and a prestigious bloodline, but that doesn't mean they judge every non-titled person within the Three Kingdoms."

I arch a brow. "Right... And just because there are storm clouds in the sky doesn't mean it's going to storm."

Gray sighs, loud and drawn out. "So you agree with the boy's mother, then? You believe she was right about him needing to give up?"

"I agree that she is right to have concerns for his future. I agree with her if she wants to prepare him for the heartbreak he may inevitably face when he realizes how divided, how biased and hierarchical the world is."

"The boy has talent," Gray pushes.

"And yet place him between two noble children, and he will be overlooked every time."

Gray remains silent, his face scrunched with thought. The sound of the horses is my only companion for a long while. Finally, feeling slightly guilty for bringing such pessimism into our final day together, I let out a quiet breath. "Wanna race horses?"

He slides his eyes to me, a fresh smile already tugging at his lips. "You don't even know where we're going."

"Give me the due direction, and I'll be able to manage."

Gray boasts a fully-formed smirk now. "You're always so confident. Tell me, is the confidence real, or is it hollow?"

I bark a laugh. "That's a secret I'll never tell."

He smiles. "North. We continue due north. But when I win, don—"

I kick my heel into the side of the horse, not even waiting for Gray to finish his sentence.

The wind beats against my flushed cheeks as my braid flaps behind me and my hips move with muscle memory on the saddle. It feels like flying— like I'm defying the bounds of mortal limitations. A feeling I find empowering, invigorating—utterly freeing.

I bask in it.

Gray knows I'm the better rider. Once I was placed as a ward with his parents, Sterling saw to it that, alongside my thorough education, I also received proper riding lessons. I never understood why, but I never complained, either. By the time Gray and I turned fifteen, I was already galloping through the Free Lands while he was still learning to control his mare.

And some things never change.

When Gray finally arrives at the end of the tree line, the Arteman Sea humming in the background, I have already dismounted and tied up my horse.

I shoot him a sharp grin and waggle my brows. "Better luck next time," I sing.

Gray dismounts from his gray-speckled stallion. "You cheated," he grumbles, tying his horse next to mine.

I smile with victory. "But haven't you heard? Fortune favors those who don't play by the rules."

Rivara's lore is steeped in stories of gods and mortals, of love, betrayal, and bloodshed.

And before us stands a crumbling remnant of one such tale.

Broken columns of eroded marble sag and crumble, piles of rubble littering the spaces in between. Vines and twigs twirl and tangle along the edges of the remaining marble structures, and once grand statues now rest beheaded, or otherwise handicapped, in pools of water filled from the rain.

It is said these ruins were once a great temple dedicated to worshiping the gods. That when the Three Kingdoms were still united under one king, two children stumbled into this temple and were Blessed. But then the two children grew up, and they each fell in love...with the same person. The story branches into many variations from there—ranging from a murder, a wedding, a dagger plunged into a heart. Yet the version I choose to believe is the one where they battled at this temple—at the place where it all began—where one fell to the other, turning it into the ruin it is now.

I turn to Gray, a humored smile pulling on my lips. "So, you wanted to spend your last day amongst ruins?"

"Not exactly." He motions for me to follow him.

I tug at my brows, a wave of curiosity washing through me, and trail behind Gray as he escorts me down a pebble-filled path. He leads me to a small water basin, where a creek flows over rounded stones stacked atop one another.

I arch a brow at him. "Alright, time to spill. Why'd you bring me here?"

He bites down on his growing smile. "Naturally, I wanted our final day together to be memorable."

"Naturally," I echo through a laugh. "And this creek run-off is what satisfies your vision?"

His smile widens. "No," he drawls, extending his hand out to me. When I place my hand in his, he squeezes. "One last adventure, Lyra. My final surprise."

My brows twitch, but I allow him to guide me forward, around the basin, to directly beside the water trickling over the large stack of rocks.

He drops my hand. "Did you know the ruins aren't actually from the sacred temple? They're from the forecourt that was open to everyone. The *real* temple—open only to its dedicated priests and priestesses—was kept a secret, hidden away."

My brows furrow, confused as to why he's giving me a random history lesson. "Your point being?"

He grins. "Well, I was doing some light reading in the restricted section of the king's library—"

My brows lurch. "—Have you lost your *mind*?" I interrupt. "The king would have your head if he knew."

Gray waves me off. "Neither here nor there."

I fold my arms over my chest. "So you mean to tell me Gray Nightenjoy, the habitual rule-follower and do-gooder, has found the line he's willing to cross, and it's for *books*?"

His grin is cheeky and proud as he arches a brow. "Is that a problem?"

I shake my head and laugh, gesturing for him to continue with his entertaining speech.

He chuckles. "As I was saying, the temple was kept a secret, and has remained a secret for many, many years. Most thought the knowledge to be lost, but it turns out, the king clearly has more books than he and his archivists realize."

I finally put the pieces together. "Don't tell me…"

Gray is beaming. "Oh, yes. Today, you and I are going into that temple."

CHAPTER SIX

The temple, hidden underground and remaining oddly preserved, was beautiful.

As Gray and I explored it, slipping effortlessly into a childlike giddiness, we left no stone unturned, studying the pillars, illegible scribbles, altars, and half-filled pools.

It was a fitting last day for us. A day of highs I know both he and I will cling to after Gray leaves. And as it draws to a close, we attempt to squeeze out the last remnants of joy the fleeting hours can offer.

Lying on a blanket beneath the crumbling remains of my favorite ruin, a sole lantern our only source of light, Gray and I consume the night sky through the exposed domed roof while waves crash against the sandy shore in the background and the breeze hums through the grass.

I stare up at the glittering sky, feeling a sense of longing in my chest. Though, for what exactly, I'm not sure. "Tell me a story."

He glances at me, surprised. "It's been ages since I've done that. I think the last time was…"

"It was two years ago," I finish for him. "When I had a night terror that kept me from sleeping."

"That's right," he murmurs. "Well, what story would you like? One of love? Of heartbreak? Perhaps of heroism or great betrayal?"

"Tell me a story about a beginning, so I won't focus on an ending." My voice sounds like nothing more than a soft note in a sad melody.

Gray turns to me, his eyes soft as his face fills with understanding.

"Alright," he agrees. "How about the story of Morwenna?"

I bite down, a laugh on my lips. "Remind me who she is again?"

Gray shakes his head, amused. "You really didn't ever pay attention in our lore and mythology studies, did you?"

"It's why I always cheated off you whenever Sterling gave us an assignment," I coo.

He rolls his eyes, his smile soft. "I'll never understand why you find such little interest in the lore of our lands."

I stretch my arms above my head. "I have my reasons. Plus, there's a lot to keep up with. I pick and choose as I please."

"I'm sure you do," he mutters with an arched brow. But ultimately, Gray draws in a breath and begins the story.

"Long, long ago, the gods frequently visited the mortal realm. A goddess, Morwenna, Daughter of the Moon and goddess of water, favored a mortal girl who would sit on a moonlit shoreline and sing. Morwenna, wide-eyed and full of jubilance, loved to dance. She would twirl across the sparkling veil of the sky to the mortal girl's song. As she danced, it was said her eyes would swell with joyous tears that trickled from the horizon like scattered raindrops."

A helpless smile breaks free while I stare at the colored stars, listening.

I've never told Gray how much I love it when he tells me stories. How he's always been able to soothe any restlessness within me when he does.

"One day, as Morwenna danced fervently to a song of great beauty, her tears slipped from her eyes like a gentle stream. For that night, the mortal girl sat perched on a stone overlooking the sea and sang out a ballad for the one she loved, hoping her beloved would soon return to her.

"Morwenna, stricken of the heart, was moved far greater than she had ever been, and she lost herself to her dance—to the song that became known as the Ballad of the Tides. And as her tears landed atop the mortal girl's head, the moon stirred, and the tides shifted. For unknowingly, the mortal girl had suddenly been kissed by the passion of the Daughter of the

Moon, resulting in her hair turning stark white beneath the moon's glow.

"Curious by the shift in the sea, the girl reached her fingertips out to it, swearing she heard the tides singing back to her, responding to her song. The mortal girl never expected the sea would listen to her—that she would move the very water crashing to shore, forever changed by Morwenna's fallen tears."

Gray looks away from the sky and down at our interlaced fingers.

I'm not even sure when I reached for his hand.

"And that," he murmurs softly. "Is the story of how the first water-wielder came into existence."

An inexplicably sad feeling begins to form in my chest, but I drown it before it can ever know life. Yet I feel Gray watching me—can sense the sudden heaviness hanging in the air between us.

I squeeze his hand. "What is it?"

He looks at me, and his expression splits apart slowly—like the first cracks in fracturing ice. "I'm not sure if I can do it," he whispers. "I don't know how I'll be able to." He lifts himself from the blanket, dropping his head in defeat.

I sit up and place a comforting hand on his arm. "All great things must end eventually. Even if we're not ready to let them go."

Gray turns his chin over his shoulder, meeting my gaze. "But why? Why must good things end simply because they are good?"

I'm not sure if I smile or frown at him. My lips move in an attempt to smile, yet my heart aches in the way it would when accompanying a frown.

To see the world through Gray's rose-colored eyes.

"Because if things were good forever, then the world would be a paradise. And sadly, Gray, this world is not paradise."

He leans his forehead against mine, and I have to squeeze my eyes shut against the emotion attempting to crawl up my throat, swallowing it back into the abyss from which it came.

"If I stay, we could make it one," he breathes. "You and me, Lyra. We can carve out our own paradise."

What I want to say back to Gray is simple: *I am blood-bound to the king, forced to serve him for the rest of my life. You are a Nightenjoy who has his whole life in front of him. There is no paradise here for us, because this world is cruel, and you won't find your idyllic end within it.*

Yet instead I force my lips to forgo their confusion and smile, even if they protest, claiming sadness has told them they wish to frown.

I lift my fingers to Gray's cheek and reply in a falsely promising voice, "Someday, perhaps. But for now, you do not miss your opportunity to become something great."

Gray pulls his forehead back from mine, his gaze holding steady. "I will come back for you. Whether it's a year from now or five, I will not leave you behind."

I bite down on the inside of my cheek. "I know you will," I say to him, my voice a shade more than a whisper. "And I will count down the days until you return."

Gray looks as though he is about to speak when a smudge of rosy color materializes in the charcoaled sky, reorienting our attention. The glossy pink expands and morphs into glowing rods composed of teal and turquoise.

It is the Great River of Light.

Gray shifts his gaze from the sky onto me, and he slowly lays back down, stretching out his arm beside him—a silent invitation.

One I gladly accept, taking my place nestled into his side.

We lay in silence, watching the dancing colors zip through the inky blotches of night. Regal blues undulate into jade and lilac as dazzling whites soar through the sky. They move and flow as freely as I imagine Morwenna did as she danced across a glittering horizon.

And for the briefest moment, it almost feels like everything might be okay.

Until a loud crack of magic erupts through the air, and a swirling portal of black and silver opens across from us.

The horses, spooked by the sudden outburst of magic, protest and stomp, and Gray and I scramble upright. He steps in front of me, instinctually shielding me with an outstretched arm.

Klytis, the king's resident aether-wielder—a type of magic that allows a wielder to create portals to and from places—appears.

"There you are," he says, breathless. "I've been looking everywhere for you two."

My brows scrunch together while Gray takes a step forward. "Why?"

"The king decided to entertain tonight. He called for Lyra, but when she did not come, he lost his *mind*. He sent me to find her. She...." He exhales a long and heavy sigh. "Well, she's been summoned."

My stomach plunges into a free fall as fear, the resilient spider, keeps crawling into my chest no matter how aggressively I try to keep it down.

Gray turns to look at me, his eyes already filling with a mix of horror, apology, and regret. I know he will blame himself, even if I don't blame him in the slightest.

How do you teach a wolf who's never been hunted to suddenly think like a sheep? You can't.

But I know better. I shouldn't have acted as though I have such freedoms—I have no true freedom.

Klytis drags out a long breath. "We should go. The longer you wait, the worse it will be."

I nod my head, glancing at the horses. "What about them?"

Klytis jerks his chin at Gray. "He can bring them back to the stables."

"No," Gray counters with a level of force that catches me off guard. "I am coming with her."

Klytis arches a brow. "That...is not a very good idea."

Gray folds his arms in protest. "I don't care. I'm the reason Lyra is being summoned, so I am coming with her."

Klytis opens his mouth as if to argue further, but just as quickly snaps it shut, clearly thinking better of entering a verbal tiff with the son of Sterling Nightenjoy, who's nicknamed the wielder of cunning words for a reason. "Very well," he concedes. "I'll take care of the horses."

He throws out his hand, and a portal of swirling black and silver appears. "But for the love of the gods, when your father asks you what the hell you were thinking, please make sure to mention that I tried to talk you out of this."

CHAPTER SEVEN

I step through the silver and black portal and enter directly into the king's throne room.

From beside me, Klytis whispers, "Good luck," before stepping backward, vanishing into the swirling silver.

Gray subtly brushes a comforting hand across the small of my back. I glance at him, and he nods. I blow out a quiet sigh through tightened lips, and then, together, we strut forward.

Immediately, I glimpse Sterling standing to King Alastair's right. He waits patiently with his hands folded in front of him, his face carefully neutral—though I can spot the lecture and worry streaking through his eyes. One glance at Gray, and I know he sees it, too.

The king watches us with a narrowed gaze, perched haughtily on his throne. "Oh?" he coos, ice snaking over his words. "What's this? I have summoned one but received two." Eyes remaining glued to us, he chides, "Sterling, why does your son stand before me?"

Sterling releases a measured breath. "I have no idea, Your Majesty. As you have said, you summoned one but have instead received two."

Oh...

Sterling's pissed.

So rarely have I seen Sterling mad. He's always said that the moment you lose your temper, you lose the battle. And though his temper remains in check, there's a terrifyingly silent fury in his eyes—though no one could probably spot it but Gray and I.

"Hm," King Alastair hums. He locks his eyes on me, pinning me with his cold gaze. "Where were you?"

I take a few steps forward, attempting to put distance between Gray and me. When he insisted on coming—a foolish decision—I quickly recognized he was not going to be talked out of it. So the least I can do is make sure the king keeps his attention on me, and *only* me.

I walk until I am at the foot of the dais, a small knot twisting in my stomach as I realize Gray will have to see me like this.

Has he ever seen me acting out my role, playing the part assigned to me ever-so-dutifully? I can't remember...I don't think he has. Sterling always tried to keep him away from the king's parties—away from his court.

Still...

He certainly will see the degradation now.

"I was at the temple ruins, My King. I offer you my humblest apologies; I did not know you planned to entertain tonight."

He glares at me. "I don't remember letting my little birdie out of her cage, so how is it she flew away?"

I take another careful step up the dais, lowering my gaze and altering my voice to his liking. "You are right, My King. I should not have been so bold. How can I show you my remorse for making you wait?"

His lip curls. "Remorse is for the weak," he spits.

Another step up. Then another. I kneel at his feet and slowly glide my hands from his ankle up his calf, lifting my eyes with caution. "Of course, My King." Once my hands reach his thighs, I slowly rise from my knees, letting my fingers linger on the inside of his legs. I pull my hands back and fold them in front of me, bowing my head. "I will do whatever I can to satisfy you."

I dangle the bait and pray to the gods, hoping it'll be me on my knees stripped bare in his private chambers instead of me on my knees stripped bare in this throne room.

But sometimes the gods do not listen, and prayers are nothing more than hollow wishes.

I glance up just in time to see the king's lips curl into a sharp, taunting smirk. "Guards," he practically sings. "Prepare the chains." His eyes hover back to me. "Strip," he commands.

I clench my teeth so forcefully, I fear they may crack and shatter—much like my pride. "Your Majesty," I plead, my voice already shaking.

His eyes flare, and mine go wide at the recognition of my slip. "I–I'm sorry. I didn't mean—"

"—Do *not* address me as anything other than what I've instructed. I am your *what?*"

My bottom lip begins to quiver, and a deep loathing reawakens within me. "King. You are *my* king."

"And what has your king instructed, my little toy?"

I have to suck in my cheeks to keep my lip from quivering further. "To strip. My king has commanded that I strip."

"So then strip you shall."

He says it with such finality, I don't dare utter a response. Instead, I swallow against the overwhelming dryness in my throat, release a trembling breath, and I slowly peel away the clothes from my body. When I'm fully bare, my cheeks flush with heat. Not from desire, nor fear, nor even bashfulness from being nude—it's from the humiliation of knowing that a pair of mossy gold eyes is watching, witnessing things I never wanted him to bear witness to.

Please don't think less of me. Please don't think less of me. Please don't think less of me.

The king drinks me in like a thirsty traveler gulps water from a fresh spring. And then he smiles contentedly—satisfied—before he tsks softly. "You know I hate to do this to you, pet. But I am nothing if not a man of order and strict discipline."

Lies.

He rather gets off on inflicting pain. I've seen the evidence—*felt* the evidence—on numerous occasions.

He angles his head, his eyes holding mine. "Shackle her," he demands without breaking his gaze.

As the guards step up the dais to restrain me, Sterling's voice cuts in. "Perhaps it is best if I take the boy and offer you privacy as you impart your judgment."

From over his shoulder, the king growls back, "You will stay right where you are. The boy, too. She was your ward after all. Bear witness to her disobedience."

Sterling inclines his head in submission. "As you wish, Your Majesty."

The guards grip my arms and tug me backward, and I despise the small whimper that escapes my lips. I despise even more that Gray heard it, because it results in him losing his rational thought.

"Wait," he shouts, his voice echoing off the marble walls. "Let her go."

King Alastair waves a dismissive hand. "Restrain him."

Guards surround Gray and yank his arms back, holding him steady. From the corner of my eye, I glimpse him thrash and buck against their hold.

Please, I want to say to him. *Don't fight.*

But I know if I address him, it'll only make it worse.

"*Stop!*" Gray shouts, still jerking. "Please...it was my fault. Not Lyra's."

As my wrists and ankles are being locked in chains that lick my skin in a frigid kiss of promised pain, my body now outstretched like a star, I catch it when King Alastair slides his eyes to Gray, finally addressing him.

"If you do not cease speaking, I will have you gagged and whipped next. I will deal with your presence once I am done punishing *my* blood-sworn servant."

Gray's jaw ticks, but he doesn't speak further. Though, he does attempt to wrench himself free of the guards. They just tighten their hold on him in response.

Now bound in chains, my front side bared to the king so he can watch my face twist with pain, I grit my teeth in anticipation for what's to come.

"Count your lashings aloud for me, pet. You will be given fifteen with the Shredder so that you will remember yourself and your duties to me."

I always want to roll my eyes when the king uses one of those gods-awful names he's given to his whips. The Shredder, both fortunately and unfortunately, is one that has never been used on me before.

King Alastair flicks his eyes to the guard now holding the glass-laced whip. "You may proceed."

Every time my clothes have been stripped from my body and the tip of a whip has bitten into my skin, my mind attempts to protect what remains of my withered heart by disassociating—by detaching my human elements.

I am not a person with dignity; I am a blood-sworn servant to a king.

It is the kindness my mind offers me to get through these encounters. Yet this time, my mind doesn't do that, incapable of shutting off, circulating on high alert instead. I am keenly aware of every inch of my exposed body. I absorb every chiding word, feel every sneer—see every demoralizing detail.

And for the first time, I want to bury my face in shame. I want to wrap my body in a dense cloak and hide from the humiliation, from the guilt and the embarrassment, as questions of my self-worth scribble across my skin in bolded script.

I never wanted Gray to see this. I never wanted him to be privy to my treatment from the king. Knowing and seeing are two very different things, and now that he's seen, will he ever be able to look at me the same? *Please don't think less of me.*

The first kiss of pain slices diagonally across my back. Tears prick in my eyes, but I'm not sure if they are the result of the searing pain I feel on the outside of my body, or from the jagged pain on the inside.

Numbly, I do as the king instructed, and I count. "One."

The next strike of the glass-laced whip kisses the back of my thighs. My body buckles, but the chains keep me upright. I grit my teeth, my face twisting.

I always somehow forget the way a whip's touch exists like a phantom limb; the feeling still very much on my skin—fresh and hot—long after the cords have receded.

"Two," I grate, my voice rough and dead.

On the third strike, a cry of pain echoes in my mouth. The glass wedges into the skin at my nape, the whip dragging its teeth over my shoulder, caressing my collarbone, shredding my body—hence its silly name. The room starts to spin, and everything grows fuzzy.

Something snaps—no, *clicks*—inside me, and a surge of pain invades my veins.

And I don't realize how muffled the world has become until one sharp sound tears through the imaginary cotton in my ears.

Gray's voice.

"Please," he begs, thrashing to break free from the guards. "*Please.* Listen to me. Listen to what I have to say."

When my eyes finally manage to lift from the ground, I find King Alastair studying Gray—appraising him with a measured gaze. After a long moment, the king releases an exasperated sigh. "Out of respect for your father and your bloodline, I will hear you. Now speak before I change my mind."

Gray jerks his arms out of the guards' hold, shooting them a sharp look after. He steps forward and kneels before the king. "I understand that a price is owed for what happened tonight. I understand you seek to teach your servant a lesson, but…I humbly request that you allow me to step in and receive the punishment in her place."

My heart falls into my stomach while my eyes bulge, and my chest fills with weighted lead. I glance at Sterling and find the blood leaching from his face, though his features remain perfectly neutral.

The king arches a brow and chuckles, strangely amused. "And why would I do that?"

Gray pauses, and I suddenly become keenly aware of what he's doing. *Gray Nightenjoy, son of the wielder of cunning words.*

How they underestimate him.

Gray is the *true* wielder of cunning words—when he wants to be. Most often, he is so true of heart that he chooses not to use his abilities because he doesn't like *manipulating others*, in his words. But that objection is cast aside as he turns his tongue silver. I can *feel* it—alongside my own pain—in each measured movement he makes.

"Because I am asking you for the sake of my honor as both a man and a Nightenjoy. It was I, Your Majesty, who goaded Lyra into leaving. I who implied she had no responsibilities."

The king rests his cheek on his fist. "You can take a man into the king's coffers, but you cannot make the man steal his wealth."

Gray bows his head lower. "All the same, Your Majesty. I fear I would feel less of a man if not granted this request. That is why I kneel before you, begging at your feet. Please..." He finally looks up and meets the king's glowing gaze.

King Alastair loves to watch people beg.

"Please," Gray repeats, emotion beginning to betray him, rattling his voice. "Allow me to take her place." He steadies himself, clearing his throat. "For the sake of my honor, and to preserve the integrity of my bloodline's virtue."

The king watches Gray for a long moment, and as he does, my heart is an erratic flutter of broken wings.

The king sucks in a loud breath. "Very well. I cannot deny a man on his knees, begging to retain his honor." A slimy smirk spreads across his face. "Go release her then, boy, and be chained in her place."

Gray rises, bowing deeply at the waist. "Thank you, Your Royal Grace." Slowly, he turns on his heels and approaches me.

As he does, his eyes never leave mine. He does not glance down, to the side, along any ridge of my body—only at me, at my face. Just mossy gold gazing into a frozen sea of amethyst.

He takes the key from the guard and begins unlocking my shackles. Under his breath, so low I barely catch it, he murmurs, "I am so sorry, Lyra. I am so unbelievably sorry."

When the last shackle has been undone, my knees have an infuriating bout of weakness, and I buckle. Gray catches me under the elbows, holding me steady.

"Not yet," he whispers against the top of my head. "Stay strong just a little longer."

Just a little longer.

Gray pulls off his tunic, exposing his perfectly unblemished skin, and he gently places it in my hands. "I've never been so glad to give you this before." His eyes hold onto mine for as long as they can, sure and true.

Tears give a warning prick along the shore of my eyes, and my bottom lip quivers.

It's the same.

Gray is still looking at me the same way.

But I shove the thought down and tug Gray's tunic over my head, covering my exposed body—the fabric like a hot, sand-coated brand on my oozing lacerations.

I bite down on the skin of my cheek and lift my chin. I will be strong for Gray. I will be strong because I owe it to myself to not let the king watch me crumble. To make sure he knows he can't make me shatter into fragments. Even if I would barter with any god, monster, or sorceress to stop Gray from doing this.

It should be me.

No. Gods no. It is all coming back...familiar yet distant. The pain is old, yet is as fresh as the bleeding wounds on my back.

It should be me. It should be me. It should—

The cracking sound of the first lashing snaps me back to the present. I hadn't even seen the guards lock Gray's shackles.

He grits his teeth, but nothing else. Not a single noise slips past his lips.

"Impressive," the king comments. "Most unfamiliar with the touch of a whip squeal at first contact."

Despite knowing that I shouldn't—that it'll only bring me more pain and heartache—I glance at Sterling. There is a wrinkle in his brow as his lips part slightly, fear and worry being the iron pry bar to crack him open.

The king's rough command jolts my eyes back to Gray. "Again."

After the whip lances across his back—Gray again only wincing in pain, not giving anything more—King Alastair lifts his chin. "How many is that, boy?"

Beginning to shake, whether from pain or something else, I can't be certain, Gray lifts his chin and meets the king's eyes. "Two, Your Majesty."

The king hums with pleasure. "Let's make it three."

Without further warning, the glass cracks against Gray's skin, and a few pieces wedge into the crimson seams of his once unblemished flesh.

The guard yanks the thong of the whip back, and pieces of Gray's skin detach with it—flying through the air like chunky snowflakes.

He grunts, the pain becoming too much, and I instinctively step forward. But he jerks his head up and shakes it.

I'm okay. He mouths the words with gentle conviction, and an invisible knife twists in my heart at the sight.

Four lashings.

Five lashings.

Six lashings.

On the seventh, Gray wails in pain, his back a bloodied, mangled mess of zig-zagging marks oozing clumps of skin and blood. I can tell his body is giving out from the way he's buckling. Yet the shackles won't let him fall.

Cruel—the King of Rivara is so, so cruel.

Flames dance in my mind, twirling around my skin in a taunting reminder of a night from my past. One where tiny fists beat against the ground and a strange feeling appears.

So long it's been since I've thought about that strange feeling. I've never given light to the events that transpired back then. I only buried them in the shadows, wishing them away, denying their existence.

 But watching Gray suffer—seeing his body twisted and mangled because of me—is the shovel digging up the grave of memories I buried long ago.

Eight lashings, and Gray screams—a sound that will haunt my nightmares.

That clicking feeling intensifies, and something begins to bubble in my stomach, spreading to my veins. My chest rises and falls with erratic breaths, and a tingling feeling shoots down my spine, spreading to my fingertips.

Am I about to pass out? Is it from the pain—from the resurfacing memories I am still unable to face?

My breathing grows shallow and my skin warms, growing as hot as the boiling waters of Illithious Lake. Frightened, I look to Sterling—to the only father figure I have ever had.

He looks pale and...

Perplexed.

Am I imagining that? Is my broken mind playing tricks on me? Sterling never openly wears such damning expressions.

The clicking sensation rises to my chest, and it is behind my breastbone that I feel it lock into place. A surge of electricity floods my veins, lacing around my spine, twirling as it rises up, up, up to the nape of my neck.

My head swims with a surging high, buzzing and tingling.

I return my gaze to Sterling, and he looks...strained? Why does he look haggard all of a sudden? Like he barely has the energy to continue standing?

Nine lashings.

Gray, wrecked with pain, lets out an ear-splitting cry. And the king laughs. He *actually* laughs.

The feeling inside of me crescendos, and my vision begins to blur and throb. Sterling collapses beside the king, steadying himself with an outstretched hand before he can fall on his face, drawing the attention of King Alastair.

And it is in that moment I explode.

CHAPTER EIGHT

A network of twisting vines and woody roots pour from my palms like living serpents, coiling themselves around the entirety of the throne room.

Thorns spring up from the marble floor, jutting upwards like jagged teeth, creating a maze of sharp edges between Gray and the king. The once glimmering moonstone pillars are swallowed by a sea of twining green—the light slowly disappearing as they unfurl their spindly bodies, clogging the glass roof in a gnarly bundle of overlapping flora. The king's royal banners tumble from the walls as trailing ivy and tangled threads scale the marble surface, eating everything in their wake.

The walls groan as the weight of the emerald tendrils overtake the space at horrifying speeds. They shoot for the king, snaking up the dais—twisting around his throne. Black venomous flowers sprout to life, and when their petals unfurl, a gray vapor is revealed—lazily floating into the air like nothing more than an inconsequential fog.

And the sudden realization that all of this is coming from *me* is so jarring, I stumble backwards, tipping myself over from shock. I outstretch my hands, but it's too late—my body plummets to the ground in wide-eyed dismay.

"What *is* this?" The king shouts, rising from his throne.

Sterling clutches his chest, his breathing ragged. Slowly, on shaky legs, he rises. And then his eyes fall directly onto me—an undeniable worry resting within them.

King Alastair follows his gaze, his eyes narrowing into a sharp dagger of accusation.

Which...the evidence is pretty damning.

I glance down, turning my palms over, inspecting the strange network of silver mingling with gold as it runs beneath my skin. The light is like a glittering river, coursing upstream from the tips of my fingers to the veins in my forearms.

My mouth opens and closes, and as I search for words—any singular syllable—I find that I am utterly speechless.

Could it be...was I a late-bloomer after all? It is rare, but there are known records of wielders acquiring their magic late—something Gray always tried to remind me of while growing up.

I had just given up any hope it would happen to me.

I fervently scan my arms for a wielder's mark. When magic manifests in a wielder, their wielder's mark—a unique mark that appears on the wielder denoting their magic type—almost always manifests with it.

Yet I find nothing.

Though it could be somewhere I can't see. Is it on my back? On my—

The king's growling threat snaps me back. "Restrain her!"

Before I know it, guards are tugging me up from the ground and twisting my arms behind my back. As they do, like obedient soldiers, all of the winding roots and twisting vines, thorns and flowers—everything—it recedes back to me, disappearing like smoke into my palms.

And like a fool, all I can do is blink.

As if on instinct, I look to Gray. He is entirely hunched over, being held upright only by the shackles confining his wrists and ankles. His back is mutilated—the sight gruesome. But his face has become gaunt and pale, to an alarming degree.

He didn't look like that before. Has he lost too much blood? Was the glass laced with something? No, that's not it. I would have noticed such a thing sooner.

My neck tingles, floating with the lightness of clouds yet swaying as though it is supporting bricks. Before I know it, my vision assumes a strobing effect, and my chest feels as though it's hollowed out—almost like I've been kicked.

Tired.

I feel so tired all of a sudden.

I wobble like a shaky branch in a hailstorm, swaying on my feet. And as my eyes roll to the back of my head, bringing a cover of darkness with them, the final thing I see is the row of the king's royal banners lined along the wall, undisturbed, as if nothing has happened at all.

How strange.

I could have sworn I saw them fall a moment ago.

※ ⁊※

"Please. There is no one else I can entrust this to."

The tone of my mother's voice made me shift on my feet. Hidden within the shadows, tucked away behind a cracked wooden door, I listened in on the conversation as it carried on late into the night.

I'd had a strange dream that woke me from my sleep. Plus, Gray was snoring in bed next to me, which made it next to impossible to return to the dreamland. So, when I heard the adult's whispering in Gray's parent's living chamber, I couldn't help but to crawl out of bed and eavesdrop.

"Perhaps you could ask...him," Azalea offered. "You've said it yourself that he is a good man—an honorable man. I understand it would not be easy to gain an audience with him, but maybe he could help—"

"Don't you dare bring him up," my mother chided in a harsh quiet. I watched her shoulders rise and fall with her emotion-laced breath. She dropped her voice even lower, and I had to strain my ears to hear her murmur, "She must never know about him. You swore to never tell a soul."

I wondered who they were talking about.

Azalea reached out and took my mother's hands, cupping them between her own. "Railiana, I would never. I swore the unbreakable oath to you, and even if I hadn't, I would never betray my Sister in Ahlai like that."

My mother's shoulders drooped, and she was silent for a long moment. "I have told you what I've seen in the fog. The Veil...it is a distorted place of hazy imagery. Most times, all a Veilreader can hope to do is interpret patterns or catch a fleeting glimpse of things to come." She lifted her head, and she locked eyes with Azalea, and then Sterling. "But I saw it in full color, clear as the channels flowing through Keziah."

Sterling's back was to me, so I could not see his expression—though, I didn't particularly need to see it. I had spent so much time with him and Azalea, I could practically replicate any of their expressions to near perfection.

His voice was soft and filled with a gentle optimism as he supplied, "The act of Veilreading is anything but concrete, Rai, and impressions are subject to change. Perhaps what you saw is not what you've interpreted it to be."

My mother shook her head, as if resigning herself to something. It was strange seeing her make such a foreign gesture. "You know a Veilreader cannot control how precise the vision is. Tell me, Sterling, do you think I wished to see that in the fog? Don't you think if I could have interpreted what I saw as anything else, I would?"

He did not answer right away. "I do not doubt you, Rai. But please understand that I am a man of reason and logic, and what you have just told us defies any semblance of either."

My mother sighed, long and deep. "I know...I do not take burdening the both of you with this lightly. But...when I was last in the Veil, I saw something else as well. Something I will not share. I just...I had to tell someone, and you two are the only people I trust with my family's life."

Azalea's brows furrowed as her mouth fell into a frown. "The way you speak... You're scaring me, Rai."

My mother only glanced at Azalea before she again locked eyes with Sterling. "Somewhere, there is a record of everything, and it will confirm what I have told you—what has mostly been lost to neglect and time. I have good reason to believe it is in the king's restricted section of his library, in the archival records. Promise me you'll search for it."

I could see the bob of Sterling's head. "You have my word."

A long-legged spider tip-toed along the skin of my exposed leg, and my immediate reaction was to stomp it away. I kicked out my leg in an attempt to shake it off, somehow finding the self-control to stifle my rising shout.

But I wasn't nearly as quiet as I thought. My mother stood up abruptly and called out my name. "Lyra?"

Before I could get busted, I scurried back into bed, throwing the covers over my head, pretending to be as sound as asleep as Gray—who was still snoring.

※ ✦

When I come to, my hair is bunched in a guard's fist, and there is a dagger at my throat.

"How gracious of you to finally wake from your slumber." The king towers over me—which isn't saying much considering I'm being forced to my knees—and leans down, his lip curling with rage. "What did you do to my advisor, and how long have you been hiding your magic from me?"

I feel like a fish out of water, unable to function—to *breathe*—properly. There is a pounding headache expanding behind my eyes. My muscles are fatigued for reasons I am entirely unsure of, and I must have just collapsed onto my raw, bleeding back, because it *burns.*

"Answer me, girl!" the king snarls.

"I–I...I don't know. I—"

He glares at me as though I've grown another head. "You don't know? *You don't know?*" His voice elevates with anger. "You just turned my whole throne room into a gods-damn jungle, and you expect me to believe that you don't *know?*"

Yes?

The guard yanks my hair, tugging my head back, forcing my chin to lift toward the king. "I swear, My King. I don't know."

"*Liar!*" he seethes. He lifts a hand and slaps my face, the bitter sound echoing. "If you will not tell me the truth, perhaps a few nights spent in the dungeons will loosen your tongue."

A panic seizes me, and in a moment of weakness, that panic reveals itself with the twists of my features.

The king smiles, delighted to have glimpsed my displeasure. "Oh, yes. The dungeon is exactly what you need. Perhaps I'll put you in a cell with the other bastards, and you can offer them some entertainment."

I open my mouth to protest—to lie, to do anything to prevent myself from being placed in the mildewy dungeons, but the sound of Sterling clearing his throat has me quickly snapping my mouth shut.

"If I may, Your Majesty."

King Alastair turns on his heels, sweeping his eyes along Sterling. "You may speak."

Sterling inclines his head. "If the girl were lying to you about having magic, she most certainly would have manifested her wielder's mark. Given she was just nude before you, and there was no mark..." he trails off, allowing King Alastiar to put the pieces together himself.

Which he does, his brows furrowing as it clicks into place. His head swivels from Sterling to me, back to Sterling. "So how would you explain this, then?" He speaks to Sterling, thank the gods.

Because I sure as hell don't have an answer.

Sterling's voice is smooth and neutral. One would never know he just suffered a bout of...of...

What *did* happen to make Sterling collapse like that? The king pinned the blame onto me, but surely I hadn't been responsible.

Right?

Sterling clasps his hands. "It would appear that the girl unexpectedly falls into the rare category of late-bloomers."

King Alastair wrinkles his nose at the words. "A wielder comes into their magic at puberty. Everyone knows this. If after maturity they still do not wield, they were simply born without lakti. Those are the known ways."

Sterling nods his head, agreeing. "You speak true, Your Majesty. However, there are recorded cases of wielders that came into their magic late in life. It is a phenomenon known as the Surge. The magic quietly builds beneath the surface, only to suddenly surge into existence with remarkable force."

The king looks back to me, assessing me through narrowed eyes as if he is only now seeing me for the first time. "Is that so..." He begins pacing, rubbing his chin in thought.

I flick my eyes to Sterling, whose gaze is now fixed on me. My brows twitch, and I squint to catch the word Sterling is mouthing at me while the king's back is to us.

Bathara.

Bathara?

The academy Gray departs for in the morning? The one known for its deadly entrance exams. The place where Jurafen are trained—where those with magic go to become something great. If they can get admitted.

Why is he...

The gears start turning in my head, and suddenly, I see a new path emerging from the shadows. One where gilded bars are melted down into molten gold, and dreams of a better existence do not die of suffocation.

I now possess the ability to wield. Which means I can access magic. Flora magic at that. Which means...

Subtly, with a newfound understanding, I dip my chin at Sterling. He lets a near-imperceptible smile flicker across his lips in response.

I glance over my shoulder and am just barely able to glimpse Gray. He remains shackled, his head still slumped, his body slack. As if sensing my attention, he slowly drags his eyes from the ground, his exposed chest raking in wheezing breaths. When his glassy eyes meet mine—when I glimpse all the pain, the silent terror and rage, all the stubborn resilience still simmering in his eyes—a fire ignites deep in the pit of my stomach.

Two things happen simultaneously.

The first is I swear a silent vow to myself. Someday, I will take revenge on King Alastair for all he's done. And the world will be a better place because of it, allowing the Rivara Kingdom to flourish under the reign of an entirely new king. For King Alastair has yet to produce an heir—rumored to be barren and incapable—which means his bloodline's reign will end with him.

The second is a flood of determination that washes through me so forcefully, it temporarily numbs the pain. And as my eyes bounce from Gray, to Sterling, then back to the king, I am suddenly reminded that I was raised by both a cunning mother and the Nightenjoys, and though my tongue may not be coated in fine silver like Gray and Sterling, it certainly has a silver edge.

And I see my opening with undaunted clarity.

"If I have magic, that means I could become a Jurafen." The guard gripping my hair jerks me back, and I grit my teeth against the jolt of sharp pain, flicking my eyes down at the cool metal still positioned at my throat.

The king spins on his heels, a mocking sneer already twirling his lips. "*You?* A Jurafen?" He claps his hands together and barks a loud laugh. "Oh, my ignorant little pet. Just because you have suddenly manifested your ability to wield does not mean you are even remotely capable of becoming a Jurafen."

Words I buried long ago suddenly surface within me.

I will not cower. I will not yield. I will not falter.

I lift my chin as much as one can with a blade at their throat. "You're wrong."

The guard tightens his hold on me, and the king raises a disarming hand in response. He lowers the dagger and releases me, throwing my head forward. When I reorient myself, glancing up at the king, his eyes are brimming with cold amusement, and his arched brow climbs even higher when I look up at him.

"What's this?" he asks, his tone deceptively calm. Your ability to wield appears, and suddenly you think you can refute a king?"

I shake my head. "No, My King. But..." Moment of truth. "I'd wager that, if you permitted me, I would pass the upcoming entrance exams and gain entry into Bathara."

The king tips his head back and laughs—deep from his gut, as if I just told a crude joke in a tavern. "Your disconnection from reality humors me, truly. But you know nothing, girl. You possess no chance of passing, and even if you *did* manage to somehow skirt through the exam, they'd never permit you entry. You are a servant. No, you are a king's entertainer—a whore. What business do you think you have in receiving the honor of being titled Jurafen?"

I bow my head. "All the same, I'd wager otherwise. I believe I can."

I've dangled my bait carefully, wrapping it in a skin most appealing to the king—something he can never resist.

Wagers.

King Alastair loves to make wagers.

60

He hums with patronizing amusement. "Is that so? And what would you wager on this delusion of yours?"

Leaving my head bowed, my eyes still glued to the marble floor, I alter my voice to his liking. "What is it that would entice My King?"

"Well you see, pet, the thing about enticing a king is you must offer him something he does not already possess. Something he desires. And seeing as I already own you—that you are *blood-sworn* to me—there is little you can offer me that I simply cannot already take."

I speak on instinct. "An heir. I will promise you an heir."

"No." Gray's broken rasp barely penetrates the sound barrier. And it is a struggle to not turn to face him—to keep my feet from lifting with their own mind, stumbling to his aid.

"Silence, boy, or I'll take the whip to you again." The king refocuses on me, a malicious curve tugging at the corner of his lip. The realms of hell burn within his eyes. "And how is it you can promise such a thing when no one else has been able to?"

I clamp down on my bubbling anger and give the performance of a lifetime. "Before her death, you had my mother working on an elixir that could aid you in your quest for an heir."

His annoyance grows palpable. "I do not make a habit of discussing those in the grave." King Alastair cocks his head, a wry smirk spreading across his lips. "One might think you'd avoid such topics as well."

I will not cower. I will not yield. I will not falter.

And I sure as hell am not backing down here.

I maintain the illusion of submission. "She discovered a viable elixir that could ensure you an heir with your next... release. She left all the instructions behind in her work journal—a journal I still possess. She had just successfully finalized the recipe around the time of her passing, so you were never made aware of it."

King Alastair flexes his jaw. "And why am I just now hearing of this?"

"I only recently discovered the journal in a pile of her old work aprons."

Lie.

All of it—every last bit.

The king is silent for a long moment. For a *very* long moment. He rubs a finger over the top of his lip, humming with thought. Finally, he huffs a laugh—seemingly more amused with himself than anything else. "I do love a good wager," he muses. "Very well. I will indulge this silly game. You may depart for Bathara and participate in their entrance exams. Then, *when* you fail, you must swear that you will return to me immediately, and you will fulfill your promise in providing me with an heir."

I raise my eyes from the ground and lift my chin. "If I pass, you must swear to release me from my blood-oath to you."

The king's smile is baleful. A patronizing condescension sings in his eyes as a smug expression settles on his face. "If you pass the exam and are *offered* a place at Bathara, I wouldn't even really have a choice, now would I?" He chuckles, and my bones begin to hum with the anger lacing through my filaments at the sound. "But very well. I will swear it."

He smiles, but I do not return the gesture. "Then it would seem we have a wager, *My King.*"

His brows jump at my sudden boldness, but it seems he's presently too amused with the recent turn of events to be angry. "What a convenience that we have a Sealer in our midst to finalize this sweet treat." Still smiling, King Alastair peels his eyes from me and glances back at Sterling. "Would you mind?" he sings.

Sterling inclines his head. "Of course, Your Majesty." He steps down the dais and halts directly between the king and me. He unsheathes a dagger from his hip and meets my eyes. "May I?" He nods toward my hand.

Swallowing back any lingering hesitation, I lift my hand and place it in the palm of Sterling's. With the cool tip of the dagger, he knicks my finger, drawing blood. After, he does the same to the king, pressing our fingers together, coalescing the tiny pools.

Sterling's palms warm, and that warmth funnels around the king's and my connected fingers. Hazy white light appears, cocooning our hands—the small pool of crimson dribbling from our skin. "This wager will be sealed in blood. If one forfeits the terms, they forfeit their life." He turns to face the king. "Your Majesty, do you agree to the terms that, if Lyra completes the entrance exams and is offered a place at Bathara, you will release her from her blood-oath, thus relinquishing her from her servitude?"

King Alastair's silver eyes do not break away from me. "I agree to those terms."

Sterling swivels his gaze to me. "Lyra, do you agree to the terms that, if you fail the exams or do not receive a formal offer of admittance into the academy, leaving you Unselected, you will return to the king without delay and fulfill your promise to ensure that he receives an heir?"

I lift my chin. "I agree to the terms."

"Very well," Sterling says. "Then the blood wager is sealed."

The light intensifies, and with it comes a wave of tingling heat. It boils the small pool of blood gathering on the pads of our still-touching fingers. Feeling something like a creeping insect, the blood seeps beneath our skin, forming a small crimson tattoo of a blood droplet on the corners of both King Alastair's and my index finger.

Which means the seal is final—there is no going back now.

King Alastair pulls his finger from mine and inspects his new mark. Once finished, he flicks his eyes up at me and huffs a laugh. He leans forward, his lips grazing the skin of my ear. "I look forward to watching you fail, little pet. And receiving an heir in the process." He pulls back and smiles.

And it is an act of the gods that I do not spit in his face.

The king reorients his attention to the two guards posted beside Gray. "Unshackle the boy. I'm done here." Without so much as another word, the king saunters away—as if he's just finished a mundane meal on an ordinary evening—whistling low and rhythmically as he goes.

When the two towering doors are pulled open, revealing a luxurious hall lined with priceless paintings, arched windows, and relics, King Alastair halts and turns his chin over his shoulder. "Oh, and pet? I demand you have salt rubbed in your wounds before allowing any healers or remedies to touch you. Do not think I have forgotten how you spoke to me a moment ago." He pauses, and the corners of his lips tighten with anger. "And now, as you depart from this kingdom, I will not let you forget it, either."

Then he's gone, the doors groaning to a close behind him.

I don't realize I've been biting the inside of my lip so forcefully until the tangy, metallic taste of blood swims along my tongue. I unclench my jaw, blow out all the air and tension that's built up in my chest, and I race for Gray—

Not stopping for even a single moment to think about what the hell I've just done.

CHAPTER NINE

There are moments.

Moments when the weight of one's damaged self becomes so overwhelming, so daunting, all one can do is idly float through it, as if untethered from their own body, moving through the haze of sorrow and regret, mindlessly—numbly.

The proceeding hours following what happened in the throne room were composed of such moments.

It hadn't been my ears listening to Gray scream as healers mended him. Those hadn't been my hands cradling his head in my lap. Hadn't been my fingers uncorking a vial of sleeping tonic I'd originally prepared for other uses, forcing it down Gray's scratchy throat, plunging him into a hazy unconsciousness so he wouldn't have to feel the pain. Those hadn't been my strangled cries as Sterling—gently as he possibly could—rubbed sea salt into the lacerations on my back, because I'd asked him to be the one to do it.

Those now permanent trails of war wounds along my back and lower thighs hadn't been earned, merely given, and it surely hadn't been my body that experienced the pain from them. Just like it hadn't been my body being mended once the salt crystallized the skin into beautiful flakes of marred ash.

No. It had been a variation of me—some version that is conjured to be a stand-in when the weight of painful realities press too heavily against my heart and mind, plunging me beneath the waves of awareness, sinking me into a sullen state of oblivion.

And once I'm tethered back to my body, it's like waking up from a strange, vivid dream.

The hearth is roaring, the sounds of crackling flames and pops of wood a welcome background noise to the blaring silence in my head.

Sterling approaches on light feet, resting a gentle hand on my shoulder as he passes, making for the chair across from me. I lightly touch my fingers to his hand before they drop back into my lap, as if they are too heavy to hold upright.

"How are you feeling?" he asks, his voice soft as feathers. "Is your back troubling you?"

I snort a hollow laugh. "I'm alright."

My eyes drift across the room to Gray, who sleeps soundly on a cot the healers brought out for him. The walls of my heart constrict when I glimpse his smoothed-over face. The outlines of pain have finally melted away.

When I return my attention forward, Sterling is watching me with a gentle expression. One I know sees through me—gleans down to my very core. So it is for that reason I openly speak.

"What Gray did for me...the fact that he stepped in..." My mouth flounders, unable to find words, and the pain in my heart somehow signals my eyes to well with tears.

Sterling leans forward and places his hand over mine. "He did exactly as Azalea and I have raised him to do."

I swallow back the rising lump in my throat. "Sterling...what the hell just happened?" My question squeaks out of me. "What have I done?"

Understanding the real underlying question, he squeezes my hand a final time before leaning back into the oversized chair. "You have done what a person who is willing to fight for their freedom would do. And you should not feel guilt, nor shame, nor any other emotion outside of pride for it." He does not waver. "Tonight, you stood up to a king. Something men raised in court all their lives only dream of doing."

I shoot him a dry look. "I think you're confusing courage with unfounded confidence. I've never even left the Rivara Kingdom before. And now?" I scoff, disbelieving. "Now I can wield magic after twenty-one years, and the world beyond these borders suddenly feels real. Like a fairytale brought to life. And I have no idea what to do with it."

I can wield magic.

I can *wield magic.*

What a strange, foreign sentence that would have been only a day ago. It would have also been a falsehood—a lie.

Now it is an unequivocal truth.

How odd, the way a lie can turn into a truth so quickly.

Sterling tilts his head. "All the same, you saw the situation for what it was, and you took advantage. You did well, Lyra. You thought quickly and rationally." His eyes soften as a small curve pulls at his stubbly lips. "I am quite proud of you."

My eyes snap to his—emotion I am incapable of expressing swelling in my chest—and I observe Sterling as if for the first time.

Sometimes, it's strange watching him—taking in his features. It's like I've glimpsed into the future and am seeing the man Gray is destined to become. They have the same coppery flare of moss and gold in their eyes. The same nose. The same infectious smile that immediately disarms a person. The only real difference between them lies in Sterling's aging lines and the silver threading through his fading brown hair.

"I only acted on what you suggested," I say after a passing moment. "I would have never thought of something as ludicrous as me participating in Bathara's entrance exams had your fascinating mind not thought of it."

Sterling arches a brow, a slight chuckle trickling into his words. "Right. So you made a blood wager on your ability to pass them and gain admittance into the academy instead."

A dry laugh blows from my lips. "Fair point."

He smiles, bringing his thumb up to his mouth in thought. His brows wrinkle, and his whole expression—demeanor, even—shifts. "Lyra, I must confess something to you."

The sharp change in his tone has me tugging at my brows. "What is it?"

He releases a drawn out sigh. "That night with your mother, when the king—"

I cut him off with a raised hand. "I'm aware of the night you're referencing."

I don't attempt to mask a single fracture as it leaks into my expression at the mention. He knows what happened that night with my mother—knows my deepest scars, what plagues my most terrifying nightmares.

Understanding washes through his features, and he nods—as if more to himself than anything else. "That night, after all was done, there was a peculiar shift in the air. I quickly realized the shift was coming from you—was *because* of you."

I blink, confused. "Me?"

He dips his chin. "Yes, you. The king felt it, too. He was departing but stopped. And in that moment, I saw two paths emerge before me."

A knot forms in my chest as a creeping fear blooms in my stomach.

Sterling draws in a slow, measured breath. "Before her passing, your mother suspected your wielding would be...special." He chooses the last word carefully, and my brows twitch at his choice.

"Special?" I repeat. "How so?"

I mean, I know flora wielders aren't as common as water or fire-wielders, but they aren't necessarily *rare*, either. Certainly not rare like Gray's illusionary magic or Sterling's ability to Seal. So what could possibly make my magic more special than types like theirs? Other than the fact that my ability to use it manifested so late.

Sterling rises from his chair. Silently, he moves to the hearth and, to my surprise, pulls a hollowed-out tome from the shelf. Inside it rests a smaller leather book, worn with age. He retrieves the tattered thing and repositions the larger tome on the shelf. On his way back, Sterling gently rests the journal in my lap before returning to his chair.

Once settled, he peaks his fingers over his lips. "Lyra...I did something that night. Something I have pondered over for many years." He pauses, an indent forming between his brows. "In your heightened emotional state, you manifested your ability to wield, and I...I sealed it

68

away, erasing any lingering traces of it from your veins." He releases a loaded breath. "I had a decision to make, and I made it. I will not sit before you and argue I made the correct one, but I will sit here before you and tell you I made the decision I thought would keep you safe—would best protect you from the king."

The world tilts, the fabrics of my understanding with it.

A spectrum of emotions rip through me within an instant. Betrayal, anger, confusion, frustration—yet, regardless of how viscerally each and every emotion hits my heart, my body seems to settle on one. The least suspecting of them all.

Acceptance.

I could get angry with Sterling. I could kick and scream and yell, making declarations like *you ruined my life* or *you lied to me*. But what would that really accomplish? What would be the point?

Sterling still took me in as his ward. Still raised me as if I was his own daughter. He and Azalea provided me with a home, with love, with an education—a family. I'm not going to spit on those selfless actions for something I long ago decided is not a necessity to my life. Besides...

Would I have chosen any differently if presented with the same choice?

Sterling's seen more than I can imagine, being King Alastair's right hand and all. So, despite my head telling me I should be angry, it's the absence of doubt resting in my heart, knowing Sterling made the decision he truly believed would be best for me, that settles me into a calm resignation for that which has passed.

Still, thinking of the past makes that resurfaced memory gnaw at my chest. The one where Sterling, Azalea, and my mother sit in front of the same hearth I sit beside now. Their whispers. My eavesdropping. My mother's pleas for aid. It was a memory buried deep within me. One I had completely forgotten, until it surfaced in a fog of color behind my shut eyes.

I thumb through the yellowed pages of the small book. "So my mother suspected my magic would be special, and you sealed it away to protect me from the king."

Though I don't say it like a question, Sterling still answers, "Yes."

I do my best to let the weight of that realization settle. "Thank you," I murmur. "For protecting me when there was no one left to."

Sterling's eyes shudder before falling shut, and he looks...relieved. Unburdened, even. Like I've just handed him the key to free himself from weighted shackles.

When he reopens his eyes, he appears brighter. "I want you to read that journal in your lap. I suspect you'll find important answers in doing so." He nods his head in the direction of the leather-bound pages. "Read it thoroughly. Read it wholly. But more than anything—" a sharp, knowing look "—make sure you actually *read* it. *All* of it."

"Whose is it?" I ask, cracking the cover for a peek.

"It belonged to the son of the first Rivarian king, King Isaphus. Casimir Vivaldri was his name."

"Casimir Vivaldri..." I repeat the name slowly. "And why give his journal to me? More importantly, how did *you* end up with it?"

Suddenly, my mother's request to Sterling—plucked from the seams of that memory—echoes through me.

Somewhere, there is a record of everything, and it will confirm what I have told you—what has mostly been lost to neglect and time. I have good reason to believe it is in the king's restricted section of his library, in the archival records. Promise me you'll search for it.

Sterling gave his word to her that night, and Sterling *never* goes back on his word. This must be what my mother wanted him to find. I'm not the least bit surprised that he managed to recover the item, but what I can't deduce is why she asked him to find it in the first place.

What had she seen in the Veil?

Veilreaders sip from a potent elixir, allowing them to transcend the fabrics of this world and enter into a place known as the Veil. Little is understood about the Veil. The consensus is that it's beyond mortal comprehension. Yet, some wielder's possess a special type of laktî—the substance in a wielder's veins that allows them to access magic— permitting them to see imagery and patterns within the fog of the Veil. It's all a rather abstract artform, really. Different from Seers and Diviners.

Seers gaze into the future with a clear eye. Diviners congregate with the gods—are a medium for which hidden knowledge is passed and exchanged. But Veilreaders *experience* the future as a swirling, abstract possibility. They don't receive concrete answers, but instead are presented with fragmented glimpses that must be interpreted like a riddle. The Veil is full of potential, yes—but it is also full of ambiguity.

They often work hand-in-hand with Gardners, typically serving kings. Though King Alastair never learned of my mother's gift to enter the Veil. He only knew her as an exceptional Gardner.

Sterling sighs, rubbing a hand along his stubble-filled jaw. "Lyra, I fear you will soon find yourself at a crossroads. You will face things far greater and more dangerous than just King Alastair now. Things that, as much as I wish I could, I cannot protect you from." He pauses, his eyes falling downwards with something that looks a lot like sadness. "I wish I could save you from your fate, but what is chosen by the Cycle cannot be undone. Besides, I fear they already know you've awakened."

They?

My brows furrow heavily. "Sterling, what are you saying?"

He shakes his head, and the corners of his lips twitch with an attempt at a smile. "Nothing. Forgive me. Just...read the journal. *All* of it."

My brow curves up at him. "Cryptic words from a cryptic man," I mutter.

He chuckles. "You are a smart girl, Lyra. I have no doubts you will find your way."

That makes one of us.

There is a brief silence that passes, and Sterling sucks in a loud breath, clapping his hands to his knees as he does. "I know there is still much to discuss—"

"—Like how I plan on winning a blood wager dependent on me passing a deadly entrance exam that people train their whole lives for when my ability to wield magic has only manifested this evening?" My voice is dry, sprinkled with humor.

"Yes," Sterling says with an incline of his head. "Things like that." He rises and sends a warm smile in my direction. "We will discuss more in the morning. For now, get some sleep. You will have a long day of travel tomorrow." He presses a kiss to the top of my head before turning on his heels and heading to his bedchambers, where a sleeping Azalea waits for his warmth.

I call out to him, halting his steps. "What if I lose this blood wager?" My voice drops to a meek, vulnerable whisper. "I can't... I can't give the king what I've offered."

Sterling slowly turns his chin over his shoulder, glancing back at me. "Then you mustn't lose."

He retreats into the shadows of his bedchamber, leaving me overflowing with thoughts. I stare at the dark threshold for a moment longer, until I glance down at the journal resting in my lap. To the thing that, according to Sterling, will all but decide some life-altering decision for me.

Curious, and with a wrinkle wedged in my brow, I pull back the cover.

First impression? The pages are old as dust, but the hand-writing is immaculate.

Finding myself washed in a wave of intrigue, I crack the leather spine open to a random page and read.

When I rest my eyes, all I can see is the look in the man's horrified stare—gone before he even had time to register what was happening.

Did he have a family? Did he have a son or a daughter that would wonder why their dad has never returned home? Sure, that man was the same man I caught pinning Sitara against a wall one drunken night. The man the servants whispered about for taking too much interest in young children.

But did any of that justify me taking his life?

If we all believe we are right when we seek the highest price to quench our thirst for revenge, where does the line begin, and where does it end? For even a hero, from the villain's eyes, may be equally as cruel in his quest to achieve what he believes, disguising his actions as noble under the name of justice. For that matter, what are heroes and what are villains but two titles given to characters in a story meant to label their deeds as "right" or "wrong"?

See, the trouble I have always found is neither right nor wrong point true. It is the storyteller who gives those two words direction. So, I can't help but sit and wonder... What if we read the story without the titles? Who would we deem the villain? If we were privy to the reasonings behind every action, would we deem anyone a villain? Perhaps we would instead discover what broke. Learn how to fix it.

More than that, if someone scribed the story of my life, would they deem me a hero or a villain for what I've done?

And am I nothing more than a heartless monster for thinking he deserved it?

    Casimir

My breath catches in my throat, and I slam the journal shut.

That was a hell of a page to turn to. But...noted. No more skipping pages.

Finding myself unbearably exhausted and not wanting to leave Gray alone, I collect a pile of fur blankets from around the room and pile them on top of each other next to Gray's cot. I grab a feather pillow off the chaise, and I lay down beside him, letting my eyes fall to rest.

Despite being drained, despite my body and mind begging for the reprieve of sleep, I can't get Casimir Vivaldri's words out of my head.

Would they deem me a hero or a villain for what I've done?

The question stirs a restlessness inside me—mostly because, in an odd way, reading his words felt inexplicably familiar. As if they were strung together from the very essence of my soul, forged from the same material as my own thoughts.

A gnawing feeling grows in my chest, swelling into a persistent weight behind my ribcage. It creeps up the bones of my spine, pressing up against the boundaries of my mind, shifting into a question without form, persistent and maddeningly incomplete.

And am I nothing more than a heartless monster for thinking he deserved it?

I wonder what my answer would be.

CHAPTER TEN

There is a silver candlestick resting on a table.

There are two bodies. One with closed eyes, and the other with open eyes that are unseeing.

A small girl charges. Blood pools on the floor. And then the tiny room containing her tiny feet erupts with flames. They dance and twirl around her. Lick her until she is bathed in vermillion. But the flames do not burn her—no. Even though she wishes they did, the flames instead burn those who bear the unseeing eyes.

The tiny girl stretches a hand out. She opens her mouth to call a name—a title. Yet a wall of fire keeps them apart. Cruel laughter cackles in the air as words boom through every crevice. *It should be you, you know. It is all your fault.*

The flames brighten—come alive with a hypnotic quality. The girl begs them to burn her instead. Still, they do not. The cruel voice spews malicious words, and the girl absorbs them into the layers of her skin. She hears the words, *Burn. Burn. Burn.* Just as the girl is ready to concede to the voice behind the flame, another calls out to her. The girl whips her head and sees—

"Lyra," Gray's gentle voice and soft touch to my shoulder jolts me awake.

I sit up and blink, scanning the room while mussing a hand through my disheveled hair. I blow out an exasperated sigh.

A dream.

It was all just a dream.

Except…

It wasn't.

I rub the blurry exhaustion from my eyes and lay back down. "What time is it?"

"Early," he answers softly. "Too early. Especially for you." He drops his voice into a gentle whisper. "You were having another nightmare."

Though my eyes stare up at a ceiling, a ceiling is not what they see. They still see flames curling, dancing higher and higher into the air.

"I was." I blow out a sigh and turn onto my side, facing Gray. "Thanks for waking me up," I murmur.

The hearth has died down into softly glowing embers, casting the chamber in a dim red-golden light, flickering faintly across the stone walls and wooden beams. It casts a curling shadow over Gray. He stretches a hand out and lightly grazes his thumb across my cheek, brushing away a tiny remnant of a runaway tear. "Whenever you're ready to tell me about them, I'm ready to listen."

I chew on my lip. "I know."

Flashes of the glass-laced whip slashing Gray's skin flicker behind my eyes. His pain, his cries—they echo mercilessly in my mind. "How are you feeling?"

His voice is so, so gentle when he answers. "I'm okay."

"Does it…do you still feel any pain?"

He shakes his head. "None in the slightest. Healers are truly a wonder, aren't they? I can see why you wanted to be one when we were kids."

I muster a weak laugh.

Gray spreads his fingers across my cheek, cupping my face. "Thank you for staying with me while I was being mended. And for the sleeping tonic, as well."

"It was nothing compared to what you did for me," I rasp.

He drops his hand from my face and tucks it snugly beneath his head, not looking away from me as he does. "And I would do it all again if it meant you remained unharmed."

My brows pinch together. "You shouldn't have to suffer."

"And neither should you."

A lump rises in my throat. I roll onto my back so I can once again stare at the ceiling, a heavy ache throbbing beneath my ribs. It swells so forcefully that, for a moment, I wonder if my chest might explode.

I am so lost in the sensation, I don't notice the rustling of blankets and the small creak of the cot. Not until Gray slides into the fur blankets next to me and wraps his familiar arms around me.

And it's strange. The way the action makes me feel better and worse all at once.

He holds me against his chest as he whispers onto the top of my head, "Go back to sleep, Lyra. And know that I'm here if the nightmares return."

Tears prick in my eyes, begging to be released. But I force them away, back to the duct from which they came. I will not cry. I will not give life to the painful feelings. I will not give the king power over me. Crying means he's won—that he got to me.

I refuse to let him win.

Sterling came and woke Gray and me right as the sun crested over the horizon.

In the wee, bleeding hours of the morning, he proposes a simple solution to help with my inexperience as a wielder—having Gray train me before and between tests, teaching me the fundamentals of both magic and combat needed to survive.

When I ask how he knows it'll be enough, Sterling simply shrugs. "Because it will have to be."

After we finish strategizing, I beeline for my room and gather the remaining supplies I have readily available—wrapping them carefully, tucking some neatly into a lidded box, and placing the rest in my pack. Once I have everything, I walk briskly to the stables before my absence is noticed.

I find Delroy brushing a beautiful silver-speckled mare. "Ah, Lyra," he chimes when he sees me. "To what do I owe this pleasure?" He sets his brush on a stool and hobbles over to me.

I smile when I notice his movements are less rigid.

"I–uh…I am leaving for a trip, and so I wanted to leave this with you." I hold up the box for emphasis before setting it gently on top of a rough-hewn wooden shelf mounted on the wall.

His eyes linger on me before he grabs the box and rummages through it. "So it would seem that you are. The whole bloody city is already talking about you."

My brows lurch before wrinkling. "What? How in gods-veins do people already know—"

"—About your magic and blood wager with the king?" Delroy glances at me, arching a bushy brow. "Guards are big gossips."

I don't even know what to say. Thankfully, Delroy speaks instead.

"There are a lot of tonics and healing supplies in here, dear girl. Supplies that would fetch a pretty coin for their potency and abilities." He closes the box and returns it to the shelf. "Why have you brought them here? Why not take them with you?"

"I won't have any need for them where I'm going. Or at the very least, I'll have access to the supplies to make more if I need to. I want you to have them." At his sharp gaze, I quickly add, "Please."

I've always believed Delroy's stubborn pride made life harder for him than it needed to be. Though, it's not like I fault him. We all have something.

He sits on a small wooden stool directly across from the stall housing Rylier, a large black stallion. "And why give them to me?"

I approach Rylier and run a hand down his neck. "Because I know you will use them well. If not for yourself, then for others." I drop my hand and face Delroy. "Tell the servants you trust what you have. Let them know they can come to you after one of the king's summons. Give them to a family. I don't care what you do with them, Delroy. Just see to it they do good. Most here already trust you."

He releases a long sigh, rubbing a hand across his head. "Alright."

Not wanting to push my luck, but knowing it needs to be done, I also add, "And I'd like to change your bandages and apply more salve before I go."

He glances at me pointedly, but I shoot him an equally sharp look back.

He chuckles. "Fine."

Without wasting a moment, I gather what I need and silently work with a swift pace, knowing I need to get to the atrium soon to meet Gray, Sterling, and Klytis so we can depart for the academy. Sterling hates tardiness, yet time is not on my side, as I still have one other errand I need to do before leaving.

I've just finished tending to Delroy when Thestis, the errand boy, sprints inside.

"I...caught...you," he says through winded breaths.

I laugh, walking around Delroy to stand in front of Thestis. "And why was I in need of catching?"

"I...heard...about...Bathara."

"By the gods, boy. Give yourself a second to catch your breath," Delroy chastises.

I place a hand on my hip and watch—a humored smile curling my lip—as Thestis slowly lifts his hands off his knees and draws in a few gulps of air. Finally, seeming to have his breathing under control, he lifts his chin and waltzes right up to me. "Is it true?" He asks with wide eyes.

"Is what true?"

"Did you really make a blood wager with the king? Are you really going to compete for a place at Bathara?" He leans forward onto his tippy-toes, and I can make out the splatter of freckles sprinkling across his cheeks.

His words to Gray flash through my mind.

My 'Ma told me I shouldn't hold onto such silly hopes; she thinks it's nice you train me in your free time, but she also thinks it's a waste of time.

Because nobody like him has ever done it before. Because this world has written off those without titles or noble blood. Because we are told we can't.

But I'm tired of being told what I can and cannot do.

I hold Thestis's wide-eyed gaze firmly. "It is true. I am going to compete in Bathara's entrance exams, and I am going to pass them."

"But...you're like me. A servant. A...nobody."

His words don't hold a single bite of malice nor a sliver of resentment. Instead, his voice is airy and light. He has the same cadence a child uses when they question the phenomena of the world around them; like how the stars burn and float in the sky, and how it is possible to wield magic in this realm of mortals.

I rest my hands gently on his shoulders. "All the same, what I've said remains true. I will pass. And I will be admitted into Bathara."

He stares at me curiously for a long moment. Finally, he rustles around for something in his trouser pocket, pulling his hand out and uncurling his fist to reveal a dainty necklace. "I was out late in the night running an errand for one of the king's courtesans when I overheard the guard's talking. When I got home, I woke my 'Ma and told her everything. She helped me make this for you." He lifts his hand up to me, silently urging me to take the jewelry, and I glimpse the red staining his cheeks.

With a swell in my heart, I take the necklace and hold it up to the light. Made of dark, supple leather—probably scrapped from worn boots or something similar—it features a small, oblong shaped stone suspended on a small loop at the necklace's center. The stone is crystallized into a near-translucent pale blue, coated in what looks like a sheet of shimmering ice, cracks branching like icy veins, wrapping around like glittering spiderwebs.

Thestis shifts on his feet, wringing his hands. "The stone isn't anything special; it's just a rock I found. I imbued it with my ice magic to make it look like that. I'm still learning, but it should remain that way."

I marvel at the dainty piece resting between my fingertips. It is perhaps one of the most beautiful works of art I've ever seen. Suddenly, I remember what Gray said about Thestis.

His ice magic is something special. I think that even a Fjolla would find themselves impressed by it.

Impressive, indeed.

I pull the necklace over my head and tighten the bead at the back to secure the cord around my neck. It rests perfectly at the base of my throat. My fingertips graze the icy stone, finding it cold to the touch, but not uncomfortably so. "Please don't misinterpret my confusion as ungratefulness because this—" I clutch the stone for emphasis "—this is the most amazing necklace I have ever seen. But why give it to me?"

Thestis's cheeks burn bright red. "My 'Ma said if you make it—if you actually get accepted into Bathara—that maybe there will be hope for me after all. She's going to allow me to train with a real tutor if you're admitted. Said that it'll be the start of a new future." His eyes dart to the side as he shifts on his feet. "She serves in the kitchens, so you probably don't remember her, but she remembers you. My 'Ma...she says you've always had this fire about you. She thinks if anyone can do it, you can."

"I'm inclined to agree with the boy's mother," Delroy chimes in from the stool, leaning forward with his arms braced on his thighs. A small, assured smile rests content on his lips.

And if I were someone comfortable with allowing the weight of emotions to be felt, I may have cried right then and there.

"The necklace is for good luck." He averts his eyes again, speaking while his fingers twirl over themselves. "We said a prayer over it to the Mother Goddess, Ahlai, because we know your mom was a Gardner. We also prayed to Raffir, the god of luck and good fortune. It probably didn't work but—"

I kneel and throw my arms around Thestis's tiny neck. He stiffens at first, but eventually, he squeezes me back with all the force in the world, nuzzling his chin into my hair.

"Show Bathara we matter, too," he murmurs into the crook of my neck. "That we aren't lesser than the others." He squeezes tighter. "Make them see us."

I pull back to meet his eyes, gripping the edge of his shoulders with my fingertips. "I promise I will."

CHAPTER ELEVEN

I leave the stables, saying goodbye to a hopeful Thestis and a smiling Delroy, and I immediately make my way to the attendant's wing.

Taking cautions to remain unseen, I slip my remaining sleeping tonics, paired with their anonymous note of instructions, under my fellow night attendants' doors. For an attendant named Tali—a beautiful dark-skinned, dark-haired night entertainer—I slip in detailed instructions on how to create the simplest sleeping tonic I could think of. She shows promise in the arts, and now, she can attempt to at least make *something* for the attendants to have as a safeguard.

When I finish, I exhale deeply—exhausted, yet content—and head briskly through the corridors toward the atrium. At least now, I can leave knowing they'll have supplies to last them a while longer and the means to make more. As I walk, my fingers won't stop toying with the icy stone now resting at the base of my throat.

I reach the atrium and pull back the crested wooden doors, revealing a large room filled with paned-ceilings and windows, greenery as far as the eye can see, and statues of the gods. Gray spots me first, and a humored smirk pulls at his lips. It doesn't take me long to realize why.

Sterling turns around, hands braced on his hips, a lecture waiting in his eyes. "Where have you been? And where is your travel pack?" He sweeps his eyes up and down, looking for the missing item I didn't think to bring.

"I went to see Delroy. I wanted to say goodbye." I stand a little straighter and flash an unconvincing smile, not daring to offer any information about my parting gifts to the other attendants—or the fact that I've neglected to pack.

Gray tilts his head, a silent laugh dancing on his lips, twirling into his eyes. "I have her travel pack." He unfolds his arms and slides it off his shoulders, handing it off to me. "Here you are," he says as he places the strap in my hand, his eyes holding mine steady with that quiet amusement. "As *requested*."

I flash him an exasperated look of gratitude.

Thank you, thank you, thank you.

"See," I chirp to Sterling after I sling it around my shoulder. "Good to go."

Sterling, looking unconvinced of my preparedness, hums. "Be that as it may, there is still the matter of Klytis."

My eyes rove across the room, and I realize Klytis is indeed absent.

Strange.

Klytis is never late—mostly because he can just open portals to and from places as an aether-wielder.

I begin to walk around the room. "Well then, it would appear I am perfectly on time." I glance over my shoulder and catch Sterling rolling his eyes, and Gray snorting a laugh. A pointed smile tugs at my lips, and I clasp my fingers behind my back and continue strolling.

Standing proud in front of each arched window, surrounded by rose vines, are beautiful white jade sculptures depicting the primary gods—also known as the Canamae, the pillars of our mortal world. To the left are the male gods: Merikh, god of death and war, Algol, god of trickery and deception; Raffir, god of the harvest and prosperity, as well as luck and fortune, and Astralis, god of the stars and justice. To the right are the goddesses: Adhara, goddess of love and beauty, and Araceli, goddess of health, fertility, and purity; Saffi, goddess of cunning and knowledge, and Ahlai, the Mother Goddess who oversees all.

I stop in front of the Mother Goddess's statue. Gardner's are said to be Ahlai's children, and within Eden, the garden oasis city where people go to train to become Gardners, there is a sacred ritual that Blesses those who complete their training and are deemed worthy by the Masters there. My mother wouldn't tell me what the ritual was—she was forbidden from it, as all who become Gardners are—but she always said after receiving her Blessing, she never once couldn't feel the Mother Goddess's presence within her.

A swirling portal of silver and black appears, and Klytis emerges. I turn back to Ahlai's statue, press a kiss to my two fingers, and lightly place them at its base, hoping she will share the gesture with my mother.

I waltz back over just in time to hear Sterling chide, "And where have you been?"

Klytis—only a few years older than me—rubs the back of his neck. "I was in a meeting with the king."

Sterling pauses before sighing. "Out with it, then."

Klytis drops his hand from his neck. "I've been commanded by His Majesty to only transport them to the entrance at Foreigner's Valley."

"Foreigner's Valley, huh..." Sterling rubs his stubble-filled jaw. "What about the outskirts of the Cliffs of Yilandra or at least to the outer edges of the Endymion Mountains?"

Klytis shakes his head. "His Majesty was adamant. I am to take them to the entrance of the valley, and only to the entrance." He pauses, and flicks his pale blue eyes to me, sympathy resting within them. "He said, 'Tell my pet the game has begun.'"

Sterling pinches the bridge of his nose. "I suspected he'd have *something* up his sleeve." He reaches into his tunic and pulls out a tiny vial strung with twine, like a pendant on a necklace, filled with a deep green liquid. Sterling locks eyes with Gray, and then me. "I need the both of you to listen carefully and heed my next words. There have been recent reports of creatures awakening in that valley. It is imperative that you take precautions and always remain on guard. Stay together. No matter what. Find a cave to rest in overnight, always quell your fire when the moon finds its peak, and *never* travel through the night. Understood?"

Gray and I both dip our chins in acknowledgment.

"Good," Sterling replies. "Now take this." He gently places the vial in my hand and guides my fingers to a fist. "This is a paralyticus potion Azalea made. One drop on the tongue, and it would paralyze even a bull for at least an hour. Be wise with how you use it."

My heart squeezes at the mention of Azalea. Saying goodbye to her this morning had been unbearably hard. Still, I again dip my chin. "We will," I assure him.

Klytis picks at his nail and muses, "Hopefully you won't have to use it at all."

Gray shoots him a side-eye. "Yes, hopefully. Though it would be great to *not* be transported into the valley."

Klytis arches an auburn-colored brow. "Would you like to go plead your case to the king, then? I'm just following orders here."

"Klytis is right," Sterling supplies. "It is not his fault for what the king has decided."

Klytis winks at Gray; Gray rolls his eyes. And then they start bickering some more.

It makes me giggle, watching the two of them. Though I may have no one else outside of Gray, the same isn't true for him. Besides me, Klytis has always been his closest companion. Certainly his closest *male* companion.

Sterling taps my shoulder, redirecting my attention. "While they squabble, might I have a word? There are a few things I wanted to discuss with you privately."

I nod, and he guides me over to the other side of the room. Once safely out of ear-shot, I ask, "What is it you'd like to discuss?"

He clasps his hands behind his back and draws in a deep breath. "Firstly, I'd like to provide you with a warning. I've heard Erandor Kingdom's Supreme Commander often frequents Bathara. I hear he offers stratagem advice to the council at times. I would like to warn you to avoid him at all costs, but I fear that is not entirely feasible. So instead, I'd advise that, should you ever cross paths with him, mind your words, and remember that everything is a game of wits with that man." Sterling watches me closely, ensuring I absorb his guidance. "Under no circumstances, ever, should you trust him. The Dalmar bloodline is not only known for their peculiar dark magic, but also for their ability to wear many masks."

I've heard of Erandor's tyrant commander. The Great Leader of Legions, he is called. Hailed wielder of the most powerful magic known to the Three Kingdoms—dark magic. He is said to be a master strategist with an almost preternatural sharpness of mind. He is also the head of House Dalmar, another Great House, and the third and final remaining bloodline constituting the Archbloods, alongside the Sulien and Fjolla lines.

Tynan Dalmar.

Despite being an Archblood and honored for his progenitor bloodline, Tynan is a man known for his delights in bestial acts, said to have a fascination with human nature that expands beyond acceptable curiosity. He is also a man swimming in controversial rumors—the most prominent being that he abused his son, his heir, to turn him into an emotionless weapon.

Yet Tynan Dalmar is too powerful—too formidable— for anyone to care.

Even if Sterling hadn't warned me, I would have done my best to avoid anything to do with that man and his bloodline at all costs.

"I understand," I say to Sterling. "Is that all?"

He sighs. "Not quite. I have one last thing—a favor to ask of you, really."

I tilt my head. "What is it?"

A poignant smile pulls at his lips. He glances over his shoulder toward Gray and Klytis, who are laughing about gods only know what, before looking back at me. "Take care of him for Azalea and me," he requests in a gentle murmur.

Understanding who he means, I slide my eyes to Gray—who is now speaking in animated gestures with his hands—and a small, wistful grin sweeps across my lips. "He doesn't need me to take care of him."

"No," Sterling agrees through his fleeting smile. "But he does need you to aid him. Sometimes, his deep conviction to do what he feels is right can cloud him from making the hard choices. He sees right and wrong, morality and justice, in shades of black and white. While you, Lyra, understand they are not." He pauses, thinking for a moment. "Those who live in the gray have much less to lose than those who build their foundations using black and white stones. So in that sense, my dear girl, I ask you to help guide my son. Promise me you'll help him if he ever loses his way."

The thought of Gray wandering lost provokes a sudden ache in my chest. "Of course I will. I will always be there for him, no matter what."

"Thank you." Sterling inclines his head. "I will sleep better through the nights knowing you two will be looking out for each other."

I snort a laugh. "That makes two of us."

His eyes crinkle. "Parting hug for a nagging, aging man?" Sterling outstretches his arms to me, and I gladly step into them. When he lets me go, he clears his throat and addresses Gray and Klytis. "Now, then. It's time to depart."

We emerge from the portal of swirling black and silver.

"I'm afraid this is where I must leave you," Klytis says from behind us as Gray and I adjust to the blinding rays of shimmering light.

After Sterling said goodbye to Gray—Gray holding his emotions deep inside his chest, made evident by the constant hitches in his breathing—we offered our final farewells, and that had been that. We followed Klytis through the portal he summoned and emerged beneath a gilded sun and sea-licked breeze.

"Thank you, my friend." Gray extends his arm, holding Klytis's eyes.

Klytis clutches Gray's forearm in return. When he pulls back, his sleeve shifts, and I can see the details of his wielder's mark. Resting in the center of his forearm, a swirl of misty black and silver meet inside the shape of a small keyhole. Flecks of white splatter along the blackness.

"Bathara would be lucky to receive you," Klytis muses with a large grin. "Though the Rivara Kingdom and Keziah mourn losing you."

For a brief moment, my heart feels the weight of a tiny fracture splitting its damaged frame. I've been so occupied with the thought of Gray leaving *me*, I never considered all the others Gray was leaving behind. Naturally, I knew Azalea and Sterling would be difficult, but they have also always held aspirations for Gray to someday become a man who assumes a full and prosperous life of his own—whatever it may look like for him. Yet, I never considered he is leaving Klytis behind, his other best friend. That he has to say goodbye to the tutor he's had since he was a mere boy. Hell, even Thestis would be difficult to say goodbye to, with his wide eyes, scattered freckles, and charming persistence.

Does it make me selfish that I never considered the ramifications outside of myself?

For some odd reason, the passing question surfaces a sentence from Casimir Vivaldri's journal.

More than that, what if someone scribed the story of my life—would they deem me a hero or a villain for what I've done?

And suddenly, my fingers twitch with the desire to reach for Casimir's journal, securely tucked within my personal pack.

"Maybe someday you can leave for Bathara as well," Gray offers. "You're certainly skilled enough."

A rueful smile sweeps over Klytis's lips. "Can't."

I think he's going to elaborate, but then he just...doesn't. Instead, he turns to me, reaches for my hand, and presses a light kiss to the back of it. "Best of luck, Lyra Izacalli. May the gods shine their favor upon you."

Gray rolls his eyes.

When we were teenagers, Klytis was a shameless flirt with me. Until one day, Gray and him had a "talk". He stopped the open flirting, moving instead to small provoking gestures that irk Gray.

And like always, his lips curve up pointedly as he drops my hand. I bite down against my answering smirk, fighting the urge to chuckle at Gray's displayed annoyance and Klytis's delight in it.

"Thanks, Klytis. I left healing supplies with Delroy, should you or anyone you know be in need of them."

"Well, let's pray to the gods I don't." Klytis inclines his head. "But thank you for the information just in case I do."

I dip my chin.

Klytis claps his hands together, and his gaze bounces between Gray and me. "Well, it appears this is goodbye, then." He smiles a final time, his eyes bright. "Give Bathara hell."

He steps backward through the swirling portal, blinking it out of existence.

And Gray and I are officially left to face the valley alone.

CHAPTER TWELVE

F oreigner's Valley.
They tell stories of this place. How it got its name. Why travelers far and wide know to travel cautiously through its deceptively beautiful terrain.

Wedged between the Cliffs of Yilandra and the Endymion Mountains, Foreigner's Valley overflows with lush, sprawling grass, vibrant wildflowers, and towering pines and cedars. There is a sparkling river, split into two separate streams that weave through its center. An assortment of vegetation and herbs sprout along the lands, and it is inhabited by many animals—birds, gazelles, wolves, foxes, and the like. From the outside looking in, it is a peaceful place filled with great beauty.

But on the inside...

The story goes that a foreigner once lost his way in the valley. A foreigner with a twisted and strange sort of magic. Legends claim he heard voices whispering to him. Voices that told him different directions and forced him to walk in circles. After the seventh day, the foreigner—on the verge of madness—went across the valley instead of going through. He hiked to the highest cliff in Yilandra and cursed the valley before jumping from the ledge into the Turely Sea, landing among the jagged rock formations.

Now, it is said any traveler wandering through the land hears those same voices. According to legend, if one is not careful, the trees, flowers, and streams will actually shift direction—changing from east to west, guiding a traveler north whilst they think they're going south. It was the final mark of the foreigner; his curse to those who wander through this forsaken valley.

The legend used to be regarded as nothing more than a mere bedtime story. That is, until the disappearances of travelers in the valley continued to grow—their remains never found again.

"It certainly doesn't look frightening," Gray observes while we walk down a dirt path surrounded by fluffy grass sprinkled with pink and purple flowers.

The Endymion Mountains tower in the south, clouds covering the onyx-colored anthracite composing the mountainside. The valley's river runs east, a vast amount of flowers and vegetation growing along its bed. Birds chirp, blades of grass whistle, the river sings.

It's the perfect alluring trap.

I arch a brow at him. "I think that's kind of the point."

He chuckles lightly, folding his arms across his chest as he walks. "I suppose it is."

I snort a laugh and roll my eyes. "Bathara is due east through the valley. Should we just follow the river and see what happens?"

"I don't see why not. There's no sense in creating solutions for problems that don't yet exist. We'll stay close to the river and follow my father's instructions—making sure to stop when the sun rises and quench our fires when the moon peaks—and we'll see what happens." From my peripheral, I see Gray glance at my throat, a smile tugging at his lips. "That's new." He tilts his head in the direction of my necklace.

My fingers clutch the icy stone as if on instinct. "It was a gift from Thestis, believe it or not."

Gray arches a brow. "Thestis?"

I squeeze the stone a little tighter, the chill of its touch biting into my skin. "His mother said if I'm accepted into Bathara, she'll have him continue his training with a tutor. The necklace is for good luck."

At Gray's silence, I drag my gaze toward him and find he has a giant, goofy grin painted across his face, observing me with a gleam in his eye.

I click my tongue and shove him.

I get it.

I, the pessimist, am giving Thestis's mother a reason to be optimistic. But it doesn't mean he needs to smile at me like that.

After a passing silence, Gray muses in a soft voice, "It is very pretty."

I again graze the glittering stone with the tips of my fingers. "It is," I agree. "Though I think I'm going to need more than just luck to be accepted into Bathara."

With a humorous lilt in his voice, Gray asks, "What else is there besides a little luck?"

I scoff a dry laugh. "Oh, I don't know...actual skills, training, combat ability, magical knowledge." I arch a brow at him. "Shall I continue?"

His lips curve upward with amusement, and he suddenly stops walking.

I halt, slowly turning to face him. "What are you doing?"

With a pointed grin, he claps his hands together. "Well, there's no time like the present, so might as well begin some of your training now."

"What, right here?" My eyes scan the landscape.

Gray shrugs. "It's as good a place as any."

I sigh, feeling a slight nervousness creep into my veins. "Of course you'd say that," I mutter.

"We'll start simple," Gray assures me. "I'm going to restrain you, and I want you to break free and dislodge me."

I lift a suspecting brow. "That's all?"

"That's all," he confirms.

I eye him for a long moment. "Alright. Tell me what to do."

Gray wags a finger at me, instructing me to come near. I approach him, watching him assume a spread out stance. "To start, I want to see what you do. What your instincts tell you. We'll talk about it after the first go."

I nod, and Gray takes that as confirmation to wrap his arms around me, cocooning me inside of his powerful embrace.

"Break free," he commands.

I wiggle, writhe, try to push his arms off by attempting to press my elbows outward, but nothing works. I am helplessly restricted—caged by his strength.

I suck in a breath, not willing to admit defeat yet.

I squirm and twist some more, attempting to buck against him, but Gray simply doesn't budge. I exhale, frustrated, and concede. "I can't."

Gray releases me and steps back. I turn on my heels to face him, and am surprised to see his face assuming a more serious expression, slipping seamlessly into the role of tutor. "There are different strategies for getting out of different types of holds," he begins. "The way I just held you is one of the trickiest to maneuver."

"Okay," I say, a wrinkle forming in my brow. "So what do I do?"

Gray steps forward. "May I?" After a confirming dip of my chin, he steps forward and again embraces me from behind, wrapping his arms tightly around me in the style of a bear hug. "What I want you to do is drop your hips, take a step that reaches outside my legs, and move it behind my feet."

I slowly go through the motions.

"Good," he approves. "Now, when I say so, I want you to grip behind my thighs and, in one quick movement, drop your weight to the ground while sweeping a leg behind me. Okay?"

"Okay."

"Go through each step slowly first," he suggests.

I take a steadying breath and slowly do as he instructs. I drop my hips, slide my foot across the ground and step outside his leg. I reach for behind his sturdy thighs, and I imagine dropping my weight, feeling the phantom sweep of my leg to come.

Gray smiles. "That was great. Now, on my cue... *Go.*"

Using swift, fluid movements, I complete all the steps just as Gray instructed, dropping my weight to the ground and sweeping my leg behind him. He plummets to the soil as a result, still attempting to clutch onto me. But his grip is awkward and loose, and I wiggle free from his hold. I scramble upright, then I whirl back toward him, feeling strong and ready to pounce.

Gray sits up, draping his arms over his bent knees. "You're a natural," he praises, looking up at me with a proud grin.

I fight the urge to roll my eyes and stretch a hand out to him. "And you're biased."

Gray grabs my hand, and I help him stand. He glances down at his rumpled tunic and brushes the dirt from it. "Your doubt in my ability to scout talent wounds me."

I snort a laugh, and he smiles in response.

"That move can drop anyone, no matter their size," he continues, his voice again shifting to a more serious tone. "Whoever it is will try to hold onto you—will try to keep their grip secure—but as soon as they hit the ground, that's when you break free and run."

"Why run? Can't I fight back?"

His eyes soften, and he lightly grips my arms with his fingers. "Eventually. But for now, and while at Bathara, you run."

A small seed of disappointment roots itself in my stomach.

Gray squeezes my arms gently, noticing. "The time will come when you can fight back. But first, you need to learn how to walk before you try to sprint."

Though I hate the taste of it, I know he's right. It's just I've always believed something so different. That running is never an option, and one should simply sink their feet deeper into the mud, standing their ground, and *fight*.

Never let them win.

I tuck a loose strand of hair behind my ear. "What's next?"

❦

Gray and I work through multiple types of holds.

He shows me what to do when someone wraps their arms around my neck. How to tightly pull down their arm as far as I can and drop into a low stance; the art of reading the push and pull of my opponent's energy—deciphering if I should flip them forward or swing my leg behind them and pivot, twisting them to the ground. He also shows me how to break free when someone embraces me around the hips, equipping me with different techniques based on both my stance and my enemy's.

We walk through different simulations, Gray highlighting certain patterns to look for. He focuses on explaining the movements—the tells—of the enemy's intentions. Showcases the way their body will adjust to my movements, and then teaches me how to counter those movements to my benefit.

After we finish, we continue traveling a few miles farther, only stopping once the sun dips beneath the horizon. We locate the mouth of a small, damp cave to rest in for the night, and I collect sticks for the fire while Gray traps fish in the river to eat for dinner. We work efficiently, not stopping until both of our tasks are complete.

Utterly exhausted from a long day of travel and combat training, we eat our charred fish mostly in silence. Once nothing but bones remain, Gray tosses his stick into the flames. "We're going to wake up at first light tomorrow and go over those moves again. I plan for us to stop for three training sessions per day. One in the morning to cover your defensive skills, one in the afternoon to go over combat and offensive moves, and in the evenings, we will work on your magic."

My eyes remain glued to the flickering flames. "Do you think it'll be enough?"

Gray releases a loud sigh. "I think it is exactly as my father said—it will have to be." He turns to look at me, and I let go of my hold on the flames to meet his mossy gaze. With a soft smile curving his lips, he jerks his head toward the cave. "Come on," he says softly. "Let's get some sleep."

We quench the fire and shuffle into the cave, where we lay out our bedrolls side-by-side in the small center. Within minutes, I can tell Gray is asleep. Yet there is so much on my mind, I remain awake, thinking about Bathara, the blood wager—if I have what it takes to really do this.

I stare into the black voids of the cave's ceiling. As sleep lingers in the pervading dark, I focus on the steady rhythm of Gray's breathing, naming off different flowers in my mind.

At some point, my eyelids finally close, leading me into the sweet delights of a peaceful slumber.

¤

I jolt awake as the feeling of burning ice spreads through my veins.

My fingers reach for the necklace at my throat, clutching it with my fingers. I glance around the cave, completely blind in the dense darkness. I count to ten, taking slow, deep breaths between each number, just like I've done after so many other nightmares. My ears tune in to every faint sound, but all I hear is Gray's steady, rhythmic breathing.

Swiping a hand across my forehead, my skin collecting beads of sweat like a harvester gathering crops, I lay back down on my bedroll and calm my pounding heart.

I am so close to attributing the chilly feeling to another nightmare. One fragment away from chalking up the noises grating my ears and raising the hairs on my skin to nothing more than a simple bad dream.

Until I hear a loud scraping noise outside of the cave.

Until I hear a sharp, shrieking howl belt into the night, echoing as though it fills the entire valley.

Until I inhale the face-puckering stench of rotten, decaying flesh.
I don't fall back asleep after that.

CHAPTER THIRTEEN

"You look terrible," Gray says to me as we break from our training for water.

The afternoon sun is high in the western sky, shimmering and pulsing with astounding brightness. I pour some water into my hand and splash it onto my sweat-slicked neck. "The exact words every girl dreams of hearing," I mutter back, the dryness in my tone thick and glaring.

Gray laughs, folding his arms across his chest. "What I mean is you look like you didn't sleep at all last night."

"I didn't." I fiddle with my waterskin, lifting it into the air and inspecting the remaining liquid.

"Why not? I've seen you sleep in far more uncomfortable places. For example, atop that gravel roof you adore so much."

I shoot him a pointed look.

He raises his brows in silent challenge.

My eyes go for a spin, and I sigh. "I...heard something last night."

He pulls at his brows. "What do you mean, *something?*"

I lazily shrug my shoulders. "I don't know. Something that smelled like rotting flesh and howled like a large wolf. Something that felt...cold."

Gray is silent for a moment. "Well, let's thank the Mother it didn't come into the cave."

"Yet," I mumble under my breath.

He clicks his tongue at me before strolling over to the large rock I've been using as a seat, bracing his hands on each side of me, boxing me in. He levels me with a challenging stare, and his voice is deceptively calm when he muses, "You have ten seconds to assume your fighting stance before I throw you into that river."

I arch a brow. "You wouldn't."

"Try me."

⁂

Gray doesn't throw me into the river.

He does, however, make me continue throwing punches into the air until my shoulders ache for mercy.

Today's training consisted of reviewing my defensive moves bright and early, Gray quickening the pace of our simulations to a more realistic speed. Then, after a lunch consisting of dried jerky and nuts, I learned where to keep my feet and where to hold my hands; the importance of rotating my foot outward at a slight angle for balance and allowing my body to flow like the river I train beside. He showed me the basics of throwing a punch and blocking one in return. All the foundational pieces I will need to survive.

And then we trekked on through the valley, continuing towards Bathara.

Now, after marching through the valley for miles—the sun beginning to hum goodbye, stealing the light of day with it as it goes— Gray and I sit criss-crossed in a field of overgrown grass and weeds, a decorum of white and yellow flowers sprinkling through.

"Tell me everything you know about magic." He faces me head-on, our knees touching each other as we talk.

I blow out a breath, puffing my cheeks. "Let me think..." My fingers glide across my lips as I attempt to recount what little knowledge I have. "First, there are the basics most everyone knows. Wielders are only capable of wielding one type of magic, and it is whatever magic manifests within them. A wielder's mark denotes their magic type, and a person can't officially be categorized with a specific magic until the mark appears." I pause. "Though, to be honest, I've never understood why a certain wielder manifests a particular type of magic over another."

Gray leans back, supporting his weight with his outstretched hands. "Your guess is as good as any. Some believe it to be a matter of destiny or fate. Others believe it's determined by the gods themselves. But most scholars nowadays theorize that it's embedded into our genetics—a trait in the blood or heritage of the wielder that feeds the magic. Hence the powerful bloodlines. The ideas are endless, but the answers are scarce." He tilts his head at me. "What else?"

I suck in another bout of air. "I'm aware a person's laktî is what gives a wielder their ability to harness the properties of magic, but my understanding of it is rather...limited. All I know is the laktî in our veins is attuned to our magic types, and without it, we would be unable to wield."

"Do you know how laktî works?"

I snort a dry laugh. "Not even a little bit."

Gray nods, shifting his weight forward. He tucks his knees into his chest, leaning toward me. "It's a good start, what you know."

"I have the magical knowledge of a child," I flatly retort.

He chuckles softly, but shakes his head. "Having any sort of knowledge is better than no sort of knowledge at all."

"Spoken like a true Nightenjoy," I mutter.

His lips kick up with a small smile as he continues. "Laktî does indeed allow us to wield. Put as simply as possible, it is attuned to your magic's capabilities—like a sort of frequency. But it is a finite resource, and it can be drained."

"Does that mean every wielder's laktî is different?"

Gray considers my question. "Yes, I would say it mostly is. Though the governing principles are largely the same. Think of it like...wine."

My nose scrunches. "Wine?" I ask, humor coating the word. "Really?"

"Actually, yes. Wines differ in their potencies and abilities to get you drunk, right?"

I lift a brow, still not entirely convinced this is about to make sense. "Yes," I answer, my hesitation obvious.

"Well, the same is true for laktî. Think of it like sipping nobility's expensive Sparkling Ecstasy versus a commoner's house wine. Because one is of better quality, it will get you drunk faster with less consumption. It may seem strange, but that is similar to using laktî. Though the resource may be finite, when you train it, the strength and quality of it becomes greater, making you a more powerful wielder."

"Is that why some wielders are more powerful than others? Because they have more laktî than another?"

He blows out a breath, raking his hand through his unbound hair. "Not exactly. It's like..." Gray pauses, pinching his chin between his fingers as he thinks. "Okay—think of the jug containing the wine. Your body is the jug, and, as we've established, laktî is the wine. The jug has a set capacity for the amount of wine it can contain, right? And no matter how many times the jug is drained empty or replenished to be full, its capacity for the *amount* it can hold will always remain the same. Are you following?"

Maybe? Kind of? A little bit?

"Yes," I reply, instead.

"Good. See, having more laktî than another certainly gives the wielder a considerable advantage. The sheer *volume* of magic they can wield at a time would be greater than someone with less laktî. But all of it means nothing without training."

"Right," I drawl with hollow confidence. "Because training..."

Gray lifts his brows and leans in with anticipation, waiting for me to finish my sentence.

I don't.

After a quiet laugh, Gray finishes for me, "Because training will allow you to not rely solely on the *amount* of laktî you contain, because it will increase its *potency*, allowing you to get more for less. In doing so, you not only lessen your chances of draining all your resources, but you will also have more control over your magic as well."

I sit in silence for a moment, taking it all in. "Alright," I declare after a long bout of thought. "I think I'm following."

"Don't worry," Gray assures me with a soothing smile. "You'll learn a lot more as you progress. Learning the basics always seems the most daunting because it's like setting the foundations for learning the old language—nonsensical and confusing. But—" he braces his hands on his thighs and rises "—the best way to learn is through application." He stretches his hand out to me.

I stare at it as if it were coated in poison, resulting in Gray's smile quickly falling into a frown.

And I'm not sure what to say to him. Not sure how to convey the turmoil turning inside of me, sitting like lead on my tongue.

How does one explain that they fear attempting the very thing that might save their life because, if they realize they are incapable of doing it, then at least living in ignorant bliss for a while is a hell of a lot better than drowning in a burning sea of anxiety and loathing. How do I look Gray in the face—the person who has always said I was bright like the sun and gazed upon me like he meant it—that I fear failure to a crippling degree, and it will be the stormy rain cloud to hide my shine?

As if hearing my thoughts, Gray squats down beside me. "You have nothing to fear, Lyra." He says it with such a tender voice, I wonder if every person is privileged to experience such a softness. "I'll be with you every step of the way."

My breath hitches in my chest before finding its release. I slip my hand into his, and he helps me rise.

Just as he has done so many other times before.

※ ↘ ↙ ※

"Before you can access your magic at will, you need to understand it."

Gray paces in front of the glistening riverbed, his hands clasped behind his back.

The moon has begun peeking over the horizon, and the evening air spreads thin. There is a gentle breeze blowing through the valley tonight, and it is a comfort against my skin as I listen to him speak.

"You must become familiar and intimate with its touch—with its unique feeling, sometimes referred to as its essence." Gray halts in front of me and opens his palms to the sky. He makes a silver comet appear between them, flames of ice and fire forming at its tail, and the comet circles around its own star-flecked patch of darkness. With the last shred of light remaining—and because Gray has rolled up the sleeves of his tunic—I can see his wielder's mark on his forearm: an eye enclosed in a circle of precise black lines, with four small dots descending to meet a slithering snake. It glows with golden light.

We watch the comet ride an invisible orbit in his hands. "This used to be your favorite illusion," he muses in a soft whisper. "You had just learned of the Ardoris comet festival in the Anatolé Kingdom. You all but rioted when my father explained you weren't allowed to attend." A nostalgic smile tugs at his lips. "Do you remember?"

A weak curve tugs at the corner of my mouth. But where Gray's smile was sewn from warm remembrance, mine is strung from the threads of frayed, wistful strings. "I remember. It was how I found that spot on the roof. I wanted to be alone—wanted to gaze at the colored stars."

Gray nods. "But..." he trails off, allowing me to finish the story.

My chest tightens. "The sky was cloudy, and the stars weren't visible that night. I descended the roof in a rage and fell off the ladder. I was fine, but..."

"You sobbed hysterically."

I shoot him a look. "I was twelve. Cut me some slack." But my features soften as I continue gazing at the silverlight comet in his palms. "I was so upset for so many reasons. My mother was gone. The king was forcing me to shadow his current night attendants. Falling...it just felt like a catalyst—an excuse to finally feel all the pain I'd been harboring on the inside." I huff a hollow laugh, shaking my head. "I remember crying until I felt empty. And then you were there. Your mother sent you." I flick my gaze up from Gray's glittering illusion and meet his eyes.

His impossibly kind eyes that burn with the gold of sunlit meadows.

"It felt like it had been so long since I'd last seen you cry. There for a while, you were just...hollow." His eyes round in a sad sort of way. "I remember being conflicted, happy to see you finally feel something. But it killed me to see you cry like that. So I created this illusion to soothe you." The comet flares brightly a final time before rippling and disappearing. "Something about it made everything click into place for me. I became familiar with my magic's touch. Knew exactly what it felt like—suddenly understood how to call on it the way a wielder should." Gray drops his hands to his side. "And now I am going to help you do that very thing."

A frenzy of nerves ricochets beneath my skin. "Tell me what I need to do."

"I want you to close your eyes and recede deep inside yourself. As if your consciousness is a flowing stream, and you are pouring it into your veins. I want you to inspect the contents residing there, and then bring them back with you as you open your eyes."

I arch a brow. "That...makes zero sense."

He chuckles, amused. "It will."

I suck in a breath and loudly blow out all the consumed air from my lungs. I shake out my hands, hoping that will help with the nerves.

Gray, picking up on my nervousness—though, it's not like that's particularly hard to do right now—takes both my hands in his. "Close your eyes," he instructs in a whisper.

I follow his instructions.

"Now," he continues with a feather-light tone, "feel yourself drifting away from my voice. Drifting away and into yourself. You are searching for something. Something foreign yet utterly familiar. Find it."

I focus inward, allowing Gray's words and the sounds of the rushing river to fade softly. A whipping breeze pushes hair from my shoulders, and I inhale the scent of the white pines mingling with cedar and sweet lush grass—breathe in the smell of crackling embers and ash as they swirl up toward the heavens. Slowly, I begin to ebb and flow in the expanse of myself.

There is a blotch of darkness—a whisper into the void—and then like lights being turned on, stars blink into existence. One small flicker, then ten, then a hundred. One after another, until the depths of infinity are filled with glowing, luminous balls of light. They twinkle and glimmer, some silver and gold, others violet and sage. And then they *burn*. They burn violently. They burn with a cold flame—a flame that is destruction and rebirth.

The ceiling of colored stars illuminates a network of glowing threads wound with every color, twirling over themselves like the braided rivers found in Tuarana's River Lace. Most are too far for me to reach, flowing in the distance into something that appears like a loom. Yet there is one that hums directly in front of me, golden and bright.

At the base of my feet, there is a pulsing thread lacing itself around my body, flowers of every color blooming throughout as if it were a vine. I pluck the thread, causing a sudden burst of glittering light to funnel inside my skin, flooding my veins. As it pours its thrumming energy into me, I see flashes of rippling power waving into the colorless depths in hues of fiery blues and glowing violets and burning orange. It radiates like heat from a flame, and then it shifts, and I am soaring through infinity as ice and burning stone—dust trailing in my wake.

And I feel...

Endless. Boundless. Like the energy of light that illuminates the vastness of night. I feel like I could conjure anything—an envelope of glittering power.

"Lyra." Gray's voice leaks back into my mind. "Lyra," he says again.

Like a wave, I recede from this place of star and thread. I kiss the inky depths goodbye and ride the wind back until I feel the heat wrapping around my cold bones.

"Open your eyes and look down," Gray murmurs.

Slowly...oh, so slowly, I blink my eyes open, waiting for the blurriness to fade. I glance down and see the faint hint of silver lining my veins. Like the first time, it mingles with streaks of gold. Yet what is most notable is the way I can *feel* it humming underneath my skin.

Gray grins at me with unabashed pride. He folds his arms across his chest—a bead of sweat hovering above his brow—and he dips his chin. "And now I give you permission to sleep."

Chapter Fourteen

Within the damp, chilly cave, Gray sleeps as soundly as ever. Yet, as the moon glows in the dark sea of night, my fingers twitch with the urge to read Casimir Vivaldri's journal. I can't explain it, exactly, but it's like it calls to me. Though, I've heard Gray say different books call to him all the time, so I think little of it.

With stealthy precision, I pry myself from my bedroll and crawl over to where Gray's satchel rests against the cave wall. As quietly as possible, I unbuckle the strap and rummage for the pack of matches I know is buried inside. Once I find them, I reach for the small wax candlestick tucked into a side pocket, then crawl back to my bedroll—fully aware that if anyone were here to see me, I'd be met with a pointed brow and a curious look.

I resituate myself, pull the journal from my pack, strike the match against the stone, and kiss the sparks to the wick, washing the cave in a warm glow. I wince and glance at Gray, worried the sudden brightness will wake him. Yet he remains sound asleep on his back, a hand resting against his chest while the other is bent at a strange angle near the top of his head.

A sigh of relief pours from my lips.

My eyes flick down to the centuries-old journal, and my thumb traces the worn leather. Having learned my lesson about opening this journal at random—and now committed to reading it in order—I crack the cover open and begin reading the first entry on the opening pages.

This journal was a gift from my father.

After my mother's passing, he says that he believes it could help me channel and understand my feelings toward her untimely death. I have a lot of thoughts, and I have plenty of feelings, but I do not believe either are capable of being fully articulated within the spines of a journal. I am not a poet after all.

Yet he has my interest piqued. There is something about recording life through the lens of paper and quill that appeals to me. So, I've decided I will write. I will record all that is around me. All that haunts me. Moves me. Burdens me. All the things I love; all the things I fear. I will write them, and so perhaps their words will live on in time, even though I will inevitably crumble to ash.

As the first and only son of King Isaphus, I am heir to the throne, and thus privy to much discussion. The Rivara Kingdom has been newly founded, with the other two kingdoms beginning to take on their own system of politics, trade agreements, and order. Yet already, I fear I am catching hints of discord, despite the Three King System being newly instituted to facilitate and broker peace in our lands. It is for that reason, and that reason alone, I have suggested a yearly celebration where each kingdom takes turns hosting the other to commemorate what has come to pass. "The Founding", is what I'm calling it. A grand and lavish celebration where we honor and remember the union and institution of peace through a new accord.

For someday, our mortal lives will cycle through, and what has happened here on these lands will be forgotten.

My father is rather enamored with the idea. He has already sent out communications to the other two kings. He tells me that, should they agree, he will then send correspondence to all the remaining Houses and Great Houses. Though, I hear the Anatolè Kingdom has done away with such a system under their new governances. My father also plans to extend invitations to the Archbloods, who have seemingly all migrated to be within the borders of Erandor Kingdom.

Fascinating, the way bloodlines have had a hand in the divisions of power after the fall of the last king of Solaya.

Many would look down on my father. Before his rise to power, we were not nobility, nor were we anyone of importance. My family, we were merely dedicated to the cause of the people, and we wanted prosperity to return to these lands. Yet it remains, many seek to discredit our legitimacy to the Rivarian throne because of our "common" blood.

Though, I digress, and I fear I am boring even myself with these ramblings. Besides, I *must depart to meet with Magaius and Sitara. As my best friends, they will pull me by the tips of my ears if I am late to meet with them.*

Until I scribe these pages again,

Casimir.

I glide my fingers along the artistically scribbled name.

How was this journal ever neglected or lost? It feels like I just learned more from that one entry about the institution of the Three King System than I ever have in all my years of study. I had no idea Casimir and his father were the ones behind creating The Founding.

If my memory serves, the official records state that The Founding celebration was the result of a grand party thrown the very night the Accord of Three Kings was signed. It brokered such synergy that, collectively, the first of the Three Kings declared it a yearly celebration, as important as an equinox or solstice.

Yet, Casimir claims the kingdoms were already plagued with discord, and that The Founding was his idea to diminish the turmoil. Seeing as his account was written in a personal journal, he has no reason to lie...

Still, to reconcile what you've always thought to be true as a sudden falsehood is not an easy task. And I can't help but wonder...

If the records are wrong about something as monumental as the institution of The Founding, what else are they wrong about?

I blow out a loud sigh and glance at Gray as a tinge of guilt taps at my heart. Gray loves history more than anyone I know, and I am certain he would be giddy at the chance to read this journal. Yet I have this feeling scratching at me. A feeling that tells me I shouldn't tell him or anyone about the journal.

Not yet, at least.

As I blow out the flame from the candle's wick, I wonder if that gnawing feeling is right or wrong.

CHAPTER FIFTEEN

G ray and I have just finished with our lunch and are trekking through a forest of overgrown grass and vegetation—passing around the bend of a towering anthracite mountain—when I spot ravens circling in the sky.

"Look," I say to Gray, pointing a finger skyward. "Ravens."

Gray tilts his head back, shading his eyes against the brightness of the sun. "Some might call that a bad omen," he mutters flatly.

I nudge my elbow into his side. "I disagree. Ravens are just unfairly judged. They've been crowned the markers of death simply because of the color of their feathers and the nature of their diet. But plenty of animals feast on carrion—it's not just ravens, you know. Yet a lion can be wicked and cunning, feasting on living flesh of the weak, and he is marked a king. But the raven—arguably the most cunning of all—feasts on what's around to survive and is marked a plague. Why?"

Gray glances at me, his brows high on his forehead. "I don't know. I've never considered the question before."

I tilt my head back and watch the three ravens fly in a circle, screeching. "Did you know," I muse, my eyes still fixed upwards, "it's rumored that ravens can bond with humans? That they may think and perceive similarly to ourselves."

"I did not," he answers. Gray chuckles, shaking his head and smiling. "But what I *truly* did not know is how fascinated you are with ravens."

I roll my eyes and shove his shoulder.

We walk in silence, the gurgling sounds of the river and gentle brushes of wind accompanying us over the next mile. It isn't until I see the same-looking bend at the same-looking anthracite mountain that I halt.

"What is it?" Gray asks through lowered brows.

I scan our surroundings with a sharp scrutiny. I take in the ferny, silvery foliage, rich with a balsam-like aroma. I notice the milkweeds, the bellwort, and the large-leaved asters. I spot the same hornberry tree I noticed a mile ago, standing next to a towering alder tree.

But perhaps it could be a different one. A new tree, in a new area, that looks an awful lot like the area we just so happened to pass.

A coincidence. Nothing more than coincidence.

"Lend me one of your daggers."

Through narrowed brows, Gray unsheathes one of his daggers from his side and hands it to me. The cool metal feels foreign in my grasp, but I tighten my grip on it as if it were an extension of me. I approach the hornberry tree, and I dig the tip of the metal into the bark, the wood groaning as the blade slices marks along the trunk.

"What are you doing?" Gray asks from behind me.

"You haven't noticed it yet?"

I don't need to look at Gray to know he has folded his arms across his chest. I can hear it all in his tone. "Noticed *what*, exactly?"

I give a nod of approval at my carvings marring the bark. "That everything is the exact same as it was a mile ago." I turn my attention to him and watch as he scans the landscape through a new lens.

"Shit," he mumbles under his breath.

I turn his dagger over in my hand and offer it back at the hilt. Gray takes it and sheathes the blade at his side.

"Only one way to know if I'm right or not."

He releases a deep sigh and rubs his fingers along his brow. "You're rarely wrong about this kind of thing."

My face is neither victorious nor prideful when I respond, "I know."

We walk a mile before circling back and seeing the freshly carved hornberry tree.

Gray glides his fingers along the marks on the silvery-gray bark, smooth like glass—despite the name of the tree. He glances right at the onyx-colored Endymion Mountains, the shiny black all but sparkling in the already fading sunlight, and then looks left, over the river and past the trees, toward the Cliffs of Yilandra.

"The only way through the valley and to Bathara is forward," he contemplates aloud, the remnants of worry leaking through. "And if we continue in circles, that prevents us from moving forward. So how, then, do we proceed?"

I can't recall the last time I've seen Gray's eyes filled with such uncertainty.

Just as I'm about to respond, a slithering voice skulks through the wind.

"*Neither here nor there,*" its snaky voice hisses. "*Neither friend nor foe. You wish to pass, don't you?*"

Gray's eyes immediately lock on mine, and he shakes his head at me once—firm.

He doesn't wish for me to answer.

I hold his gaze a second longer before slowly drawing in a steadying breath. I shoot Gray a quick look of apology before projecting my voice. "Yes. We do."

A brush of delighted wind kisses my neck. As if that voice—ancient and cruel, both man and boy—wishes to show me its pleasure with me answering.

"*And why should I help you?*" the voice croons. "*Why you, when I have let so many others wander lost?*"

"Perhaps we can offer you something."

I hear Gray's palm smack against his forehead. I shoot him a pointed look before refocusing my attention to the faceless voice in the wind.

"*And what, pray tell, do you believe you could offer me, mortal?*"

The air around us plunges into an icy chill. The hairs on my body rise as gooseflesh lines my skin. "What is it you desire?"

I feel a flickering inside me—an instinct.

Run. Run. Run, it seems to say.

I glance over at Gray—whose eyes watch me with concerted focus—and I see the snake on his wielder's mark glowing with a deeply golden light.

I glance down at my veins, but glimpse no traces of color.

Another chill snakes down my spine, and I whip my head to the right, swearing I can feel the weight of a person next to me. But nothing is there except the towering anthracite mountains.

"A dangerous request."

"There is no danger in the request. I can't promise we can fulfill your desire, but I also don't see the harm in knowing what your desires are. Wouldn't you agree?"

I feel a crawling sensation—like a creeping spider—float down the length of my arm, until it reaches the very tips of my fingers.

"The thing I desire most is the very thing I can never have. I am forever intertwined with these lands, and here I will forever remain."

"But you don't wish to remain here?"

Gray is staring at me through furrowed brows, a thousand thoughts racing through his eyes.

A gust of frigid wind that feels unnervingly intimate brushes across my skin. *"She was right about you. You* are *different,"* the ancient voice purrs with a poisonous curiosity. *"Did you know, girl, that someday, a child will come— defined by a name both two and one—born from the ashes of a great love, whose untamed power can raise or crumble kingdoms."*

I pull at my brows. "I haven't the slightest idea what you're talking about."

"You will soon enough." A low hum rumbles the ground. *"Yes, I can see why she sent me, indeed."*

I blow out a frustrated breath and steel my nerves. "Who sent you?"

Another swirl of wind sweeps against me. *"Did you know the wind whispers to me? I have heard whispers of rising armies, creatures unseen for centuries, dark and forbidden magics moving through kingdoms. What strange times we've stumbled upon."*

"What's your point?" Gray asks, his voice tight with frustration.

That brush of wind leaves me, and I watch as it wraps around Gray, circling him so forcefully, he stumbles backwards. That sharp wickedness returns to the voice of man and boy, filling the world in a blanket of ice. *"The scales are tipping, the fate of the kingdoms with it. What should happen if the two join together? Better yet, what will remain if they don't?"*

Question upon question streams through my mind. Though I get the distinct impression that this voice is not one to patiently answer them. So, it is for that reason I ask, in my mind, the most pressing question at the moment. "Why are you telling us this?"

A low chuckle comes from nowhere, yet fills everywhere. *"You'll find out soon enough. For the strings of Fate are bound by threads of fire, ice, and shadow, and there is no escaping when they pull at you."* Like a wind blowing from the salty seas, a chilled kiss sweeps across my cheek. *"In the far north is an island. On that island lives a Diviner. She is the one who sent me for reasons only known to herself."*

"And why do as she asks?"

"Consider it a favor to an old friend."

I arch a brow. "I'm surprised you ever had any friends."

I swear I hear laughter echoing behind the mountains in response.

Suddenly, violent winds whip through the valley. The trees creak and moan as they sway, and the river roars in response. My braid flaps against the gust of cold, and Gray shields his face from the slicing ice laced in the air.

That ancient voice echoes loudly, but it drifts away from us, fading. *"Remember this, Threadweaver: love is no lesser force than hate, and a scorned heart does not wither—it burns. And fire does not choose sides."* I feel a soft touch caress my cheek—like a finger gliding against my skin. It strangely reminds me of what I felt during The Founding celebration.

"I have now said what I've come to say. The way forward is not through. Try as you might, it will only confuse you."

And then, as if out of nowhere, the wind ceases, and the voice disappears.

The descending orange sun warms my skin once more, and the river slows to a softened melody of water over rock. The milkweeds, bellwort, and blades of overgrown grass finally still, and a lull of noiseless calm sweeps over the valley—a welcome reprieve from the sweeping winds.

Gray shifts to face me. "What the hell just happened?"

"I think he was trying to...help us."

"I don't know," he retorts. "My magic roared the moment his voice slithered into the air. Not to mention all those cryptic words of his." Gray shakes his head, clearly bemused. "And why did he call you *Threadweaver?*"

A good question.

"I don't know," I mutter. "But I believe his parting words are true; we won't make it out of this valley if we continue forward."

Gray hums his agreement and rubs a hand along his jaw. "What do you propose we do, then?"

I survey the lands. The rivers, trees, neighboring mountains and cliffs. And then the words from the tale of Foreigner's Valley ring in my head. *After the seventh day, the foreigner—on the verge of madness—went across the valley instead of going through.*

It hits me then.

"We cut across the valley," I suggest. "To the Cliffs of Yilandra."

He takes a measured breath, deliberating. "If we do that, we won't make it to Bathara in time. Not unless we travel through the remaining nights." He pauses, his eyes sharp with warning. "You know what my father said."

Sterling's warning echoes in my mind. *Find a cave to rest in overnight, always quell your fire when the moon finds its peak, and* never *travel through the night.*

Still, I see no other options. Not unless we want to be mice in a maze, playing at the whims of whatever magic curses this valley.

I express as much to Gray, holding his gaze firm all the while.

Gray pinches his chin between two fingers as he considers the options. "You're right," he concedes through a sigh. "I don't see a better choice. We'll change course for the cliffs, traveling through most of the night, stopping for rest intermittently." He looks at me with wary eyes. "Let's pray my father was being overly cautious with his warnings."

Yet he and I both know Sterling is not an overly cautious man, but simply a wise one.

Chapter Sixteen

Crossing the river was difficult.

Even though the air was pleasantly warm despite the coming shift in seasons, the river was *freezing*.

We had to backtrack, following the length of the river for what felt like miles, until we spotted a place for safe crossing—a wider passing downstream where the current slowed. But finding that safe passage cost us the rest of our daylight, and we had to make quick work of crossing the frigid river to avoid being cast into total darkness while in the water.

Now safely on the adjacent bank—our only casualty a cut sliced down my calf by a jagged rock beneath the surface—we change into dry clothes under the glow of the moon and continue hiking through the thinning pines and into the denser silver birch and cedar trees beyond.

For a while, everything feels like it's going to be alright. That we're making progress and our solution is going to work.

Until the familiar bone-chilling sound of claws on stone pierces the quiet, and a rancid smell clots the air.

My spine straightens at the traveling howl, not far from where we walk between the trees.

Close.

The sound is *way* too close.

The smell of rotting flesh overtakes the once sweet breeze, and my eyes water as I force back the gag threatening to rip from my throat. Twigs creak and snap behind me, a bundle of fallen leaves snagging.

Then comes the clicking of sharp claws rasping against each other.

Gray, only a few paces in front of me, turns his head at the eerie sounds, and I don't need to turn around to know whatever creature lurks in the darkness is one of nightmares.

The blood draining from Gray's drawn face and the panic overflowing in his eyes tells me all I need.

"*Run*," he demands.

But my body refuses to move. Instead, slowly—much too slowly—I creak my head and glance behind me.

To find a pair of eyes, glowing like molten lava, staring back.

The creature is only about twenty paces away, and the overwhelming smell of rotting flesh almost makes me puke. Its body is shaped something like a wolf, but three times the size. It has ashen looking flesh with sunken, glowing eyes like a snake. The creature has no lips, and a slew of jagged, razor sharp teeth jut from its gums, exposed to the world. Two large, pointed horns tower on its head, accompanied by two smaller horns on each side.

I need to move. I need to *run*. But my feet are planted into the soil, defiant to my will. I find I'm only capable of gaping at the creature as it moves with unnatural swiftness—unnatural predatory grace.

It isn't until the creature stands upright, towering on its hind legs, and closes the gap to six paces in two, fluid steps, that I feel a pull on my arm, dragging me forward.

"We have to *move*, Lyra." Gray's voice bounces as his feet pound against the ground in a sprint.

It takes me a moment to realize my feet are doing the same.

We sprint through the trees, up a hill, and then take a hard left; Gray tightly clutching my wrist, guiding me the whole way. We descend down a back slope and meet a fresh patch of overgrown grass and vegetation. Gray halts and stuffs me into the green thicket. He pushes my shoulders toward the ground, silently commanding me to crouch.

"Do not move," he whispers, breathless. "Wait until you see a silver comet soar above your head. That'll be your cue to run. Do you understand?"

"I can help you." I reach for his arm, but he pulls away and shoots me a look.

"Don't be foolish, Lyra. Three days of training does not make you a match for a creature of this caliber."

"But—" I begin to protest.

"Please," his voice is gut-wrenchingly soft. "Please," he repeats. "I can't bear the thought of anything happening to you. If you go with me, I'll only be distracted, worrying about your safety." He brushes his fingers against my cheek. "So please, stay hidden and be silent."

I swallow back my protests and nod my head.

That life-draining howl pierces through the wind, and the large, wolf-like creature emerges from the trees. The light of the moon slides off the creature, as if it were made in darkness and swallows any light.

Gray looks at me a final time, scanning my eyes. His mouth opens like he is going to say something else, but he quickly presses his lips together and kisses my forehead instead. "Remember the signal. Regardless of if I follow, you *run*, Lyra."

Then he unsheathes the sword from his back and runs toward the creature, whose claws are as long as the sword in his hand and twice as thick.

Crouching within the overgrown weeds, I watch as Gray charges at the beast. He must have wielded some sort of illusion on it. For one moment the creature is locked in on Gray and his movements, and the next, the creature acts as though it has lost him entirely, tipping his lipless head into the air and sniffing.

But then the creature locks in on some sightless smell, and those molten eyes reignite with wicked delight as it throws its claws out into the world.

Gray braces his forearm against the blade of his sword to stop the iron-sharp claws from piercing through his chest. He drops to the ground and slashes steel against its heel, drawing black, oozing blood.

The beast roars with fury. It thrashes its teeth toward Gray, and he has little time to evade its strong jaw. Pieces of his tunic weave through the creature's canines as bright, red blood drips down its face.

Gray's blood, I realize with no small amount of horror.

It takes every ounce of self-control I possess to not shout his name. To not stand up and run to him. But I saw the pleading look in his eyes. Heard the desperation leak through as he asked me to stay.

Gray narrowly avoids a swipe of the creature's dagger-like claws and stumbles backwards. The creature lunges forward, and Gray uses the moment to side-step the attack and slice at the ashen beast's eye.

The slice hits true, and an immediate oozing split cleaves its left eye. The creature howls in both rage and agony as it rises up on its hind legs. Gray wastes no time, gracefully striking his sword into the chest of the creature.

But the sword misses its heart—if it has one.

The creature swipes in a blind rage, this time hitting Gray directly and knocking him into the trunk of a thick tree.

The world slows to a near standstill.

I know I promised Gray I would stay hidden. I know I said I wouldn't try to help. But a once buried set of words echo in my mind for the second time, bringing me to run even faster toward Gray and the beast.

I will not cower. I will not yield. I will not falter.

My lungs spazz for air. When I reach Gray, I slide across the moonlit covered ground and grasp the back of his limp neck. I repeatedly tap his cheek. "Gray," I plead. "Gray, wake up. Come on."

His eyelids flutter, and he groans before going fully limp.

"Shit," I curse under my breath. "Shit. Shit. *Shit.*"

I gently rest him against the tree and turn back to the beast just in time to see it sniffing the air with a curious interest. The black blood oozing from its eye has already begun to clot and scab, and I can only hope it's created a blindspot.

The creature lowers itself back on all four of its legs and digs its gnarled claws into the soil. Its face twists, and if it had lips, I'd wager it was wearing something like a sneer.

I reach for the power hidden beneath my veins. I try to float down and down, searching for the magic resting in that blackened void illuminated by twinkling lights and glowing threads. I grasp at it. Pour it into my veins.

Will it to come forward.

I throw my hand out in anticipation of the power I'm about to unleash and—

Nothing.

Not even a tiny sprout of a single flower or a small vine rises from the ground.

Far cry from the magic I displayed in the king's throne room.

It's as if the beast knows it. It's head cocks in an unnerving way, and it sniffs a final time before its molten eyes seem to flare.

I try once more, begging the magic to flood my veins and pour out of me. "Come on, come on," I demand in a near silent whisper.

Yet...nothing.

The beast charges.

I dart right, back into the trees, attempting to take the creature as far from Gray as I possibly can. I figure, with the cover of night and nothing to guide me but the glow of the moon, the sea of trees is better cover than an open field of overgrown grass.

I zigzag as I run up the sloped ground, my thighs and calves screaming at me, my lungs burning like fire. I run and run until I trip over a protruding root and slam into the ground. My vision floods black and red, and my chin cries from the impact. But I pick myself up, dirt coating my skin.

As I rise, a small *clink* sounds beneath my tunic as a small vial clacks against the ground. My eyes widen as I remember the object resting at my chest. Realize I have a certain vial wrapped in twine around my neck.

Sterling's words ring in my head. *One drop on the tongue, and it would paralyze even a bull for at least an hour.*

The paralyticus potion.

Ice slices through me in that now-familiar way, and when I turn, I find the beast sniffing the path I just ran through, Gray's sword still protruding from its chest. It moves like it's in no hurry. Like it's taking its time with me, enjoying the hunt.

Within a heartbeat, I devise an entirely new plan. One that will require immaculate precision and unparalleled luck.

Under the cover of a broad cedar tree, I clutch the vial in my hand and send a prayer up to Ahlai, the Mother Goddess, and Saffi, the goddess who blesses those with cunning.

I draw in a measured breath. Then another. The third is slow and thorough—drawn with an appreciation for its fragility. After, I exhale it through tightened lips, and then I run. Down to the other side of the sloped trees, back toward the river, I run and run, willing my legs to move like the warrior race once rumored to walk this continent.

Faster. My mind screams at me. *Faster. Faster.*

I don't dare look behind me. That suffocating smell of rot and decay forcing itself into my nostrils, that slicing cold cutting into my bones, tell me enough. I know the beast is close. So dangerously close. Yet I'm counting on the creature enjoying the hunt, hoping it's the reason it hasn't struck yet.

Spots begin to form in my vision right as I see it, exactly where I remembered it to be.

I hurry toward the tree with shaggy bark, shaded in light grayish-brown. Its short petioles and oblong leaves confirm it's exactly what I thought when we passed it earlier.

Honeysuckle.

I snap the thickest branch from the base of the bush and almost cry from relief when the plant's pith is exactly as I hoped to find it.

Completely and utterly hollow.

I snap the stick in half to lessen the chance of failure, then uncork the vial and slide it into the hollow branch, open side first. Saffi must indeed be watching over me, because the opening extends all the way through and is wide enough for the vial to pass. I press my thumb against the end, holding the vial in place as I tuck the stick behind my back and wait.

Within seconds, the beast lurks toward me, its molten eyes glowing with delight. Its razor-sharp teeth—still stained with Gray's blood—glint in the moonlight. It prowls closer and closer, ultimately coming to a halt in front of me.

Within a blink, the beast pounces.

I jerk backward and stumble right as the creature pins me with its claws. They dig into my shoulder, and for a moment, I'm not sure which is worse: the white-hot pain jolting into my fingertips, or the smell of death that is so overwhelming, my body gags uncontrollably in reflex.

Its saliva, thick like paste, drips onto my cheek as it opens its mouth in a snarl inches from my face.

My brain screams at me.

Now!

In one quick motion, I bring the hollow stick to my lips, removing my thumb from the end, and blow with all the force a pair of lungs are capable of mustering.

The vial shoots out from the stick, making a soft *swooshing* noise as it soars directly to the back of the beast's throat. Stunned, the creature recoils and coughs from the impact, the slender vial tumbling from its mouth, falling to the ground.

Empty.

The vial is so beautifully empty—the residue left from the green liquid serving as the only indication it had once been full.

I stare through heavy eyelids as the creature points its black, slimy nose to the sky and howls. I fight through the looming exhaustion, ignoring the warnings my body gives me as it tries to tell me I've lost too much blood—my vision fading.

Instead, I monitor the beast as it sways, trying to fight against the effects of the potion.

But not even a creature of this caliber is able to win against a potent concoction crafted by a skilled Gardner.

The beast hits the ground with a loud *thud*, and I almost feel a sliver of pity as I watch its molten eyes rapidly shift side-to-side, its chest heaving in erratic breaths, clearly stunned and confused as to why it's no longer able to control its limbs.

After I'm sure the beast is fully paralyzed, I somehow muster the strength to peel my blood-stained body off the ground, wrench Gray's impaled sword from the creature's chest, and limp back down the slope, through the trees, back to Gray—who is still out cold.

By some stroke of luck, it is only when I reach him that my body gives out, my scratchy wheezing the only sound as I drift into the depths of a hazy unconsciousness.

CHAPTER SEVENTEEN

My eyes flutter open to the blinding rays of a midday sun. I rub the exhaustion from my face with a sweeping hand and suck in a breath. The air feels crisp and fresh, the sweet aroma of damp soil mixing with floral notes comforting.

Still lying on my back, I slowly turn my head and stretch a hand out to graze the sea of flowers surrounding me. Petals filled with soft pinks, reds, yellows, and unblemished whites boast beneath the gilded rays of a breathtaking sun. My fingers tingle at the familiar texture of soft stems, teeming with life. I smile lazily at the bed of vibrant color. A salt-kissed breeze that reminds me of the Rivara Kingdom caresses my face.

Home, I think. *Have I found hom—*

Suddenly, I jolt upright and scan my surroundings. Flashes from the night race through my mind. The creature. Gray. Blood. Sprinting through the trees. The vial. And then...and then...

I press a hand to my now-pounding head. I wince at the movement, glancing down to find my body wrapped in white bandages soaked with blood. A sharp jolt shoots down my arm, and I grit my teeth against it.

How did I get here? Why am I idly laying in a field of flowers? How am I *alive*?

I shouldn't be alive.

And Gray...

Where is Gray?

My heart cracks with panic, and I try to stand. But my body is weak, and my head is woozy. White spots flood my vision like fluttering snowflakes, and my knees buckle, sending me back down to the soft ground.

I place a hand out in an attempt to steady myself, but I can tell I'm flirting with unconsciousness again. I'm in the process of preparing my body to push through its warnings, ready to search for Gray at whatever cost, when his familiar voice sends a rush of relief through me.

"Please stop trying to stand."

I turn and find Gray knelt down, plucking flowers and placing them into his satchel.

"What happened?" I ask, pressing a hand to my head. "Where are we?"

Silently, he rises from where he was collecting flowers and approaches me, crouching down so we're face-to-face. He releases a loaded sigh. "We're only a few miles from the Cliffs of Yilandra. I saw this field of wildflowers and stopped to look for useful plants."

Son of a Gardner, indeed.

But if we are so close to the Cliffs of Yilandra, that means...

"I was sleeping for an entire day?" I ask with no small amount of bewilderment caressing my words.

Gray nods tightly, his face drawn with tension.

"How...how did we get here, then?"

"I carried you."

"You...*what*? You carried me for a whole day? For...for *miles*?"

Another nod.

Gray tilts his head and studies me with a sharpened gaze. "Before I begin, I need to first know how you feel. Anything to be worried about?"

I lift a brow. "You mean other than the puncture wounds in my shoulder?"

I do a quick inventory of my body—rotating my aching muscles, cracking my neck, squeezing my fingers into fists and uncurling them afterward. All things considered, I don't feel *awful.*

"No, I'd say I'm okay." I narrow my eyes on him. "And before you begin *what*, exactly?"

Gray's expression tightens with frustration. "Before I begin scolding you for being reckless and putting your life at risk. What were you *thinking*, taking on that creature alone?"

My mouth falls open. "What do you mean, '*What was I thinking?*' I was thinking that *thing* was about to make you its next meal when it slammed you unconscious against a tree. I was thinking that, no matter the cost, I had to *help* you."

He regards me with a sharp stare. "You do not risk your life for me, Lyra. Ever."

"Fine. Then *you* don't ever risk your life for *me*."

His brows furrow, and his face twists in frustration. "That's different. I—"

"—It's *not* different. There are no twists of logic that will allow me to believe you should have the right to put your life on the line, yet I shouldn't."

Gray's frustration spikes. "You haven't *trained*. Haven't properly learned how to use a blade, your magic. You've never even *seen* combat. Understand where I'm coming from here, Lyra. There are risks, and—"

"—I understand, and I don't *care*." I pinch the bridge of my nose and dull the sharpness of my words. "I took down that beast despite my lack of training, didn't I?" My voice is soft, the question entering the world on a calm wave. "You had your sword and your magic. Had your training. And what good was it?" I let the silence sit heavy for a moment before continuing. "There are different methods for achieving similar outcomes, Gray, and I will not let you undermine the strength of mine."

He takes a long moment to absorb what I've just said. Finally, he huffs a small laugh, shaking his head. "I wouldn't dare purposefully undermine your capabilities. You'd probably spike my next drink if I did."

His offer of concession.

"Wise man," I coo through a smirk.

Gray chuckles and positions himself on the ground next to me, raking a hand through his half-bound hair. "How'd you do it, anyways?"

"What? Save your ass?" I mock a casual shrug, sending a spark of pain shooting through my shoulder. "Like I said, I have my methods."

121

Gray lets a gentle laugh escape from his lips and nods. "Fair enough. Though I really would like to know."

I tuck my knees into my chest—resulting in another jolt of pain—and rest my chin atop of them. "Honeysuckle," I murmur. "When we were traveling, I noticed a honeysuckle bush not far from where we were. I scrambled a plan together, and ran back to it, praying to the gods I could find a hollow branch. I did, and then I used it to shoot the paralyticus potion your father gave us down the beast's throat."

Gray looks at me, stunned, until a creeping smile spreads across his lips and he gazes at me with such adoration, I have to fight the urge to fidget beneath the undeserving look. "You never stop amazing me. You know that, right?"

My cheeks warm at the compliment. But wanting the attention off me, I pivot the conversation. "What was that thing, anyways?"

Gray glances down at his palms. "It was a Wynn," he answers, his features and tone growing solemn.

A Wynn?

Surely that can't be right.

A creature of nightmares built with exceptional strength, sharp eyesight, superior speed, and hearing. And much like nightmares, it is a lethal beast incompatible with sunlight. If the sun shines on them too long, they burn and crumble to ash.

As the story goes, Wynns were nothing more than ordinary wolves until they were struck by a mad wielder who imbued their very veins with forbidden magic as a cruel experiment. To his savage delight, the pack of wolves became...different. They became lethal killing machines capable of great destruction through their unparalleled senses. The mad wielder attempted to create an army of Wynns, imbuing pack after pack with forbidden magic, thinking he would forever be their master. Until he discarded them like old toys when he soon learned they could only exist under the blanket of night.

The Wynns turned on the wielder, and they shredded him with their teeth while he slept. Thus the nightmare had been born.

I had always thought they were nothing more than creatures in a bedtime story. Something meant to make children grow wide-eyed with terror, fearing the Wynns may come for them if they misbehaved.

Something else strikes me, too. Another component of the story.

Wynns feed off of forbidden magic. It's the only way they can survive.

The implication sends a slash of ice down my spine.

"Are you sure?" I ask Gray. "I thought Wynns were just some made-up creature in some made-up story."

But before Gray can answer, the sound of thunder rolls through the valley. Only, with a quick sweep of my eyes, I can see it's not thunder at all, but rather a band of horses with hooded riders galloping toward us.

What in god's veins are riders doing in Foreigner's Valley?

Gray and I quickly scramble upright—the movement sending a sharp, slicing pain through me—and he steps in front of me, outstretching his arm. "Stay behind me," he demands in a low, steady voice. An authoritative type of voice I'm not sure I've ever heard Gray use with me before.

The horses slow to a halt in front of us, and the hooded riders dismount—some with more impressive grace than others. As a group, they approach. By a quick count, there are four of them in total, with no others in sight. Two figures seem to lead the small group. They trail in front of the other two with a kind of authority and respect I'm not sure I'll ever be able to command.

"Who are you?" Gray asks, his voice deep and unwavering.

But the voice that replies back is even deeper—firmer. "Funny, we were going to ask you the same question."

It comes from the hooded figure on the left. His cloak covers every inch of him, yet what it can't cover is his towering height—his indisputably large frame.

"Forgive me for not answering first, seeing as we are exposed to you and not hiding our faces."

Watching Gray so easily slip into this diplomatic, yet authoritative persona only further solidifies my belief he would thrive in court.

The cloaked figure to the left lets a low laugh ripple from deep within his throat. "Alright," he says. Slowly, his fingers lift to his hood, and he pulls it back, revealing his face.

And goddess's tears is it hard not to openly gape.

Night-dark shaggy hair rippling with waves tumbles against his sandy-beige skin. A strong nose and an even stronger jaw complement his full lips, carved with a deep indent.

But it's his eyes...

One is filled with a translucent seafoam green, while the other holds a soft gradient of shifting blues and greens. And branching from his pupil, like a crack in the earth, is a small fissure stemming diagonally, breaking apart the gradient with a small slit.

It reminds me of the bonaria plant, whose petals sparkle like glass and invite you in, only to stop your heart with a drop of the poison lurking beneath its beauty.

Those other-wordly eyes slide to me, and the stranger tilts his head, a wrinkle in his brow. "You."

Like an idiot, I point a finger at my face, still tucked behind Gray. "Me?"

His eyes sweep over me, and when they linger on my chest, I'm a second away from spewing sharp words. But then my eyes flick down, and I realize I'm still wrapped in nothing but blood-stained bandages. Heat blooms in my cheeks.

"You're injured," he states without a hint of fluctuation. "Are the wounds infected?"

"No," Gray replies for me, with no small amount of bite lacing through the word. "I've attended to her wounds personally, and ensured they remained clean. I was just about to redress her, but your unexpected arrival has delayed that task."

I glance up at Gray, my brow severely arched.

The stranger cocks his head at the underlying pointedness in Gray's tone. "Is that so?" His reply comes out like a sultry hum.

"It is."

The cloaked figure standing to the right of the intimidating stranger finally drops his hood, revealing shoulder-length ruby-red hair. "Now,

now, gentlemen. Claws are for beasts, and we are civilized creatures, so I suggest you put them away."

A sharp gasp escapes from my lips.

That hair. Those features. That distinctive...smirk.

I step forward and around Gray. "I know you," I breathe, my brows scrunched tightly across my forehead. "I saw you during The Founding celebration."

His wry smirk widens, and it takes all of a few seconds to realize this is a person prone to mischief. I also can't help but notice that he, like his traveling companion, is highly attractive. But whereas the other stranger is rough and unrefined, he is soft and elegant. The contrast is a little jarring, honestly. Like seeing a wild, unruly black wolf trot around with a beautiful, sly fox.

The red-haired man taps a pondering finger against his chin. "The Founding, you say? I'm normally rather drunk for those festivities. Was it a few years back when Lord Petushka almost fell on his own sword trying to perform a trick? I do recall causing quite the spectacle with my insistent laughter."

I'm normally rather drunk for those festivities.

Which means he is someone who frequently receives invitations to them. Which also probably means these two standing before us are high ranking nobles.

Still, is he being serious right now?

I arch a suspecting brow. When I glance back at the dark-haired, bright-eyed male next to him, I catch a flicker of something passing through his features, and I can't tell whether it's amusement or vexation.

I release a sigh. "The Founding celebration that just passed only a few short days ago in the Rivara Kingdom. It featured unauthorized magic. The lights went out. The king yelled." I fold my arms across my chest and cock my head at him. "You're a fire-wielder. I remember because I saw you flicking flames to life in the oil lamps."

His smirk grows. "Oh," he chirps. "That one. Yes, I remember that one." He tilts his head, amusement twinkling in his eye. "Rather astute, aren't you?"

My eyes narrow on him. "I caught you smirking at me. Why? Is it that..." I swallow. "Were you the one who touched me?"

I'm not sure why I'm so desperate to know. But for some unidentifiable reason, I cannot get that small touch out of my head. The way the simple gesture felt. Like someone whispered the words *do not let them break you* into my mind, as if they wanted me to know I wasn't alone.

His sapphire eyes do not break away from me as he coos, "I haven't the slightest idea what you're talking about."

The shaggy-haired stranger to the left frowns at me, a deeply pronounced curve in his brow. "Has no one ever smirked at you before? Is it truly such a rare occasion that you have to question why?"

My face twists with annoyance as my mouth pops open, and the red-haired stranger bites down on his grin. He covers his mouth with a fist—fighting against a laugh—and shrugs, the gesture graceful and casual. "What can I say? I'm known to always have a smirk on my face."

"A little unnerving if you ask me," Gray mumbles under his breath.

But I'm still focused on what the dark-haired male just said. I take a few steps forward, closing the distance between us, and point my finger into his chest. "I don't know who you think you are or where you come from—only that you're clearly some pampered noble who's used to speaking to people like that—but you will *not* speak to me with such disrespect."

I didn't leave Keziah behind just to be treated the same by men.

The man next to him blows out a low whistle.

Languidly, the towering stranger flicks his peculiar eyes down toward my finger and slowly pushes it away with his hand. "Hit a sensitive subject, did I?"

His brush of skin against mine sends a small shiver down my spine, putting me on high alert.

My brows furrow. "What is that supposed to mean?"

"Only that people must never truly smile at you. Go on," he says coolly. "Interrogate my traveling companion all you want. It makes sense now—why you're so desperate to understand."

"I am *not* desperate," I seethe between clenched teeth.

"No? You're not doing a good job of showing otherwise, then."

I clench my fists at my side and pinch my teeth into the skin of my cheek.

Before I can say anything else, Gray clears his throat. "Perhaps names are a good place to start. I'm Gray." He outstretches a hand. "Gray Nightenjoy."

The stare between the towering stranger and me remains gridlocked, and I am entirely unwilling to back down—I won't let him win. The only problem is, it appears he is knowingly participating in this unannounced game, because as the thought crosses my mind, a small curve tugs at the corner of his lip, as if he just read the very thought in my eyes.

The man with ruby-red hair takes Gray's hand in his. "Oh? A Nightenjoy, huh. You have quite the reputable bloodline. I'm Kiran."

The omission of his surname does not go unnoticed by me, and I'm sure Gray notices, too.

Gray turns his attention to the insouciant stranger next. Yet his eyes remain fixed on me.

"Draven," he supplies in a cool, unhurried tone, not bothering to meet Gray's outstretched hand.

Again, no surname.

When all remaining eyes slide to me, I realize I'm the only one who has yet to provide their name. I lift my chin—keeping my eyes defiantly locked on the stranger—and muster all the confidence a girl who is shirtless, wrapped only in blood-soaked bandages, possibly can. "Lyra Izacalli."

I hear the smile in Kiran's voice as he inquires, "And what is it you are doing out in Foreigner's Valley, Lyra Izacalli?"

I keep my eyes locked on the dark-haired stranger, Draven, still not backing down. "I should ask the same of you."

Kiran makes a rapid ticking noise and sings, "Uh-uh. We provided our names first. In the spirit of fairness, it's your turn to answer."

I finally rip my eyes from Draven and click my tongue at Kiran—which results in him grinning even wider.

"We are traveling to Bathara to participate in its entrance exams," Gray answers smoothly. He spares me a soft glance before returning his eyes to Kiran. "For reasons we won't disclose, we had to travel through the valley to reach Bathara."

Kiran's eyes bounce between the two of us, something that looks a hell of a lot like shock swimming in his expression. "*Both* of you plan to participate in the entrance exams?"

The underlying tone in his voice is...odd. Especially for someone just meeting us.

Gray dips chin. "We do."

Kiran's sapphire eyes flick to Draven, something inscrutable passing through them. "I see," he muses much more gently than before.

Draven folds his arms across his chest, pushing the fabrics of his cloak up, revealing a collage of black tattoos winding around his considerably toned forearms—so saturated in black, they almost seem to swallow the light. With his eyes still locked on me—his stare intense and unsettling—he inquires, "Why were you forced to travel through the valley?"

Gray opens his mouth to reply, but I comment back faster than the words can leave his lips. "That is none of your concern."

Draven lifts a dark brow, but says nothing.

And the ghost of his smirk has my blood warming with growing agitation.

Gray breathes out a near-silent sigh before addressing Kiran. "Why is your party traveling through the valley?"

A wry smile pulls at Kiran's lips. "We are on an...*undisclosed* scouting mission."

My head tilts while my brows furrow deeply. "Scouts? In Foreigner's Valley? What are you scouting?"

Draven's answer comes swift and dry. "None of your concern."

His pettiness pushes my simmering annoyance toward a full-fledged boil. And clearly, being within the valley these past few days has diminished my court training, because my lip openly curls at him while I click my tongue.

He huffs under his breath, clearly amused with himself, and the sound reverberates low and deep in his throat.

"As it so happens," Kiran drawls, his tone the exact opposite of Draven's, "we are scouting *for* Bathara." He glances at Draven, then at me, before they fall back on Gray. "Normally, we wouldn't do this. But given the nature of these circumstances, I fear I'd regret it if I did not extend an offer to have you join our party and return to Bathara with us." He pinches his chin, openly considering something. "It's not everyday a Nightenjoy attempts to enter the academy, after all. Tell me, have you considered which aggregate you'd hope to be Selected into if you pass the exams?"

I catch the twitch of Draven's brows, and I notice the way his eyes dart to the side toward Kiran. It's the sort of look that, if it ever carried a physical repercussion, would result in a stab wound.

"I haven't," Gray answers. "Why do you ask? Are you students?"

"Something like that," Kiran chirps, clasping his hands behind his back. He cocks his head. "So, what'll it be? Care to join us?"

Gray glances at me before back at Kiran. "It's not solely my decision to make. She and I need to discuss it first."

Draven's reply comes gruff and swift. "Redress her wounds and talk it over. Find us when you're finished. You have an hour." Then, without so much as another glance, he turns on his heels and strides back to his black stallion.

Kiran studies Gray and me a moment longer. As if amused by whatever he sees, he chuckles under his breath and croons, "Hope to be traveling with you soon."

CHAPTER EIGHTEEN

"What do you think?" Gray asks me as he pulls Azalea's healing salve from his satchel.

"I think the tall one could use a lesson in manners," I grumble, still frustrated.

Gray chuckles. He shifts to his knees, sets the salve down beside me, and begins unraveling my bandages. "Though right you may be, that isn't exactly what I'm asking."

I sigh. "I think, regardless of how irksome they appear to be, traveling with them would better our odds at making it to Bathara in one piece."

"But do you think we can trust them?"

Tricky question.

Do I think we can *trust* them? No, not really. They both appeared to be hiding something earlier. Whether it's the details of their scouting mission or something else, I can't be sure. But do I think they'll take us to Bathara like they say? I suppose I do.

I wince a little as Gray reaches the lower layer of bandages. "I wouldn't spill my deepest secrets to them anytime soon, but I do think they'll make good on getting us to Bathara."

"I suppose you're probably right." Gray reaches the final layer of linen, leaving nothing but my bare skin waiting underneath. He hesitates and flicks his eyes to mine, clearing his throat. "I—uh. I can turn around while you remove the last bit and wrap yourself in the first layer of fresh bandages if you want." Splotches of red rise to his cheeks.

I arch a humored brow. "Didn't you already bandage me?"

A confused look scrunches his face, as if what I've said makes no sense at all. "That was different. You were unconscious and bleeding out. I had no choice. This time, I want to make sure you have the choice."

An airy smile sweeps across my lips, and I teasingly reply, "Circumstances may be different, but my body remains the same. It's nothing you haven't seen before."

He resumes with his work. "If I had it my way, I would've never seen a single inch of you. Not unless it was you who wanted to show me."

He sucks in a sharp breath, and I never knew a human face was capable of such redness.

"That came out wrong. I meant if *you* wanted me to see you shirtless." He slaps a hand to his forehead and drags it down his face. "Wait, no. It's still coming out wrong. I mean...what I was trying to say..."

And at the sight of his uncharacteristic stammering...

I tip my head back, laughing. I laugh and laugh, until my side pinches and my ribs ache. Tears swell in the corners of my eyes, and I have to swipe them away with the crook of my finger. As I laugh, I feel the sun kissing my cheeks, and I become keenly aware of all the color surrounding me.

And for a brief moment, I feel the flickers of happiness; it feels so warm.

Have I truly become so cold that I've forgotten what it feels like to have warmth settle inside me?

When I tilt my chin back down, I find Gray watching me, an indiscernible look resting within his eyes.

"What?" I ask, the traces of laughter still bloating my words.

He observes me for a moment longer, and I notice the way the sun makes the copper in his eyes burn—the way it lightens the mossy green to near-translucent. "Nothing," he finally replies in a soft whisper.

I make a face at him. "Come on. Tell me."

He shakes his head, smiling. "Really, it's nothing. It's just...I don't think I've ever seen you laugh like that."

The words swell in my chest and press against my breastbone, aching tenderly.

He applies the healing salve to the puncture wounds at my shoulder before laying fresh bandages. When he finishes the last layer, he clips the extra fabric and pulls back to inspect the quality of his work.

Deeming it acceptable, he meets my eyes. "All finished."

⁂

Gray and I find Draven and Kiran near the river, watering their horses.

As we approach, Kiran turns to greet us, but Draven's gaze remains fixed on the coursing river, his hand mindlessly stroking his horse's strong body.

"So," Kiran coos. "What did you decide?"

Gray inclines his head. "We'd like to accept your offer, if it remains."

Kiran smiles, delighted. "Wonderful. You get to ride with me, Nightenjoy."

One glance at Gray after those words, and I have to bite down on my lip to hold in my laughter.

Kiran slides his sapphire eyes to me, a smirk already curling his lip. "I don't know what you're laughing about," he chides. "You have to ride with him." He jabs his thumb to the towering figure behind him. To Draven. "And if you haven't noticed, he's the broody, insufferable type, and they don't make for very fun company."

My smile indeed quickly falls, and now I'm fighting the urge to gulp.

Evidently, my shift in demeanor is obvious, because Kiran folds his arms across his chest and gives a confirming nod. "That's more the expression I'd expect to see."

I flick my eyes to Draven's considerably broad back, just in time to see him stiffen. And as if sensing that somehow, Kiran's smile just grows wider.

He really is always smiling, isn't he?

"When do we leave?" I ask, curious to know how much time I have to prepare before getting onto a horse with Draven.

Kiran makes a show of thinking. "Let me see…right now, as it so happens."

The blood leeches from my face, and I make a choking sound.

"It's probably best if you go and properly introduce yourself," Kiran continues. "He's rather unfriendly, and if you're going to ride him, he likes to be familiar with your scent."

My cheeks flood with scalding heat as I tug at my brows. "*Excuse me? I don't know what sick perversion makes you think—*"

Gray loudly clears his throat, cutting me off. "He's referring to the horse, Lyra."

I didn't think it was possible, but I'm certain my cheeks grow even redder than before. "Oh."

Draven finishes prepping his stallion right as I clasp my cloak.

He gives the horse a pat before turning to face me. "Do you want to get on first or would you like me to?"

I shrug. "Either is fine with me."

He studies me, his mismatched eyes striking. "Have you ever mounted a horse before?"

Though his tone wasn't condescending, I still answer with a slight defensive bite. "Many times."

He hums, the sound a deep, hypnotic tune. "And are all the wounds dressed properly?" Though one would think those are caring words, there isn't a hint of tenderness to them.

The question catches me off-guard. "They are."

"Good." With fluid grace, he mounts the horse suddenly and offers his hand after. "The last thing we need is to be slowed down by an infected wound."

I resist the urge to roll my eyes, but still swat his hand out of the way. I mount the horse, thanking the gods the beautiful stallion holds steady.

As I position myself on the saddle, I press against Draven's frame—*all* of his frame—and I have to douse the fluttering wings of butterflies in my stomach before they take flight.

I have no interest in such juvenile feelings. I especially have no interest in getting distracted by his looks. There is far too much at stake for me to get diverted by a pair of pretty eyes and a toned body.

Not to mention, our first encounter leads me to believe he's always an unpleasant ass.

Draven reaches around me for the reins, and I am swallowed by his muscular arms, embraced by his towering frame. It makes me feel all at once deeply in danger and entirely safe.

At least he smells decent—like citrus and leather mingling with the subtle smell of sweat.

Noticing how he smells makes realization smack me in the face.

I must smell terrible.

But maybe that's not a bad thing. Maybe it'll act as a barrier to make him stay away.

"Are you ready?" Draven calls out to Kiran, his deep voice rumbling in his chest against my back.

My mouth runs dry, and I have to swallow against the sudden drought in my throat.

But then I glance over at Gray, who looks positively unamused to be sharing a horse with Kiran. Not because he is frustrated with sharing a horse with a man; Gray doesn't care. But rather because he and Kiran are both large, muscular men sharing a saddle that is not fit to accommodate two people with such builds.

A giggle escapes me.

"Ready," Kiran answers over his shoulder, turning his speckled horse away from the river, eastward.

Draven kicks his heel into his stallion's side and makes a clicking noise with his mouth. We begin to move at a slow trot.

Without turning around, I ask, "Where are your other traveling companions? There were two others with you before."

"We're meeting up with them now." A pause. "How were you injured?"

I'm surprised by the question. "We had an…encounter."

"An encounter? With what?"

I huff a sardonic laugh. "You wouldn't believe me if I told you."

The horse picks up speed, and Draven shifts forward with the reins. I can practically feel his breath on the tip of my ear as he replies, "Try me."

A chill skitters down my spine, and I become keenly aware of his hips pressed against my backside. I clear my throat. "It was a Wynn."

Draven is silent for a long moment. "And where was he?" I feel more than see his chin jerk toward Gray.

"Also injured," I reply.

Draven snorts a dry laugh. "Naturally." He pulls on the reins, his arm brushing against me.

Ignoring the touch, I glance back pointedly at him. "And what's that supposed to mean?"

"What do you think it means?"

"I don't know. Hence why I'm asking for clarification."

A small bump on the ground has Draven again shifting into me. I again ignore it. "Someone who can't even defend themselves against one silly creature has no place participating in Bathara's entrance exams."

I manage to keep my words clipped. My annoyance contained. "Have you ever seen a Wynn before?"

"No. I have not."

"Then you have no right to judge him when you haven't the faintest clue what we were up against. It..." I pause, flashes of the Wynn running through my mind. "It is a creature of nightmares—of death and rot. I wouldn't wish my worst enemy to face it." I sit up a little straighter and lift my chin. "And I'll have you know, Gray is an incredibly capable wielder, and an even more talented fighter. His swordsmanship is second to none."

He huffs as if he's amused. "Is that so?"

"It is."

His low grunt is his final reply.

We continue trotting behind Kiran and Gray in silence, the clapping hooves the only sound for a long while. Until Draven's voice snaps me from my wandering thoughts. "I want you to know you'll be safe from injury for the rest of this journey."

I arch a brow—even if Draven can't see it. "Oh?" I retort a bit mockingly. "And how can you guarantee that?"

"Because I'm here now. And despite what you might think, I don't lose. Ever."

CHAPTER NINETEEN

My ass hurts more than I care to admit.

So, when we finally come to a halt in a small passing near the base of the cliffs, wedged between a line of trees, I practically leap off the saddle, desperate for reprieve. I stretch my limbs, pressing my hands into my lower back and extending my chest out. I pull my foot back, then my other foot, and am bending down to touch my toes when a shadow drapes over me.

I flick my eyes up to find Kiran standing in front of me, his arms folded across his chest as he watches me with a cocked head. And of course...he is smirking. "Soo," he coos. "How was the ride?"

I rise, arching my brow. "Fine." The curve in my brow deepens. "Why are you so curious to know?"

He drops his arms from his chest and shrugs. "No reason." Kiran shoves his hands into his pockets, turns on his heels, and whistles merrily as he walks toward a gnarled, towering tree that looks different than all the rest. "You can come out now," he drawls.

As if appearing from nowhere, two cloaked figures emerge from the shadows. They each place three parallel fingers over their hearts and drop their heads.

And it's not like I *needed* something to confirm their high status, but that gesture certainly just did.

I startle at the low voice rippling from beside me. "Report."

My eyes dart to the side and find Draven standing only a few inches away from me, his arms crossed against his chest.

When the hell did he even get there?

One of the figures removes his hood, revealing unruly, brown, curly hair, and a face full of freckles. "Here?" he questions, shifting a little on his feet. His eyes bounce to me before returning to Draven.

Gray appears then, coming around from the other side of Kiran's speckled horse. He stands on the other side of me and glances down at me the same moment I glance up at him, offering me a warm smile before turning his attention to the brown-haired man. His features stiffen into focus.

"Did you find what you were assigned to scout for?" Draven elaborates, his voice not unkind but also not warm and friendly, either.

"We did," the man answers.

"And?" Draven presses.

"I believe we'll be able to return to Bathara tomorrow morning." His eyes are filled with the ghosts of unspoken sentences.

I glance at Draven and see his eyes narrow—with thought or suspicion, I can't tell. Regardless, he exhales through his nose and says, "Good," before walking back to his stallion.

Kiran glides over and takes up residence where Draven had just stood. "Lyra," he says cheerily. "I'd like you to meet our fellow traveling companions."

The two step forward, and the remaining hooded figure draws back the cloth from his head, revealing black hair, a slender face punctuated by prominent cheekbones, and full lips.

"This is Griff," Kiran says, sweeping a hand toward the man with the unruly, brown hair. "And this is Meiji." He motions toward the man with the delicate features. "Meiji is a healer. Griff is an aether-wielder. The two essentials to any scouting party."

I dip my chin. "Nice to meet you both. I'm Lyra Izacalli, and this is my traveling companion, Gray."

Griff struts forward, ignoring Gray, and takes my hand, pressing a light kiss to the back of it. "Pleased to make your acquaintance, Lyra Izacalli." He lifts his brown eyes and locks them on mine as he smiles.

My brows jump up to my hairline at the bold display.

Meiji steps forward and shoots him a pointed look. "Ignore him," he says as if he's had to explain this a thousand times before. "Griff is a shameless flirt. But he's all bark no bite." He slaps the back of his head. "Reign it in for once, would you?"

Griff rubs at the spot. "Who said that wasn't me reigned in?"

Meiji rolls his eyes before stretching his hand out to me. "It's nice to meet you, Lyra. Please, if he continues to pester you with his hollow charm, do let me know."

Griff clicks his tongue. "My charm is not hollow."

Meiji folds his arms and chuckles. "It most certainly is. You're like an untrained pup."

"You always act like you're *so* much older than me." Griff lifts a brow. "When, in fact, you're not."

"I think the word you're looking for is maturity," Meiji supplies through a mocking smile.

Kiran rubs between his brows and sighs. "Must we always bicker?"

Meiji claps Griff on the shoulder before strutting over to stand next to Kiran. "When you bring a pup along, it's bound to bark."

Griff glowers at them. "Again," he retorts dryly. "Not. A. Puppy."

Gray clears his throat, gaining everyone's attention. "I presume this is where we'll be camping for the night?"

"It is," Kiran confirms. "You are free to do as you please for the rest of the evening. We'll depart for the academy in the morning."

I tilt my head. "If we have an aether-wielder, why not just have him open a portal now?"

Meiji grins. "Oh, do tell them, pup."

Griff rolls his eyes and sighs haughtily. "I'm drained," he grumbles. "Even if I wanted to" —he shoots Meiji a look— "though it's not like we'd be leaving *anyways*, I wouldn't be able to open a stable portal."

Curious, I ask, "Does a portal always have to be stable?"

Griff frowns at the question. "Sure, if you want to arrive wherever you're going with all of your limbs."

"It's a fair question for her to ask," Meiji says while sliding his pack off his shoulders, rummaging through the contents.

"I didn't say it wasn't," Griff counters.

I glance to the side, realizing that, at some point, Kiran walked away without anyone noticing.

He and Draven are both eerily good at moving quietly.

Gray leans down, keeping his eyes on the still-bickering Griff and Meiji. "Perhaps we should take this opportunity to train."

I watch them a moment longer, a wrinkle in my brow. I look back to Gray. "I'm in."

"Not with that wound you're not," Meiji interjects suddenly, sliding his gaze to me. "I'm mending you before you do anything."

My brows lift, impressed by how quickly he detected my injuries. Is that why he started rummaging through his pack?

"I'll find you when you're finished," Gray assures me.

Meiji frowns. "Your injuries are just as bad as hers, if not worse. I'll be mending you, too."

I shoot a look at Gray, who attempts to stifle his wince. He didn't even tell me he was injured. Knowing him, he was probably going to keep it to himself until we reached Bathara.

"Come on," Meiji says, rising from the ground and shouldering his pack. "Follow me."

※ ✺ ✺

Meiji is quick and efficient, mending Gray first.

The moment he pulls Gray's shirt from his body—revealing claw marks stretching along Gray's side, the three jagged grooves red and angry despite being cleaned—it is an act of will not to slap Gray upside the head.

Meiji lets out a low whistle. "If you waited any longer, you probably would've had an infection invade your body."

I remember Draven's words.

The last thing we need is to be slowed down by an infected wound.

Had he somehow known about Gray's injuries? I assumed he was just talking about the marks on my shoulder...

Gray glances at me through the sides of his eyes, and I fold my arms over my chest, pelting him with my stare. He sighs, his shoulders slumping forward.

Meiji chuckles quietly at the exchange. His fingers move nimbly as he pours his magic into the ripped seams of Gray's skin, stitching it back together with glittering threads of gold. After a quick few minutes, he pulls back from Gray's healed flesh and claps his hands to his thighs.

"Alright," Meiji says. "All finished. Try not to mess up my work anytime soon, okay?"

Gray picks up his shirt and laughs, nodding. "I'll do my best," he promises. "Thank you."

"No thanks necessary." Meiji turns his focus onto me. "Come on," he drawls, waving me over. "You're next."

I plop down where Gray just sat, turning my chin over my uninjured shoulder. "I'll come find you when I'm finished."

Gray's lips curve gently as he dips his chin. Then, he scuffles over to the other side of the trees, leaving me to undress and unwrap my bandages with privacy. Meiji inspects my wounds, somehow not making me uncomfortable in the slightest—the mark of a truly skilled healer.

"Not bad," he decides. "Gray attended to your wounds?"

I nod my head.

"Does he have any experience with healers or medicine?"

A warm smile tugs at my lips. "He's the son of a Gardner."

Meiji's brows skip up. "Ah. That'll do it, then."

He gets right to work, his fingers surprisingly warm and soft. We sit in a passing silence before I grow bold enough to ask, "So who are you guys, exactly?"

Without looking up at me, he hums a laugh. "I take it that neither Draven nor Kiran disclosed that information to you?"

"No," I answer. "No, they did not."

He hums again, this time a bit louder and rougher. "Then I suppose they probably have their reasons for that."

I resist the urge to wrinkle my nose at his answer. Instead, I draw in a breath and flick my eyes down at Meiji. "Well, can you tell me who *you* are?"

He huffs a soft laugh, amused. But his brown eyes meet mine, and they crinkle with warmth. "I am Meiji Himari, son of Lord Himari. I am an instructor at Bathara, and a former member of their Philator aggregate. A proud healer, and a scholar at heart, I am also an older brother, and a man who's debilitatingly in love with a woman named Nuha. I plan to make her my wife once we return from this trip, actually. Then, I will hopefully be a husband, and perhaps someday, a father."

"A pretty future," I muse, my voice distant.

"The future is like a blank canvas waiting to be painted. Pick the colors, choose your brush, and then shape it as you please. If your future is ugly, then I do not feel pity for you. You paint your picture and no one else."

I tug at my brows, his words familiar to previous thoughts of my own, even if spun differently. "Do you really believe that?"

He shrugs. "Anyone who doesn't is simply looking for an excuse to place blame anywhere but on themselves." Meiji stills, thinking. "Though, I don't suppose I blame them for it. It's easier that way for most people."

"Hm," is the only noise I'm able to muster as my mind drifts.

He slides his eyes up to me. "And who are you, Lyra Izacalli?"

A good question.

"I am the daughter of a Gardner."

"Is that all?"

"No," I answer, my brows pinching with thought. "But I...I think I'm still deciding on the rest."

Meiji hums. "The greatest questions require the greatest answers." Something like encouragement rests within the creases of his warm gaze. "Great answers take time to find."

The corner of my lip tugs with a gentle smile.

He claps his hands on his thighs. "There. All finished."

CHAPTER TWENTY

I find Gray shirtless, doused in sweat, and already running through movements with his sword.

Approaching him from behind, I clear my throat, gaining his attention.

He drops the tip of his blade to the ground and turns around, leaning against the hilt with a smile on his lips. "Welcome back. How do you feel?"

"I'll feel a lot better after I do this." I flick his nose. "If you *ever* withhold an injury like that from me again, by the gods, I will deal you your next lethal blow myself."

Gray's brows kick up as the corner of his lip curves up into a soft smile. "Fair enough."

I continue looking at him pointedly. "There is nothing noble about plain stupidity."

He exposes his raised palms to me. "I get it. Your point has been made."

I raise my chin. "Good."

He watches me for a long moment, chuckling quietly, before walking a few paces over and grabbing his scabbard. Gray sheaths his sword and returns to me. "Come on," he says with the jerk of his chin. "You can release some of that anger through training."

We go through our usual warm-up, revisit correct form, then launch into a spar. And Gray was right, throwing my fists at him *is* making me feel better—even if he easily dodges all my punches.

He counters with his own attack, and I manage to dodge it. I want to strike back, so the moment my feet are set, I charge at him. But Gray easily catches my wrists with his hands and presses them to my sides.

He shakes his head. "You shouldn't have attacked."

"You're wrong."

Out of nowhere, surprising both Gray and me, Draven emerges through the trees.

My brows twitch with confusion. How long has he been watching us?

Gray releases my wrists. "Excuse me?"

Draven approaches, his strides long and steady. "I said you're wrong. She shouldn't always evade. She should fight back. Instead of telling her otherwise, you should be teaching her when to strike and showing her where an opponent's points of weakness are."

Gray nods. "When she's ready, yes."

Draven cocks his head and folds his arms across his broad chest. "And why do you presume she isn't ready to learn something like that now? Did you not say you're traveling to compete in Bathara's entrance exams?"

Gray releases a breath, gathering his composure. "I did. But Lyra..." He pauses, clearly considering his words, not wanting to give too much away.

He doesn't get the chance to finish.

"Lyra, what? *Can't* perform the movements? Then she has no business competing. Or is it *you* who is going easy on *her*, too worried about preserving her instead of *training* her?"

Gray's mouth tightens. Draven stands his ground, his arms still folded across his chest, his peculiar eyes locked on Gray. I flick my eyes between them, the tension so thick and wound taut, a small hangnail could cut it.

God's veins...

"I'm showing her the better moves for both her stature and muscle build," Gray presses, his voice clipped.

"I disagree."

"Then I'm sorry, friend, but I believe it is *you* who is mistaken."

The corner of Draven's lip kicks up, and I have never seen a smile look so terrifying. Draven drops his arms and takes one step forward. Then another. And another. Until he and Gray are a few inches away from each other. Neither of them balk. Neither of them relent.

Draven's voice is a low, crackling melody. "First, and just so we're clear, I am not your friend. Second, I'm *not* wrong. But if you are so deluded that you can't see clearly, allow me to assist." He draws back, unsheathing his sword.

My feet move before my mind.

Within an instant, I am standing between them—Gray unflinching, eyes locked on Draven, and Draven with his sword idly in his hand, a smirk twisting his lips. I outstretch my arms as if I could actually stop them.

"Stop it, the both of you." My hands drop to my sides, and I glance between the two of them. "Really, this is childish and made of ego. It's just training for the gods-sake."

Draven snorts at me, and his features lock into something cold. "If you think that, then you are a fool and deserve to be trained as you currently are." He takes a step toward me, and I have to fight the quiver threatening to buckle my knees. "Why do you train?"

I blink. "What?"

He takes another step, lowering his head to meet my eyes. "Why. Do. You. Train." His lips are so close to me that, if he wanted to, he could easily bite clear through my lip. An animalistic action I wouldn't entirely put past him given his sharp, savage expression at the moment.

I lift my chin. "Because I want to win."

Draven's gaze does not waver. "Win what, exactly?" His breath curls against my lips.

"I...well, my..."

My freedom. My life. This fucked up game that nobles have created of worth and measure.

But he doesn't deserve to know anything about me. Plus, based on the way he is currently looking at me, I get the distinct feeling none of those answers would be enough for him anyways.

My chin falls with my eyes. "I don't know," I murmur.

"Then you are undeserving of the title Jurafen, and you have no place at Bathara." He drops his voice, and he lowers his lips down toward my ear. "Want to know what I train for? I train so no one in this world can best me. To make sure I remain the strongest. That way, I can defend whoever, whenever I need to, and no person can ever force me to my knees."

He draws back, and my breathing hitches in my chest from the cold look passing through his seafoam eyes. A look so viscous is undeserving of eyes so beautiful.

Before I can even consider a reply, Gray is there, wedging himself between Draven and me, his arm extended into a straight line. "That's enough," he warns in a low growl.

A look of indifference lines Draven's features once more. "I agree," he murmurs through a lazy shrug. "I no longer see anything worth fighting over."

The words strike me like a physical blow, and they seep beneath the layers of my skin, crawling up and up until they're like weighted knots in my chest.

⁂

The sun has gone to sleep, and the fire replacing its faded light clings to its last, crackling ember.

Meiji and Griff retire to their tent for the evening, and Kiran strolls over to where Gray and I have our bedrolls laid out, bids us goodnight, and then disappears into his own tent. I don't know where Draven is. I hadn't seen him while the tents were being erected, and only two are posted. He's probably sharing a tent with Kiran, but it's odd that I haven't seen him since training. Not that I'm in any hurry to see him again.

I no longer see anything worth fighting over.

I roll onto my back and lock my fingers behind my head, exhaling a breath. My eyes consume a star-embedded sky, and I savor the warmth the sight brings me. Unfortunately, however, it's not enough to stave off the frigid chill lingering beneath my skin.

Why do you train?

Because I want to win.

I sigh, conceding to the irksome fact I will probably get little sleep tonight. My fingers twitch, and the thought of reading Casimir's journal flickers into my mind. I sit up and scan my surroundings. Not surprisingly, Gray is sound asleep like always, and my ears don't detect any noises coming from the two tents posted a few paces away.

But just as I reach over for my pack to grab the journal, someone calls out to me. "Ly-ra...Iza-calli..."

It is a chilling voice I do not recognize.

I squint, trying to make shapes out of formless shadows between the trees. Yet I see nothing.

The hissing voice calls for me again. "Lyra...Izacalli... Come. *Come.*"

A foreign feeling washes over me, and before I fully realize what I'm doing, I'm standing upright, and my feet are guiding me into the shadows. Deeper and deeper into the line of trees I wander. It's like I'm being drawn somewhere—tugged by some invisible force.

"Lyra," the stranger hums.

I whip my head left, then right.

No one.

I steel my eroding nerves. "Who's out there? How do you know my name?"

"Because Master told me your name."

Fear pricks my skin like tiny needles, shooting down the nape of my neck, stretching all the way to my fingertips. "Who is your master? Is it the king? Has he sent you as another obstacle to indulge his petty game?" I halt in place, attempting to pinpoint where the voice is coming from.

A low chuckle rumbles from my left, and instinct has me pivoting my body, taking up my fighting stance. "King, you say? A king, a king, a king." The man's gravelly voice shrills, his speech growing erratic. "What is a king? A ruler? A title? A facade of power? Who is *your* king, Lyra Izacalli? Do you believe him to be the same as mine? If either is false, does that make the man any less a king?" The voice rounds the line of trees, now echoing from my right. "What is a king? A king, a king, a king?"

A branch cracks from behind me, and I whirl around.

Yet nothing is there. Nobody waits for me.

My breathing turns jagged, and I attempt to regulate the stuttering beats of my heart.

I straighten my back and lift my chin. "I serve no king."

"Ah," the stranger breathes with excitement. "An embodiment of ideals. To you, that is a king." Dirt and grass crunch beneath a boot, and I am scanning the land around me with wild eyes.

Why can't I see him?

A warning shoots down my spine and through my veins like a bolt of electricity. But before I can act, a hand claps over my mouth, and I am yanked backwards, landing against a chest. The smell of burnt embers, laced with something else, stuffs into my nose, and a fragment of my heart splinters beneath the weight of its strange familiarity.

A putrid, sickly sweet smell.

Burning flesh.

For a moment, I am back. I have returned to the hill where my mother is drenched in oil and tied to a stake. Where flames lick the moisture from the air, regurgitating suffering and ash instead. I am small, tiny fists beating against a cold ground. I am devastation and agony. Brokenness and regret.

My fault.

It should have been me.

A fissure cracks in my chest, cleaving my heart and fracturing the bones protecting it.

Dry, cracked lips press against my ear. "Mmm, I can taste your sorrow." Those lips split, and a slithering tongue emerges through them, tasting my skin from my jaw up to my temple. The stranger giggles like a child—no, like a mad man. A lunatic. Like someone...someone...

Someone lost to the forbidden magics.

Pure, cold dread replaces the blood draining from my face as I become aware of who—*what*—this stranger is.

An Abdite.

A corrupted wielder who is lost to the lunacies of the forbidden magics. Wielders who, despite all the warnings, all the Tani laws forbidding anyone from attempting to access such magic, still attempted to barter with their soul for power.

I've only ever seen one. He was in King Alastair's service and was in the early stages of madness. His very veins began to darken, and his skin turned sickly. I was there the night King Alastair had sentenced him to Toellor, the stone prison in the Spicere Mountains dedicated to containing Abdites. The corrupted man had smiled—exposing rotting teeth—and mumbled hysterical ramblings under his breath.

And now, such a dark and twisted wielder clutches me against his chest.

My heart hammers, my pulse pounding against my skin. The Abdite drops his hand from my mouth and glides a rough finger along my jaw. "I have the key that will unlock the door. Master will be pleased with me."

Before I can speak, he spins me around to face him. Ragged cloths drape over his body, covering his frame and shadowing his face with a fraying hood. I can't make out a thing about the Abdite prowling before me. Nothing except his eyes.

They glow like a molten flame, even through the shadows.

I dig my nails into my palms to keep myself from shaking.

"You're looking at me," the Abdite squeals with delight. "No one ever looks at me. I want to show myself to you. I want you to behold my fire."

He lets go of me, and my first instinct is to sprint off in the opposite direction. But to my absolute horror, I am frozen in place, as if cemented to the ground, glued to the sky.

"What have you done to me?" I murmur, breathless.

"Bound you," he answers, his words sounding as if they came through a frown. His fingers rise to the ragged hood, but before he can pull it back, a shrill female voice pierces the air.

"Don't you dare, Lexamon. Master will not be pleased with you exposing yourself."

I want to turn, to look behind me where the voice sounds from. But all my limbs are frozen in place. The only things I have control over are my eyes and lips—and I guess my lungs since I can still breathe.

I guess that's something to be grateful for.

"Dridus, my body sings in her presence. Let me press the melody into my flames."

"You risk the others," she replies.

Others? There are more?

Which means Gray isn't safe. Kiran, Meiji, Griff, hell even Draven… I have to warn them. I have to let them know Abdites are in the valley.

I struggle against the hold locking my body in place, and the display results in the Abdite, Lexamon, giggling some more. "Look, look at her. Tell me she isn't a riveting creature."

"Master needs her."

"Why?" I grit out, finding my voice still works. "Why does he need me? I am no one—nothing of worth."

"You are the key," the female Abdite, Dridus, answers. "And the one hunting you will stop at nothing until you are his. That's why we were sent. To recover the key."

It's as if she just spoke another language, because nothing she says is making sense. "The key? The key to *what?*"

Dridus begins snickering, her madness snapping into place. "Key to lock, key to lock. What is locked that needs a key?"

Despite my appallingly dire situation, I can't stop my grumbling retort. "I was hoping you would answer that."

Dridus and Lexamon both giggle hysterically. Through her grating laughs, Dridus answers in the tune of a child's song. "I'm not supposed to say, but you mustn't jump to conclusions. A key is many things, and locked is none when possessed by one."

A blood-curdling scream echoes from the distance, expanding into the sky and rattling my chest.

Meiji.

That definitely sounded like Meiji who screamed.

Fight, determination—call it what the hell ever. But a fire pours into my muscles, and I fight against the magic holding me in place. Still, I don't budge.

"They've started without us," Lexamon pouts.

Dridus, as if a part of another conversation entirely, starts chanting in hysteric whispers. "Up the rising goes forward. Up the rising goes forward. Up the rising goes forward. Up the rising goes forward."

Up the rising goes forward.

The words spin in my head, until it clicks into place.

The uprising goes forward.

Lexamon addresses Dridus. "Shh. Shh. You mustn't spill the game."

Dridus, as if lost in a trance, continues rocking back and forth while chanting in a hypnotic whisper. "Up the rising goes. One by one, until it unfolds. Forward we forge, just like the land before. Time rewind, magic that binds, brother by brother. My brother, oh brother." Still not able to turn and see Dridus, I figure something must be happening, because her voice cracks and shrieks as she continues to chant, gasping between words. "I'm sorry, brother. I'm sorry it had to end like this. Revenge. Avenge. A purpose to serve. A purpose to die. Reborn from death. An abomination until the end."

Lexamon begins hitting his palm against his forehead. "She's said too much. What would Master have me do?" He starts to reach for me, but quickly reels his hands back to his body as if zapped. "No—*no*. I mustn't burn the key. Master says no harm can come to the key." He hits himself harder. "But Master also said no one can know of the gathering."

I see the silhouette of flames rise in the air, and I pray to the gods those are Kiran's towering flames, not an Abdite's.

Clanging echoes, and I hear magic clash together.

Help them. I have to *help* them.

Though, what good am I? What could I do? I can't even break free from one Abdite's hold—how could I possibly help against a band of them?

Worst of all, had I led them to us? Is it my fault they discovered our camp?

The smell of burning flesh reappears, and those words float back to me.

My fault. It should have been me.

Lexamon whips his head to me and moans as if aroused. Like I have just caressed some sensitive part of him. "Oh, do you see now, Dridus? Her self-loathing is titillating. Her sorrow is delicious. It makes me ache with the desire to touch her." Lexamon steps toward me, and he leans down, until his molten eyes are parallel with my own. "I've already tasted you. Now, I will touch you how I expect you to touch me next."

He slowly stretches his hand out—his fingers twitching as they near my skin—but a slash of glinting steel forces him to jerk back. His hand thumps to the ground, detached from his body.

"You will not lay a single finger on her again."

CHAPTER TWENTY-ONE

I plummet face first into the ground, released from the invisible binds that confined me.

I guess losing a hand somehow released Lexamon's magic. Though, when I stand up and reorient myself, he doesn't seem to be bothered by his lost limb in the slightest. Instead, he appears to be rather...*eager.*

"I've been cut by the thread from the needle that's sewn you," Lexamon delights, glaring at the stump of his arm now spitting black blood. "What a pleasure."

Draven steps forward, emerging fully from the shadows, and as the moonlight sparkles against his sword, the darkness appears to ripple around him. Though it's probably some illusion from the silhouetted, moonlit trees.

Draven's low voice emerges through his frown, cutting through the air clear and sharp. "Can't say the same."

And then he moves.

But this time the Abdite all but disappears into thin air, not giving Draven the chance to strike again before reappearing across the trees.

Lexamon clicks his tongue repeatedly. "Ah, ah, ah. You've already taken one hand. I need my other."

Draven's voice rumbles from beside me. "Do you need it more than her?" He jerks his chin at Dridus, who is still lost in a mad state of hysterical chanting.

"The strings of my heart are already burnt from my flame," Lexamon says. "Pulling on them won't work."

Draven's reply comes swift and dry. "Alright, then." Within what feels like no more than a blink, Draven strides to Dridus, lifts his sword, and swipes the metal clear through her neck.

Much like Lexamon's hand, Dridus's head thumps against the ground, and her body collapses like nothing more than weighted cargo.

"Dri...dus..." Lexamon stumbles as if confused. "Dri...dri..." Faster than lightning, he appears in front of Draven and me, his eyes burning a molten color. "Thread or no thread, through the eye of the needle or not, I will tear you apart."

Draven lets out a low laugh. "I'd like to see you try."

Lexamon pulls off his ragged cloak, revealing...

Holy gods.

Gnarled veins wrap around his body like a living ribcage. They twist and knot across his arms, over his shoulders, and around his scalp. Beneath the black markings, brightening with Lexamon's every inhalation, rests a fiery glow that looks like sparking charcoaled embers. His black eyes are ringed with a matching molten blaze, and hovering in the center of his forehead, twirling across his brow bone and gliding down along his jaw, is a warped, inverted flame.

Lexamon briefly shuts his eyes, tips his head back, and exhales a breath. Afterwards, he drops his chin and tilts his head at Draven. "I'm going to enjoy this."

The mark on his face glows, and the air plummets into a piercing cold. Voices begin to whisper all around us. *Erhé akta maht. Erhé akta maht. Erhé akta maht.*

What dialect is that? Better yet, what *language* are the voices even speaking in?

My eyes dart around the scene unfolding before me, fear beginning to sink deep into the pit of my stomach. Lexamon's skin brightens, going almost translucent, revealing a smoldering fire beneath. He lifts his hand, and a burning sphere of black, inverted flames forms in his palm. His mark begins to thrum, as if pulsing against his skin, and it dawns on me.

The mark was once his wielder's mark. But since he's accessed the forbidden magics, it is...tainted, almost. Corrupted. Just like him.

The warped sphere of black flames grows into a daunting circle threatening destruction. Lexamon smiles wickedly, exposing his rotted teeth, and then flings the twisted fire at us.

It all happens so quick...

One moment, a ball radiating strange, corrupted energy is flying at my head, and then the next moment, it is being swallowed into oblivion by a rippling wall of darkness.

I blink, entirely confused.

But Draven's rough voice snaps me from my daze. "Go. *Go.* Find Kiran." When I don't move, his voice lashes at me like a spear. *"Now."*

Finding myself, I shake myself out of my daze and sprint in the opposite direction.

Lexamon's voice grows savage—twisted and strange. "You will *not* take away our key."

The surrounding whispers grow louder, more hysteric, as Lexamon's mark burns brighter with a silver glow that is...wrong. So wrong.

Erhé akta maht. Erhé akta maht. Erhé akta maht.

Draven, seemingly unbothered, replies, "And who's going to stop me? You?" He pouts at Lexamon, clicking his tongue after. "Not in this realm of hell."

Lexamon hisses at him. "Stubborn thread. Allow me to fray you a little bit."

Draven snorts at Lexamon, as if amused. "You're welcome to try. But I promise you won't harm me."

I hear nothing more of their conversation as I emerge through the trees, refusing to turn around.

Not even when I hear powerful magics clashing. Not even when I hear an earth-shattering shriek. Not when birds disperse through the trees, nor when a wave of chill-inducing energy warps past me, making the hairs on my arms rise.

With my lungs burning like the waters of Illithious Lake and my calves screaming at me, I slow only when I glimpse ruby-red hair bathed underneath the moonlight, standing behind a towering wall of burning flames. Just nearing it makes my body prick into a sweat, and I stagger at the sight.

For Kiran to be capable of something like this...

Kiran whips his head behind him, finding me immediately.

It is the first time since meeting him that I've seen him without a trace of a smile or smirk. Instead, his sapphire eyes are lined with concentration and...rage.

"Are you injured?" he asks first.

I shake my head.

"And Draven?"

I gulp down air, trying to steady my needled breathing. "He's..." Another gulp. "He's fighting an Abdite."

Just saying the words feels ludicrous. Like I suddenly inhabited a body—hell, a *world*—I do not belong in.

Kiran just nods—swift and firm. "He'll be fine."

How is he so confident? It is an *Abdite*. And his magic...it had been so cold and strange. Like it drained life from the very world around it. Just the wrongness of it was enough to freeze me with fear.

Gray appears suddenly, dropping what I realize is an illusion he cast to make himself disappear into his surroundings. "Lyra," he breathes, immediately pulling me into his chest. "I was so worried." He squeezes me, and for a brief second, I allow myself to be held.

Gray drops his arms and pulls back to scan my eyes.

I shake my head at him, still trying to process everything that just happened. "Abdites. There are Abdites in the valley. They—they..."

"We know," he says with as gentle a voice as he can.

My eyes rove to Kiran, fire pouring from his palms and into the burning wall of mammoth-sized flames, the sight unlike anything I have ever seen. But then I realize....

I whip my gaze back to Gray. "Where are Griff and Meiji? I–I heard him scream."

Gray's eyes fall to the ground. "They're on the other side of this wall."

"What? *Why?*"

Instead of Gray answering, it is Kiran's voice echoing into the night air. "Because an Abdite took Meiji, and Griff went after him."

"So why aren't *we* going after *them*?"

Gray rests a hand on my shoulder, shaking his head like he's resigned to whatever it is he's about to say. "We can't drop the wall, Lyra. Not until Draven returns. To do so...it would be suicide for us all. We counted twelve Abdites, and those were just the ones we saw. Kiran's wall is the only thing keeping us alive right now."

"So you're just going to let them *die*?!" I couldn't believe what I was hearing.

"Of course not," Kiran shoots back, turning his chin over his shoulder. "But what good are we to them dead?"

"We can't just do nothing," I plead, my voice cracking.

"This isn't nothing," Kiran grits back, his voice uncharacteristically rough. He returns his attention to the wall of bright, roaring flames, and I look back at Gray, incredulous.

His gaze is soft as he watches me through sympathetic eyes. "He's right, Lyra."

A pitchy female voice carries on the wind through the flames, wrapping itself around our bodies. "Do you want him? Your healer? Then come get him, girl. I'll even tell you where I keep him."

Both Gray and Kiran jerk their gaze to me.

"Lyra," Gray cautions. "Do not do anything rash."

I blow out a breath, shaking my head. "I'm sorry. But I can't just stand here doing nothing like some helpless fool."

And then I sprint straight through the flames, ready to singe my skin with welts and burns. Yet the flames part for me, and as I cross through the burning threshold, I come out unscathed. Shock courses through me, but I do not let it delay me. I charge forward.

That voice fills the air once more, deepening with authority. "Let her pass," she demands.

With a quick scan of my surroundings, I see Abdites returning to the shadows, bowing their heads and drawing back. Fear rattles through me, but I ignore the voice in my head telling me to turn around and go back behind the wall.

I won't leave them.

I won't just stand idly by and watch them die. Too many times had I cried—*begged*—for someone to come after me. Too many moments where a whip cracked against my skin, or a guard pinned me against a wall that left me begging for help from someone—*anyone*. And I know I'm not much, but...

I will not cower. I will not yield. I will not falter. Not today, at least.

"This way. This way." The voice guides me, steering my path to wherever it is she wants me to go.

It leads me back to that large tree, different from all the rest.

Cloaked, the woman gasps when she spots me. "You came!" she exclaims with no small amount of shock.

As if she didn't direct me the whole way here.

"Where are they?" I demand, not mincing words.

"Where is anyone, really? Here, there, in the wind. You must be more specific."

"Lyra..." Meiji's weak voice sounds from the right, and my eyes snap to where it came from.

I spot him slumped against a tree, and I sprint to him, sliding across the ground on my knees. Blood drenches his tunic, and I lift the fabric up, scanning for a wound. A task made much easier by the lightened sky from Kiran's wall of flames. But even despite having the bright orange glow, I see no wound—no source to explain the pool of blood.

Until Meiji lifts his arms and croaks, "No. Not there. *Here.*"

He holds up his hand-less arms, bright-red blood spouting from the amputated stumps. My eyes bulge in my skull while the blood drains from my face, and I whip my head back to the humming Abdite.

She smiles when she sees my stare. "Oh, just wait. The show will get better. Much, much better."

Ice fills my veins, but I still manage to focus on Meiji. "I'm going to get you out of here. Where's Griff?"

His eyelids flutter, and his head lolls to the side. I snap my fingers aggressively in his face. "No—*no*. Come on. Stay with me. Where is Griff?"

"Behind...hind..." He slumps forward, and I curse under my breath. Blood. He has lost *way* too much blood.

The Abdite steps forward and giggles like an innocent child. "See what I can do, Master's Chosen. Watch what power I've discovered in the dark." She drops her hood and removes her cloak entirely, revealing an arm with a gnarled hand tattoo running along her forearm. Iron-colored, shifting light funnels in the palm's hand, awakening with an eerie glow. And just like Lexamon's mark, her wielder's mark has been corrupted.

My heart thunders in my chest because I'm still able to recognize what remains of her wielder's mark. I had wanted to be one of them once upon a time. Typically, it's a variation of a hand or folded hands with pure white light formed in the palms. The mark of a healer.

But what happens when a healer is corrupted?

The Abdite stretches out her hands, a vile smile tugging at her chapped lips. "It demands to be fed. It demands to be unleashed. Demand, demand, demand." Her head tilts at a weird angle as she swivels her gaze to me. "Are you ready, Lyra Izacalli?"

My name on her lips is like a shock to my system.

"Whatever you plan to do, please, I beg you...don't do it. I'll go with you. I will. But not if you harm anyone else."

She angles her head further. "The key will come with me?"

I swallow against the dryness in my throat and dip my chin. "Yes. I'll go with you."

The Abdite pauses, considering my offer. "This will please the Master. Very well." She lowers her hands. But within a second, they rise back up, as if with a mind of their own. She inhales a loud, scratchy breath, and her neck cracks as her head suddenly bends backwards. "Feed me. Feed me. *Feed me.*" Her voice is low and raspy, and it sounds like she's never been given water a day in her life.

The palm on her arm glows once more, and it stretches to her fingertips, her skin lightening to a state of eerie translucence. Those voices return again, and they sing alongside the hysterical mumblings the Abdite rants under her breath. *Erhé akta maht. Erhé akta maht. Erhé akta maht.*

Brilliant white light seeps from Meiji's skin, and it enters into the Abdite's fingers like a coursing stream.

"Watch me siphon. Watch me steal." The Abdite's eyes roll to the back of her head, and she sucks in a pleasured breath. "Delicious. His vitality tastes so delicious. A healer's life essence is always the best, so pure and full. I want to taste more. More, more, *more.*"

She pulls more aggressively with her fingertips, the brilliant light thickening into something like strings.

I blink, stunned at what I'm witnessing. She...she is siphoning the very life from Meiji's body, pulling it into her fingertips like nothing more than a puppeteer tugging on its marionette's strings.

And with stark clarity, I realize—

Healers give life; corrupted healers take life. Instead of possessing the magic to cure and give back, she's corrupted her magic to destroy and take. But I will not watch her drain Meiji's life force before my eyes.

I find my feet and rise, and I open my palms, willing my magic to surface. I think of the vines and thorns I summoned in the throne room. Think of the way they speared through the air like weapons at my command. Still, nothing happens; nothing comes.

Fuck it.

Not having magic has never stopped me before.

I sprint at the Abdite and knock my full weight into her, throwing her back. We both land on the ground with a loud *thud.*

The Abdite squeals with delight. "You've figured it out, haven't you? That I can siphon a person's very life away. It feeds me. Feeds my magic." She squeaks with joy again. "Ah, clever, clever girl. The Master will be most enamored with you."

I spring to my feet, looking around for anything I can use as a weapon. "I have a hunch the feeling won't be mutual."

With another quick sweep, I catch the blue-stoned, hilted dagger glinting under the moon, strapped to Meiji's thigh. I scurry for it, unsheathing it and holding it at the ready between the rising Abdite and me—even though I haven't the slightest idea how to use it.

But the concept is pretty straightforward, right? Use sharp point and stab.

She giggles. "That won't do anything to me. Do you see my skin? You can cut and cut, but it won't hurt me."

I click my tongue. "Doesn't mean I won't try." And then I charge at her—recklessly, I'll admit.

She grabs my wrists and holds me at bay, giggling all the while. I dislodge from her hold, and I manage to plunge the knife into her side. But, for some ungodly reason, it's like stabbing jelly. Her translucent skin swallows the cold metal like nothing more than a fish on a hook.

Her shrill voice pierces the night air. "I told you. I told you. That won't hurt me." She cranes her neck and stretches out her arms again. The string of light begins to flow into her fingertips once more, thickening, growing denser like a braided cord.

A savage cry escapes me, and I lose myself in a blind fury. I plunge the dagger into her side, her arm, her chest. Again, and again, and again. All the while, she is giggling, overjoyed at the display.

A loud boom sounds in the distance, and the night air suddenly dims back into darkness.

Kiran's wall of flame is gone.

The Abdite whips her head toward the sound and hisses. I seize the moment and ram my blade into her left eye.

The Abdite jerks back from the impact, alarmingly silent. Slowly, she tips her head forward, the knife jutting out of her eye socket like a gnarled limb. "You. Can't. Hurt. Me," she seethes.

An airy, boyish voice hardens into a weapon of its own. "I can." And then within a blink, steel sweeps through the Abdite's neck like a knife easily cutting through warm butter.

The shock remains on her face as her head tumbles to the ground.

Griff and I lock eyes, his stare impossibly saddened yet lined with a cold rage. And then, to both his and my horror, breathy words spew from the decapitated head. The same frenzied words I've been hearing since the Abdites arrived.

"Erhé akta maht."

And then life finally fades from the Abdite's eyes.

Griff pants in ragged breaths, staring coldly—distantly—at the severed head. Crusted blood pools along his temple, trails of fresh blood still trickling down his cheek. He slides his gaze back to me. Then, those cold-set eyes roll to the back of his head as he collapses.

It takes me a moment to fully come through the disorienting haze of everything that's happened. A second too long to process. A moment too long to reorient myself to the chilling reality awaiting me.

My feet move quicker than my mind, dragging me to Griff. With two fingers pressed against his neck, I sigh with relief when I feel his pulse hammering steady. I fall back for a moment and tip my head, only to shift my gaze afterward toward the tree.

Meiji has tipped sideways, his body slumped at an awkward angle.

My heart plummets into my stomach as I rush toward him. This time, I kneel gently beside him, and I loathe my wince at the gruesome sight. His skin is paper-thin, lined with age. His muscles have atrophied almost to the point of eradication, leaving nothing but bone beneath the surface. Every weak intake of scratchy breath is wet and rattles.

Through painful wheezes and stuttering attempts at words, Meiji gurgles, "Po...cket. My...po...cket."

Through lowered brows, I search the pockets of his breeches. My fingers land on something cool and circular, and I tug it free, revealing an emerald ring. My fracturing heart deflates. His words clamor through me, leaving behind a trail of needles in their wake.

I am Meiji Himari, son of Lord Himari. I am an instructor at Bathara, and a former member of their Philator aggregate. A proud healer, and a scholar at heart, I am also an older brother, and a man who's debilitatingly in love with a woman named Nuha. I plan to make her my wife once we return from this trip, actually. Then, I will hopefully be a husband, and perhaps someday, a father.

Meiji holds my eyes with his yellow, crow-lined stare. "Tell...her...I love," he pauses, his breaths growing sharp and ragged. He fights against it. "I love her, and...that I am...sorry...I couldn't...couldn't uphold...my...promise."

His breaths come in quick wheezes now, the effort to speak clearly torturous. I clutch the ring in the palm of my hand and nod. "I will," I swear. "I will make sure she knows."

Meiji attempts a smile before his eyelids flutter closed. He rasps two final words. "End...it..."

A series of hurried footsteps approach, crunching against the grass. They halt not far behind me, but I don't turn to see who all is there.

"What in the realms of hell..." Kiran's voice is breathless—awed, but in a heart-wrenching way.

Without a word, without a single expression of emotion, I rise and yank the dagger from the eye of the fallen Abdite. Not once do I flick my gaze in the direction of the silhouettes I see observing me. I return to Meiji and clutch the weapon in my shaking hands, hovering the metal tip over his chest.

Should I pierce through his heart? Is that the fastest way? What would allow me to give him the quickest death; would offer the least amount of pain? The temple, the neck? No, no...I think the heart is the right thing to do.

Gray's gentle words come from directly behind me, followed by a soft touch to my shoulder. "You don't have to do it, Lyra. I can be the one who...offers him peace."

I inhale trembling breaths through my nose. The dagger remains firmly in my grip, still hovering in midair, as Meiji's wet rasps fill the space like a crushing sound of sorrow. My fingers squeeze the hilt of the dagger more tightly, and my knuckles turn white.

Gray tries again. "It doesn't have to be you."

"Yes," Draven's voice carries, low and solemn. "It does."

"You can't force her to take a life," Gray counters, but not aggressively. I think everyone is too filled with...exhaustion, sorrow, remorse?...to even attempt fighting right now.

"I promise you," Draven replies, holding steady. "I would not force her to do this. But we weren't here; she was. We were not the ones who spoke with the dying; she was." He pauses. "If she can't, then I will do it. But first, you must offer her the chance to see this through. It's the way of the Jurafen."

Gray sighs and drops his hand from my shoulder, receding.

Draven's right—I was the one who saw the events unfold. I am the reason things ended this way. It has to be me.

Only me.

My fingers settle on the leather, and I gently shut my eyes and whisper the ceremonial words under my breath. "In Death you walk. In Life I remain. Bound together, yet neither the same. Safe travels, weary soul, for I shall see you soon. But until that day, I'll give you life by remembering you."

I plunge the dagger through Meiji's heart.

CHAPTER TWENTY-TWO

G riff comes to not long after Meiji draws in his last breath. Watching him take in the devastated condition of Meiji's body is not an easy task, and Griff's remained silent ever since. I find myself wondering if it's out of grief, or from the heartbreak that accompanies a goodbye-less parting.

With everyone helping, it doesn't take long to collect and assemble a make-shift pyre. During the process, I spot scattered headless bodies littered across the ground. I count sixteen. *Sixteen* Abdites. And that's not even including the Abdite Griff beheaded, Dridus, or Lexamon.

To be honest, I'm not entirely sure what to do with that knowledge. It seems like some fictional story the people of Solaya would tell its children before bed. A band of Abdites, totaling nineteen corrupted wielders, was in a cursed valley, attempting to kidnap their "key"—whatever the hell that even means—but then three wielders were able to make their stand and emerge victorious. If this is what you call victory.

That is perhaps the bit of information I find the hardest to reconcile. That somehow, Gray, Kiran, and Draven were able to defeat them. Three wielders overcoming nineteen Abdites is entirely unheard of.

Which leaves me wondering...

Just how strong *are* Kiran and Draven?

Because I know Gray is both a strong and competent fighter and wielder, but I also know he's not of the caliber to accomplish that sort of feat without considerable aid. Though I guess it's not like they got away unscathed. They look like they went through hell and back, and without a healer, they have to endure whatever still afflicts their bodies.

I make a silent note to offer to assess their injuries and create some sort of tonic or salve from the plants Gray collected this morning.

This morning.

A jarring realization.

Though perhaps it is more like yesterday morning now that dawn is on the horizon. Regardless, it feels like worlds away—almost like an entirely different life. Perhaps it was. Perhaps leaving that field of flowers behind was like leaving my old self—my old life—behind with it.

Once everything is ready, Draven and Kiran—as delicately as they possibly can—carry Meiji's deteriorated body onto the pyre. With heavy eyes and silent mouths, we all watch as fire pours from Kiran's palms, igniting the wood that will help guide his path to the afterlife. As the pyre goes up in flames, swallowing the final remains of his existence, the sky awakens with first light, casting the world in a hazy gray.

Strange, really. The way the forming colors of the rising dawn paint such a beautiful backdrop for something so horrific. It reminds me of something. Of a blotted red sky that also boasted behind wicked flames, incinerating the innocence from my veins, leaving me inexplicably empty.

Griff breaks the weighted silence first. "He didn't deserve this."

"No," Kiran agrees, his words sewn with the threads of grief. "He did not."

I look away from the flames and to Kiran, who stands to my left, then to Gray, who remains on my right. When I glance down, I'm shocked to see Gray holding my hand, quietly offering me comfort.

How had I not felt his touch? Not noticed his fingers intertwined with mine?

Griff, positioned on the other side of Gray, mutters, "Who is going to tell Nuha?"

"I will," Draven answers in an uncharacteristically soft voice, standing to the left of Kiran.

From the sides of my eyes, I glimpse Kiran rest a hand on Draven's broad shoulder. "I'll be there as well. No reason for doing it alone." I could have imagined it, but the last sentence sounded a bit pointed.

Draven says nothing.

"She's going to be crushed," Griff murmurs. "I've never seen anyone look at someone the way they looked at each other."

Kiran's tender voice drops an octave. "Indeed." A pause. "Do you know if there were any temples he had hoped to be burned in?"

Griff rubs at the back of his neck. "Nuha would definitely be better suited to answer this, but I believe so, yes. He once spoke of someday venturing to the Elwood Forest to find Araceli's waters. He also frequently made offerings to Morwenna. So...maybe both were options?"

Both deities do make sense for a healer to align with. It is also not uncommon for a healer to dream of venturing to find the legendary waters located somewhere deep within the Elwood Forest. It's rumored the water possesses unparalleled healing properties, and perhaps even more. But his intrigue with myth probably doesn't equate to him wanting to be burned in Araceli's temple.

"If he made offerings to Morwenna, I'd wager his preference was to be burned in the goddess's temple," I murmur.

Kiran continues staring at the building flames. "Does anyone know one of Morwenna's hymns?"

Gray clears his throat. "I—uh...I don't know the words, but I do have my double-flute with me. I'm familiar with *Ballad of the Tide*, Morwenna's favorite song. I can play it, if you like."

"Please," Kiran replies through a soft breath. He sounds so tired.

Gray wordlessly unlatches his satchel, rummages through its contents, and then pulls out an instrument featuring two elongated flutes fused side-by-side, carved from pale wood, with staggered finger holes. Ornate carvings line the wood, and leather pieces are strapped around it.

I remember the day he received the instrument. Azalea's eyes welled with tears, and Gray's were not far off.

Gray wets his lips, and then the haunting melody echoes through the wind as he plays. Between the burning pyre, the grief hanging heavy in the air, the streaks of dawn zipping across the horizon, and the lingering notes of the double-flute, it's as if a hypnotic trance falls over everyone. Nobody moves. Nobody speaks. We just stand and stare. Some with tears spilling over the rims of their eyes, others with hollowed expressions.

Before I know it, the song is finished, and Gray is putting his double-flute away while Griff swipes tears from his cheeks. Kiran clears his throat, sweeping his emotions aside.

"I suppose I should collect the Abdites' bodies and burn them as well," he murmurs.

"I'll help you," Gray offers.

"Me too." Griff's voice is raspy, thick with lingering sadness.

They shuffle in the opposite direction, their movements stiffened and slowed by the night's events.

Only Draven remains.

My eyes stay glued to the flames. "I understand what you mean now." I surprise even myself at how hollow I sound.

He is silent for a moment. "About?"

"Training. You told me you train so you can protect anyone. So you'll never be forced to your knees." I finally tear my eyes from the fire and look at him, surprised to find his gaze already pinned on me. "I'm not only going to best them," I continue, holding the weight of his stare. "I'm going to get *revenge*. On all of them. On the King of Rivara. On the Abdites. On the nobles who treated me like I was worthless. I am going to pass the entrance exams into Bathara, refine my magic, and then someday, I am going to make them all cower at my feet."

Draven remains quiet, something inscrutable passing through his eyes. Finally, he murmurs, "Revenge isn't everything, and you shouldn't get caught up in it." His brows lower with thought. "What did the Abdites say to you, exactly?"

I huff a sardonic laugh. "You really want to know? They told me I was their 'key', and that, 'the one hunting me won't rest until I'm theirs.'"

"Does that mean anything to you?"

A heavy curve forms in my brow. "I haven't the *slightest* clue what that means. My magic just manifested a few days ago. I have no wielder's mark. I possess no noble heritage. No qualities or traits worthy of comment. I'm nothing—a nobody. Why anyone would go through such trouble to kidnap me is beyond my comprehension; I'm not worth it." I feel a drop in my chest, followed by a subtle ache, and suddenly, I am so exhausted. My voice softens. "At one point, I thought King Alastair sent them to indulge his twisted sense of entertainment, but...that wasn't him. I know it wasn't."

Draven watches me closely. "Why would you suspect King Alastair? What does he have to do with any of this?"

I return my gaze to the burning pyre. "You know I plan to compete for a place at Bathara, and I tell you my magic manifested only a few days ago with no mark, yet that's what you focus on?"

I glimpse his shrug through my peripheral. "It's the only thing I find relevant at the moment. Plus, I already knew something was off with your magic. Not only from its feel, but by the fact that, even in the face of an Abdite attack, you never once wielded it." I glance at him sidelong and see him tilt his head. "Which, by the way, you really need to get that figured out. You won't make it through the exams if you can't even draw on your magic at will."

"Naturally," I mutter, unenthused. A beat of silence. "Wait, you can feel my magic?"

He nods. "Most wielders can. Laktî senses laktî. I just happen to be exceptionally good at it."

I slide him a look, a deep curve in my brow. "Of course you are."

A low noise hums in the back of his throat, and Draven folds his arms across his chest. "You're avoiding the question. What does King Alastair have to do with anything?"

I rub at the spot between my brows. Yet I give in, deciding there's really nothing to lose at this point. I lift my finger, revealing the tiny blood droplet inked into my skin.

Draven steps toward me and leans forward, his face scrunching. "A blood wager."

"A blood wager," I repeat dryly.

"Why?"

My teeth sink into my bottom lip as I consider whether or not to tell him—*how* much to tell him. But it seems my exhaustion from the night's events has loosened my tongue, because I share almost everything.

"Before my magic manifested," I begin. "I was a night attendant for the king, blood-sworn to serve him. But I was nothing more than a decoration for his parties. I hated it. Hated him. So, I made a blood wager: if I pass the entrance exams and am offered admittance into Bathara, he'll release me from his service and grant me my freedom. But if I fail, I must give him an heir."

Draven's brows furrow. "It's rumored the king is sterile."

I scoff, the sound bitter. "Those are no rumors. He is."

He hesitates, his eyes narrowing on me. "And yet if you lose, you're expected to give him an heir? Not even the best healer is able to do that. Not yet, at least."

I'm quiet for a long time. "I may or may not have led him to believe otherwise."

"And he believed you?"

My shoulders rise and fall with a careless shrug. "He had good reason to."

I can practically feel Draven's stare boring into me. "And that is?"

I glance at him sidelong. "I've already shared enough with you—a complete stranger for all intents and purposes. Forgive me if I don't feel like sharing anything else."

Something flickers in his expression, but ultimately, he sighs and turns back toward the pyre. "You know the penalty for breaking a blood wager, right?"

I numbly stare at the glowing flames. "I do, but it doesn't matter. I'm not going to lose. I will not let King Alastair win."

Draven nods. "Good."

CHAPTER TWENTY-THREE

S leep does not find me easily.

In fact, for a long while, it felt nearly impossible to rest after Draven and Kiran declared we should sleep a few hours before officially departing. But eventually, like a shepherd finding its lost sheep, it came for me, and it guided me away from the looming darkness.

In my fitful state, I have strange dreams. Dreams of fire and ice shooting like spears across an ash-ridden sky. Dreams where I am running through some foreign place, screaming for something precious to me. Dreams where I meet an old friend on rubble-littered ground. I dream of Meiji. Of the Abdite plucking life from him as easily as plucking the string of an instrument. Of my fingers gripping the hilt of a dagger, but really they are gripping the tethers of a life.

And then the true nightmares come.

Flames that grow wider and taller devour me, but they do not burn. Gods, I *wish* they would burn me. Clattering voices, heavy silver, a bedroom, and a dead stare. Voices swim in my mind, haunt my dreams. But there is something different about this familiar nightmare. A shadow lurking in the dark, watching. It calls to me. Says my name. Tries to tell me something. I…

"Lyra." The gentle voice is like a bucket of cool water, refreshing my senses.

I blink my eyes open, the golden sun a shock to my nerve endings, and I'm surprised to find myself gasping for breath, my entire body slicked with cold sweat. It takes me a moment, but everything comes into focus, and Gray's pinched face enters my line of sight.

"You were having another nightmare," he murmurs.

He isn't asking, but still I nod my head.

Gray's lips thin. "You were talking. In your sleep, I mean. You were saying something strange, and you were fidgeting like crazy. Are you...are you okay? Do you want to talk about it?"

I tug at my brows and sit up. "No," I rasp, my fingers gliding across my clammy forehead. "What was I saying?"

He watches me for a long moment. "I'm sorry, but I couldn't figure that out. I did try, but...it was like you were speaking in some foreign language."

My cheeks puff out from my exhale. "Great," I drone, dry and flat.

"Oh, good. You're both awake." Griff appears in front of us. He tries to smile, but I can see through it. It's easy to glimpse the way the curve no longer rises enough to frame his mouth. The way the gesture no longer makes his eyes crinkle. "We're going to leave for Bathara soon. You might see to your needs and attend to whatever else before then." He begins to turn on his heel but stops short, glancing over his shoulder at me. Griff clears his throat and rubs at the back of his neck. "Listen...I—uh, I wanted to thank you for what you did for Meiji. That couldn't have been easy for you. And also for the tonic. I'm not sure if I would have managed to sleep without it."

Before everyone took to their bedrolls, I offered to take a look at their injuries and prepare something for them. Gray was in remarkably good condition, and between Kiran, Draven, and Griff, only Griff accepted my offer.

My eyes drop to my palms. "You don't owe me any thanks," I mutter.

A sad smile flits across his lips. "Funny," he says, his voice far quieter than before. "Meiji used to say the same thing."

Leaving "soon" is a bit of an understatement.

It's much more akin to, *leaving right now, at this very moment, as soon as everyone stands, ready.* I barely have time to attend to myself before Gray is calling after me, urging me to meet back up with everyone. The remains of our campfire have been buried, the tents deconstructed, and the supplies packed.

They move quick, I have to give them that.

I shuffle over and find all the boys waiting for me, packs and satchels strapped across their chests. Gray glances at me and smiles. My lips tug up at him in return as if on instinct, but my eyes drift over to where Draven stands, locked in conversation with Kiran, whose ruby-red hair is half-drawn. I can't help but notice how regal it makes Kiran look—like a true highborn noble. Draven's shaggy hair, on the other hand, tousles messily with waves, and his jaded features make him appear anything but. Though, the structure in his every move gives him away. Not to mention the brash and authoritative way he speaks to people.

Griff claps his hands together. "Alright, gentlemen." He flicks his eyes to me and smiles. "And lady."

I snort a laugh and mock a curtsy.

This time, his answering smile meets his eyes. "I'm going to open a portal to Bathara. Now, I've been everywhere on the grounds, so does anybody have any place in particular they'd like to be dropped off at?"

I'm happy to hear a bit of the bounciness return to his voice. Still, his phrasing snags my attention. "What does your being everywhere at Bathara have to do with anything?"

"Because an aether-wielder can only open portals to places he's been to. Or at least seen with his own eyes."

I blink at him, a little stunned. "Huh...I didn't know that."

Griff braces his hands on his hips. "Doesn't surprise me. Most of us don't like to talk about it since it's typically seen as a weakness." He puffs out his chest and lifts his chin. "But I like to think of it as a necessary handicap to keep our strength in check. Like the gods knew we'd be far too formidable without something anchoring our magic."

Kiran strolls over and claps Griff on the shoulder, tilting his face toward him. "Is that what it is?" That taunting lilt of his has returned, along with his signature smirk.

Griff's brows pinch together. "What else could it be?"

"A weakness," Draven answers. Coupled with his dry tone and arched brow, I have to stifle my rising laughter. Draven slides his eyes to me before back at Griff.

And I'm glad to see them returning to themselves, even if shocked at the speed of their recovery. Though, I guess death is more normal for them, for a Jurafen—even one in training. Which means it'll become normal to me.

Terrifying, the way the thought doesn't phase me.

"A friend of mine is an aether-wielder," Gray muses. "He says the magic resting within a place can determine whether or not you can open a stable portal. Is that true?"

Griff tilts his head, considering. "That's true for any wielder's magic, if you think about it. All magic can be overwhelmed by stronger magic, rendering it useless. The same is true for us."

Kiran snorts a laugh and folds his arms over his chest. "How very diplomatic of you."

Griff's eyes roll around in their sockets before he sighs. "You know, I could always just leave you stranded in the valley," he mutters.

Kiran's brows do a little jump. "Ah, gone is the diplomacy. There is the Griffith I know and cherish."

Griff winces at the use of his full name and glances at me.

My mouth curves into a smile as I rest a hand on my popped hip. "Griffith?"

He flicks his eyes up to the sky before back down at all of us. "Fine," he grumbles. "To the surrounding hills of the academy it is." He throws his palm out, and just like Klytis's portal, it is a vortex of swirling black and glittering silver.

"Ladies first," Griff instructs.

My mouth parts in rhythm with my rising eyebrows. "Uh-uh. I am *not* walking through that thing first." Griff looks to Gray, who looks more than happy to oblige, but I tug on his arm, pulling him back to my side.

"And neither is he."

With surprise rearranging his features, Gray studies me before blowing out a conceding breath.

Draven steps forward and glances sidelong at me. He clicks his tongue. "And here I thought we were starting to trust each other." He steps through the portal without another glance.

Kiran rests a gentle hand on my shoulder and smiles at me, then Gray. "I'll see you both on the other side. Though, the circumstances may be...different."

Before I can ask what the hell that means, he steps through the swirling portal next. Which just leaves Gray and me.

He turns to face me. "I can go first, if you'd like."

I shake my head. "No. We'll go together."

Gray smiles at that and offers me his hand. I gladly take it, twining my fingers through his as a thousand thoughts race through my mind. Are we wrong to trust this so easily? What if this portal doesn't lead to Bathara at all, but somewhere else entirely? What if it's all some trap?

What if? What if? What if?

Gray squeezes my hand, silently telling me to breathe.

"You know," Griff says. "Your lack of faith in me is hurtful."

Despite myself, a laugh escapes me. I quip back, "Excuse me for having trust issues with the shameless flirt."

A sad look flickers in his eyes, and for a moment, I wonder if I shouldn't have spoken the words Meiji used to describe him. But then the expression passes, and like a hidden sun emerging through rain clouds, Griff's smile returns—different, yet still bright.

He shrugs. "Fair enough."

Gray turns his chin over his shoulder to look at me. "Ready?"

I pull my lip between my teeth and nod. "I'm ready."

I catch the twitch of his fading smile before we step forward to the portal.

And then, we pass through.

When we emerge on the other side, my eyes flutter as they adjust to the glaring sun. Once they do, once I am able to fully take in the sight before me, a soft gasp escapes my parted lips.

An afternoon wind transports the delicious notes of soil and flora, caressing my skin with its gentle touch. A kaleidoscope of butterflies—wings of blue and black, sage and white, lavender and silver—flutter overhead. There is a powdery blue sky and clouds that look like candy. I look left and see verdant hilltops rolling as far as the eye can see; I look right and see more mounds lost in a sea of lush green. But when I look directly in front of us...

In the distance, surrounded by cascading waterfalls that seem to spill from the heavens like liquid silks—the water pouring into a network of streams winding through the hills—nestled comfortably amongst the verdant swells of land, stands Bathara Academy.

It's a sprawling complex that looks part manor, part castle, glinting iridescent against the morning light. Majestic towers and spires forged from natural stone branch into their own wings, encased by an architecturally astounding wall made of glimmering moonstone, carved with ornate decadence.

A dazzling academy, astounding waterfalls, and one thought: *Am I dreaming?*

It is everything and more I ever fantasized it could be.

I glance up at Gray, who is just as wide-eyed and slack-jawed as me. "I never imagined it would be so beautiful," he murmurs.

Someone clears their throat, and when I glance toward the sound, I find Kiran and Draven standing off to the side, a few paces ahead with their arms crossed.

"Remarkable, isn't it?" Kiran asks.

I huff a laugh, absorbing all I possibly can of the sight. "Remarkable is an understatement."

One side of Kiran's mouth curves. "I understand entirely."

Griff appears, and the portal blinks shut behind him. "Well then, shall we be on our way?"

When we reach the front of the academy, Draven and Kiran excuse themselves, saying they have other matters to attend to now that they're back at Bathara.

My heart deflates as the question forms in my mind: are they going to find Nuha and tell her about Meiji?

On instinct, I grip the ring in my pocket.

I wonder if I should give it to them? I know Meiji handed it to me, but I was his only option. Kiran and Draven...they seem to *know* Nuha. And even if they aren't familiar with her on an intimate level, at least it won't be a complete stranger offering Nuha her fallen partner's ring—quite possibly the only remaining item left of Meiji for Nuha to keep.

Deciding, I quicken my steps to catch them. "Wait," I call out.

Draven and Kiran stop. Kiran turns fully, while Draven only shifts partway. But Draven is the one closest to me, so I pull the ring from my pocket, hold it up for them to see, then gently grip Draven's wrist, lifting his hand to place it in his rough palm.

"Where did you get this?" he asks me in a low voice.

"Meiji gave it to me. He asked me to give it to Nuha, and to tell her that he loves her, and he's sorry he couldn't keep his promise." I pause, swallowing against the lump clogging my throat. "I figure his final words will mean more to Nuha if they're not coming from a total stranger."

Draven stares at the ring for a long, silent moment.

Kiran steps forward and observes the ring with a wistful stare. "Before burning his body," he supplies quietly, "we searched him for this ring. We knew what it meant to him—what it represented. We thought it was lost." Kiran looks up from the ring and at me. "Thank you."

The quiet earnestness of his gratitude catches me off guard.

Draven's fingers slowly close around the object, and he drops his fist to his side. His expression remains unreadable as he studies me in silence for several seconds. Eventually, he tears his gaze from mine and redirects it to Kiran. "Come on," he says with a jerk of his chin. "We've got to go if we want to make it in time."

Kiran nods at Draven before offering me a parting smile. Then, with closed mouths and silent steps, they turn and continue walking ahead toward the gated entrance. I stay behind, absently observing them as they go, a strange numbness drifting through my chest.

As I watch, I notice the quiet look of deference lingering in the eyes of the guards standing vigil at the academy's gates as they let Kiran and Draven pass. Afterward, confusion ripples across their features as they notice that both men had been traveling with me only moments before.

Odd...the way the guards almost seem protective over them.

I jolt at the sound of Gray's voice. "Everything alright?"

I hadn't realized he and Griff caught up with me. "Yeah," I assure him through a series of rapid blinks. "Of course."

Griff stretches out his arms and grips both Gray and me around the shoulders, guiding us forward. "Come on," he whispers. "I'll escort you two to the check-in table before leaving you to your own devices."

I'm not sure what I was expecting—maybe for the academy to be packed with scary people—but everyone looks so...normal. Not to mention, the academy grounds are so large, it doesn't feel crowded at all.

My eyes bounce around, drinking in all they can. The courtyards are beautiful. The fountains are lavish. The marble walkways, enclosed by sprawling bushes, are decadent. And I count five impressive wings in total—or at least, the ones that are visible.

Groups of people stand scattered around, laughing or whispering. I catch more than a few girls watching through lowered lids as Griff and Gray pass by, smiling with fabricated innocence. It takes a feat of strength not to roll my eyes at the display—clearly, a strength the noblewomen here lack, considering they do exactly that to me, paired with a lovely sneer.

Typical.

A movement catches my eye, and I flick my gaze between Gray and Griff, finding them both standing a little straighter, their chins lifted.

I arch a brow. "Really?"

"What?" Griff challenges through a laugh. "Might as well give 'em what they want."

"Shameless flirt, indeed," I mutter. My eyes slide to Gray next. "You, too? I thought you had more dignity than this—you know, honorable

Nightenjoy and all."

Gray chuckles. "I haven't the slightest clue what you're talking about."
I click my tongue at him.

When we approach the line formed in front of a large table, Griff claps his hands together. "Well, friends. It's been fun."

My brows skip up. "I don't know if 'fun' is the exact word I'd use."

He pinches his chin. "Fair point." A pause. "It was nice traveling with you, then." Griff rubs the back of his neck. "Good luck on the exams. I hope to see the both of you in aggregate uniforms after the Autumnal Equinox." He glances to the side before back at us, leaning forward and cupping a hand over his mouth. "All I'm saying is," he begins in a whisper, "if the opportunity arises and you find yourself Selected by the captain of the Castaria aggregate, you should accept."

My face scrunches. "What? What does that—"

His loud, cheery whistling cuts my question short, and he stuffs his hands into his pockets before turning on his heels and walking away. He throws up an idle hand as a final goodbye.

"He really is quite the character, isn't he?" Gray muses from beside me, humor leaking into his words.

"Something like that," I say through a smile, watching him wander farther and farther away.

※ ❧ ❧ ※

The long line moves quicker than I expect, which is equal parts a good thing and a bad thing. It gives me time to settle my growing nerves, but it also gives me time to marinate in my own pointed thoughts. Before I know it, Gray is next in line.

"Name?" A man in his mid-twenties with long, mousy-brown hair asks Gray while staring down at a piece of parchment.

He wears a stone-colored tunic paired with a fitted, deep pine-green robe trimmed in crimson. An emblem featuring a white eagle with outstretched wings is stitched in gray and red over his left pectoral. Above the eagle, a banner of burnished bronze unfurls, the word *Elefet* scribed artistically within. Below the eagle is another banner, angular and sloped to a point. Inside, the word *Glory* is elegantly written in bold print.

Gray's voice is steady when he responds. "Gray Nightenjoy."

The man looks up, his head cocked. "Nightenjoy, eh? We haven't seen someone from your bloodline in a while. What type of wielder are you?"

"I wield illusionary magic."

The man leans back in his chair and folds his arms. "No kidding? We haven't seen someone with that type of magic in a long, long time. Do you have a particular aggregate you're hoping to be accepted into?"

Gray shakes his head, and I wonder if he, too, wonders why everyone keeps asking that question. "Not particularly."

The man with amber eyes huffs a laugh. "Well, if you're worth a damn at all, you'll no doubt be accepted into at least one aggregate with that magic. I'd wager you wind up with the Castaria aggregate. The captain likes to collect unique wielders, you see." He records Gray's name and magic type onto a piece of parchment. Once finished, he gives Gray a close-lipped smile. "Good luck."

Gray nods his thanks and then veers off to the side. I approach the table as Gray did.

Without looking up, the man again asks, "Name?"

I lift my chin. "Lyra Izacalli."

"What type of wielder are you?"

Fighting the urge to shift on my feet, I chew on my lip instead. "Uhm...flora-wielder, I think."

His head jerks up from the parchment, and he narrows his eyes at me. "What do you mean you *think*?"

My hands clench together before I make them go slack. "As in, my wielder's mark hasn't manifested yet, so I don't know my wielder-type for certain."

The man studies me carefully, looking positively dumbfounded. "You don't have a wielder's mark? When the hell did your magic manifest?"

Do I tell him the truth? Do I lie? Or at least, embellish reality?

The truth makes me seem weak, yet a lie implies I have some strange defect. How else do I explain the lack of a wielder's mark without raising suspicion?

I decide on the truth, settling on the simple fact that perceived weakness often leads others to underestimate a person—which, honestly, is probably better for me anyway.

"A few days ago, actually."

The man stares at me for a long moment before tipping back in his chair and howling with laughter. "Okay, who set this up? Was it Ryndall? The little prick. Well, the joke's over because I've caught on. Really, what is your wielder's mark? I've got a job to do here."

I arch a silent brow at him, giving him time to put the pieces of reality together himself.

He leans forward and drops his voice. "You're actually *serious?*"

He catches on faster than I thought he would. Good for him.

I do a little bounce on my toes. "Yup."

He sweeps his eyes slowly from the tip of my head down to my feet. "You have to be one of the oldest late-bloomers I've ever seen. What in god's veins are you doing here?"

"Competing."

"*Competing?*" he repeats. "You manifested your magic this late in life—mere *days* ago, as you say—and you intend to take the entrance exams into the most prestigious magical academy in the whole gods-damn Three Kingdoms? A task examinees will spend the better part of a decade, if not their whole lives, training for?"

I fold my arms across my chest. "I think saying 'this late in life' is a bit dramatic," I grumble, a frustrated sigh sneaking past my lips. "But you've spelled it out perfectly. Now, will you just record my name so I can move along with my foolish plan?"

His face falls into a scowl, but he scribbles my name and alleged magic type onto the parchment. "Fine," he mutters. "It's your funeral."

I dip my chin at him. "Thank you."

I'm just turning to walk away when he calls out to me again. "Izacalli. I don't recognize the name. Where is it from?"

I lift a lazy hand and shrug. "From my mother, I suppose."

His frustration becomes palpable. "Not what I meant. Do you come from a noble house? Is the name from some new cadet branch? What's your heritage?"

"The truth?"

He arches a pointed brow. "I don't know why you'd assume I want anything else."

I huff a weak laugh at the reply. "The truth is I know nothing of my heritage." A small smile tugs at the corner of my mouth. "But no, I'm not from a noble house. Just a plain, lowborn commoner is all."

As I turn on my heels, I hear him mutter under his breath, "Your funeral, indeed."

I'm laughing quietly to myself, my fingers lightly grazing the ice necklace resting at my throat, when I spot Gray locked in conversation with an older gentleman. Curious, I wander over.

Gray turns his attention to me, a smile stretching his lips. "Lyra," he says, strangely jubilant. "Come meet Josiah. He's a long-time friend of my father's."

The man, Josiah, turns to face me. "Lyra Izacalli," he coos in a soothing, regal voice. "It is very lovely to make your acquaintance." His tanned skin is a beautiful backdrop against his rich blue eyes and long white hair. In a way, the wear of life looks good on him. Gives his face a sort of inviting appeal.

My brows dip as I observe Josiah more closely. He looks familiar. Like I've seen him somewhere. "Have we..." My head tilts with my growing curiosity. "Have we met before?"

He clasps his hands behind his back. "Not in any way of consequence. Though, I do remember you from my time spent in King Alastair's court recently. You were his prized night attendant, if I recall correctly."

I blink at him, my memory lagging.

Until it finally hits me.

He was there the night Gray told me he was leaving. The king had been hosting travelers from Bathara and emissaries from Erandor. I remember a man with salt-and-pepper hair talking to another with long, white curls. They were discussing Sterling and the Nightenjoy line, along with their noble titles—or lack thereof, I guess.

"I remember you," I inform him with a slow drawl. "You were with that man who had gray and white hair."

"Vague description, but yes. His name is Cahlmon. A bit ill-tempered at times, but overall a good man." He pauses, rubbing the tips of his fingers underneath his lips. "I must admit, I did not expect to see you here. It's not often a king relinquishes one of his most cherished servants." His eyes hold onto me. "Yet here we are. What a twisted, unpredictable thing fate is."

Gray crosses his arms, the corner of his lips tugging up. "My father told me to find him once we arrived. It appears he has done us a service and found me instead."

Josiah chuckles, the sound warm. "You have grown since I last saw you. Why, you were no more than a couple feet tall back then. I apologize for not seeing you during my last visit. It was brief and centered around political matters, unfortunately."

Political?

The wording strikes me.

Why would Bathara be in Rivara Kingdom on political business? Let alone with Erandor emissaries present. If it had something to do with the Jurafen, then emissaries from the Anatolé Kingdom would've had to be present as well. Bathara and the Jurafen answer to no king; they do not involve themselves in politics in order to better protect and serve the Three Kingdoms of Solaya.

Strange, indeed.

"Your hair is fully white now," Gray says through a taunting smirk.

Josiah nods, amused. "Indeed it is."

"You're officially an old man it would seem."

"At last," Josiah sighs. "Your long-running nickname for me is a fitting one." He folds his hands in front of him. "Your father told me you traveled through Foreigner's Valley. As it so happens, Bathara also had scouts in the valley. If it's alright with you, I'd like to speak with you in a more private setting about your time there."

I catch the slight twitch of Gray's brows. "Of course," he agrees.

"Excellent. If you'd follow me, then." Before he goes, Josiah faces me and inclines his head. "Lyra, it was such a privilege to finally meet you. I've always heard such wonderful things from Sterling."

My heart strings feel like they've suddenly been pulled taut. "You have?" The words slide from my tongue faster than I can think better of it.

"Yes," he replies through a soft smile. "I have." And then with fluid grace, Josiah turns and saunters off toward Bathara's inclining marble stairwell, to what I'm assuming is the main entrance.

Gray reaches for my hand and squeezes. "This shouldn't take long. Will you be alright by yourself?"

I lift a brow. "Think I can't take care of myself?"

He plants a kiss to the side of my head. "Never." Then he flashes me a parting grin. "I'll be back before you know it."

Gray jogs to catch up with Josiah, following him up the stairwell and through the towering doors. Through a long-winded sigh, I turn back around, scanning my surroundings.

To my surprise, I find eyes of many colors watching me, scrutiny simmering in their stares.

My guess?

Word must have already spread about my magic and less-than-glamorous bloodline. A feat that might surprise someone who hasn't spent the last four years in direct service to a king, attending to his courtiers, emissaries, and appointed nobles. But for someone who has—someone like me—it's not the least bit shocking.

Women, for some reason, have been bestowed the reputation of being gossipers. But all it takes is an hour in a room with men to know that isn't the least bit true. *Men* are the real gossips. They just take the action and dress it up using the word *politics*.

I glimpse a bench wedged between rose bushes, and I've never been so relieved to see an isolated stone structure before. I make my way over, but pause when I overhear a booming female voice.

"I said," the voice echoes in a way that leaves no room for questions, "I'm fine. *Thanks.*"

I peer around a waterfall of wisteria and see a girl with coppery-red curls brace her hands on her hips.

A loud voice spews from a tall, blonde-haired man. "Come on. It's my duty as a noble to ensure the commoners stay fed. The rich exist to help the poor. It's a system as old as the god Raffir himself. Don't be prideful. Let me help you."

From my viewpoint, I see the backside of his head and arm as he attempts to shove meat into her hand. "Take it. It is dried venison seasoned with the best Juniper berries your lips will ever have the privilege of tasting. I ask nothing in return."

Her voice cuts like a lethal blade. "I have no desire to feast on your provisions. I have plenty of my own."

"Stop being difficult and just accept my generosity."

"I do not *need* your generosity, nor did I *ask* for it."

"Well, the loose-fitting rags hanging from your slender body say otherwise."

I watch as she turns away from him and walks in the opposite direction. He reaches out and grips her arm, yanking her back toward him. "I'm not don—"

Before he can finish his sentence, she cocks his wrist up and swings around behind him, bending his arm at an angle that makes my insides twist. He grunts in pain. She tugs harder.

"Touch me again, and I will snap your arm like the little twig you are. Understood?"

Red-faced and eyes watering, the blond-haired man nods and whimpers a small, "Mhm."

"Good," she chirps as she drops his arm and boasts a delighted grin.

He mutters a string of curses under his breath and scurries away.

Once he's out of sight, I step out from the wisteria, garnering her attention. "Can you teach me that?" The words come out awed— breathless, almost.

She observes me with her vibrant cobalt eyes for a long moment, a notch in her coppery brow. After an excruciating silence, her head cocks to the side. "Have you received any previous training in self-defense or fighting systems?"

"A little."

Not entirely a lie. I have—a few days' worth.

She continues watching me, a curious expression in her eyes. "Show me what you know."

"Excuse me?"

"Show me one of your moves," she elaborates.

Now it's my turn to arch a brow. "Are you sure? I don't want to accidentally hurt you." Not that I'm some incredibly trained fighter, but still...

She smirks and pops a hip. "Don't worry," the woman assures me, her tone a bit wicked. "You won't."

I chew at my cheek, thinking about which move I should use on her. Judging from what I witnessed, she'll know the basic moves Gray taught me. But isn't everything I know pretty basic? I search my brain, replaying all the lessons, all the skills Gray drilled into my muscles. Eventually, one move in particular shines above the rest. A move he taught me because I requested to know.

"Choke me," I instruct.

She inspects her nails. "Sorry, but that's not really my kink."

I roll my eyes and click my tongue. "You're the one who asked me to show you something."

She drops her hand back to her side. "Fair enough." The girl strides over to me and forcefully—plus with admirable strength—grips me by the throat.

Following Gray's instructions, I grip her wrist, reach for her fingers, and yank them backwards, bringing her to her knees. I twist out of her hold and swing back, kicking her directly in the shoulder, making sure to pull my kick to prevent her actual harm.

A tiny grunt escapes her lips at impact, but nothing more. She braces her weight on her knees and gets right back up, as if the kick was nothing at all. Which, I know I pulled the force of it, but the ease of the gesture is still a little disheartening.

She brushes strands of her coppery-red hair from her alabaster skin.

"Impressive."

The satisfying warmth of a small victory floods through me. "Thanks. So, you'll teach me that move?"

She dusts off her blue and black tunic, a lopsided smirk tugging at her lip. "Only if you teach me yours."

I grin, extending my hand. "You've got yourself a deal."

Our hands meet in a firm clasp, and we shake on it.

"I'm Lyra."

"Marcella," she replies.

The lack of a surname confirms to me what I just witnessed between her and that man—she is like me. Someone without titles, without some noble name to wield or hide behind. It brings a smile to my face— different from the one I wear around Gray, or that finds me in moments of happiness. This smile is...appreciative, perhaps? Grateful, even?

Her eyes hold mine, and she assesses me with a discerning gaze. As if finding an answer to some undisclosed question, she hums a laugh and shakes her head, deciding something.

My face scrunches together. "What?"

Before she can answer, a booming voice echoes through all of Bathara. *All wielders partaking in the entrance exam are to report to the Arena immediately. I repeat, all wielders report to the Arena immediately.*

When I glance back at Marcella, I find she is already three steps ahead, strutting forward toward the Arena.

I scurry to catch her. "Hey, wait. What was that look about?"

She glances at me sidelong. "Why do you think it was anything worth sharing?"

"Call it intuition."

Marcella keeps her pace quick, eyes forward. Still, I catch the subtle curve forming at the corner of her mouth. "You're a fighter," she supplies. "I can see it in your eyes."

My voice is soft. "How?"

She halts—only for a moment—and faces me. "Because those stitched from the same threads will always recognize each other."

CHAPTER TWENTY-FOUR

Two massive arched doors, hewn from dark wood and traced with intricate arabesques, open to a granite corridor lined with torches. Hopeful examinees funnel in, some murmuring anxiously while others laugh, giddy and overflowing with confidence. A few walk in stony silence. Marcella and I keep pace together, exchanging occasional glances, walking in our own peaceful quiet. When we emerge on the other side of the torch-lined corridor, the brightness is so sudden and jarring, I shield my eyes with my hand while my pupils adjust. I catch a blurry glimpse of Marcella doing the same. It takes a few seconds, but my eyes adapt, and the sight before me sharpens into stunning clarity, unlike anything I have ever seen.

The walls of polished marble rise high, seemingly into the cloudless sky, gleaming under the soft glow of a circle of braziers. Above, a grand dome composed of glass allows the sunlight to cascade through, bathing the space in a kaleidoscope of colors. The outer-circle of the arena is divided into four sections with tiered seating that spirals up and up. Grand, milky columns rise in seemingly endless rows. I glimpse a slew of balconies, one significantly larger and better crafted than the others, its marble railing adorned with twisting banisters. Adjacent to that balcony rests a mezzanine. On that mezzanine, five empty, lavish chairs wait beneath their respective banners, each one boasting unique colors and emblems. I recognize one of the banners as the same emblem from the uniform of the man who checked me in.

Marcella lets out a low whistle. "Fancy."

I chuckle while scanning all the faces, looking for Gray. But all I manage to find are unfamiliar eyes, unfamiliar lips, and unfamiliar bodies.

Marcella tilts her head, her brows pulling together. "Are you looking for someone?"

"Yes. A friend of mine. We traveled here together, but we were separated just before I met you."

"What does he look like?"

I arch a brow at her. "How do you know it's a he?"

She just snorts a laugh and arches a challenging brow right back. "Well?"

I eye her a moment longer before sighing. "Shoulder-length brown hair that's almost always half-pulled back into a bun. He has hazel eyes that are a rich mix of moss, copper, and gold. His tunic is brown with gold stitching, and he almost always has his satchel strapped across his chest. Tall, muscular build, he—"

Marcella pins me with her humored gaze, a teasing smirk dancing on her face.

My arms fold over each other while my eyes do a spin. "What? *You* asked what he looks like."

Her voice drips with honey as it pours through her saccharine smile. "He sounds *very* handsome."

I click my tongue. "Don't get the wrong idea. We were practically raised together. He..." My voice softens. "He's the only family I have."

Marcella's guarded features loosen, and those sharp cobalt eyes turn gentle, as if the harshness of the world has been suddenly smoothed away. "I grew up in a large family. I'm the only daughter, but third oldest, and I still have three younger siblings below me. I can't imagine enduring this life without them." The corner of her lip flickers with the ghost of a smile. "I'm glad you have him."

I study her closely, surprised by her admission. My lips part to respond right as the hums of chatter disappear, an overwhelming quiet replacing it. I follow the fixed gazes to the large balcony, and to my surprise, Josiah is there, gripping the marble railing with his hands,

188

watching the crowd of examinees.

But if Josiah is there, where is Gray? Not to mention, *why* is Josiah on the balcony, observing us? Just who is he, exactly?

Josiah addresses the room, his soothing voice filling every bit of space. "Examiness, welcome to Bathara Academy. I know most of you have traveled far and wide to participate in our humble exams, and for that, you have my gratitude." He pauses, his eyes roving the arena, locking eyes at random.

"To be Jurafen is to assume responsibility for the continent. It is to pledge yourself to the good of the Three Kingdoms, submitting to honor and duty. You are the defense to all that lies Beyond. Magic, creatures, Abdites, the evils of men... Once sworn in as a Jurafen, you are bound to fulfill the obligations of the title, no matter the costs." A pause. "It is not easy. It is not a decision that should be made lightly. So I warn you now: if you are unable to commit to these responsibilities, unwilling to give your heart, your blood, and every ounce of laktî you possess, then I suggest you walk away while you still can."

He scans the room with calculating eyes. Some people glance around, clearly considering his offer. A few go pale at the mention. Yet no feet turn to walk back through the corridor that led us into this grand arena.

"Very well," Josiah says with a nod. "Then you all have made your decisions."

He raises his hands, and the braziers roar with a building flame. Heads whip in every direction as rapid murmurs swirl in the air. Josiah slowly lowers his hands, and the flames in the braziers settle back into a calm, warm glow.

A small smile plays at Josiah's lips. "Allow me to introduce myself. My name is Josiah Hartley, and I am the Keeper of Bathara."

My eyes practically bulge from my skull while my jaw pops open. *Josiah* is the Keeper?

The man responsible for all of Bathara. The man who must answer directly to the Tani, the highest order of governance over magic, and act as the diplomat who speaks for the Jurafen on behalf of the council. The man who must supersede virtually all wielders—a Master of Magic—and determine the consequences for Jurafen's actions.

It's hard to believe that Josiah is the Keeper. But I guess that at least explains why he was in Rivara Kingdom, even if it still doesn't explain why the Anatolé Kingdom was absent. I wonder if Gray was aware of Josiah's role when he introduced us. If he was, why didn't he say something? Offer me a warning or *at least* a hint.

And where the hell *is* Gray?

Josiah's voice echoes off the marble. "The entrance exams are composed of three unique tests. Each test is designed to measure the vital abilities and characteristics required of Jurafen, and will vary in length. You will be given seven days of rest between each test to replenish your magic. If you make it through to the next round, that is."

Buzzing whispers—like a swarm of flying insects—overtake the room.

With a concerted sternness, Josiah continues. "The captains of the five aggregates will determine who passes each finished trial. Collectively, should they determine your performance acceptable, you will be permitted to continue on in the exams. Should they find you an unqualified candidate for Bathara, and thus for a Jurafen, you will be dismissed from the exams and asked to leave Bathara. Once all tests have been cleared, a captain may Select you into their aggregate, or they may not. Acceptance is at their discretion."

"And if we pass all three tests and none of the captains offer us a place in their aggregate?" A sour, female voice questions.

Josiah shrugs—a graceful gesture. "Then you have no place at Bathara."

A male voice shouts back, "You would have us risk our lives during the exams, even knowing it might all be for *nothing* because a captain doesn't personally *select* us?"

"Precisely," Josiah replies coolly. "I assure you, as a Jurafen, you will risk your lives for much less." He takes his time, letting his long pause weigh heavy on the crowd. "The captains of Bathara's aggregates are unparalleled, highly-trained wielders. They were all once the top of their class, and they exhibit some of the most powerful magical capabilities

Bathara's ever seen. You should not show such disrespect by discrediting their judgement so quickly."

Despite Josiah's words, the crowd erupts with hissed complaints, rising in volume like a well-fed flame. A flurry of disgruntled shouts bounce off the marble. *Unfair. I am noble. My father—*

Marcella and I exchange unsteady glances. Her fingers slowly crawl toward the sheathed dagger at her side, and I take inventory of who surrounds us and their temperaments. But the whispers and shouts are muted by an emerging darkness that suddenly appears at our feet, floating in an eerie fog, rising and consuming every inch of space in the arena. It is like standing in a void of nothingness. A blackness so thick, it rivals that of a starless sky.

Marcella reaches for my hand and squeezes, the gesture comforting. Even if, for some reason, nothing about this darkness frightens me. Perhaps I've grown used to the dark. Still, I clutch onto her hand tightly, letting her know I'm here with her.

As the darkness recedes, Josiah is the first to emerge from its embrace. He stands tall and steady, his sharp eyes assessing the panicked faces. His keen gaze flicks to me, and his facial expression shifts in such a minor way, most wouldn't detect it.

But I do.

Though, I don't know what to make of the ambiguous look.

He addresses the room once more. "Speaking of the captains," he begins with a wry smile. "It appears they have finally arrived and are ready to greet you." He gestures to the mezzanine on his right, and standing in front of each chair, the banners of their aggregates boasting proudly behind them, are the captains.

And if my eyes didn't bulge out of my skull before, they *certainly* do now.

No. Fucking. Way.

In front of the banner boasting the emblem composed of pine and crimson—the same emblem worn by the man who checked me in—towers Draven. Wearing something like a loose hemp sweater and breeches, his arms are folded across his broad chest, his features set with a cold indifference. I catch him observing me, expressionless.

And next to Draven is Kiran, wearing a finely woven black tunic trimmed in ruby. Not surprisingly, he studies me with that familiar glint in his sapphire eyes, boasting a lopsided smirk. Though, I notice it looks...different. Off, almost. Normally, his smile looks effortless and natural, but this one seems forced. Still, Kiran clasps his hands behind his back and winks at me so subtly, I think I'm seeing things.

I fight the urge to laugh at the gesture.

When we all met in the valley, I knew they were hiding something— or at the very least, omitting information. But I had assumed it was related to their scouting mission or their heritage, not wanting us to know which noble house they came from. I never imagined they were hiding their titles as captains over some of Bathara's aggregates.

Even *I* have heard the emissaries and the courtiers whispering about the rumored strength of Bathara's current captains.

I guess that at least explains how Kiran was able to control such a staggering wall of fire, keeping the Abdites at bay, and how they were able to defeat the corrupted wielders. Because I never did get to see Draven's magic, and I'd be lying if I said my mind didn't randomly wonder what it is. Though, I guess I have a glimpse at my answer as the dark vapor fades away, returning to Draven's fingertips like an obedient pet.

And for some ungodsly reason, as it does, his sharp gaze remains fixed on me.

Slightly annoyed by his unrelenting observation, I arch a pointed brow and stare back. I understand he thinks I have no place here, but I'll be damned if I let him intimidate me. I'm not giving him the satisfaction, not letting him win.

Until it hits me that he is one of the people holding my fate in his hands. And if he doesn't think I belong here, then he holds the power to make sure I'm not accepted. But he also knows what's at stake for me— what I have to lose.

I exhale a frustrated sigh through my nose.

Marcella's eyes bounce between the two of us. Subtly, she points a finger up at Draven. "Uhm, do you know him?"

"No," I answer, truthfully. "I know nothing about him."

"Hm," she hums while flicking her eyes to Draven, to me, then back at Draven. Her brow rises. "Okay...then why are you staring at him like you can't decide if you want to slit his throat or rip his clothes off? And why is he staring at you like..." she tilts her head and pouts "...what the hell even *is* that look?"

I scoff. "I do *not* want to rip his clothes off." My lips twitch fondly at a passing thought. "Though, the idea of stabbing him once or twice has a particular appeal."

I no longer see anything worth fighting over.

Bastard.

She chuckles and flashes her palms. "Don't shoot the messenger. I just call it how I see it." She pauses, again sliding her gaze to Draven, a flirtatious smile now twirling her lips. "Besides, *I* certainly want to rip his clothes off." Her eyes slowly scan the mezzanine. "In fact, I wouldn't mind ripping *all* of the captains' clothes off. Is being attractive a requirement for being in charge around here or something?" She snorts a laugh. "I mean, goddess's tears, they are all brutally good-looking."

I clamp my lips together to contain my laughter. But damn it all if Marcella isn't right. They all look like lesser gods on that mezzanine. Beautiful, sculpted, and teeming with power.

Closest to Josiah is a woman with luscious black hair and brown skin, whose purple and gold attire accentuate her considerable curves. The banner behind her possesses an emblem shaped like a shield, trimmed in winding gold whirling like vines up into a point, purple filling the space inside. A teardrop sits at the center, also outlined in valiant gold, with markings I can't quite discern scribbled into the outlines.

I squint at her, trying to get a better look. She looks...sad, almost. It's hard to be certain from this distance, but it looks like her eyes are swollen, and her face is strained from the effort not to fall into a frown.

Standing next to her is a man with white hair, and at attention next to him, in stark contrast, is Kiran—whose banner's emblem is actually my favorite. Stitched entirely in gold, it boasts the rays of a shining sun encircled by golden markings. Rising from the base is the golden blade of a sword, its tip pointing to a burst of radiant light encircled by gilded leaves of an olive tree.

Next to Kiran stands Draven, and next to Draven stands a girl with beautifully bronzed hair and skin, paired with honey eyes. Her banner is an emblem with sprawled golden wings, a small shield wedged in the center with colored crystals peeking out below. Rather pretty, that banner.

"Now that you all know how your fate at Bathara will be determined." Josiah continues. "It's time you're introduced to your first test." He looks to the mezzanine. "Finlay, would you care to explain?"

A man who looks about the same age as Gray, with the flowing white hair, pure like the first fall of snow, steps forward and dips his chin at Josiah. Braids pull at one side of his head, and his clothes are luxurious and beautiful—the white stunning against the shimmering golds and blues lining his surcoat.

His banner showcases a sapphire shield, its silver edges curving elegantly, outlined and crowned with what looks like white flames. In its center, a lattice of line work adorned with patterns twirl in a mix of blue and white, arching out to resemble wings, surrounded by crossed swords and flowing, petal-like motifs.

"I am Finlay Fjolla," he says to the room. "And I am captain of the Skyborne aggregate."

Marcella hisses under her breath while I lift a brow, surprised to see a Fjolla here.

"What?" I ask in a low whisper, curious at her unhappy noise.

She remains standing stick-straight and admirably still. With a hushed tone, she responds, "I've heard rumors about the Skyborne aggregate. They only accept those with reputable noble bloodlines. The highest of highborns, if you will." She scowls in Finlay's direction. "Which, considering it's captained by a *Fjolla*—" her lips pucker like she's just tasted something sour "—I at least now understand why."

As an Archblood and a Great House, House Fjolla is richer than a king and practically as powerful as one. They are the progenitor bloodline of ice magic, and thus, no one wields it as skillfully or with as much power as they do. They are also somewhat of a mystery. The Fjolla line resides at Aderwynn Castle located in the far, wintery north, on the very outskirts of Erandor Kingdom's borders. Surrounded by the treacherous Wolfgaith Mountains and enclosed by Tuarana's River Lace, they are somewhat isolated from the rest of Solaya, making them rumored recluses and...unpleasant. Though, it could be debated whether the root cause of that is from their isolation or self-imposed importance.

Well, that at least explains Finlay's all-white clothes and hair. And the freaky, icy blue eyes.

"For your first test," Finlay declares in a rigidly poised voice, "you will be tasked with recovering an item. A flower."

"But not just any flower." Kiran steps forward and smiles lazily at Finlay. Finlay returns the look with a scowl, and...I'm sensing some tension there. "You will recover an *essence* flower from the Whispering Grove." Kiran's voice is charming and brimming with life, the complete opposite of Finlay's rigid and stiff tone.

Kiran opens his mouth to continue, but Finlay interjects instead. "An essence flower," he begins, shooting Kiran a warning glare, "is a flower that will only bloom when someone who shares its essence nears. They are a rather peculiar magical phenomenon, but ultimately, the flowers represent the essence of that which lingers in your veins." Finlay lifts his chin and observes the way his words resonate with the examinees. "Your task is simple: detect your essence flower by attuning your magical energy to it, pick the flower, and then bring it back to us within three days."

"Those of you who succeed will present what you return with to us. Afterward, we will deliberate and determine whether you proceed in these exams." Kiran scans the crowd, a curve tugging at his lips.

And there's something oddly comforting in knowing he truly never loses that wicked smirk of his.

In tune to the thought, as if some cruel smack from the universe, Kiran's smirk falters, and he swivels his attention to the woman with dark hair. The one with sad eyes.

"Nuha," he murmurs, softening his voice into something kind.

Ice strikes my heart, spreading through my veins and down to the tips of my fingers.

Nuha.

Meiji's partner. The one he planned to marry. The woman Meiji loved so fiercely, it took me only seconds to feel his devotion. The woman who, once upon a time, in a world where cruelty didn't steal, would wear a ring proudly on her finger. As if on instinct, my eyes glance down to her hands—specifically to her fingers.

There is no ring on them.

Nuha lifts her chin, and I glimpse the subtle rise and fall of her shoulders as she draws in a steadying breath. "Your every action, every decision, will be monitored through the use of these." She holds up a small, braided bracelet interwoven with small stones. "It is an amplifier embedded with anthrine mined directly from the Endymion Mountains. It will allow us to keep tabs on you for the duration of the exams." Her hands drop back to her sides, and she lowers her head, clearly finished with speaking.

And I feel both sad and heavy watching her wear the fabrics of repressed sadness—of hidden pain. It forms a sharp cracking sensation in my chest, knowing what she's going through and still having to be here, addressing a room like nothing has happened. Like she hasn't just lost the love of her life. It reminds me of a cold fact that once threatened to unravel me: the world goes on, whether or not you're ready to go on with it.

A blurry image of a dagger gripped between my fingers appears in my mind, and I am helpless as it shows me the story of how it plunged into an undeserving heart.

My fault.

It should have been me.

"Your test begins tomorrow," Josiah informs us. "You must be standing in this arena, flower in hand, before the third moon rises. Should you succeed, the captains will evaluate you. Should you fail, you needn't bother attending the judgment." He glances over at the five captains, silently weighing something over. "Draven will escort you to the guest wing, where you will find your accommodations." He gestures the salute of the Jurafen—three fingers over the heart—and then turns his back to the crowd, disappearing into the shadows.

I shake all the lingering thoughts and emotions from my head, glancing up just in time to see Draven shoot a pointed glare at Josiah as he saunters away. I also catch the tiny, taunting smile Kiran flashes Draven before shuffling from the mezzanine with the other captains. A gesture that results in Draven wearing an even more annoyed expression, if such a thing is possible.

He runs a hand through his shaggy hair and releases an irritated sigh. When he speaks, I'm unprepared for the voice that ripples into the room. "Okay, listen up."

Everyone goes still. Utterly silent. Slowly, as if any sudden movements may cause them unsolicited harm, the crowd turns toward the booming voice.

"I'm Draven, captain over the Elefet aggregate. All of you are going to follow me to your temporary living quarters. You will sleep two to a room, and the rooms are pretty cramped, so most of you shouldn't bother with unpacking." His eyes slowly rove across the sea of faces. To my absolute delight, they don't stop on me. "Meet me in the courtyard in two minutes." Then just like that, he turns and walks away without so much as another word.

Yeah, he's still the same as he was in the valley. A bit colder and more clipped—who knew that could happen—but the same, nonetheless.

As the examinees scramble toward the corridor—probably in fear Draven will take their heads or worse if they're late—I huff a dry laugh and sarcastically mutter to Marcella, "He has a real way with people, doesn't he?" We follow the crowd, shuffling awkwardly as we go.

Marcella drops her voice. "I hear Elefet is an aggregate filled with barbarians. That they recruit the most ruthless, skilled fighters in every entrance exam."

I scoff, unsurprised. "Fitting he's their captain, then." Though, the nature of Marcella's information strikes me. "How is it you know so much about the different aggregates?"

"My family operates a spice farm. My two older brothers travel along the trade routes to sell our spices at different markets. A few years back, the lead chef at Bathara purchased some of our spices and was so impressed, he sent a messenger back a few days later requesting we be his permanent supplier. Now, we have a trade agreement with him, and my brothers deliver the supplies to Bathara personally when they can." She lifts a lazy hand and shrugs. "They try to keep information locked down around here, but my brothers have made some friends along the way. And let's just say, sometimes, those friends like to gossip." She pauses, considering. "Though, what I know barely scratches the surface. Makes you wonder what all goes on around here, doesn't it?"

That it does.

She blows out a longing sigh. "At least it keeps things entertaining."

We funnel out of the arena and scatter around the courtyard. True to his word, Draven appears right at the two minute mark, arms folded and lips stretched tightly into a straight line. "Let's go." Without any further elaboration, he turns and strides off.

Marcella and I trail behind the masses as we follow Draven to a large stairwell leading to one of Bathara's many wings. He pushes against the large doors with two hands, swinging them open, and the hinges squeak with greeting while the wood groans. We step inside, and Marcella lets out a low whistle that echoes off the walls.

The foyer is the size of perhaps three Great Halls and basks in the warm glow of countless flickering torches. Pulsing globes emit a soft, white light, suspended from the ceiling. The walls are adorned with tapestries depicting the five emblems of the different aggregates, and beneath our feet is a mosaic of swirling patterns, the tile filled with whites, beiges, and grays. Rare woods detailed with gemstones form the backbones of plush, velvet chairs, and directly in the center lies a glittering fountain ensconced between balance scales.

"This way," Draven calls to the group without even sparing a glance over his shoulder, not giving us time to marvel at the sight.

He escorts us into a corridor lined with stained glass windows, whose panes depict artwork of the Canamae, the primary gods. Ornate, candle-lit chandeliers hang overhead and guide us to another narrowing hallway that veers left and then right, leading us to a large open space with a trail of doors lining the walls.

Draven halts without warning in the middle of the opening and finally turns to face us. "This is where you'll be staying. Bathing chambers are down the hall and to the left. Pick someone to bunk with, find a bed, and try not to bother anyone in the process."

A slender girl with bobbed, black hair raises her hand, the gesture slow and timid.

Draven releases a breath—as if even the smallest question is the largest inconvenience to his day—and folds his arms. "Yes?"

The girl's cheeks color with red splotches. "Do we, uhm...are we allowed to bunk with *anyone*?"

Draven blinks at her before arching a brow. "Do as you wish. We're not here to babysit you or your—" he tilts his head, considering his word choice. "—activities."

Her face heats with a red so deep, it borderline looks purple. She loudly clears her throat and replies with a brisk nod.

Marcella snickers beside me, and I nudge my elbow into her side, shooting her a wide-eyed look. She flares her eyes back at me, as if to silently protest, *What? It's funny.*

I roll my eyes in response, but accidentally let a bout of laughter slip from my lips. Draven's sullen stare whips to Marcella and me.

Oh, shit. Not good.

Marcella audibly gulps as he approaches, and I press my lips tightly together to prevent any other noises from slipping out.

"Something funny?" Draven purrs with a misleading curiosity.

Marcella and I exchange hesitant glances before shaking our heads in perfect synchrony.

He leans back and folds his corded arms over his broad chest as he eyes Marcella, dragging his eyes to me next, where they remain. "No? That's a shame. I was really hoping for a good laugh."

My lips move faster than my mind. "You certainly act like you could use one."

Marcella snorts a laugh next to me, immediately clapping a hand over her mouth afterward.

Draven cocks a brow while a low hum rumbles in the back of his throat, and I swear I hear the breath whoosh from the person next to me. He takes a step toward me. And then another. And another. Until his towering figure is no more than a few inches away from me. Slowly, he leans down and brushes his full lips against my ear. "If you want to make it around here, I suggest you learn to keep that sharp tongue of yours on a leash. We're not in Foreigner's Valley anymore, and I'm no longer some stranger on a scouting mission to you."

He pulls back just a few inches, allowing his eyes direct access to my own. My breathing catches in my throat, and I send a prayer up to Algol—the god of trickery and deception—that Draven doesn't notice.

The corner of his lip twitches with a smug smirk.

Bastard.

He noticed.

Draven recedes, clearly satisfied, and turns to leave, offering no more than a parting wave over his shoulder. "If any of you need anything, find someone else to bother."

Everyone sits in a few, tentative seconds of silence before exploring the area and resuming conversation.

I suggest you learn to keep that sharp tongue of yours on a leash.

I click my tongue as the words simmer in my stomach. There is something peculiar about Draven's presence. It's hard to place, but it's like a contradiction of ice on a flame. A tamed rage. He was already mildly unpleasant in the valley, but here? Here it's like all the walls and jadedness are fortified and put on full display.

Marcella speaks, and I twitch at the sudden remembrance that I'm not alone. "I'm not sure if I'm scared of him, or *really* turned on by him."

I scoff a laugh and shake my head at her. "If you were wise, you'd be the former, not the latter."

She exhales a dramatic sigh. "Alas, I am not known for my wisdom." A wicked curve tugs at her lips. "I have a crippling weakness, you see, for always wanting to know how those brooding men are in bed."

"It's always the quiet, brooding ones that make the best lovers," I muse with humor, solely to entertain Marcella.

She tilts her head, as if contemplating, and says through a sigh, "Their inner-demons are my inner-pleasures."

My brows skip up, and I bark a laugh. "If we were *truly* wise," I begin, veering down a different path, "we'd search for a room near the bathing chambers."

Marcella hums with approval. "Clever." She regards me, a smile blooming across her lips. "I knew there was a reason I immediately liked you."

The words spark a sudden warmth in my chest. I've never had a real friend outside of Gray. Not really, anyway. Nor have I ever met someone brimming with such raucous life and unyielding tenacity like Marcella. Finding both in one person feels like a gift I don't deserve.

And as I follow Marcella down the corridor toward a small room on the left, the scent of nobles' lavender soap already drifting in the air, I can't help but notice how quickly life can overturn itself—whether by divine force or mere chance. Not so long ago, I served a king who cared nothing for my fate beyond the next assignment he gave me.

Now, here I am, dusting off a thin sheet on a narrow mattress in Bathara, alongside a copper-haired girl whose wicked tongue and warrior spirit overflow with such raw vitality, my heart tightens just at her grin. Someone who doesn't see me as King Alastair's lowly night attendant. Someone who doesn't sneer at my lack of titles, common blood, or lowborn status. She regards me as if I matter.

And I'm not sure whether to cling to that feeling or let it slip away. Part of me still believes I have no right to the feeling—that it'll end in flames, just as it did before.

Still, the thought tugs at the corners of my lips, as if they are connected by a string.

My first friend outside the shadows of Rivara.

CHAPTER TWENTY-FIVE

Tonight, sleep and I are long-lost companions who, at the current moment, are not on cooperative terms.

I think my still-active brain is partly to thank for that. On the one hand, it frustrates me endlessly. But on the other hand, how could I not be wide awake with thoughts? I never was able to find Gray, making his whereabouts unknown. And even if I know he's completely capable of caring for himself, that doesn't keep me from worrying about him.

Then there is the matter of the first test: detecting my essence flower.

Somehow, I have to skillfully tap into the magic I can't access at will and know nothing about—not really, anyway—and attune its energy to...to...its match?

How *does* that even work?

My mother told me stories about the essence flowers; a delicacy born from magic that cultivated a breed of flowers that glow with different colors and properties. Properties that fall in perfect alignment with the essence of a wielder's magic and soul. Some variations claim they were bred from the blood of fallen stars. Others say they were the sister seeds to the very magic that rooted itself into our veins. Regardless, they are a sanctioned rarity, highly revered across the Three Kingdoms.

A dusty memory creeps into the front of my mind. Of a night spent in the royal greenhouse with my mother, pruning flowers and collecting herbs. There was a strange, white-speckled plant I had never seen before, and she had thumbed it fondly.

"It reminds me of the essence flower I once received," she had murmured, her eyes going distant as she drifted into a memory. "It bloomed while cupped in the palms of my hands." She had chuckled, shaking her head. "I couldn't believe it."

I remember asking her what she meant by *received*. I thought it odd that someone would gift her something so rare—wondered *how* someone would even be able to gift such a thing in the first place. But she had merely shaken her head, claiming the answers to those questions as irrelevant.

A sudden ache envelops me, constricting my chest to the point of pain. I squeeze my eyes closed, fighting against the demons that always seem to surface in the night.

But the demons whisper. And this time, they whisper the words of the gods that damned me. The words that condemned my mother—haunt my dreams.

A soul for a soul, sanctioned by the gods. But only fire can wash away the stain of what the child has done.

Slowly, flames flicker to life in my mind, and screams echo through me. I breathe against it, willing it all to evaporate—to go away. But the words press against me, demanding to be remembered, demanding to be felt.

I do not wish to feel.

You do not let this break you. You do not let them win.

I love you.

My eyes rip open, and I jerk upright, gasping. I press my clammy palm against my sticky forehead and glance over at Marcella, who's sound asleep, arm draped over her face. For a moment, everything feels fuzzy and distorted. It takes seconds—maybe even a minute—before my heartrate settles and my breathing goes back to normal. Yet a lingering anxiousness remains wedged beneath my skin. An anxiousness I'd do anything to eliminate.

I scan the room through the darkness, searching for my pack. Finding it with surprising ease, I quietly get out of bed and rummage through it, until my fingers graze against old, bounded leather. With stealthy steps, I sneak out of the room, not caring that I'm in the sleeping attire Bathara provided us.

The braziers remain lit, so wandering the corridors is easy. Moonlight leaks through the windows in hazy streaks as I attempt to remember the turns Draven made while leading us to our quarters. But somewhere, I take a left when I think I should have taken a right, and I wind up at the foot of a large staircase, wrapping round and round like a coiled snake. Naturally, curiosity gets the better of me, and I follow the stairs all the way up, until I reach a small room with no furniture or features outside of a nondescript door.

I glance down at Casimir's journal wedged firmly in my grip before back at the door. Exhaling a clipped breath, I approach the arched wood and slowly turn the brass knob, creaking it open. To my complete surprise, it reveals a square balcony. My lip twitches with satisfaction at the discovery, and that tiny twitch spreads into a full-fledged grin when I step outside and consume the night-sky strung above me.

Stars scatter across the dark like sand spreads across the bottom of the sea. Thousands—*millions*. All shining against the night, waiting for hungry admirers to stop and appreciate them. They may not be colored like the stars in Rivara Kingdom, but these stars are brighter and more numerous in number.

And there is this hypnotic quality about being out here.

The many waterfalls surrounding Bathara compose their own melodies, playing in tune to the chirping insects and rustling grass, sounding like a peaceful trickle from this distance. It seems like the perfect place to think—or better yet, to read.

I sit cross-legged on the edge of the wide balcony railing and fold open the journal's pages. Between the natural light emitting from the stars and moon, coupled with the lit sconces mounted on the stones, the words are remarkably readable. I begin where I last ended.

Magaius won't see reason.

I understand the discord is growing, and that soon, we will be forced to choose: squelch the uprising and deal with the Restorationists, or choose a path of peace and continue negotiations through the means of compromise.

 Magaius believes in the former and spits on the idea of backtracking; I believe in the latter. My father is in the middle. It's like he's teetering on a parapet, waiting for the wind to blow him in one direction or the other. Magaius does not believe we should concede a single thing to the Restorationists. That they are simply unhappy children, and that one does not reward children's bad behavior. But I see compromise differently.

 I see it as a way to prevent a potential war. A way to reduce tensions. I see a family whose father kisses his children on the head before they go off to sleep, warming his wife's bed at night instead of lying on a cold battlefield. I see a son who returns to his mother, or a sister who celebrates her next birthday. These fragile lives must be protected from conflict.

 Why am I the only one who sees that?

 Casimir

I huff a deep breath, puffing out my cheeks. Still, that was a short entry, so I turn the page and read the next.

 I watched two ravens today. They were fighting over scraps left out on the street. It seemed pointless to me. Why can't both birds pick from the scraps? Why must they attempt to hoard the entirety of resources for themselves when they can simply share, maintaining peace between themselves?

 I wasn't sure if I wanted answers to these questions, or if I merely wanted to ask them. Yet an answering question floated into my mind: is this the fate of all living creatures? To fight for scraps, blind to the harm that's inflicted as a result?

 What does the answer change?

 Casimir

I turn the page again.

 A Diviner spoke of a great war—of a war where the gods fight alongside the mortals. I fear there is nothing I will be able to do to stop it. Desperate, I sought out a Veilreader from the famed Izavarda bloodline and asked her to enter the Veil for me. I thought perhaps she could see something different. Diviners commune with the gods, after all, and maybe the gods want us to be tricked into thinking a great war is our only fate.

 But the Veil showed the reader images of blood-soaked grass and arrows arcing through a sky. She said she saw three shadows—three figures—that would determine the outcome. Whether they were gods, mortals, or creatures, she didn't know; the Veil would not show her. But the acrid smell of death wafted through the fog, and she knew with unquestionable certainty that what the Diviner had spoken of was true—that it would indeed all come to pass.

And that is what frightens me more than anything. For the Diviner did not just whisper of war, but she spoke of a chilling prophecy as well. One that, at this present time, I do not wish to record in ink. Still, the truth of the coming reality remains...

War is coming.

And something terrifying with it.

Casimir

I close the journal, my heart racing. For a moment, I sit and absently stare out over the hills in a loud silence.

It simply doesn't make any sense. We were always taught that the Three King System was a peaceful division of power. That the Great Clamaté War came first, and the Accord of Three Kings came after. Why...why *lie* about something like that? What is there to gain?

Casimir speaks of Restorationists, yet I have never read any historical texts recording a group who opposed the new system. I could ask Gray, but doing so would require me to tell him about the journal.

Up the rising goes forward.

The obscure sentence echoes in my head, as loudly and clearly as if it were just murmured by the Abdite named Dridus.

The uprising goes forward.

It's the only thing that makes sense. But what uprising? The Three Kingdoms have been in the Era of Peace for centuries. Since...well, since Casimir's father, King Isaphus, assumed the first-ever Rivarian crown.

Something else strikes me. Casimir wrote of a Diviner who whispered of war and spoke of a prophecy.

All at once, words the voice at Foreigner's Valley spoke swirl in my head.

In the far north is an island. On that island lives a Diviner. She is the one who sent me for reasons only known to herself.

A chill skitters down my spine, erecting the hairs on my arms to a point. Surely it couldn't be the same Diviner...right? I mean, Casimir Vivaldri lived *centuries* ago. I've never been as skilled with history as Gray, but if my memory serves correctly, four-hundred-some-years is a long time for a Diviner to exist.

And as another interlocking fragment lays itself flat against the puzzle unfolding in my mind, my heart picks up speed in my chest.

Did you know, girl, that someday, a child will come—defined by a name both two and one—born from the ashes of a great love, whose untamed power can raise or crumble kingdoms.

I hadn't thought much of the information. So much happened in Foreigner's Valley, it all felt overshadowed. Yet what Casimir wrote...

I could be stretching. My mind may just be spooked and tying strings together that don't belong. But the voice's cryptic words sound an awful lot like words that would be uttered in a prophecy. What if it isn't a coincidence? The mention of the Diviner, the voice's choice of words.

The words Sterling said to me the night before I left the Rivara Kingdom echo in my mind next.

I want you to read that journal in your lap. I suspect you'll find important answers in doing so.

That's another thing I never gave much thought to because of how quickly everything happened. Why did my mother want Sterling to recover this journal, and why did Sterling think it belonged with me? What purpose—besides inciting major trust issues regarding the credibility of recorded history—does it serve for me? Unless...

The wooden door to the balcony groans, and I slam the journal shut and swivel off the flat railing, jumping to my feet. My brows furrow deeply at the person I see.

"You." It sounds like part question, part accusation.

Draven folds his arms and tilts his head. "Funny. I remember saying something similar to you when we met."

Ignoring him, I press, "What are you doing here?"

He strolls toward me and leans against the railing. It makes him look so casual—so much younger. He can't be more than twenty-four or twenty-five. "It's my job to know who wanders Bathara's grounds at night." With an arched brow, he pointedly adds, "And you are no exception."

"Never said I was," I grumble back.

"What are you doing out this late?" He pauses, and I catch the tiny twitch at the corner of his mouth. "Better yet, what's that you're hiding from me behind your back?"

My mouth pops open, and a tiny scoff escapes from my parted lips.

How the hell did he know I had something behind my back? I even angled my body when he approached to remain inconspicuous.

"It's nothing," I lie.

His brows do a little jump. "Oh," he patronizes through a mocking smirk. "You and I both know that isn't true."

Gods, he really is an infuriating bastard.

I heave a sigh and roll my eyes. Ultimately, however, I pull my hands forward, revealing the journal.

He tilts his head, a frown pulling on his lips. "What is that?"

A wrinkle forms in my brow. "It's a journal," I reply in a flat voice.

"Yours?"

My eyes narrow on him. "Does it matter whose journal it is? You asked what it is, not who it belongs to."

He blows out a breath that almost sounds like a laugh—almost. "Fair enough." Draven cocks his head and observes me. "What do you plan to do about your first test?"

I prop myself back up onto the railing, setting the journal down in my lap and tilting my head back to look at the stars. "To be honest," I murmur, "I haven't the slightest clue. But losing is not an option, so I guess I plan to do whatever it takes to win."

Outside of Gray, and as strange as it is to consider, Draven knows the most about my situation. About what I stand to lose and gain—the truth about my magic capabilities. Perhaps that is why I answer him with full honesty.

He hums—the sound deep and almost enchanting. "Being able to attune your magic properly is already not an easy task. Attuning it to an essence flower is an even more difficult one."

I glance at him with a pointed expression. "Gee," I drone flatly. "Was that supposed to make me feel hopeless or helpless?"

"Neither," he assures me. "It was merely a fact."

"A depressing one," I mumble. "Especially given my circumstances."

Draven glances up at me the same moment I flick my eyes down toward him. His left eye is the heterochromatic one, and there's something hypnotic about the way the blues and greens mingle together, appearing almost fused by the small fissure branching from his pupil.

He does not pull his entrancing gaze away from me as he says, "Exactly. Which is why you need me to train you if you're going to survive."

I reflexively jerk back and blink. "What?"

He glides a hand along his sharp jaw before re-tucking it under his arm. "I've thought about it, and you need my help. Both for protection and instruction. Me training you can kill both those birds with one stone."

I don't think I'm hearing him correctly. "Wait, what?"

He lifts a dark brow. "Did you hit your head recently? It seems incapable of processing things at the moment."

That snaps me out of it.

I click my tongue at him and quip, "My head is very capable of thought, thank you very much. I'm just confused why you think I'm in need of your protection or your training."

"Hmm," he begins, rubbing his fingers across the top of his considerably defined lips. "Well, it certainly has nothing to do with the band of Abdites trying to kidnap you. Nor the exam you've enrolled yourself in, which requires considerable mastery over one's magic and a high level of precision to execute each test well enough to be considered worthy of progressing." Draven mocks a shrug. "Yeah, I can see what you mean now. There's nothing implying you need me or my talents."

"Your sarcasm is a delightful quality," I mumble dryly. A brief pause, then I arch a brow at him. "Talents? Really?"

"Yes, talents," he defends. "I have many of them."

"I'm sure you do," I mutter under my breath.

"Oh, I do." And there is a particular undertone there I don't even want to think about. He blows out an irritated sigh. "You have an interesting way of showing gratitude, do you know that?"

A wry smirk tugs at my lips. "Some may say it's *my* most delightful quality."

"Charming," he retorts flatly.

Despite myself, I laugh.

Through my peripheral, I see Draven slightly lift his chin to study me. Though his expression remains unreadable.

"There's a rule against captains helping examinees during the exams," he informs me. "If I am going to train you, there will have to be good cause for the other captains to go along with it." He shifts his weight forward and turns his body so he is looking outward over the rolling hills, bringing us face-to-face. Draven braces himself against the railing, flicking his eyes up to the star-coated sky. His features almost seem to soften at what he sees.

"What if you just told them about the Abdite attack?"

He shakes his head. "That poses too many problems. One, not all of them know the details of the scouting mission we were on. Kiran was telling the truth when he said it was an undisclosed mission. Second, admitting Abdites are after you raises too many questions, and during these exams, the last thing you want is to be scrutinized under a watchful gaze."

"Careful," I joke through a soft laugh. "Say any more, and I might think you actually care about what happens to me."

He slides his eyes to mine and tilts his head. I realize then how close our faces actually are. "And what makes you think I don't?"

I arch a challenging brow. "Do you?"

The corner of his lip twitches. "No," he says, the words far gentler than I expect. "Not particularly. But that doesn't mean I want to see you dead, either."

I rest my chin in the palm of my hand. "The cold, stoic scout has a beating heart after all."

He drops his arms from the railing and leans back, his lips slightly parted. "You know, I *am* a captain over one of Bathara's renowned aggregates, not a scout."

I shrug. "I think I liked you more when I met you as a scout."

Okay, this time that is definitely a laugh blowing past Draven's lips. "Be that as it may, you need training and quick. Specifically, *my* training. I'll figure out a way to make it happen."

My brows twitch in tune to my passing thought. "Why help me?" I ask him. "What's in it for you?"

Now his smirk is unmistakable. "I'm sure I'll think of a way you can repay me."

"Ah, there it is." I exhale a loud sigh. "And here I was, beginning to think we were actually becoming friends."

"I don't have friends."

"Because you don't want them or because you're incapable of making them?"

Draven's response comes in the silent form of an arched brow and pointed stare.

I huff a clipped laugh. "I'll warn you now—I have very little I can offer you." My word choice unnerves me, so I quickly add, "And just because you know of my past as a night attendant does *not* mean I'll offer you any similar...services." As embarrassing as it is, my cheeks warm at the mention.

"I would never ask you to do that in exchange for my protection. Ever." I'm taken aback by the harshness of his tone.

Confused, I blink at him, my voice softening. "So, what do you want then?"

With his arms still folded across his chest, he continues staring up at the sky. "I'm not sure yet." He answers in a way that convinces me there is complete truth in the statement.

My brows pinch together. "So, I'm just supposed to agree to some undisclosed cost? That doesn't seem like very smart bargaining."

Draven huffs, amused, and returns his gaze to me. "Would you like to set boundaries on the price?"

His taunting voice has me lifting my chin and straightening my spine. "I would, as a matter of fact."

He waves a lazy hand. "By all means."

His wry tone is irritating, and I shoot him a sharp look. "First, the cost cannot be related to anything sexual. Second, you cannot ask me to lie, cheat, murder, or steal for you. And third..." I expose my palms to myself, glancing down at them. "You cannot ask me to do anything that makes me feel as though I've been stripped of choice."

"Done." There is no hesitation in his reply—as if he answered without a shred of thought.

My brows kick up to my hairline, and I whip my gaze to him. "That's it? No counteroffers or haggling to change any of my limitations?"

He glances at me with a heavy arch in his brow. "Do you want me to do those things?"

I blink. "Well, no. Obviously not."

"Great," he drawls. "Then we're in perfect agreement. I find a way to train you and keep you protected from the Abdites, and in turn, you'll repay me in the way I eventually choose, so long as it's in accordance with your boundaries."

I hold his gaze—his eyes almost glowing in the darkness, the blues and greens clear like glass. "You have a deal." I extend my hand to him.

He glances at it, then meets it with his own calloused palm. "You know," he muses in a wry tone. "It's a shame you decided to become a Jurafen. You would have made one hell of a merchant."

"I'm taking that as nothing but a compliment."

"Take it however you like," he quips back.

We both observe the other for a long, silent moment. With stark realization, I notice our hands never let go. They remain clasped together, still locked in an unmoving handshake. I tug my hand free of his. As I do, a loud, piercing noise suddenly splits the night air, oscillating between different pitches. A voice soon follows the wailing sound.

All examinees report to the Arena immediately. I repeat, all examinees report to the Arena immediately.

But...it's the middle of the night.

I whip my eyes to Draven. "What the hell is happening?"

"Your first test."

CHAPTER TWENTY-SIX

D raven walks with me down the stairs. His eyes scan the area before sliding back to me. "Your Nightenjoy companion," he whispers, his tone devoid of leisure. "You'll need his instruction to pass this first test. Or at least someone with his knowledge. Allow him to help you." And then, just like that, he recedes into the shadows, his final words a fading echo. "Good luck."

I follow the growing noises to escape the maze of corridors. My heart pounds in my chest, both with anticipation and nervousness. Thankfully, it doesn't take me long to find the crowd shuffling out. It does, however, take me a bit longer to go against the crowd and return to my chambers to change out of my sleeping attire and into the clothes Bathara provided us.

My cheeks burned the moment I realized the whole exchange with Draven had transpired while I was in sleepwear.

I halt in my tracks when I creak the door open and find Marcella standing in the middle of the room, her hands braced on her hips. "Are late night strolls a frequent habit of yours?"

"I couldn't sleep," I mumble as I rummage around, peeling the clothes from my body and dressing myself in the new ones. As subtly as I can, I tuck the journal underneath my pillow.

"So you think exploring an ancient magical academy in the middle of the night was a good idea?"

My lips kick up. "I never said I thought it was a good idea."

Marcella huffs a dry laugh. "Come on," she chides with a shake of her head. "Hurry up. You're going to make us late."

My fingers move quickly, twisting my hair into a sleek braid, and then I shove my feet into a pair of combat boots. How the academy knew our sizes, I haven't the slightest idea. But all I know is one moment Marcella and I chose our rooms before heading to the bathing chambers, and the next, there were clothes and shoes folded neatly on our beds when we returned.

Though, I have to admit, I kind of like them. The flowing, billowing trousers are loose yet structured, offering freedom of movement, and the wide legs taper at the ankles giving me a sense of security. The shirt is long-sleeved with soft fabric, resting comfortably around the shoulders. There was also a leather belt-contraption-thing that Marcella told me was called an Armsling Belt, meant to carry all the weapons a Jurafen may need. I have no weapons nor knowledge of how to use them, so I tuck that underneath my bed.

Marcella is already halfway out the door, watching the last wave of examinees shuffle from their rooms. When she slides her gaze back to me, she offers a brisk nod. "Ready?"

No.

Not at all.

"Something like that," I reply.

I follow her out of the room and through the corridors. When she makes a right, I realize I had indeed made an incorrect left earlier. We walk at a brisk pace—examinees both in front of us and a few trailing behind us, giving me a sense of temporary calm knowing we aren't the last ones. From the sides of my eyes, I catch Marcella looking at me.

"What?" I ask.

"Why couldn't you sleep?"

I can tell the vague question is intentionally neutral. I respect the approach, honestly. So I answer truthfully. "I was a night attendant for the King of Rivara before coming here. I'm used to being awake through the night."

Marcella gives nothing away, her face the perfect mask of calm. She does not push, but she does not recede, either. "Wanna tell me about it?"

And for the first time, I think I do want to talk about it. Or perhaps it's simply that I want to tell *her* about it. So as we walk, I tell her everything about my time as a night attendant. I tell her about the nobles, the courtiers, and the emissaries I entertained. Tell her about the good ones, some of the bad ones—though I omit the worst ones. I tell her about the sleeping tonics. That I'm the daughter of a Gardner. I even tell her about the anonymous notes, and about how all of the night attendants began using the tonics to protect themselves.

"How'd you manage to never make them question things?"

I huff a humorless laugh. "The tonics I made contained a blend of sedatives and a plant that, when ingested, disrupts the memory consolidation process. So, the next morning, all I had to do was blush a little when I saw whoever I "entertained" and bat my eyes. A person's pride is a powerful weapon to wield against them; it clouds their judgment and makes them see only what they wish. They were always more than content to puff their chests because of their *performances*."

Marcella clicks her tongue. "Pride is a distorting mirror reflecting only the image we crave. That's what my mother told me, anyway, when I was a girl." She blows out a haughty breath. "I'm glad you got out of there. That idiot Rivarian king can rot in hell for all I care."

The tips of my lips curve with a wry smile. "Careful," I warn. "You just committed high treason against the King of Rivara. He does not take kindly to such things."

She snorts a laugh. "Let's see him attempt to capture me, then. He'll be fed his own skin before he gets anywhere."

My brows lift as the thought settles pleasantly within me. "I'd pay good coin to watch that."

"You and plenty of others." She glances around, making sure we are still a good distance away from the groups of examinees. "In fact, maybe I should seek him out and demand penance for all the harm he has caused my new friend."

I bark a sardonic laugh. "You'd have better luck speaking to one of the gods than that happening."

She hums a tune of wicked laughter. "I have a way of making things happen."

I observe her more closely, then. Boisterous confidence rolls from her like waves crash to a sandy shore. She holds herself with such an elegant grace despite coming across so masculine. And with her curls sleekly braided back, I can see she really is quite pretty. Her face is round and soft, her cobalt eyes large like a doe. Her skin is pale and unblemished, save for the freckles dotting her slender, button nose.

A nose which she scrunches at me. "What?"

"You are quite pretty, Marcella."

She sticks her tongue out and makes a sour face. "The day I care about what my face looks like is the day you can burn me in Amala's temple."

"Amala?" I question, lifting my brow. "You want to be burned in the goddess of earth's temple?" My eyes narrow on her. "What's your wielder's mark, exactly?" My eyes flick to her arms, but they are covered by sleeves.

"What's yours?" she shoots back through a half-formed smirk.

Touché.

I incline my head, silently saying as much. The next time I open my mouth to speak, her pointed gaze has me quickly snapping it shut.

"If you so much as suggest I wield fire magic because of my hair, I will slice you."

I chuckle. "Noted."

Our continuing conversation makes the journey to the Arena pleasant and quick, but there is a sharp shift in the air once we enter those towering doors and walk through the corridor that opens to the jarringly large space. Examinees are groggy and unhappy, a twisted mix of dread and annoyance clotting the air. We find our own corner, away from the grumbling groups of people awaiting instruction, and mind ourselves silently.

Until my peripheral vision catches a glimpse of half-drawn, shaggy brown hair. I whip my gaze over and find Gray scanning faces in the crowd.

My body slacks with relief. "Gray!" I call out to him.

He snaps his head toward the sound of my voice, and the lines surrounding his features soften when he sees me. Within a handful of seconds, he is in front of me, pulling me into his embrace.

"Where have you been?" I ask into his shoulder. "I was starting to worry something happened." My voice holds steady, and I shield out the unexpected emotion I feel rapping at my chest.

He gently places one hand on the back of my head and squeezes tighter with the hand still wrapped around the small of my back. "I'm okay," he assures me in a whisper. "I'm sorry for making you worry."

I pull away to see his face. "So what happened? What did Josiah want with you?"

"To know what happened in the valley."

I blink, stunned at first. Until I remember Josiah is the Keeper, and he was probably the one who dispatched Kiran, Draven, Griff, and Meiji on that scouting mission in the first place.

A pang pulses along the seams of my heart as I think of Meiji. "But why you? Kiran and Draven are *captains* here for gods-sakes." My brows wrinkle with thought. "Why ask for your account?" When I catch the tiny arch of his brow, I quickly add, "No offense."

"None taken," he assures me through a tiny laugh.

Marcella takes a step forward, a curved brow and a humored smile filling her features. "Is this him?" she asks while jabbing a thumb in Gray's direction.

"That's him," I lilt back, amused.

Gray's brows pull together as he flicks his eyes between Marcella and me. "Well, since you seem to know who I am, might I know who you are?"

She stretches her hand out while wearing a boisterous grin. "Marcella Lynderful. Pleased to make your acquaintance."

Gray shakes her hand, a puzzled expression lingering on his face. His gaze slides to me, and he flares his eyes, silently urging for a more thorough explanation.

I glance at Marcella and find myself surprised at the genuine smile tugging at my lips. "Marcella and I met yesterday at the commencement, and well...became friends. She and I are bunkmates now."

His brows raise slightly. "Oh. I..." He clears his throat. "I had assumed we would be bunkmates." A subtle red tint blooms across his cheeks.

Marcella throws an arm over Gray's shoulder—forcing him to crouch down at the height difference. "There's always room for a handsome man like you in our chambers. Right, Lyra?"

I chuckle at the display. "But of course there is."

"You and I can share a bed," Marcella continues, wagging her eyebrows at him.

Gray escapes her embrace and clears his throat again, attempting to hide the embarrassment tinting his skin. He readjusts his tunic. "That's a generous offer, but I'll be fine. Josiah made sure there was a room left for me."

Marcella's grin flirts with sin. "The offer always stands."

Just when I think Gray is about to implode from embarrassment, the captains emerge on the mezzanine and save him from his discomfort. They line up in front of their banners like yesterday, and the room fills with the sort of silence that makes your skin prick. And I still can't shake the strangeness of seeing Kiran and Draven up there. Which is odd considering I've only known them a short while.

I suppose it just goes to show how powerful first impressions can be.

"Examinees, we apologize for waking you, but such is the life of a Jurafen. Whether in the dead of night or in the blooming life of morning, you must be prepared to fight." Nuha's striking eyes scan the room. "Welcome to your first test."

People in different colored uniforms shuffle into the arena and wordlessly clamp those sparkling black bracelets on our wrists. A girl with streaky red and white hair clasps mine, and I recognize her uniform as belonging to the Elefet aggregate. Draven's aggregate. I offer her a sheepish smile. She does not return it.

Against my better judgement, I flick my eyes up to the mezzanine—more specifically, to Draven. He watches the girl lock the bracelet on my wrist with an expressionless face.

The girl standing next to Draven—gorgeous, with her bronzed skin and almost perfectly matching bronzed hair—steps forward. "I am Arden, captain over the Iradine aggregate," she declares in a raspy voice that somehow manages to feel smooth against the ear. "Our aether-wielders are going to open portals that will transport each of you to the Whispering Grove so that you may find your essence flowers. Remember, to be considered *yours*, it must bloom for you. If it doesn't, and you return with a sleeping flower, you will not receive judgment, and thus fail the first test." She pauses. "There is only one rule to these exams: do not cause intentional harm to your fellow examinees. Past that, you may do as you please."

Finlay steps forward. "Open the portals," he bellows.

One by one, swirling portals blink into existence. Some are large and swirling like a sea of oil and smoke. Others are smaller, but sparkle like the anthrine now clasped around my wrist. My wandering eyes still when they land on a guy with unruly, brown hair.

Griff stands at attention in front of his portal, dressed in a white and gold uniform. His lip kicks up with a proud sort of smile when he notices my attention.

"Form your lines quickly," Finlay commands. "And we will see those who succeed by the time the third moon rises."

People scatter for different portals. Despite my initial desire to go against the grain and head for Griff's line across the arena, I settle for the aether-wielder who opened his portal close to where Gray, Marcella, and I stand. He's a rather large, hairy man who doesn't seem to smile often. I catch his name floating in the whispers of those who lined up behind me: Archennon.

Gray, without fully turning, tips his chin over his shoulder and murmurs, "They've likely instructed each wielder to alter their portal so that once an examinee steps through, they land in a different part of the grove—scattering everyone for the test. From what Griff said—about aether-wielders having to visit a place physically before they can open a portal—I'd guess they've split the grove into multiple sectors and assigned an aether-wielder to each one."

"Okay," I draw out. "So, what do you think we should do?"

Still staring straight ahead, Gray says, "I have a plan for us to stay together. I know detecting an essence flower will come naturally to you." He casts a brief glance over his shoulder and gives a gentle smile. "But not without someone guiding you on exactly what to do—or rather, what to look for."

He isn't wrong. Even Draven said as much.

"What do you plan to do?"

I hear the confident edge in his laugh and can picture the faint curve of his lips. "Cast an illusion, of course."

I blink. "Are we even allowed to do that?" Another thought springs to mind, knitting my brows. "And you hate casting illusions on people. You say it feels exploitative and dishonest."

"I'll do it to ensure you survive." He pauses. "And you heard what Arden said. There are no rules to these exams outside of not harming your fellow examinee."

I give him a long look—though, he doesn't see it considering I'm staring at the back of his head.

"Just walk through directly after me. Don't hesitate, and don't look uncertain. Go straight through."

The line moves faster than I expect, and as Marcella—who stands ahead of Gray—reaches the portal's entrance, my heartbeat quickens. She winks back at me before slipping through, and suddenly it's Gray's turn. Yet Archennon doesn't spare him a glance; his muddy, beady eyes remain locked on me—like nobody else is there.

"Well?" he rasps. "What are you waiting for? I haven't got all day."

My gaze flicks toward Gray just in time to see him vanish into the swirling onyx and deep silver of Archennon's portal. At the same moment, Archennon snaps his focus to the portal, confusion twisting his features when he sees nothing but empty space. Shaking his head, his eyes sweep upwards at someone before he turns back to me.

"Well?"

I scurry forward, stepping through the portal.

The hush greeting me when I emerge on the other side brims with a choir of voices, beckoning me deeper into the unexpected mist.

CHAPTER TWENTY-SEVEN

The Whispering Grove.

Located in the heart of an ancient woodland—old like Elwood Forest, yet not nearly as steeped in magic—the grove is a place rumored to have astounding beauty and confounding trickery. Travelers come here to whisper their questions and interpret the riddled answers, despite countless warnings to stay away. For the grove is divided by a powerful force that bore witness to the dawn of humanity: good and evil.

I've always wondered how much of the tales were true. I've heard of the Breathing Trees, with leaves that refract light like a clear stone, and how the grove is rumored to supposedly smell of each visitor's favorite scent—leading me to believe it must indeed be beautiful.

But the place I've arrived has none of those wonders.

Well, save for one distinct feature, lingering unmistakably: the whispers.

They hiss through the stagnant air like hurried secrets no one was meant to hear—fleeting, breathless murmurs that rise and fall with the shifting mist. Each half-formed word seems to quiver on the edge of audibility, a frantic chorus of voices tangled in the shadows, never quite finishing their whispered confessions.

At least the grove lives up to its name.

The thick, humid air is heavy with musk and filled with a collage of decay and stifling sulfur—the rot so pungent it leaves a bitter taste upon my tongue. Mist hangs like a veil in the air, and I can barely see the gnarled trees towering around me. I swivel my frantic gaze left and then right.

"Gray!" I shout.

Yet it's as though the mist swallows the sound of my voice as hungrily as a starved crow picking at scraps.

I see a shadow running in the mist before it disappears. Voices follow the shadow, whispering and giggling. I follow the voices.

They lead me through the milky fog and guide me to an expanse of water that appears contaminated—venomous, almost. An icy dread skitters down my skin as I realize where we were transported.

Of all the places in the Whispering Grove, there is one spot no traveler ever dares to wander, its creatures and evils known to many: The Bog.

The Bog sprawls in an expanse of murky water and tangled vegetation, the surface shrouded in a thick haze. The water gleams a sickly shade of green, thick with algae and coated with mats of decaying vegetation. Dappled light falls onto random patches of the stagnant water, and they shimmer with an oily sheen. An assortment of reeds and cattails rise from the depths, twisted and gnarled, and clumps of sodden vegetation teeming with crawling insects litter the land.

The malevolent energy thrumming through this place makes my blood run cold. Like a venomous heartbeat sounding from the pit of these lands, it pulses. Moves. Calls.

I stick to the Bog's outer edges, gingerly testing each step on the sodden ground before placing my full weight. The terrain is flat and vast, and I scan it with anxious eyes, desperate to spot Gray. I can't see him, but I hear him.

"Lyra? Where are you?"

"Over here!" I shout back. "I'm in the mist!" But, as before, the mist seems to be a wall, bouncing my voice right back at me.

I hear no reply for a long moment, but then Gray's voice sounds again. "Lyra, if you can hear me, I can hardly see anything through this fog, but I'm here."

I attempt to pinpoint the general area it sounds like Gray is shouting from, and I venture toward it. As I creep forward, The Bog's whispers fall silent, leaving only the sounds of chirping insects and croaking frogs. The oily water ripples with movement, and I jerk my head toward the noise—just in time to glimpse a slimy tail the same sickly green as the water.

Suddenly, it feels like my ears are cupped, muffling every noise. I spot an overgrown patch of decayed vegetation rustling. Heart pounding, I ease closer and slowly part the leaves.

"Gra—"

A small, bloated creature leaps from the undergrowth, oozing sores glistening with slime.

"Person, person," it shrieks. "Person for me to eat."

Despite myself, I scream—a loud, piercing shriek that finally penetrates through the dense mist. The creature's breathing is a wet rasp, and its stench is so vile, I nearly retch.

"Meat. Meat. Flesh and bone. So long it's been since I've tasted your kind." It lunges forward, launching itself upward using my arm and scrambling onto my shoulder. Razor-sharp nails punch into my skin, drawing a startled gasp from my lips. "Yes. Yes. Pain. So much pain," it croons, voice thick with twisted pleasure. "I can taste your pain. Scream for me again."

Another hand digs pointed nails into the nape of my neck. I try to swallow my cry, but a strangled sob escapes me instead.

"Yes. Yes. Me like this. Your pain tastes good."

My vision blurs, and only then do I catch the tang of something acrid in the air.

Poison.

Its nails are tipped with poison.

Desperation flares hot. I claw at the creature, thrashing to free myself. "Get off me!" I seethe, heart pounding.

The creature's black eyes grow wild with delight. "Yes. Yes. You have figured it out, haven't you? Us Mirefiends have poison running through our veins." It jumps up and down on my shoulder and thrusts its nails into my skin over and over. "Yes. Yes. Potent poison. But it will not kill you quickly. No. No. We Mirefiends like to take our time. Yes. Yes."

My mind reels, the world collapsing into a cruel blur. I swing blindly at the Mirefiend, fueled by a bitter mix of anger and desperation.

A voice calls for me from somewhere in The Bog, and I drop to my knees, pain flooding my vision with pulses of red and black. Yet I finally see Gray through the mist. He clutches his sword in front of him, black blood splattered across his face as he defends himself against the Mirefiends attacking him.

A mounting pressure fills my veins, surging like a storm, and I wince. My head spins—threatening to go dark—and I'm suddenly overwhelmed by images of that place within me. The place where Gray once guided me to find my magic, where a network of threads waits for me. I clutch at the waterlogged grass, my fingers digging into rotted earth, and bare my teeth as a pained scream rips from my throat.

I manage to catch the blur of Gray whipping his head toward the sound.

The Mirefiend leaps, stopping inches from my face. With me on my knees, we're nearly eye to eye. "Friend, I see. Yes. Yes. I have more friends, too." It tips its small, bloated head back and exposes its tiny, serrated teeth. Without warning, it lets out a sharp, ear-splitting scream, and a hundred Mirefiends emerge from the mist, echoing the same piercing cry that just rattled my ears.

The Mirefiend before me swings back to face me, black eyes gleaming with a ravenous hunger. "Yes. Yes. We shall enjoy this very much."

My body—thrumming with pressure but battered by pain—is shutting down.

So. Much. Pain.

Violent. Sharp. Consuming.

Images flash through my mind as the world fades to black. Dark, insidious scenes of a man with a sword plunged through his heart. Of fire raging while distant screams echo. I see Death.

A voice calls out to me, distant yet determined, from somewhere I sense I was meant to reach, to do...something.

"Lyra! If you can hear me, do not let them touch you—their nails are poisoned."

Lyra.

Is that my name?

I fall flat against the ground as my body begins convulsing—my mouth covered in something sticky—and the pain constricts my chest, latching a lock onto my lungs, preventing them from expanding fully.

The Mirefiend in front of me giggles with joy. "Yes. Yes. Good. So very good." Somewhere on my lower half—though I can no longer pinpoint where, exactly—I feel something sharp penetrate my skin. "More. More. Yes. Yes."

My body jerks with involuntary tremors.

The haze in my mind grows darker and darker—shifting from white to murky gray until it becomes an impenetrable wall of black. Nothing remains except a faint light flickering against the darkness, straining to remain lit against an unseen wind.

But it loses.

The wick dies.

True darkness looms.

It parts for me as I move toward it, welcoming me, craving me. A thin layer of fog floats in the void, color shimmering into existence behind it. A low, rippling voice, as calm as still water yet as solid as stone, speaks. *"At last, you're here. Come closer. I have much to show you, starting with what you're truly capable of."*

The voice is strangely familiar, even to this disembodied version of myself. Though the sound of it is as foreign as anything else. As if compelled, I drift toward the smoky veil hanging in the darkness.

But then I hear that other voice again, faint but urgent. "Give me something to go off of, Lyra. Shout, cry—anything. I'm close to you. I know I am."

It called me by that name again.

Who are you? I want to ask both voices.

The first tugs at my heartstrings; the second jerks at them like a puppet master. And when the first voice speaks, I see...

Moss-covered stones glowing in sunlight. Flecks of copper rain falling from a golden sky into a crystalline river.

There is such warmth there.

Like bathing in a perfect, gilded sun.

And something inside my chest says it wants to return to the sunlight.

I begin to recede, but black tendrils lash at me, gripping my wrists and beckoning me back toward the fog. *"Stay. There is much you must see first."*

I waver, a strange curiosity tugging at me.

Until the sun shines again. "Wherever you are—win, Lyra. You must win."

You must win.

The words stir something within me. And like a missing piece slotting back into place, I remember why.

I will not let them win.

Like a flame shifting course, I wrench myself from whatever— whoever—waits for me in the dark and step back. Behind the smoky veil of shifting color separating us, I swear I hear a drawn out sigh. *"Fine. Then this is all I can offer you for now."*

Somewhere beyond this space—in my body, I think, in a distant reality—pressure collides with pressure as something foreign floods a river...no, veins. *My* veins.

A war ensues.

The poison against something...powerful. More poison pours in, corrupting everything it touches in its attempt to decay life.

Yet a vision takes shape.

A garden.

A woman with hair more silver than lilac, her mauve eyes warm as she hums softly. As she appears, a rush of something unknown courses through me. I sense the fragility of this moment, a tentative happiness draped over roaring flames. I reach out to her.

She sees me and smiles.

"Come," she whispers with gentle joy. "Come see how this flower has blossomed, my sweet Lyra."

Lyra. That is my name.

Lyra Izacalli. Daughter of a Gardner, mothered to know the ways of every plant and herb. Raised not to cower, not to yield, never to falter.

Someone who will not lose.

That crushing pressure dissolves, replaced by a sudden wave of heat coursing through my veins. As if seared by an invisible flame, the poison slowly disappears, its black fragments flaking away like charred paper. A tingling sensation pricks my skin as something feels like it's exploding from me. After, my eyelids flutter open, revealing the hazy glow of a half-veiled moon, mist-shrouded water, and scraggly patches of vegetation. The smell of rot and decay slams into me once more.

I draw in a foul-tasting breath and realize I'm back.

Relief floods my body, and slowly, with a woozy mind, I sit up and glance down at my hands and arms. I nearly choke at the sight.

A warm, golden covering surrounds me in a thin layer. It radiates heat, mending the countless puncture wounds littering my skin.

So many wounds.

How many times did the Mirefiends jab their wicked nails into me while I was lost to the poison? The marks scatter relentlessly across my arms and legs, marring my skin. Yet the dim light makes them all disappear, leaving nothing but my tattered clothes.

I press a hand to my forehead and scan my surroundings.

I freeze at what I see.

Everywhere—through the water, across the spongy vegetation, along The Bog's borders—rest the bodies of the Mirefiends.

Singed. Charred. *Burned.*

Some remain on fire, sizzling under a translucent blue flame.

Did I do this? No...that's not possible. I'm not a fire-wielder. I wielded flora magic in King Alastair's throne room. It was flora magic that made those vines and thorns emerge from the earth and twist around the room...

Right?

The misty fog slowly evaporates. Gray finds me immediately, his chest rising and falling heavily as ragged breaths puff from his blood-stained lips. His expression is grim, his face haggard and worn. How many Mirefiends did he fight off? From the looks of him, it had to have been *hundreds*.

And the fact that he was able to do so without letting them claw him once, without letting their poison slip into his veins...

At first, Gray is so focused on scanning me, ensuring I am unharmed, he seems to not register all the singed Mirefiends surrounding us. Until his eyes finally do a quick sweep of the land, and he takes in the dozens of bodies. He whips his gaze back to me. "What happened here?"

I shake my head, and my mouth opens and closes like a floundering fish. "I...I don't know."

"You didn't see anything?"

I debate telling him I was under the poison's influence, delirious and not of my own mind for an unknown amount of time. But then I realize that would require explaining how I was able to escape the poison's death grip on me—how I was healed.

And that is an explanation I don't have. One that I do not understand.

The voice that spoke to me behind that smoky veil rings in my head. *Fine. Then this is all I can offer you for now.*

Could it be that whoever spoke to me *actually* exists? Is that...even possible?

My head pounds just trying to unravel the loaded thought. I swallow, my throat unbearably dry. "No. I..." I sigh. "It was like I was trapped in that wall of mist."

Not entirely a lie.

Gray's brows knit together as he attempts to make sense of everything. "Maybe there was another wielder here then, also shielded by the mist." He runs a dirty hand through his matted hair. "Whoever it was, they did us a huge favor by eliminating all of these creatures."

I stare off absently at nothing, tucking my knees into my chest.

A squishy noise fills the air as Gray approaches me. He crouches down and glides his thumb across my cheek. "Hell of a start to these exams, huh," he muses gently, attempting to fill his tone with a tinge of humor.

When I don't respond, I glimpse his lips falling into a small frown. "Come on," he murmurs, offering me his hand. "Let's go find a river to clean up in."

We find a clean creek near the eastern part of the grove, thankfully far away from any chanted whispers or malevolent creatures. Just moonlit trees and grass the normal shade of green.

Gray suspects the creek we found is composed of runoff snow from the Wolfgaith Mountains or a trickling limb from Tuarana's River Lace. Though regardless of the water's origin, I'm grateful for the chance to wash all the muck and grime from my skin.

I am silent for a long time. Gray tries to fill the silence—whether through random deductions about the creek's water source, lighthearted comments and observations, or simply one-sided conversation, he continues speaking despite my lack of responses. Eventually, he suggests we rest, even if only for a small number of hours.

We position our bedrolls on a flat patch of land side-by-side, crawling into them with exhaustion weighing heavily on our bones. Still, Gray does not press me to use my voice. He simply stretches his hand across the small space between us, keeping his palm open.

I exhale a loaded breath as I watch the sky begin to lighten, strange emotions clogging my throat from all that's happened these past few hours. Within minutes, I was almost killed by this exam, and this is only the first night of the first test. And I was just...helpless, unable to use my magic at will or fight back.

The thought cruelly burns me: *was King Alastair right about me? Am I destined to fail?*

Is he going to win, and will I lose?

Not to mention all my other lingering questions. But I am far too exhausted to even attempt to unpack what may or may not have actually happened in my poison-induced state of delirium.

No, those are thoughts for another night—for a version of me that isn't dampened by the feelings of defeat.

I curl into myself even more, and my chest quakes as the feeling of a small crack forming appears behind my chest. I have the distinct feeling that emotion holds the hammer.

Yet I swallow it down, forcing it to go somewhere far, far away, not willing to feel it. I know what comes from feeling, and it is never anything good.

My eyes squeeze shut, and a small tremor rocks me. Crumbling, I pry my clenched hand from my chest and place it in Gray's open, waiting palm. He wraps his fingers around it and squeezes. I hear the silent words in his gesture as clearly as if spoken aloud.

I'm here. You are not alone.

CHAPTER TWENTY-EIGHT

Golden rays seep through my fluttering eyelids. I glance over and find Gray still sleeping, my hand still securely tucked in his. Some of the heaviness from last night has lifted from my chest, though weighted fragments still linger. But I inhale a deep, pine-scented breath and blow it out slowly, determined to do better today. And that starts with scavenging some breakfast.

Yet when I sit up, all promises of peace shatter as my heart rate spikes at the sight of coppery-red curls twisted back into a braid, its tip blowing in the morning wind.

"Good morning," Marcella chirps.

I rip my hand away from Gray's and press it against my chest. "How long have you been sitting there?" I ask, remnants of my temporary fright leaking into my voice.

She picks at her nails. "Oh...I don't know. Only for a little while."

I arch a brow. "'Only for a little while?'" I repeat back. "You realize how that sounds, right?"

Her flashing grin is her only response.

Gray rustles, jerking upright once he squints his eyes open. He is silent a few seconds as his eyes dart around, his brain clearly trying to piece together the meaning of the scene before him. His mouth thins into a straight line as he—quite unenthusiastically—asks Marcella, "When did you get here?"

She puckers her lips, as if thinking about her answer. "That does seem to be the golden question around here."

Gray presses a hand to his shaking head and blows out a sigh, revealing his exposed arms and chest.

Marcella cocks her head and lifts a coppery brow. "Well there's a sight I could get used to."

I flick my eyes over to Gray, holding in a laugh. His tunic currently hangs on a tree, drying after being washed in the creek. I glance between the two of them, and between Marcella's teasing eyes and Gray's unamused expression, a small giggle slips out of me.

An action that results in Gray huffing a breath and rolling his eyes. Which only makes me giggle harder.

Marcella smiles, seemingly proud of herself, and saunters over to the nearby tree, plucking his tunic from an extending branch. She tosses it into Gray's lap and mocks a frown. "Sure you want to put that on? I think I like you better with your shirt off, actually." She tilts her head, as if really considering what she sees. "Who would have thought you, of all people, would have such nice muscles?"

A full-blown laugh escapes my lips now, and Gray arches his brows even higher as he shoots me a pointed look that he soon turns onto Marcella. "I'm not entirely sure what to make of that comment, but I think I'll put the shirt on, thank you."

Marcella feigns disappointment and swats a hand at him. "Fun-killer."

"Sleep-ruiner."

She whistles low and under her breath. "Good one."

I clutch my stomach from laughing so hard, water pooling in the corners of my crinkled eyes. It takes a moment, but I finally regain control of myself and clear my throat. "It's not that I'm not thrilled to see you, Marcella, but what are you doing here? Better yet, how did you even find us?"

Marcella plucks a yellow flower from the ground and twirls the stem between her fingertips. "Well you see, I played a game of riddles with some forest spirit and won, which prompted her to tell me you guys were in danger." Marcella sweeps her cobalt eyes over the two of us. "Though you both look perfectly fine to me." She lifts an idle hand and shrugs. "Plus, the trees talk."

"And what did the trees say?" Gray asks, half teasing. He tugs his shirt over his head and rises.

I glance at him and dryly mutter, "That's what you're focusing on? *Not* the casual mention of playing a game of riddles with a forest spirit?"

Marcella snorts a laugh and shoots Gray a look after. "They *said* little. Just provided me with a direction that helped me discover which part of the grove you were in. I tracked the two of you from there."

"I didn't know you were such a skilled tracker," Gray replies, packing our supplies and tying half his hair back after.

She smirks and tilts her head. "You make such assumptions, yet *you* don't even know anything about me. Is it because I'm a woman?"

Gray doesn't take the bait. Instead, he snorts a laugh and shakes his head. "Two of the best trackers I've ever met were women."

She narrows her eyes at him. "Good. Because you will find, Gray Nightenjoy, that I have many skills to offer. Castles and estates aren't the only places where one can learn things."

"I never said you didn't, and I never said they were."

She hums, her gaze lingering on him a moment longer. Sucking in a breath, she turns her attention onto me. "Found your flower yet?"

My brows tug together. "It's only been a few hours," I mutter back. "Has *anyone* had enough time to find their flower yet?"

Her grin is sharp enough to cut. "I have."

And the arrogance on her face...the confidence and pride mixing with the challenge gleaming in her eyes.

She is telling the truth.

"God's veins," I drawl, rising from where I sit and shuffling toward her. "Will you show it to me?"

Her arrogant smile grows wider as she rummages through her pack. "I suppose I will," she replies in a sing-song voice.

Gray is next to me within seconds, watching.

She unfolds a small linen cloth, and the air is sucked from my lungs.

"Shit," I breathe. "It's *actually* bloomed for you."

Marcella smiles. "Of course it has. It is *my* essence flower after all."

And there is no mistaking that it is indeed an essence flower in Marcella's hands, nestled gently between her palms. Still attached to a sturdy, thick stem—vibrant green leaves dancing along the stalk—the petals overflow with a riot of colors. The bottom layer is the darkest, filled with a deep blue. As the layers of the petals narrow and thin, the colors lighten—shifting from violets to powdery blues to pale yellows. Along the petals runs a saturated green seam, the veins winding and extending like a network of rivers.

"Resilia," I whisper with awe.

Gray and Marcella both glance up from the flower and at me. "Is that its name?" she asks.

I nod my head. "That is a Resilia flower. Its colors are meant to reflect the richness and diversity of the natural world, carrying the scent of the earth itself within its petals." I pause and sweep my eyes over Marcella, observing her closely. "That flower supposedly only blooms for a true daughter of earth. Of Amala, one of the Four Goddesses."

Marcella covers the flower with the cloth and carefully places it back in her pack. She meets my stare. "Well, I'd say all of that sounds about right."

I tilt my head in silent question.

She sighs and holds out her forearm, pushing back the sleeve of her shirt, exposing her wielder's mark.

From the base of her wrist, a slender vine with budding leaves winds up and around her forearm and bicep, stopping as it meets the base of her shoulder, where the symbol of earth lies.

"Flora magic," Gray muses, a hint of shock leaking through his words. He glances at me before looking back at the mark wrapping around the entirety of her arm, inspecting it closely. "I can see why you choose to hide it."

Marcella smiles. "Guilty as charged."

Something like hope and excitement courses through me. "I'm a flora-wielder, too."

Marcella's brows scrunch together. "You are?" She cocks her head and slowly sweeps her eyes over me, frowning. "That could explain why I felt something from you when we met, but…you don't have the same feeling as flora-wielders."

"Like there's so many out there," Gray retorts under his breath. I hush him, but he shrugs. "What? It's true. Not even Bathara has had a good flora-wielder in ages."

Marcella's brows lower, and she jabs her thumb at Gray. "How does he know that?" she asks me.

"I'm right here," he drones flatly.

I pinch the bridge of my nose and sigh. "Gray knows just about everything when it comes to magic and the history of Solaya."

Except, he doesn't. Not the true *history, at least.*

I shake the thought away.

"Hm," she hums, eyeing him. She turns her attention back onto me. "Can I see your wielder's mark?"

Despite myself, I wince. "Uh, funny thing about that… I don't have one."

She studies me for a long moment, clearly unsure how to react. Finally, with a carefully neutral tone, she replies, "You're being serious?"

"Unfortunately."

Her brows twitch. "Then what are you doing *here*? And I won't even start on my questions about how the hell it's possible for you to not even *have* a wielder's mark, yet still claim to be a flora-wielder."

I chew on my lip. "I've told you about my past as a night attendant, but there are a lot of details I left out." I blow out a sigh. "Look, I'll tell you everything about me. The magic, my wielder's mark, my blood wager—"

"—*blood wager?*" she interjects, her brows rising to her hairline.

"Yes," I murmur. "A blood wager." My shoulders sag. "I'll tell you everything, and then I will swallow my pride and ask for your help after I'm finished. I'm not so dense that I don't realize how royally screwed I am with this test."

She observes me for a very long, very silent moment. "Tell me everything."

I don't withhold a single detail from her.

Well, save for Casimir's journal and the truth behind why my magic manifested so late. I do omit that small bit of information—revelations that would shock even Gray.

I start from the beginning. From when Gray wandered into my room, and suddenly, it felt as though everything was changing. I stop only once I reach the part where Gray and I traveled through Foreigner's Valley.

That, to me, just feels like a story for another day.

Marcella gazes at me with wide eyes. "So you truly manifested your magic this late in life, then chose to make a blood wager with a king based on your ability to gain acceptance into the most selective and revered academy in all of the Three Kingdoms, despite knowing nothing of how your magic works, *realizing* you couldn't fulfill your side of the wager should you lose, thus resulting in your own death?"

I smack my lips together and nod. "Yup, that sums it up neatly."

Marcella shakes her head and chuckles softly under her breath. "You have bigger balls than any man I've ever met, that's for sure." She flicks her eyes to Gray. "No offense."

He shrugs. "None taken. Trust me, I get it."

Marcella laughs, and then proceeds to tell us about how her wielder's mark manifested.

It happened early on. She was tending to the fields when it appeared. Her parents—poor farmers just trying to make ends meet in Rolfbear, a poor farming town in the Anatolé Kingdom—had told Marcella they were going to have to both cut back on food rations and sell some of their sheep, one of whom Marcella loved dearly. Desperate, Marcella was in the fields crying, begging the crops to flourish.

And to her amazement, they listened.

A patch of wheat sprouted to near perfection. With tears still welling in her eyes, she tried again. And it worked again. That was when the mark manifested. She raced home and showed her parents, and when they saw the sheer size of it, saw what she could do, they immediately went out to the market and sold a family heirloom to pay for a teacher. Then, as soon as she learned how to better control her magic, she used it to produce the successful spice farm her family now operates. In fact, she used it to help *all* the farmers in Rolfbear yield successful harvests. In turn, the town went from a struggling backwater to a gold mine of desirable crops.

And it's not that I needed another reason to like or respect Marcella more, but hearing her story certainly gives me one.

"So, that isn't a misconception?" I ask both her and Gray. "The size of a wielder's mark truly does indicate a wielder's strength?"

"Just about," Gray answers. The three of us sit in a small circle as we talk. "The size of a wielder's mark typically acts as an indicator of the wielder's raw potential. Since some believe it to be a pact between the wielder and their magic, it's been said the size shows the allowance of magic the gods gave you. Technically, it can manifest on any part of the body, but it most commonly appears somewhere around the wrist or forearm. To have one stretching all the way down the arm, however, is largely unheard of. It would imply the wielder's innate capabilities are...well, something to be feared, to say the least."

To my surprise, Marcella does not boast or laugh at the subtle compliment. Instead, she simply elaborates on what Gray said. "At first, the wielder's mark just reflects a wielder's magic type. Like flames for fire or waves for water. There are all kinds of different variations, but most appear with a similar foundation. But—and this is a rather recent revelation proposed by scholars—the mark isn't static."

My brows furrow. "What does that even mean?"

It's like Gray is zapped with energy, and his eyes round as he comes alive with intrigue. "You know about this?"

Marcella arches a brow at him. "Why are you surprised by that?"

"Because it's so new. Because it's not something publicly accepted as fact yet. People fear that particular advancement in our understanding of our marks because, to them, it resembles an Abdite corrupting their mark too closely."

"Most people fear what they don't understand. I'm not one of those people."

I bounce my eyes between the two of them, noting the small tilt of Gray's head as he studies Marcella as if for the first time. "So uhm, for those of us who still don't fully understand, can someone please elaborate?"

"As a wielder develops and their magic strengthens," Gray begins, turning his attention back onto me. "Scholars now believe the mark can evolve—can change. But in order for it to do so, the wielder has to enhance their wielding abilities by such a significant amount, most don't even believe it's possible. It's part of why the theory is so divisive—many think it's a waste to theorize on something others already consider an impossibility. That—" He stops when he catches the lifted brows on both Marcella's face and my own. "Sorry," he mumbles. "I got carried away, didn't I?"

Marcella's eyes soften, if only a little. "Don't apologize for being passionate. I'm only stopping you because firstly, it'll confuse Lyra if you continue on, and secondly, we are operating on a time limit here."

Gray nods, shifting his gaze to me. "Sorry," he says again.

I offer him a reassuring smile before circling back to the earlier point in the conversation. "So, that's why you hide your mark? Because it gives away how strong you are?"

She nods. "You got it."

My brows furrow. "But why hide something like that?"

Gray is the one who answers. "Most wielders choose to hide their marks if they can. It's easier that way. You either put a target on your back for being too strong, or you put one on your back for being too weak. Regardless, it's not something most wielders like to discuss."

I clamp down on my growing smile. I can't help myself. "So, to be clear, I shouldn't go up to a guy and ask him how big his mark is?"

Marcella howls with laughter.

Gray tries not to laugh, but ultimately caves. He covers his mouth with a fist, attempting to hide his growing smile. "No," he responds through his chuckle. "No, you should not."

The three of us laugh together in our tiny circle like we've been friends for ages. Though I suppose Gray and I have, Marcella fits in as seamlessly as a sky fusing its light with a horizon. It feels...nice.

Once Marcella's laughter dims, she exhales a long breath—her demeanor taking a sharp shift—and turns to look at me. "All that delightful information to say, a wielder's mark is heavily intertwined with a wielder's magical capabilities, and you are at a serious disadvantage without yours. Right now, asking you to detect your essence flower is like tying a hunting dog's legs together and telling him to go track his prey."

Talk about a mood killer.

"But can it be done?"

Marcella's answering smile is sharp. "With both his instruction and mine, it certainly can." She shifts her gaze to Gray. "Tell me, have you detected your essence flower already?"

My eyes whip to him. Has he? Why wouldn't he say anything?

Gray drags his hand through his hair. "Yes," he supplies softly. "I believe I have."

Her lips flatten into a thin smile, and she nods her head. "Thought so." She turns back to face me. "We'll definitely be able to help you. Starting now, even. Take a deep breath, close your eyes, and sink down into your magic." A pause. "Wait, you have at least figured out that part, right?"

I squint an eye open and look at her. "Mhm. Gray taught me."

"Fantastic," she chirps.

Shutting my squinted eye, I spiral down and down into that magical place within me.

Marcella's voice sounds distant when she asks, "Are you there?"

I nod.

"Then let this be a quick lesson on control: laktî runs through us much like a river streams through earth. We are its vessel, and it is our vital source. You must steer it, mold it—take *charge* of it. You are its master, not the other way around. Remember that."

"The beauty of magic," Gray adds from the other side of me, "is the way it is both dependent and independent of our very selves. It has its own heartbeat, but your veins give it purpose."

Feeling slightly overwhelmed by all the information I'm receiving, I attempt to heed their words. I plunge into the flowing river of laktî within me, and I wrap myself in its feeling, twining it through my bones. A warm feeling washes through me.

"Now," Marcella says. "Pretend there is a small piece missing from your magic. Pretend that you want it back—*need* it back. Where does your magic tell you to go?"

I do as she says, and I'm shocked when I feel a tug on some unseen thread in the center of my chest. "South," I murmur, my eyes still closed. "I think I'm being pulled south."

I open my eyes to find Marcella wearing a look of unbridled approval. "You figured that out much faster than I thought you would."

I smile, then look over to Gray, who watches me with soft eyes. "Where is your essence flower pulling you?" I ask him.

"North," he supplies, his voice gentle. "Up the trail and toward the mountains."

"Oh," I reply. "I'm not sure how far south I'm supposed to go, or whether I should venture east or west, just that—"

"—Lyra," Gray interjects softly. "You did great. You'll hone in on specific directions more once you get closer to your flower." I attempt a smile, but it's weak and unconvincing. Gray scoots closer to me and tips my chin up with the crook of his finger so that I have to look at him. "You can do this—with or without me by your side. You are capable, and smart, and brave. You have nothing to fear."

Except I do. There is much I fear.

Marcella's pointed cough loosens the air. She looks at me, but points a finger at Gray. "Where can I find one of those?"

Marcella and I watch Gray venture northward, following the pull toward his essence flower.

He glances back at us a final time, and I offer him a parting smile, while Marcella gives an overly animated wave, her other hand resting on her hip. Gray shakes his head, laughing, and turns back around to head off on his own.

Still watching him, I say to Marcella, "You don't have to come with me. You've already done enough to help. You should go back to the arena. Hell, you might even get bonus points with the captains for your speed."

"I know," is her only reply.

"I don't want to cost you anything."

"I know," she says again. Marcella eyes me sidelong. "But as a fellow flora-wielder, I'm dying to know your essence flower. Plus, any minute spent with those stuffy highborns is a minute too long. I'd much rather slum it with you." She nudges me with her elbow and winks at me.

A laugh rises in my throat as I turn away from the north trail. "Thank you," I say, my voice far more loaded than I would have liked.

The corner of her mouth tugs upwards. "You and me? Untitled lowborns that nobility think shouldn't be here...we are going to prove them wrong."

My fingers clutch at the ice necklace resting at the base of my throat. Thestis's sweet face appears in my mind paired with a simple thought—

I will not let them win.

CHAPTER TWENTY-NINE

The path kicks out wide before narrowing and winding like a snake. The trees whisper two riddles to us—one I solve, the other Marcella. Their cryptic guidance leads us to a long-forgotten trail, nearly invisible beneath the overgrown weeds. Following it, we emerge at the grove's edge, where the trees thin before vanishing altogether, as if marking a boundary. Beyond the opening, the descending sun bathes the snow-capped peaks of the Wolfgaith Mountains in red-gold light, the spread breathtaking.

That's when the thread tugging at my magic goes slack, severing my connection to the flower, and we've been stagnant for hours since.

"Anything?" Marcella asks from her chosen resting spot—a patch of overgrown grass and wildflowers, her back leaning against a thick tree trunk. She rolls the stem of a plucked yellow flower between her fingers, inspecting it with furrowed brows.

Frustrated, I shake my head. "Not yet. How is this supposed to work, anyway? Like a child's game of hot and cold? I get warmer when I'm close to the flower and colder when I'm not?"

When Marcella doesn't respond, I glance at her and find her still intently examining the cheery yellow petals.

"Heartleaf," I offer.

Her eyes shift from the flower to me. "Come again?"

I nod toward the flora she's practically pressed against her face. "That flower. It's called heartleaf."

She twirls the stem, making the petals dance. "Oh." Her cobalt eyes flick back to me. "Daughter of a Gardner, indeed," she muses under her breath. Marcella pockets the flower and fixes me with her full attention. "There's no right or wrong answer here, Lyra. That's why this is the first test to enter Bathara. The Captains and Masters expect you to have a full understanding of your magic—and that's the bare minimum."

I know she's right, but that doesn't soften the sting of feeling incompetent.

She opens her palms, and a fluorescent light begins to glow. With fluid, dance-like movements, she glides her hands, and a nearby branch creaks downward, bending toward her. A freshly ripened apple dangles from its tip. She plucks it and takes a loud, crunching bite.

"Your magic has an intended frequency—one that matches the core of its ability. Find that."

"How?" I ask, frowning.

Marcella takes another bite before tossing the apple over her shoulder. Wiping her hands on her pants, she rises to her feet. "Everything in this world is made of energy, vibrating at different frequencies. Those with laktî in their veins can manipulate these energies. It lets us harness and channel power by matching those vibrations."

I blink at her.

She pinches the bridge of her nose. "Look, this is really advanced stuff here—stuff they'll teach us more thoroughly at Bathara. But what you need to understand for now is that magic is not just some tool or force to be wielded; it is the manipulation of *energy*. And it is all around you, waiting to be molded. You just need to tap into that reservoir of magic, and channel it to shape reality according to your will. Make sense?"

No.

Not even a little bit.

"Sort of."

She rests a comforting hand on my shoulder. "It's one of those things that sounds really complicated when you try to explain it, but feels like second nature once you do it. It's much easier when you just put it into action." She drops her hand and tilts her head, thinking. "Why don't you try something simple, first. Perhaps a bed of those heartleaf flowers or an apple—whatever comes to you most easily. With the magic fresh in your veins, I think you'll have an easier time finding your flower."

"I can do that."

I think.

I shake out the rising nerves from my hands before clenching them together. I glance at Marcella. "Thank you," I murmur. "For helping me."

Marcella snorts. "Don't thank me yet. Just remember: feel the vibration of your laktî. *Listen* to it. Then command it."

Feel. Listen. Command.

Got it.

I open my palms skyward and draw in as much pine-scented air as my lungs can hold. Focusing on my veins—on the peculiar feeling within them I'm beginning to recognize as magic—I hone in on the tingling sensation.

An image takes shape in my mind. A plant I've worked with so often, it just feels natural to attempt it first. I will it to grow, commanding the vibrations humming in my skin to obey.

To my absolute surprise, unlike every other time, it actually listens.

Creamy-white, oblong petals sprout from the earth on a thin green stem, and my brows jump to my hairline as I realize they're truly there—that I've actually used my magic.

Marcella smiles, her expression brimming with pride—though I can't help but notice a faint indent between her brows. "See?" she teases, her tone like usual, but...not. "Not so hard, is it?"

"Not when I have such a talented teacher." I study her more closely. "Are you alright?"

"Me?" She waves a dismissive hand. "I'm fine. Just a passing moment of fatigue, that's all. Now, tell me—where are we heading next?"

I eye her a moment longer before blowing out a long sigh and focusing.

And it takes all of minutes until I hear something humming softly, as if calling to me. *Here*, it seems to say. *I am over here.*

I grab Marcella by the wrist and yank her forward, not wanting to risk losing the connection again. I scurry through the trees, down near the southern border of the mountains. I stop only when I reach a bed of flowers with star-shaped, honey-golden petals. They glow in the night, flecks of white dotting the flora like freshly fallen snow clinging to grass.

The Gardner's Diamond. Otherwise known as…

"Goldenstars," I breathe.

And there, at the very center, under the silvery cast of moonlight, my essence flower blooms.

Marcella's lips fall into a frown. "Well, that's…interesting."

🌿🍃 🍃🌿

Marcella and I prepare for the night, spreading out our bedrolls under a starry sky, where a doting moon casts the only light. My thoughts grow quiet, too tired to scream. As I settle onto the ground, my gaze drifts absently, not even savoring the sight above.

"Do you wanna talk about it?" Marcella asks, her hands tucked behind her head. "You haven't talked about your essence flower at all." I catch her sidelong glance. "Strange, for the daughter of a Gardner."

I hum a sound of idle acknowledgement.

She is silent for a passing moment. "The plant you created with your magic—it seemed to come easily to you. What was it?"

I scoff a dry laugh. "You really want to know?

"I do."

"It's called soporis," I say. "It was the first thing to come to my mind because I worked with it so often when making sleeping tonics for myself and the other night attendants." My biting tone leaves little room for further conversation, and Marcella doesn't try to force it.

And as I consider what I've just told her, my stomach churns with both anger and disgust.

Despite the countless flowers and plants I shared with my mother, when asked to create something tied so deeply to my heart, my mind reached for something tainted. Something born of necessity, used to shield myself from the blatant disregard of so many.

When it mattered, it was the bad I remembered most easily, not the good.

What am I supposed to make of that?

CHAPTER THIRTY

"Congratulations on passing the first test."

Josiah's voice booms from the arena's balcony as he scans the remaining faces. "It appears all but seven of you have returned. Impressive."

The trek back to Bathara was a blur. We rose with the sun and pressed on with little rest, realizing we were short on time for the trip back to the academy. My mind—for one reason or another—was lost out at sea, and I was too tired, groggy, and achy to attempt to reel it back to shore. By the time we arrived—the moon just cresting above the Hills of Thanicka—I felt like a shell of myself.

Gray had already reached Bathara by the time Marcella and I returned. His face had slackened with relief at the sight of us, then broke into a proud smile when he realized we hadn't come back empty-handed.

Now, the five captains are arranged on a tiered dais that has appeared in the center of the arena. Much like when they were on the mezzanine, they sit in front of their aggregates' emblems, waiting to begin the first judgement.

Kiran again wears a black tunic trimmed with crimson. He rests his cheek against his fist, watching the examinees with an idle smile. When his eyes rove to me, that idle smile spreads to a full-fledged smirk, and he winks.

Finlay, in stark contrast, sits impossibly straight, his muscles stiff and rigid, with stony features that would make one think he has a permanent sour smell stuffed into his nostrils.

Next to him is Arden, who sits attentively, wearing a flowing white shirt tucked into cloth pants, and next to her sits Nuha, dressed in purple, her onyx hair twisted into braids. She appears calm—composed.

Though I know how effective a facade can be.

My eyes flick to her fingers. Still no ring.

And then there is Draven, who watches the group with folded arms, his expression—per usual—entirely inscrutable. The cream of his hemp shirt accentuates his sandy-beige skin, and it helps soften his otherwise rough features. His eyes seem fixed on something. I trace his line of sight, and I'm surprised to find them locked on a clean-shaven, blonde examinee who appears oddly familiar.

An examinee Gray seems to notice at the same moment I do.

A muscle in Gray's jaw flickers, and I blink at him curiously. I know Gray well enough to recognize when he's masking his features. But...what prompted it? The blonde-haired man? Why?

"I'm sure most of you are eager to rest," Josiah says, his beige robe draped loosely over his shoulders. "So I will keep this brief. Everyone present in this room—save myself and your future captains—should have an essence flower. One by one, you will line up and present your flower to the captains. I leave judgements to them."

With that, Josiah turns and disappears into the shadows beyond the balcony's threshold.

Finlay rises and clears his throat. "You will either be cleared to continue in the exam or rejected. If rejected, you may sleep in your quarters tonight but are expected to depart Bathara at dawn." His gaze sweeps slowly across the room, and I swear it lingers on me a second longer than the others. For a fleeting moment, I think I catch an actual scowl on his face at the sight of me. "Now then." He claps his hands together. "Nobility, line up on the left. Everyone else, to the right."

Kiran jerks his cheek from his fist. "Surely you're joking."

Finlay pins him with an icy glare. "I am not."

"Come on, Finlay," Arden drawls soothingly from her chair next to him. "That really isn't necessary."

"We *will* uphold tradition," he hisses in response.

"Bathara's traditions are antiquated. There's no need to judge them separately," Arden counters.

A few examinees shift on their feet. Most, however, hold their chins high in the air, claiming what they were given, some even already migrating left.

"Not to mention," Kiran adds, "they're also *pointless* and rooted in no justifiable merit. We didn't do it last year. Or the year before that. Why now?"

Finlay's cold, merciless gaze slides toward Marcella and me as he replies, "Two years ago, there were only those with titles, and last year, the untitled didn't make it past the first test. This year, there is a rather unprecedented number of...commoners." The distaste sits thick on his tongue.

Kiran frowns at Finlay. "Why should that matter?"

Finlay's jaw flickers, but it is Nuha who declares, "Tradition is tradition. Without it, there is no order. No stability." Her words are spoken with a simple logic—calm yet firm. "Past records indicate this is how our predecessors handled exams with mixed blood. It is not our job to change the ways of old, merely to uphold them."

Finlay dips his chin in agreement. "And this is why Nuha is captain of the Philator aggregate. Nobility on the left. Everyone else on the right. *Now.*"

Kiran slumps a little in his chair and mumbles something incoherent under his breath.

The masses begin to scatter, the majority heading left. I make it no more than three steps before that blonde-haired man from earlier stands in front of me, blocking my way. "I recognize you," he drawls through a sharp smirk, wagging a finger at me. His dirty-blonde hair is clipped neatly and slicked back. He possesses eyes the color of jade and a strong nose. Actually, if it hadn't been for the smug condescension tainting his face—that appears to *permanently* ruin his face—I may have even considered him attractive.

But...*why* does he look so familiar?

248

I arch a brow. "And do you want a prize for your accomplishment?"

He clicks his tongue and sneers. "Servants have no business speaking to highborns with that kind of tone. *Especially* not servants good only for a quick fuck. Though, they have no business frequenting Bathara either, and that seems to have evaded you." He sweeps his eyes along my body—head-to-toe—and frowns. "Someone from House Fjolla would never degrade nobility by intermixing us with the likes of you."

I'm too focused working out how he knew of my background as a night attendant to notice Gray stepping beside me.

"You do not speak another word to her," he seethes with as much civility as one can while fuming. "Mind your tongue, and go to your line."

The man grins at Gray, and there is a strange familiarity in the gesture. "Oh," he sings, seemingly delighted. "Forgive me. Have I offended your family's pet?"

My brows wrinkle. How does he know about that, too? Not that I'm actually the Nightenjoy's pet or anything, but he somehow knows enough to comment on my relationship with them.

Gray's jaw clenches. "I'm not doing this with you, Huxley. Just walk away and leave us be."

Huxley?

Does Gray actually *know* him?

Huxley pouts, his lips curling mockingly. "Why should I? After all, she and I do have history. Perhaps I've missed her. Perhaps I've fallen madly in love with her after our glorious night together spent fuc—"

Like a flash of lightning across a stormy sky, Gray grabs a fistful of Huxley's tunic, his voice a low, dangerous warning. "By the gods, if you say another word about her, I'll escort you to Merikh myself."

Huxley's brows flick up. "Such uncharacteristic behavior for you. Hasn't your father raised you to be more...civilized?" He chuckles. "How odd to see you throw his teachings out the window for some..." He slides his eyes to me, and a sneer curls his lip. "Servant whore."

Gray's eyes flicker a shade of gold as he yanks Huxley forward, gold shimmering to life underneath his skin.

I blink at the sight.

That's new.

"Just because I choose a path of peace does not mean I'm without the power to end you. I'll show you just how uncivilized I can be."

A challenging smirk curls on Huxley's lips. "You think so?"

"Want to try me?"

And suddenly the realization hits me like a blow. I know why Huxley seemed so familiar...

Oh, no.

Oh gods, *no*.

I've entertained him. Fully. Without sleeping tonics.

Huxley, as if sensing my realization, flicks his jade-colored eyes to me, a knowing smile tugging at his lips. "Oh, come now. Don't tell me you've forgotten about me?" He snickers, shaking his head. "You would think a servant would remember bedding a member from House Rangard—*especially* when that person is Lord Rangard's son, presiding lord of the southern Erandor territories and a member of King Erasmus's royal council."

The shock buzzes like static in my chest, but I force myself to stand tall, lifting my chin. "I assure you, of all those I've entertained, those are the least impressive accomplishments."

Huxley's laugh is sharp—defiant. Wrenching free from Gray's grip, he comments, "It seems your famed bloodline failed to teach her manners. Why is that, cousin?"

Cousin?!

As in, *Gray's* cousin?

Before I can process the revelation, a lethal voice cuts through the air behind me.

"Find your lines, or find yourself eliminated from these exams." Draven's tone is an icy blade, ready to strike. He towers over me in a firm stance, assuming every daunting inch of his height, his arms folded over his chest.

To my surprise, Huxley immediately submits, inclining his head to Draven before sauntering to the other side of the room, where he cuts to the very front of the line. And something a lot like disgust bubbles in my stomach.

I've never really allowed myself to think too deeply about what I've done with my body over the years—perhaps because it gives me some illusion of autonomy. But seeing Huxley outside of Keziah, realizing he's been privy to parts of me he does not deserve...

I have not and will not feel shame for my past, but this moment is certainly the closest I've come.

Another tiny fissure cracks open behind my chest.

When I turn back, Draven is already seated. He hunches forward, resting his chin on his interlocked hands, his eyes pinned on me and Gray.

And for a few, slow-passing seconds, I feel too disoriented to move.

Marcella places a hand on my shoulder, her voice unusually soft. "Come on," she murmurs. "Let's find our place in line. I'd hate to end up at the very back."

🌿 🌿

There are six examinees in our line.

That includes Gray, Marcella, and myself. The other three—two girls and one boy—identify themselves as a daughter of a merchant from the Anatolé Kingdom, a son of a king's man for King Erasmus, and the daughter of a talented blacksmith in Erandor.

Huxley presents his essence flower first. He walks up the few stairs leading to the center of the dais and takes a knee in front of the captains. Cupped between his hands, he extends his essence flower out to them. Its petals are filled with a deep navy blue and trimmed in gold. They reflect with a metallic sheen and interweave, making the multilayers look interlocked. Thorns protrude from the short, thick stem.

"My flower," he says.

"For the gods sake." Kiran lifts his cheek from his fist and motions with his hand. "Stand up. We're captains, not kings. There is no need to bow."

Huxley rises, wisely schooling his scowl back into a neutral expression. Finlay glances sidelong at Kiran before returning his attention to Huxley.

"Name," Finlay demands.

"Huxley Rangard, sir."

"Lord Rangard's son," Finlay replies.

"Yes, Captain. I am his son and heir to his lands."

"My father has worked closely with Lord Rangard. Speaks highly of his commitment to honor and tradition." Finlay scans Huxley with approval. "I hope his son carries the same sentiments."

Huxley opens his mouth to respond, but Kiran cuts him off.

"Let's get on with it, Finlay," he chastises, his tone sharp. "Not everyone in the Three Kingdoms cares about titles, you know. I'd rather like to get some sleep tonight instead of watching you swoon over some lord's son."

Finlay's teeth clench as he hisses, "Yet one would think a member of House Sulien would show more respect for bloodlines and titles."

Did he just say...

House Sulien?

Kiran?

The realization slams into me. Kiran—the man who seems like he couldn't care less for rules or tradition—is a Sulien?

...*Kiran* is a *Sulien?*!

Which makes him...

A gods-damn Archblood. Kiran is an Archblood. Just like Finlay. I suspected he was a highborn, but...I never thought he was practically as high up as a prince.

Pieces fall into place, illuminating what I should have noticed all along. His formidable fire-wielding. The tension between him and Finlay.

Gray and I exchange stunned glances. Behind him, Marcella's eyes widen in shock. She turns to whisper to the girl behind her whom she was speaking with earlier—a girl with warm-brown skin and hair like blackberries.

The bloodlines flood my mind in an instant. Where Fjolla stands for regality and honor, Sulien embodies ferocity and power. Together, they counterbalance the Dalmar bloodline—the third remaining progenitor line, defined by dominance and sovereignty. To think, if a Dalmar were sitting among them right now, I'd be staring at the completed Triad.

But even without a Dalmar present, with Kiran beside Finlay, I'm still looking at two legacy bloodlines.

Two members of Great Houses. Two Archbloods.

I swallow audibly, the sound unnervingly loud in my ears.

Well, that at least explains why I saw Kiran in the king's hall during The Founding celebration. Even if I still don't understand why he looked at me the way he did.

"There has always been a rigid dichotomy between their bloodlines' fire and ice magic," Gray whispers to me. "Their constant clashing and bickering makes a hell of a lot more sense now."

Indeed.

Kiran sighs quietly before boasting a wry grin. "Such pesky things, titles."

Arden shoots both of them an unamused look. "If you *both* are finished. Let's continue."

Finlay rips his agitated glare from a still-smiling Kiran and fixes his gaze back on Huxley. "What do you know about your flower?"

"Nothing other than what I feel, Captain Fjolla. I trained extensively in the arts of magic and combat, but little on herbs and plants."

Kiran cocks his head. "Would you like us to tell you its meaning?"

"Please," Huxley replies.

They all slide their eyes to Nuha, and a tiny throb aches in my heart at the softness resting within Kiran's gaze as he watches her, a look seemingly only reserved for her.

My eyes glide to Draven next, curious. As expected, he looks at her the same way he looks at everyone else—with complete neutrality.

Ever the stoic captain.

"Wouldn't we all like to know the meaning of our essence," she muses. "Visit my aggregate's wing, and perhaps you will find those answers in our library."

A flicker of annoyance flashes through Huxley's features, but he masks it quickly. "It would be a privilege to indulge in Philator's legendary collection of knowledge."

Nuha's lip curves up with amusement.

"What is your magic?" Arden asks.

"I have fortification magic."

My brows do a little jump, and I glance back at Draven, who is leaning in his chair, pinning Huxley with a keen-eyed stare.

Huxley then goes on to explain how his magic works. After, through a series of exchanged glances, the captains agree he may proceed onto the next test. Huxley bows at the waist before descending the stairs and heading straight for the exit. I watch as he tosses his essence flower to the side, discarding it like some worthless piece of trash.

The next noble ascends the stairs, and the captains go through a repetitive back and forth with her. Uninterested, I take the opportunity to interrogate Gray.

"So...cousin, huh?"

Gray glances at me apologetically before releasing a deep sigh. "He is my mother's sister's son. My mother...she was raised in Erandor Kingdom with her sister before leaving for Eden to become a Gardner. She left to forge her own path; her sister chose to marry a wealthy lord." He rakes a hand through his hair. "That's all I really know. She didn't like to talk too much about her past. She always said her life—her *real* life—began when she got to Eden." He shrugs. "I've had the misfortune of crossing paths with Huxley a few times. I used to pity him when we were younger because his mother died giving birth to him, and I think he secretly blames himself for that. But you can only offer someone so much pity."

I'm not sure what to do with all the knowledge. Knowledge that, despite being raised by her, I never knew.

It's not like Azalea originating from the Erandor Kingdom is an earth-shattering revelation or anything. It's just...it feels difficult. To reconcile someone you've known all your life—someone who had a hand in shaping who you are today—has a past, a life, you know nothing about.

In some twisted way—a way I recognize is illogical and probably selfish—it makes me feel lonely. Like I'm being forced to recognize things

I was perfectly content to turn a blind eye to.

I am not truly a part of the Nightenjoy family.

Azalea and Sterling are not my true parents.

My only parent is dead, the entirety of my family buried with her.

That small fissure in my chest cracks a little wider as emotion pounds a little harder. I blow out a loaded breath, shaking all the intrusive thoughts and damning feelings away. "Why weren't the healers able to save his mother?"

Gray rubs at his jaw. "I don't know," he admits. "That was always the unanswerable question."

I glance at him and catch the shift in his features. Attempting to lighten the mood, I lean into his side and ask, "So, any other arrogant and cruel family members I should know about?"

He huffs a laugh and knocks his shoulder into mine. "Gods, I hope not."

CHAPTER THIRTY-ONE

O n and on and on the judgements proceed.

I watch nobles grovel after facing rejection. Watch some throw tantrums from their first taste of being told *no*. One wildly foolish examinee, who presents an essence flower with venom seeping through its petals—an essence flower known as the Abdite's Bloom for its sure omen that a wielder will cave and access forbidden magic—actually attempts to strike at the captains with a lash of their magic.

It is met with an impenetrable shield of fire, ice, darkness, light, and air in an instant.

Within a blink, and with resounding force, a spear of darkness soars through the air and pierces his heart while an arrow made of radiant golden light shoots through his temples.

Chaos erupts.

Chaos that Draven immediately squashes. "*Enough,*" he snarls. "If you can't handle *this*—" he points at the dead body for emphasis— "then you should walk out now."

People remember themselves, settling down and thinking better of their loud murmurs. Two rejected nobles—I'm assuming friends of his— drag the body out of the arena, cursing the captains as they go.

I watch the lifeless body being hauled across the floor like nothing more than heavy baggage. A trail of blood follows it like a red shadow, and unlike most in the room, my eyes aren't turned down with pity or wide with silent horror.

Maybe watching someone die once is all it takes to forever be desensitized. Maybe my heart simply stopped lurching at the sight of death after that night of fire and regret. Maybe plunging a blade through someone else's chest—whether a mercy or not—makes me immune to the sorrows for the fallen.

Besides, his death had been quick. Painless. I will not waste my sympathies on such a pleasant way to go.

Though I will light a candle for him tonight so his soul may find its path to the afterlife. So that he will not remain in the dark, trapped.

Arden, now known to be a light-wielder, looks at Draven with amorous, expecting eyes after their display of teamwork. Draven merely gazes numbly at the lifeless body being dragged away. And that is something I'm not even going to attempt to dissect.

Fifty-five.

Of the one-hundred and nine starting examinees, and then after the seven who didn't make it back, the captains had only passed fifty-five wielders from the left line.

Now it's the turn of those in the right line to present.

"I can go first, if you'd like," Gray offers.

Wordless, I nod my head, grateful for his offer.

Gray ascends the stairs and stands tall in front of the captains. His astounding posture is natural—his regal grace undeniable. As I watch him, all I can think is that he seems like he belongs up there.

At the sight of Gray, Kiran sits up straighter in his chair. His mouth quirks up, and there is a new alertness in his eyes that hadn't been there before.

"Name," Finlay drawls unpleasantly, not bothering to hide his disdain.

He is no longer addressing the nobles' line, after all. Now, he addresses our line—those without titles or respectable bloodlines.

But only the former is true for Gray.

"Gray Nightenjoy," he declares levelly.

Kiran doesn't even bother trying to hide the smile spreading across his lips.

"Ah," Finlay coos, his tone shifting drastically. "So you are the

Nightenjoy who has come to us this year."

Gray dips his chin. "At your humble service."

Finlay peaks his fingers and presses them to his lips before pointing them at Gray. "You have quite the remarkable bloodline for magic. It is a baffling phenomenon why your line has not been officially titled."

"My father denies the rank and titles."

"Wise man," Kiran chirps. "Perhaps he could teach us all a thing or two."

Finlay shoots him an exasperated, pointed look. "Foolish is more like it." He swats at the air. "But that is neither here nor there. We are not judging you based on the decisions of your father. Though...I do hear he is *quite* the advisor. Sought out by many, I'm told."

With a clear, steady voice and a lifted chin, Gray replies, "I wouldn't know. He doesn't discuss such matters with me."

Arden, her voice heavy with exhaustion, interjects, "What is your flower?"

Gray reaches into his satchel and pulls out a cloth. He peels it away, revealing a medium-sized flower with petals resembling glass. They layer and twist in a seemingly infinite pattern. Within those translucent petals, light shifts constantly—vibrant blues melting into deep purples, transitioning into saturated greens and golds. At the flower's center rests an unchanging core of pure, brilliant light, encircled by intricate crystalline structures weaving together like a lattice of prisms.

My breath catches in my throat.

It's beautiful.

All the captains lean forward, their features twisted by equal measures of shock and awe. All except Draven, whose narrowed eyes are his only sign of interest.

"The King's Reflection," Nuha breathes. Her face scrunches together. "But that...that's...." She doesn't seem capable of finishing her sentence.

Finlay looks positively dumbfounded.

Not bothering to mask her growing irritation, Arden glances at Nuha and chides, "Care to explain to the rest of us how this is possible?"

"The King's Reflection is a flower that only blooms for those deemed worthy to be a king," Nuha elaborates. "Its lore and history date far, far back."

"That much I know," she responds in a short-tempered tone. "But deemed worthy by *who*? And *how*?"

"Does it matter?" Nuha counters. "The gods, the mystical forces at play in our world, the incomprehensible nature of magic...whatever it is, *whoever* it is, a person is deemed worthy. From there, the flower is meant to reflect the raw essence of that person and their relationship with magic. Who they *truly* are, down to their very soul. I..." Her eyes glance back to the flower then back up at Gray, curiosity framing her every feature. "I've never seen one bloom with such clarity...with such *purity*."

At those words, my chest swells with pride so immense, it nearly splits me open. I've always known these truths about Gray—have always seen the light and the goodness in him. Now everyone else knows, too. And it's indisputable—made incontrovertible by an essence flower.

Nuha seems like she's wrestling with a complicated equation. "What is your magic?" she finally asks, astonishment coating her every word.

Gray's tone remains calm. "Illusionary magic, Captain."

If Nuha, Arden, and Finlay weren't floored before, they certainly are now.

Nuha's brows knit together, as though trying to reconcile a glaring discrepancy. "But...that doesn't make sense. Someone with illusionary magic should have found some hallucinogen variant, or Phantom's Trap, or Murmuring Mirage." Her expression hardens. "You swear this flower is yours?"

Kiran scoffs. "Of course it's his flower. Have you, captain of an aggregate famed for its love of knowledge, suddenly forgotten that an essence flower blooms only in the hands of its rightful match?"

Nuha blinks, speechless, and Finlay remains uncharacteristically silent.

It's unsettling, actually—seeing him so silent.

"You all know what this means," Nuha murmurs so low, I can barely catch the words. "I'm not even sure when the last time something like this—"

"—It's only if it comes to that," Finlay interrupts. "If he"— he jerks his chin at Gray—"wants that."

Whether Gray understands the magnitude of his essence flower or not—though I suspect he does—his posture and expression give nothing away.

"I move to pass the Nightenjoy on to the second test," Draven says, lifting his hand.

"I second," Kiran chimes.

"Third," Arden adds.

Finlay leans back in his chair, dragging a hand over his face. "Fourth."

Nuha stares at Gray, still visibly perplexed.

Arden prompts, "Nuha?"

A sharp inhale paired with a long blink has Nuha snapping her attention back into focus. "Fifth."

Gray offers a deep bow at the waist. "Thank you for the opportunity." Carefully tucking the flower back into his satchel, he descends the stairs to stand at the end of our line, flashing me a quick, assuring smile as he passes.

Which means I'm next.

My knees wobble as I ascend the stairs, but I roll my shoulders back and keep my chin high. I wait for Finlay to ask my name as he has done with every other examinee, but it never comes. He just stares at me with cold judgement brimming in his icy eyes. Somehow, despite the growing tightness in my chest, I hold his scornful gaze and manage to suppress the urge to shift beneath the weight of it.

Finally, after an uncomfortable amount of passing silence, Kiran slices a disdainful glare at Finlay and addresses me. "Tell us your name, please." His voice is gentle.

I swallow back any remaining nerves. If I am to not let people like Finlay Fjolla win—to not give them any power over me, or let them best me in any way—it starts with going toe-to-toe, gazing at one another on equal ground.

Or at least, presenting the illusion that that's actually true.

I will not cower. I will not yield. I will not falter.

"Lyra Izacalli," I supply, holding my voice steady.

"Where do you come from, Lyra Izacalli? I do not recognize the name." Nuha's question enters the air softly.

My heart squeezes as Nuha addresses me.

Does she know I am the one who plunged the blade through Meiji's chest? That I am the reason the Abdite's ambushed us, forcing us to fight? I wonder how much Draven and Kiran told her...

My bout of strength is diluted by the haunts of that night. But I blow out a stabilizing breath, clenching and unclenching my hands.

"Rivara Kingdom."

Finlay makes a tsking noise and looks at me with such distaste, it's hard not to feel like I'm covered in dirt and grime. "I have seen you before, fluttering about in King Alastair's hall, entertaining drunken men for sport."

Arden tilts her head with interest. "Are you a courtesan?"

I do not let any emotion seep through my words. "A night attendant, actually."

Her brows pinch together as her lips tilt. "How interesting. And King *Alastair* let you go? Allowed you leave to compete in these exams?" Her features shift as a fresh line of thought clearly takes her in a different direction. "Or did you sneak away to be here? You can tell us. Jurafen serve no king, after all. But if you're a stowaway—"

"—That's enough, Arden." Draven bites the words out.

And Arden looks like he just openly wounded her.

Draven ignores her. "Perhaps we'd be better suited to focus on the task at hand—which is judging her based on her flower—instead of quizzing her about the king she served." He flicks his seafoam eyes to the honey resting within Arden's. "You said it yourself—Jurafen serve no king, so this conversation is irrelevant."

Did he just do that to help me? It's not that I had any intentions of telling them about my blood wager with the king, but his intervention sure made that task a hell of a lot easier.

"I cannot say that I'm in agreement," Finlay objects.

"Of course you're not," Kiran mutters under his breath, rolling his eyes.

Finlay shoots him a look. A look that is soon sharpened—if that is even possible—and redirected to me. "People expect Jurafen to be of a particular caliber. We garner respect—trust. Some king's whore that has fucked her way through every courtier and emissary within the Three Kingdoms is not exactly fitting of that description. In fact, she does it a great disservice by even being here, tarnishing the sanctity of the name. No one in their right mind will feel safe with some servant protecting them instead of a properly bred noble."

The ice necklace suddenly sits heavy at my throat. My fingers reach for it, clutching it gently. Thestis's freckle-filled face and tiny voice fill my mind.

Show Bathara we matter, too; that we aren't lesser than the others.

Make them see us.

And I promised him I would, and so I will.

I lift my chin and address Finlay. "With all due respect, if we are discussing the fate of my future, then why are you so focused on my past?"

Finlay grinds his teeth. "Because the past is a medium for which one can better understand the possibilities of the future, and we would be fools to ignore it."

I do not balk. "So is a fractured past a sure indication of a fractured future?"

"Fractured is as it sounds—broken. You can try to piece it together, but it will never be as strong and effective as something not already broken."

My eyes remain locked on him. "Do you know anything about plants?"

Finlay's white brows lower. "I beg your pardon?"

"Plants," I repeat. "Do you know anything about them?"

His lip curls as confusion pinches his face. "What nonsense is this?"

My hand lifts in tune with my idle shrug. "Nothing. It's just if you think broken things always remain weaker, you should really learn more about plants. A stem snapped clean in half, when given proper care, can mend into a more resilient version of itself."

His lips thin into a fine line. "Your point being...?"

My eyes do not leave Finlay Fjolla as I give him my answer. "Just that past damage does not imply permanent fragility. Nature shows us that." I make a show of frowning. "But by your logic, that isn't possible. So I ask you, *Captain*: who's correct here—you, or the forces of nature?"

Finlay's face practically goes purple from anger, and I don't fight the small curve tugging at the corner of my mouth. I glimpse at Draven, and I'm surprised to find him with a similar smirk on his face.

"As entertaining as this debate by analogy has been," Nuha begins, glancing between Finlay and me. "I'd much rather focus on the present. What is your flower?"

My heart picks up speed as I pull the wrapped flower from my pack.

Well, here we go.

I unveil it, and every Captain's head cocks.

"What...is *that*?" Arden asks, her brows scrunched.

Nuha leans forward in her seat, and her green eyes narrow on the flower.

Finlay slides his gaze toward her. "Nuha, do you recognize that? Is it *even* a true essence flower?" He sneers in my direction before glancing back at her.

Nuha takes her time before responding. "I...can't be sure. I certainly don't recognize it."

Resting his cheek on his fist, Kiran comments, "An unidentifiable essence flower? Finally, some fun around here."

All the captains shoot him a look. Well, all the captains except Draven, that is. With his elbows braced on his thighs and his fingers peaked at his lips, he watches me with silent interest.

I allow my eyes to linger on him for only a moment before I blow out a quiet sigh. "If I may," I say to them all, though I position my gaze on Nuha.

She inclines her head.

I remove the flower from its cloth and place it gently in my palm. Time to show them what Marcella and I discovered when I plucked it from its home.

The layered petals, which look as if they've been stitched together with dull, black threads, warm under my touch. Within seconds, some of the threads come alive with green and gold, while the others remain stagnant and black. The color pulses along the flower's seemingly living seams, glowing with a glittering light.

To be honest, if it hadn't done this, I also wouldn't have believed it was an essence flower. I would have remained certain that I had simply failed to detect my real one.

But now the looming question remains: what the *hell* is it, and what does it mean?

Truthfully, I'm far more frustrated than I care to admit not knowing about this particular flower. Because *of course* the one flower that perplexes me is my own. Though I at least hoped one of the captains might have answers.

But instead, they sit before me, looking every bit as dumbfounded as I feel.

Draven leans back in his seat, and I swear I catch a small twitch at the corner of his lips.

Arden glances between her fellow captains. "When is the last time an examinee has presented an unrecorded essence flower?"

Nuha studies me with scrutinizing eyes. "I'm not sure," she murmurs. "I will have to search through Bathara's archival records."

"And the records of every essence flower we know of," Finlay adds.

Arden's brows lower. "So how do we proceed? We cannot judge her on a flower we know nothing about."

"But we can judge her on the basis of her ability to detect and return with that flower," Kiran counters.

My eyes bounce between them, watching—waiting. I quickly glance at Draven, wondering if he'll ever add any input. But he remains still—focused. Almost as if he is waiting for something.

"I say we simply cut ties now and fail the girl." Finlay locks his aqua-colored eyes on me. "Let's be done with this fool's endeavor and prevent the girl any further..." He tilts his head with thought. "...humiliation." His nose wrinkles as he practically spits the last word.

"Such a brilliant idea," Kiran retorts dryly. "Relinquish the thing you know nothing about, simply because you don't understand it." Kiran cuts Finlay a pointed look. "I know I'm not alone in sensing there is a great magic simmering beneath her skin."

I blink, stunned at the words.

There is a...*what?*

"Which makes her all the more dangerous and further solidifies my reasoning."

"Reasonings that steer you in the wrong direction. *Again.*" Kiran quietly bites out the last word. The sentence feels oddly personal—laced with a familiarity exceeding mere camaraderie.

"There is no way to guarantee she won't become a threat to us, or a danger to those at Bathara." Finlay slides his eyes to me. "Tell me, girl—what is your wielder's mark?"

Shit.

"Unmanifested at the moment." The words tumble from my mouth a lot weaker than I'd like.

Even Kiran seems taken aback by that. He didn't know, after all. Only Draven did. His sapphire eyes round with apology as he watches me, as if to say, *I'm sorry. I tried.*

Finlay sits straighter in his chair. "My point has been made. There is no way to keep a check on the girl. To ensure she doesn't become a danger. Bathara has no room for wildcards. I move to officially fail her."

And just as my shoulders are about to sag from the weight of this failure, Draven's voice finally fills the room. "What if I train her? Assess her magic and observe her for the duration of her participation in these exams."

I have to actively fight against my jaw as it threatens to drop. Realization dawns on me, and his words from the other night clamor through me.

There's a rule against captains helping examinees during the exams. If I am going to train you, there will have to be good cause for the other captains to go along with it; I'll figure out a way to make it happen.

That's what he was waiting for.

His moment to manipulate the situation into exactly what he wanted. Terrifying...how good he is at that.

All the captain's eyes whip to Draven, and Kiran's heavily arched brow does not go unnoticed by me.

"You?" Finlay questions, disbelief clinging to his every word. "*Why?*"

Draven shrugs. "Because as Kiran said, it's unwise to eliminate something just because we don't understand it. The risks associated with a decision like that are too great." He turns to Nuha. "Nuha, can you track down any record of this essence flower before the exams end?"

Nuha glances at him. "I can certainly try."

Draven nods, as if that's all he needed to hear. "In the meantime, I will train her. It will allow me to keep her under constant observation while also reducing any associated risks. Considering every angle, it's our best option."

Arden's brows pinch together so forcefully, an indent forms between them. She frowns at Draven.

Kiran claps his hands together, that signature smirk of his already tugging at his lips. "Perfect. I move to pass her then."

Arden drags a hand down her face, her features suddenly appearing far more exhausted than before. "I will second the motion."

Nuha slides her eyes to Draven, where they linger silently.

He calmly shrugs under the watchful gaze. "My vote should be implied. Third."

Nuha's eyes remain on him, her expression giving nothing away. "I'm not sure what your motivations are for this...*uncharacteristic* display of yours, but I guess I don't need to understand you to support you." Her voice softens. "Will you provide us with reports of your observations when prompted? At least until I can locate any knowledge of her essence flower."

Draven dips his chin. "Of course."

She exhales a long sigh. "Then I see no reason to worry. I support passing her."

All eyes glide to Finlay, whose cold eyes remain locked on me.

I do not buckle beneath the weight of them.

"Fine," Finlay reluctantly agrees. "Let's indulge this silly game just a little bit longer."

In the quiet, dark hours of the night—or perhaps in the frigid, early moments before the inevitable dawn—I lie awake, staring at the ceiling, drenched in cold sweat.

Somewhere between tracing moonlit shadows and replaying the night's events—Gray passing, me advancing, Marcella being cleared to move on with flying colors, the captains once again left slack-jawed by her flower—I had drifted into a deep void of sleep.

In the gripping abyss, I had a blurry dream of shadows, ice, and fires. Arrows and daggers. Sobs and graves. So many graves. I heard echoes of screams and pleas for mercy. Shrills and shrieks reverberated from fallen bodies. Bones, clattered and broken, spread over the ground like trampled flowers across a field.

Two figures clashed. Magic swirled through the air like a hurricane of power.

The world burned.

The dream felt so real, yet so distant. Like I was there, watching, but had yet to truly reach the destination.

There were melancholy hums of laments for the lost and lullabies for the restless. There was a composition of scars. Stories of old mending with stories of new in hurried whispers of voices gone and present. The stars had sung a requiem in tears for the fallen. The darkness sang out a ballad for those broken. A hymn was played for that which was forgotten.

Someone calls out to me, waiting with an outstretched hand.

In the back of my mind, a haunted scream pierces through the void. Flames flicker. Something irreparably breaks. A heart never recovers.

Finally, at some point, my mind lulls and again gives way to the dark. Whether that darkness is from my eyes finally closing or succumbing to the scream in my head, I don't know. I just know that when I finally drift back to sleep, it is deep and dreamless.

CHAPTER THIRTY-TWO

I 'm eating in the mess hall the next morning when he finds me.

"Come on," Draven orders from behind me. "Let's go."

I pause, a bite of bread hovering midway to my mouth. "But I'm eating breakfast."

Draven arches a brow, heaves a long sigh, then grabs me under the arms and hauls me upright. My bread slips from my fingers, landing back onto my half-filled plate as he drags me forward. I throw a longing glance at it over my shoulder.

Across the table, Marcella elbows Gray. With a mocking swoon, she lilts, "Have fun!"

Gray glances at her and chuckles before offering me a sympathetic look as I'm dragged out by the six-foot-something tyrant.

Draven doesn't drop my wrist until we're out of the mess hall, through the winding corridors of the guest wing, and beyond the academy walls. To a place where the hills rise around us and the sound of a soft, trickling stream fills the sun-kissed air.

When he finally lets go and turns to face me, I look at him pointedly.

"What?" he asks, folding his corded arms across his chest, the fabric of his form-fitting, short-sleeve shirt doing nothing to hide the muscles beneath it.

Honestly, it's the first time I've noticed just how defined they truly are. Which I guess makes sense considering I've never seen him in short sleeves before. It's also the first time I've seen this much of his tattoo. The intricate design snakes up his arm—from the back of his hand, coiling around his wrist, winding over his forearm, up to his shoulder—disappearing beneath his shirt. As I study it, I realize that, given the way it's been inked to his skin, I can't actually distinguish it as a tattoo or a wielder's mark.

I wonder if that was intentional, and if so, why...

I brace my hands on my hips. "I tend to at least prefer a nice greeting before being dragged away from my breakfast."

"Maybe you should have woken up earlier," he counters.

"Maybe you should have told me you planned to start training first thing this morning."

He frowns. "When else would we begin? We only have seven days between now and your next test."

Fair point.

My gaze drifts around the space, and my lips curve at the sight. "This is pretty. It feels secluded, too, being tucked between the hills. It's nice."

He follows my gaze, nodding. "I figured you'd like training here. It helps me focus sometimes when I need to get away from the academy."

His admission catches me by surprise.

"Anyways," he says. "I did some thinking last night."

My brow curves up. "We didn't finish with judgments until the middle of the night," I point out. "When exactly did you have time for some thinking? Do you not sleep?"

He blows out a clipped noise that is beginning to sound more and more like a laugh. "Sleep finds me when it wants to. And when it doesn't..." He shrugs. "I think."

I study him a bit more closely. "Okay," I reply, the word drawn out. "And what is it you were thinking about so late in the night?"

"You," he answers matter-of-factly.

A hearth lights beneath my cheeks. "Oh?" I question. "And what about me?"

He makes a show of sighing, and he shoves a hand through his tousled waves. "Why were the Abdites after you? I've gone through potential reasons again and again, and it doesn't make any sense."

He begins to pace, and my warm cheeks are quickly doused. I swivel my eyes, following him as he strides back and forth.

"You claim to have recently manifested your magic. You don't have a wielder's mark. You don't come from any noble heritage or exceptional bloodline like your...*companion.*" There is an odd bite to the word as he mentions Gray. "So, why you?" He stops pacing and squares his shoulders to me as if I might actually have an answer.

But I think he quickly realizes my blank face is as clueless as the empty answers he keeps reaching for. "That's what I'd like to know," I mutter.

He bites his lip, brows pulling tight. "There has to be something. Something that made them search for you."

The way he says it...

My eyes narrow with quiet accusation. "Is that why you goaded the captains into letting you train me? So you can figure out what it is that makes them want me?"

His expression remains unreadable. "I'd be lying if I said it didn't add extra incentive, but... I told you I'd find a way. Your..." he pauses, considering his word choice, "...p*eculiar* flower simply provided me with the perfect opening." The corners of his lips tug upwards just slightly.

I click my tongue at the smugness in his tone.

He huffs with pleased amusement.

Draven claps his hands together. "Now, all of that aside, it's time to get to the reason we're out here—your training."

I fill my lungs with a deep pull of crisp air. "Alright. What's first? Sparring? Magic lessons? Weaponry?"

Draven grunts a low laugh under his breath. "You're not even remotely ready for that."

Despite myself, my mouth pops open. "What? I was learning to spar with Gray, and—"

"—and I am not him. I'll be training you how *I* see fit." He turns, surveying the surrounding hills as if looking for something. "Besides," he continues, glancing at me sidelong, "he coddled you. I assume it's because he's your lover, but he does you no favors by not pushing you."

I choke. "My...*what?*"

Draven's brows lower, and he frowns at me. "Your lover. It was obvious he was going easy—"

"—No, no, I got that part. What I can't understand is where you got Gray being my *lover* from?"

"Well, is he not?"

"No," I say through a choked laugh. "I mean, there was this one night after we both consumed *way* too much wine where we fooled around, wondering if maybe..." My eyes go distant as I drift into that memory. It's hard not to laugh at it now. I shake my head, amusement tugging at my lips. "Anyway, it was weird, and we both agreed never again."

"So he's truly just a friend? The two of you seem closer than that."

I hesitate, thoughtful. "Gray and I... I've never quite known how to define us, honestly. He's more than a brother to me, and I suppose I do love him as deeply as anyone could ever hope to be loved, as he does me. But there are no romantic feelings between us."

My heart squeezes as—for once—it considers what it feels for something. For someone.

"If love could ever be reduced to a connection that simply exists between two souls, that is what we are. An unbreakable bond, tethered together, willing to share in all of each other's good and bad."

Draven's jaw flexes—subtly, but enough. His gaze drops to the ground. "I understand completely." Then, without warning, he sucks in a sharp breath. "So, about that training."

❧ ☙

"What in the realms of Kala is the *point* of this?" I whirl around on Draven, who stands with a smug grin and a curved brow behind me.

He chuckles lowly and lifts a lazy hand. "I've already told you. It's your training."

I turn back around and blink at the scene. Wedged between two large hills, above a constant stream pouring from a nearby waterfall, is a thick, fallen tree covered in lichen.

I point at it. "And how is crossing *that* supposed to help me become a better wielder?"

He sighs. "I just explained that to you. There are four key elements to becoming both a skilled combat fighter and a formidable wielder."

"Yes," I confirm, pinching the bridge of my nose. "I know. Balance, endurance, strength, and control."

Draven lifts a challenging brow. "Well if you know, then why are you asking me?"

I click my tongue at him. "Because," I reply. "I thought the things we did would be related to *actual* combat."

Draven's eyes don't waver. "Who said they're not?"

I cut him a sharp glare. "Don't patronize me."

"Wouldn't dream of it."

I bite down on my growing irritation and resist the urge to roll my eyes. "You know," I challenge a bit haughtily. "I still don't know *anything* about you. How can I even be sure I should trust you to train me?"

"I can make that question easy for you: you shouldn't."

I wait for him to crack a smile or huff even the smallest of laughs, but he doesn't. "Alright," I drawl. "Be that as it may, I would feel a hell of a lot better knowing at least something about the person I'm placing the hopes of my future in." I pause. "For instance, what kingdom do you come from?"

Draven lifts a dark brow. "Answering questions about myself was never a part of our deal."

"We can change that," I bait with a cloying tone. "Perhaps a wager of sorts."

He huffs a laugh and flicks his peculiar, mismatched eyes to the blood droplet resting on my finger. "I would think you were through with wagers."

"Consider this an exception."

He shifts his weight back on his heels and folds his arms. "Alright. What do you propose?"

I hum with thought and pinch my chin between my thumb and index finger. "For every task you give me that I successfully complete, you must answer three questions of my choosing."

Draven's brows shoot up. "Three?"

I nod, reaffirming the number. "Mhm. Three."

He watches me for a long moment. "Alright," he replies. "Three questions." Just when I am about to lift my chin with victory, his low voice counters, "*But* if you're unsuccessful, *you* have to answer three questions of *my* choosing."

My feet guide me forward toward the horizontal tree, and I huff a laugh. "Fine. It's not like you don't already know all there is to know about me."

"I highly doubt that."

I glance at him over my shoulder, the ghost of an inscrutable smile resting on his lips. My brows pinch together, but I reorient my gaze forward and bend down to remove my combat boots and socks. A warm wave floods through me as my bare feet kiss the ground. I've almost forgotten how much I love the feeling.

Carefully, I step up and onto the large, waxy tree trunk.

Draven stops me. "What do you think you're doing?"

Confused, I turn and blink at him. "Uhm, what you told me to do?"

He strides over, closing the distance in remarkably few steps, and tilts his chin up to look at me. "Oh," he drawls in a voice that sends warning signals skating down my skin. "Surely you don't think my task for you is as simple as just walking across a fallen tree, do you?"

Yes?

Not that I would exactly call the assignment "easy" by any means. The bark is slick and caked with lichen—which retains moisture. Not to mention, it's not that the tree is far enough to make the fall into the stream deadly or anything, but it is certainly high enough to make it unpleasant.

"Considering the way you asked that," I grumble. "I'm going to guess no."

"Smart girl," he muses with far too much enjoyment.

This time I let my eyes roll. "So, what's the twist?"

Draven's smirk turns pointed. Without further explanation, he pulls a black, silky cloth from his back pocket and dangles it in the air. "You will cross while wearing this."

I cock my head and frown. "Is that...a *blindfold?*"

Draven's tiny huff of laughter is his only confirmation.

My gaze shifts from the silky blindfold to him. I arch a suspecting brow and point at it. "Do you always carry that thing around?"

He shrugs lazily. "When I need it."

My brow arches higher. "And how often is that?"

Taunting lines curve his lips as he just watches me with wry amusement humming in his eyes.

"Staring at me is not an answer," I point out, lowering my chin further to fully meet his gaze since, propped up on the tree, I'm about a head taller than him.

"You haven't earned the right to ask a question yet," he taunts. And I swear he flicks his eyes to my lips. But it's so quick, I'm convinced I simply imagined it.

I hold his lingering stare defiantly. "Well, I'm about to." I snatch the blindfold from his fingers. "Now, will you at least explain to me the *point* of wearing this?"

Draven's gaze doesn't let go of me. "People rely too much on what they see, and that becomes a weakness. Our minds twist images into what we *want* them to be—or at least what we think them to be. Seldom does reality truly align with our perceptions. That—" he nods toward the blindfold resting between my fingers "—will help you distinguish between lies and truths. It will also force you to sense. To feel."

The way he says those last two words does not go unnoticed.

Still...he has a point, actually.

I glance down at the blindfold. "Unfortunately, your reasoning makes sense," I mumble dryly.

Draven's head tilts, and I realize he still hasn't looked away from me. "Unfortunate for who, exactly?"

My brows lower. "Me, obviously." Then, I blow out a sigh and turn back to face the length of the sprawling tree—fig, maybe?—and tie the blindfold over my eyes.

Darkness consumes my vision, and suddenly, every sound sharpens while sensations hum with clarity. The air is rich with earth and damp moss, grounding me as I take my first determined step forward—

Only to immediately slip on a patch of lichen.

My stomach lurches, and then I'm falling.

But before the stream can claim me, an arm hooks around my waist, yanking me backward into something solid.

The impact steals the breath from my lungs, and for a dizzying moment, the only thing keeping me upright is the arm braced around me. Heat seeps through the fabric of my shirt, and when I realize it is coming from another body—*his* body—my mind isn't focused on the near fall. It's sharpened into jarring focus on him.

The broad chest pressed against my back.

The steady rise and fall of his breathing.

The way his fingers tighten—just for a second—before settling flat on my waist.

And then there is the sensation of something soft grazing the tip of my ear as a brush of air caresses my skin. "Looks like I'd better start thinking of my three questions," he teases in a low voice.

My breath catches, and a shiver races down my spine, the traitorous thing.

Yet a defiant fire flickers to life inside me. I clear my throat, ignoring the way my pulse stumbles and the warm thrill humming beneath my skin. I lift my chin and keep my voice smooth. "Don't get ahead of yourself. I haven't fallen yet."

I shift, signaling that I'm ready to step forward—ready to be released and to try again.

But he doesn't let go. Not immediately, at least.

"Because I chose to catch you," he points out. I can hear the wry smile clinging to his words.

His fingers stay at my waist—a sensation that is heightened with my sight stripped from me—just long enough for me to feel the calloused tips of his fingers, the press of his palm on my body.

Then, as if the moment never happened, he releases his grip on me entirely and steps back. From somewhere behind me, Draven chides with humor, "But I won't catch you this time. Balance, or fall."

Bastard.

I blow out a steadying breath and feel around with my feet, trying to memorize exactly how many steps stand between me and falling. I give myself somewhere around a half-step margin for error.

Fantastic odds.

There was once an entertaining troupe King Alastair hired for one of his parties. They had a woman who could walk across a string. Baffled and awed, I found her at the end of the party and questioned her extensively about how she did it. She provided me with a few techniques—a few tips and tricks. But when I tried to balance across a small gardening ledge, Gray my "wide-eyed" audience, I fell into moist soil and caked my face with dirt.

No matter.

I at least remember one of her biggest tips: spread your toes and stay centered.

Keep center, I can do that.

I take a small step forward, and relief calms me when I don't immediately slip and fall. I splay my arms out, attempting to steady myself, and my toes creep forward inch after inch, staying in line with the heels of my feet.

It's a rather interesting sensation, walking across a mossy, algae-ridden fallen tree trunk. My feet feel every impression with stark clarity, and I now notice the undertones of smells that weren't there before. Every rustled leaf, shift in the stream, chirp from a bird—my ears hear it all. Hell, even my skin picks up on sensations—a dip in the breeze's temperature, a trickle of moisture in the air from the flowing stream.

Maybe Draven, despite all of that smugness, is onto something here.

At the thought of Draven, my mind can't help but replay the moment he slammed my body into his, catching me. The way his fingers twitched at my hip, like they were in a war with themselves to hold me tighter or let me go. And I am certain those were his lips that grazed my ear. But what's more concerning than the touch itself is the way my body reacted to it. The way it hummed. Awakened. The way I—

My foot slips, and I fall into the stream.

Chapter Thirty-Three

I'm wringing out my hair besides Draven in a patch of fluffy grass wedged between the hills.

Dozens.

I attempted to cross dozens and dozens of times. And not once could I do it.

Draven attributed it to me relying on my sight too heavily. According to him, it's not that I'm incapable of balancing, it's that I'm incapable of doing it without my vision.

I fight the urge to groan with frustration.

The roar of the waterfall is a pleasant hum from this distance, and the grass features sporadic bursts of wildflowers. Draven is laying casually a few feet from me, his hands interlocked behind his head. I flick my eyes to him and don't attempt to mask my dry sarcasm. "If that was only my first task, I'm brimming with excitement for the next three."

Draven's amused grunt is his only reply.

I bite down on my lip, stealing another glance at him. He looks so peaceful right now. "Any chance I can get a hint?" I push.

"You'll find out when you find out."

"Goodie," I grumble.

My fingers are twisting my damp hair back into a braid when the grass rustles, and Draven sits up, resting his forearm against his propped knee. "I believe I'm entitled to three questions now."

"And I'm sure I have three answers," I reply with no small amount of sass. I catch the subtle curve of his brow, and it makes my lips curl with delight.

"We'll see," he counters.

I huff a clipped laugh then finish my braid. After, I stretch my hands behind me, propping myself up comfortably.

If I'm going to answer gods-only-know-what, I might as well be comfortable while doing it.

I shoot him a look. "Well? Ask away."

"So impatient," he drawls with another arch of his brow.

"Patience is a virtue," I say through a dramatic sigh. "And one I've never claimed to have."

He hums, watching me for a long moment. I am seconds away from interjecting again, when his lips part, and he asks his first question. "Why didn't you let yourself feel anything at Meiji's passing ceremony?"

The question steals the air from my lungs. "I'm sorry?" All hints of sass, sarcasm—any bit of life I was exhibiting has been robbed from my words.

"You watched his life be drained right in front you. You held him while he was bleeding. You listened to his final words and assumed the weight of a dying man's request. Then, you plunged a blade through his heart. Even a seasoned Jurafen would struggle with the emotional weight of that, but you?" His eyes lock onto mine as if he can find the answers resting within them. They do not let go. "You didn't let yourself even flinch." He does not say it like a compliment. "I'm not saying you needed to shed tears for him or react a certain way, but you just...carried on. As if nothing happened."

He certainly wastes no time getting to the point.

My gaze is distant. "So your question is what, exactly?

"What in life hardened you to be capable of withstanding the weight of something like that without grieving, if only for a moment?"

In a way, the question threatens to upend my world. Like when someone is fighting tears, willing their eyes not to betray them and leak, but then someone else asks them if they are alright, and the dam holding everything at bay suddenly crumbles. Once you've brought attention to the thing, it demands to be felt. It's like a law of the universe or something.

But I'm not one to follow laws of anything, and I refuse to feel.

I take a minute to lay brick after careful brick around any potential emotions regarding that night. I will not go there; I will not remember. But the wall is not secured fast enough, and a few shadows slip through the jagged cracks.

You do not let this break you.

You do not let them win.

I love you.

My eyes fall, staring at the emerald blades of grass as they bend and sway like a dance to the wind's song. I exhale a trembling breath. "I am no stranger to death," I murmur. "Even the devastating ones."

I feel Draven's eyes on me for a long, long time. It's like he wants to say something else, but instead chooses not to. And it's not that I think Draven is one to offer pity or sympathy, but just in case, I clear my throat, steady my jaw, and lift my eyes. "That's one. You have two left."

His head tilts just slightly as he continues watching me, and I may be imagining things, but I swear I can see the lines on his normally rough face soften, if only a little. "You have no desire to actually be a Jurafen, do you?"

I exhale slowly through my nose. "Do you want a pretty lie or an ugly truth?"

"An ugly truth." His voice softens. "Always the ugly truth."

"No," I admit. "I don't."

"So why risk death? Why forge on for a life where each breath is considered a lucky one—where Merikh watches you, waiting for you to slip so he can claim you?"

I shrug. "You already know why."

He watches me for a long time, as if trying to solve something. "Were you truly treated so poorly that this life was the better option?"

My lips twitch with the attempt to smile, but it seems those muscles are just as fatigued as my other ones. "At least this life comes with honor and respect. With people's eyes watching you with awe instead of unchecked hunger." I tug at the grass. "My life was forever forfeit blood-sworn to King Alastair. And even though it breaks my heart to admit, I resigned myself to that fate. But then a light appeared, and I simply...followed it." I glance upwards, and my eyes meet Draven's with surprising ease. Like it's the most natural thing in the world. "This is where it led me."

Our gazes linger, something tightening in my chest as they do. I blow out a breath and shrug. "Plus, I have people counting on me now, and I don't intend on letting them down." My fingers toy with the ice necklace at my throat.

"And does that make you happy?"

I huff a wistful laugh—the hollow sound wrapping around my heart with a sad ache. "I've already given you four questions," I point out, my voice a shade above a whisper.

The corner of his lip tugs up. "Might as well make it five, then."

A ghost of a smile flickers across my face. "Is anyone?" I ask him. "Truly happy, I mean."

He looks away from me, off into the distance. His voice drops into a low murmur. "I don't think I'm the most qualified person to answer that."

"Which makes you entirely qualified to answer."

His mouth curves up gently. There is a long, passing silence, and I think perhaps the conversation has reached its natural end. Until, with his eyes still locked on the distant horizon, Draven speaks again in the most tender voice I've heard him use. "Maybe happiness will find us like some phenomenon finding its sky. Maybe when...rocks fly." He huffs a laugh under his breath, as if amused with himself, and shakes his head. "Yes, that's it." He turns those bright eyes back at me. "You and I can be happy when rocks fly."

"Hmm...magic or no magic?"

His lips tug up just a little farther. "No magic."

I make a show of thinking before mocking defeat. "It appears you and I will be miserable grouches for a while longer, then."

For the first time, I realize he has a small dimple in his left cheek. "It appears so."

For the rest of the day—right up until the sun and moon pass like forbidden lovers, forever near but never touching—I attempt all the training tasks Draven has planned.

Strength? Carry two buckets full of water with a stick up a hill and down again. Twist? Do it blindfolded, and do it one hundred times.

Control? Perform a series of slow, deliberate movements utilizing precise muscle control and controlled breathing, focusing on regulating my responses and internal state. Twist? Do it blindfolded, and stand on one leg half the time, continuing the slow motion movements without falling. Oh yeah, and try not to get distracted as he lobs pebbles at my head.

Endurance? Well, that one's pretty straightforward, actually. I just run a shit ton. Until my lungs are spasming and burning like the fiery waters of Illithious Lake. And I get to do it without a blindfold, so that's nice at least. But the twenty-six mile quota he set for me isn't exactly friendly.

Now, after a long day of defeat—and questions, seeing as I didn't successfully complete one task—I am exhausted. Marcella, thankfully, senses my weary exhaustion, and as I return from the bathing chambers, she doesn't attempt to pry about my day nor discuss hers. She just offers some brief, friendly chatter before blowing out the wick and casting the room in darkness.

Every fiber in my body is ridden with fatigue, yet sleep does not lull me away. Instead, my mind—the ever-defiant thing—replays scenes with Draven over and over again.

Thank the Mother he didn't ask me any more heavy questions after that first round. Instead, the questions became silly, almost childish things.

"What's your favorite color?"

"Sage."

"What's your favorite food?"

"Pickled cucumbers."

"If you could be any animal, what would it be?"

"A wolf."

Then there was the other line of questions.

"What do you love doing most?"

"The art of Gardning."

"Oh? How did you learn that?"

"My mother was a Gardner and taught me all that she knew."

"Well, what's your favorite flower, then?"

"Nox's Caelum."

It's almost laughable, how juvenile his questions felt.

My mind shifts from his words to the moments where he was so close, I could feel the warmth of him. The moments where his citrus scent enveloped me. Where his fingers touched me—whether simply correcting my form or in passing—and seemed to linger just a moment longer than usual. And then my stomach flutters with this...feeling.

I grit out a scowl and shut both my mind and body down.

Traitors.

Desperately needing to focus on something else, I reach for Casimir Vivaldri's journal, sliding it out from beneath my pillow and setting it next to me. I lean over and relight the oil lantern next to my bed, praying to the gods I dimmed it enough to where it won't wake Marcella up. Then, I prop myself against the small headboard, slide my feet back to cradle the journal in my lap, and thumb through the pages until I find where I left off.

A quick glance at the page shows me it's another short entry.

I read it.

I fear Magaius is beginning to walk a treacherous path.

I cannot be certain. There is much he has been hiding from me lately. But he appears to be...different.

There's a caged power surging within him. I can sense it. But this power is different than how it once was. I know he loves his newly founded kingdom, and I know he will do whatever it takes to preserve it, but I fear that perhaps he has crossed a line that cannot be uncrossed. Has committed an action I don't even want to cement in ink.

I spoke with Sitara privately about the matter. She plans on speaking with him, for he will not openly speak with me—or anybody else for that matter. But if anyone can get Magaius to tell the truth—to see reason or even to turn for a new path—it is Sitara.

She consistently reaffirms that my beliefs in humankind are not misplaced.

Casimir

I search my memory, trying to place the names.

That's right—Casimir said Sitara and Magaius were his two closest companions. He had also written about Magaius before, claiming that Magaius was openly supporting war—supporting stopping those they called the "Restorationists" with swift, brute force.

I wonder what Casimir meant by treacherous, and I wonder what line he suspected Magaius had crossed. He mentioned a surging power, something he did not want to write about. Could it be that Magaius corrupted his wielder's mark? Began wielding forbidden magic? What if the "treacherous path" he was on was becoming an Abdite...or something like it?

For some reason, the thought sends an icy chill skittering down my spine.

With a new wave of curiosity, I read the next entry.

War is here, officially.

I am filled with too much heartache to write about it. To discuss the politics surrounding it. But it is here, and I am forced to swallow the acidic truth that perhaps Magaius may have been right all along.

Yet even now, with the pointed future threatening to plunge through me, my mind still wonders:

Was this truly the only way?

My mind can't help but echo the question.

Was it? Was there truly no other way for them to find peace?

My eyes start to grow heavy. But I push past the sleep now threatening to claim me and read on to the next entry.

Today, I saw rivers of blood. Saw glazed over eyes staring up at a sky they will never see again.

My sword plunged into a boy—just a mere child. Life faded from his eyes like a retreating wave returning home from a shore. My stomach twisted, and the only sounds I could hear were the stuttering attempts at my own breathing. Nausea coiled in my gut, and I was overcome with the urge to vomit.

Once the battle was over, many clapped me on the back and praised me for my performance on the battlefield. They call my skills "unrivaled" and "astounding". Yet when I flick my eyes down to my blood-soaked palms, my lip curls with disgust. Are mortals so barbaric that we praise the murders of innocent children? They didn't ask for war—to be placed on that battlefield. They were probably goaded into false excitement, offered promises of honor, glory, and wealth. If I had plunged my sword through that boy's chest in the street, I'd be labeled a vicious murderer who deserved to hang. A disgrace to the gods and our mortal race. But under the terms of war, a child's murder is seen as a necessity over an atrocity, and I am praised instead of hanged.

Perhaps there is little hope for our existence, after all.

At that, I close the journal, my eyelids no longer able to withstand the weight threatening to shut them. I slide the journal back underneath my pillow, and I fold my hands together, laying my cheek upon them as thoughts that I'm too tired to fully process crash into me.

And as I am swept into Kala's, the goddess of dreams, realm, I begin to see a portrait of the words I just read. Of a man bound by duty and dedication to his kingdom plunging a sword through a child's chest, despite wanting peace. Of crimson—deep and rich—staining the otherwise unblemished hands. I see him scrubbing those stained hands in a river, again and again, the vomit coming after the panic. The scene shifts, and when I flick my eyes down again, it is I who am on the battlefield, my hands painted in warm crimson.

Then, like a passing traveler humming a distant tune, Casimir's words linger softly.

Perhaps there is little hope for our existence, after all.

Chapter Thirty-Four

Four days have passed.

I still haven't completed any of Draven's tasks. Which means over these past four days, I've been asked a *hell* of a lot of questions, and frankly, I'm beginning to wonder what Draven could possibly have left.

At this point, I think he knows more about me than I know about myself.

As I shuffle to our usual meeting spot between a set of lush, rolling hills, prepared for another day of valiant effort but bitter failure, surprise rolls through me when I glimpse multiple people waiting for me along with Draven.

I approach like a deer entering a den of lions, thrown off by their unexpected presence. Kiran halts his conversation with Draven and slides his eyes to me. He offers me a quiet smirk and a small dip on his chin. Marcella, Gray, and Griff are locked in a conversation of their own, Gray noticing me before the other two. He smiles at me sheepishly, as if he knows I have no idea what the hell is going on and is attempting to apologize for that in advance.

Marcella and Griff turn from their—what appears to be slightly heated—conversation and greet me at the same time. "Lyra!"

Marcella shoots him a pointed look before striding over to meet me. "You're here," she says, excitedly taking my hands in hers.

I arch a cautious brow at her.

What in god's veins is going on?

"I am," I confirm, my words tentative. "Though, I don't know why everyone else is." I make sure my words aren't sharp or biting.

"Ah," Marcella says with a smile. "I'll let Draven explain that."

As if summoned, Draven saunters over and stops a few feet from me, folding his arms and tilting his head as he watches me.

I look at him expectantly, and when he doesn't immediately explain, I sigh. "Want to fill me in on all—" my hands do a sweep of everyone "—this?"

It's not like I'm not thrilled to see them, I'm just...confused. Plus, the last thing I need is a whole audience watching me fail at my assignments.

Draven drops his arms from his rather broad chest. "In light of the second test happening in two days, we are not going to be working on your tasks today."

Oh, thank the Mother.

"Instead," he continues. "We are going to work on hand-to-hand combat. I've asked them—" he jerks his chin toward everyone "—to help me. You can learn a lot by observing, and often those best at combat have picked up different techniques from skilled fighters before them." He pauses. "Plus, I thought their presence might make you more...comfortable." It's not that I would call his final sentence timid or anything, but as far as Draven goes, that was pretty close.

A small wrinkle forms in my brow. "So, I'm just observing?"

Draven grunts, amused. "Oh, no. You'll be sparring. But for now, you will watch, and we will teach."

Kiran clears his throat. "To be clear, *I* am not teaching anything. After all, captains helping examinees is strictly prohibited unless specified otherwise, like in Draven's case. I am only here to spar with my fellow captain, hoping to increase my own combat abilities." His smirk widens as he makes a show of shrugging lazily. "But I can't control it if you decide to watch us and learn something in the process." He winks at me.

I laugh, shaking my head at Draven. "Your ability to manipulate the rules never ceases to amaze me."

"Actually," Kiran cuts in, a wry glint in his eye. "I am far better at manipulating the rules than Draven."

"You know," I mutter. "I don't doubt that."

He inclines his head, smiling.

I chuckle, glancing at everyone. "So you are sparring Kiran," I say to Draven. "And I can understand why Gray and Marcella are here, seeing as they're both incredibly skilled in hand-to-hand, but..." My eyes halt when they land on a grinning Griff. I jab a thumb at him. "Why is Griff here?" I pause. "No offense."

He shrugs. "None taken."

"He asked to come," Draven drones flatly.

The corner of my mouth kicks up, amused. I glance back at Griff. "You did? Why?"

"Because," he drawls through a pout. "I didn't want to miss all the fun."

✷❧ ☙✷

We all follow a weed-infested trail between the hills, leading us to a flat patch of land near one of Bathara's many waterfalls, where large river stones are positioned in a wide circle. As if following some unbeknownst-to-me, premeditated schedule, Draven and Kiran stroll toward the circle, and Gray, Marcella, and Griff line up around the sides.

A pointed smirk curls Marcella's lips. "This is going to be good."

Griff nudges her and cracks a grin. "Damn right it is. Not everyday you get to watch one captain spar. Let alone *two*."

She watches him side-long for a passing moment.

Gray cocks his head with consideration. "Truthfully, I'm excited to see how my own abilities might compare to someone of their status."

Griff snorts. "Get ready for an ego-deflating reality check, then."

Marcella barks a laugh.

And I just swivel my head as they chatter, a notch wedged in my brow.

Draven strides to one end of the circle while Kiran strolls to the other. In unison, they both pull their shirts over their heads, and both Marcella and I suck in a loud breath. Gray and Griff both arch pointed brows at us, and I simply shoot a look back at each of them.

"Don't think I've forgotten you two's victory march when we entered the academy."

They glance at each other, both their lips thinning.

"Fair enough," Gray replies, an undertone of amusement licking his words.

Marcella leans over to me, her eyes not leaving Kiran and Draven as they begin stretching their...*considerable*...muscles. "I'll share if you will," she mumbles.

I huff a laugh, my eyes still glued to the broad, impeccably defined chest belonging to Draven. My eyes flick to Kiran's toned, clearly capable body next.

Gods.

And why do Draven's arms have to be so...sculpted?

I'm also now certain his tattoo is meant to mingle with his wielder's mark, seeing it on full display.

A circular scar of mangled skin marks the base of his shoulder, and from it, whorls of black tendrils twist and lace down his arm, curling until they meet his wrist. At the crook of his elbow, the design shifts—a swirl of tiny black, dust-like dots, converging into a diamond of pure darkness. From that center, a wisp of smoke rises, unfurling into an ornate pattern stretching across his chest, twisting like roots. The design winds toward his left pectoral, where a thin-lined shield is inked over his skin, intricate script scribbled within its details. Parallel to it all, surrounding the shield, a still night sky lingers—a crescent moon and its precious stars frozen in ink.

With the design and placement of everything, it's nearly impossible to distinguish which parts are from a handmade tattoo and which parts belong to his wielder's mark.

I remember what Gray said in the valley. *You either put a target on your back for being too strong, or you put one on your back for being too weak.*

Clever solution.

Kiran's mark is also interesting. Where most wielder's marks look like tattoos—such as Draven's—Kiran's is nothing of the sort, looking instead like a burn scar branded onto his skin. It's made up of tendrils of flame wrapping along his left forearm, rising to meet a burning sun blazing at the crook of his elbow.

Draven cracks his neck, rolling his shoulders loose as Kiran bends low to stretch, his smirk firmly in place. He rises and slowly draws back his hair before giving Draven a slow grin. "This certainly takes me back."

Draven huffs a quiet laugh. "Sentimental, are we?"

Kiran clutches at his own heart. "Oh, come now, Draven. You know I've always been the sensitive one." He mocks a pouty lip, but his eyes remain sharpened with that wry glint.

They speak as if they've known each other all their lives.

Draven grunts, shaking his head. "You and I both know that isn't true."

Then, he moves.

Kiran's smirk doesn't falter as he reacts instantly. He barely deflects Draven's first strike, a sharp jab aimed at his ribs. The force sends him back a step, but he uses the momentum to pivot, already countering.

Draven catches the attack mid-motion, deflecting the blow off his forearm before driving his elbow toward Kiran's side. Kiran twists at the last second, absorbing the impact with a controlled exhale.

"Not bad," Kiran muses, stepping back into a relaxed stance, rolling out his wrist. "If I didn't know any better, I'd think you were showing off a little bit." The corner of his lip kicks up. "There wouldn't be a reason for that, would there?"

I catch Marcella's sidelong glance.

Draven adjusts his footing, a sharp curve tugging at his lip. "And if I didn't know any better," he counters, voice edged in warning, "I'd say you've gotten slower."

Kiran laughs, something awakening behind his eyes. "No, just warming up. I hate pulling my hamstring, you know." Then he attacks.

The air crackles with the force of their exchange. And god's *veins* they move with such remarkable speed—strike, counter, block, feint, counter again. Kiran's movements flow like water, elegant and fluid, while Draven strikes like a blade, sharp and unyielding.

Kiran twists, faking a low kick before snapping his leg toward

Draven's ribs. Draven barely blocks, the force making him skid back a fraction.

Draven's lips tug with the makings of a pleased smile. "Has the lion finally come out to play?"

Kiran shrugs, dusting dirt from his surprisingly defined chest. "Perhaps."

And I realize—this is nothing more than a game to them.

Draven's words from the valley echo in my mind.

I don't lose. Ever.

Well, time to test that theory.

Kiran parries, then ducks low, pivoting smoothly behind Draven. He aims a strike at his back. But Draven is already spinning, blocking mid-air. Their arms lock, eyes meeting.

Kiran's grin widens. "Predictable."

Draven smirks. "Funny. I was about to say the same thing."

Kiran reads the movement but reacts a second too late. Draven hooks a leg behind his knee, sweeping him off balance. Kiran stumbles— but it would seem he's more nimble than he looks, because he twists in mid-air, landing smoothly on his feet like a cat.

I tilt my head at the movement and can't help but to wonder if he can teach me that. It would be a hell of a party trick, if not just a powerful combat skill.

Kiran exhales slowly, brushing strands of fallen hair from his forehead. "You've always loved throwing me to my back."

Draven shrugs. "It works."

Kiran chuckles, shaking his head.

They reset themselves, and this time, Kiran takes the offensive, landing two quick jabs—one to Draven's shoulder, the other just missing his jaw. Draven catches his wrist on the third attempt, twisting it hard enough to make Kiran wince before yanking him forward. Draven drives his knee toward Kiran's ribs, but Kiran breaks free just in time, twisting out of his grip and countering with a kick.

One that Draven barely dodges, Kiran just grazing past his head.

Draven's responding smirk is razor-sharp. He moves—quick and smooth—and shifts his weight, twists, and sweeps Kiran's legs out from under him. Kiran hits the ground with a loud *thud.*

He takes a moment before propping himself up on a knee, bracing his weight on his thighs to stand. "You really must stop doing that," Kiran sighs.

Draven tilts his head, a frown pulling on his lips. "Stop letting me get away with it."

Kiran nods, flicking his brows up, before lunging again. This time faster. Sharper.

I remain still, watching how they move. Noting the way they predict, adapt, strike, evade. They waste nothing. Their every movement, every action—I realize it has a purpose.

Draven catches Kiran's next punch and yanks, twisting him midair before slamming him—quite unceremoniously—onto his back. *Hard.* The sheer force of it is enough to make me wince.

Marcella lets out a low whistle that seems to echo through the hills.

Griff, through his wince, murmurs, "That had to hurt."

Kiran stares up at the powdery-blue sky, blinking. Finally, he sits up and runs a hand through his tousled red hair. "Gods, you *truly* love doing that."

Draven's lips curve into a smile as he offers Kiran his hand. "And you truly love letting me."

Griff slides his attention to Gray and mutters under his breath, "How's your ego doing?"

Gray wears a subtle smile. "Not terrible, actually."

Kiran takes his hand, and Draven pulls him up. They regard each other for a moment, their palms clasped firmly together, before Kiran huffs a laugh and drops his hand. "I'm going to find a nice stream to freshen up in."

He heads off in the other direction, and Draven turns and approaches me. Something begins fluttering in my chest as the sun glistens off his sweat-slicked skin, and I swallow once he stops directly in front of me.

He blows out a slow exhale. "Did you learn anything?"

Gray, Marcella, and Griff swivel their gazes toward me, and I can't tell if my cheeks burn from the attention, or from the fact that Draven looks so... appealing.

I lift my chin. "I did, actually."

Draven tilts his head. "Do share."

The fluttering spreads, tightening in my stomach, but I hold his gaze. "Your movements. Neither you nor Kiran wasted anything. Every strike, every action—it was all done with intention."

A slow smirk tugs at his lips. "You have good eyes." His gaze flickers, assessing me, and I swear it lingers for a moment. "Now, let's see if you have good hands."

CHAPTER THIRTY-FIVE

I collapse onto the grass, my chest heaving, my body drenched in more sweat than I've ever produced in my life.

I spent the rest of the morning training with Gray—revisiting form, mechanics, and combat techniques, expanding on what he had already taught me in Foreigner's Valley. After that, I was granted a single hour of rest before my next session with Marcella, which focused on how to use those techniques to my advantage as a woman, regardless of an opponent's size. The sun had started its slow descent by the time we finished, the sky shifting into a deep portrait of reds and golds.

And I think Marcella may have enjoyed herself a little too much using Griff as our *play toy*, as she called him, when putting the techniques into application.

Actually...

I squint an eye open and catch Griff sitting on the slope of a hill, Marcella a few feet below him, still grumbling about how unnecessary it was for her to flip him so hard over her shoulder.

I catch the end of her reply. "—you signed up for it."

"To watch," Griff corrects her. "I signed up to *watch*. Not to be tossed around like unwanted food on a plate."

I laugh quietly, shaking my head, right as a shadow shades my vision. Gray plops down next to me, tucking his knees into his chest. "How are you doing?"

I drape an arm over my eyes and groan. "I didn't know it was possible for muscles to hurt this much."

He chuckles softly. "That'll pass." A pause. "Eventually."

I groan even louder.

I peek up at Gray from beneath my arm. "You know," I start, "we still haven't discussed your essence flower."

Gray plucks a lone white wildflower and twirls the stem between his fingers. "What is there to discuss?"

"Oh, you know...nothing major or anything. Just that you now have a claim to the throne of your bloodline's originating kingdom."

Gray clicks his tongue and dismisses the thought with a wave of his hand. "I have no desire for that."

I huff a laugh. "Any person a King's Reflection blooms for has a legitimate claim to the throne. Has the right to challenge the presiding king by Tani Law—something that's only ever happened twice since the signing of the Accord of Three Kings. You can invoke Raun."

"I know what it implies."

His terse tone has me arching a brow.

Gray glances down at me. "Why don't we instead discuss how *you* have an essence flower nobody knows anything about—a first in Bathara's history, or at least in its modern history."

When I look back up at him, I find his stare to be both pointed and triumphant. He knows he's made his point.

And I can concede that he has.

"Fair enough."

Another set of footsteps approaches, and this time, the shadow lingers over me.

I don't even need to move my arm to know who it is.

"Whatever it is," I say, my elbow still draped over my eyes, "I politely decline."

As expected, when I finally pry my sticky arm from my face, Draven stands at my feet.

He mocks a frown. "Now, where's the fun in that?"

I sit up. "I believe you and I have two very different definitions of fun."

He hums, amused. "Be that as it may, you need to stand up for your final training session of the day."

"Which would be?"

His smirk sharpens. "Sparring with me, of course."

From the corner of my eye, I catch Gray's brows rising to his hairline. An action I mirror. "You're joking, right?"

Draven curves a dark brow. "Do I strike you as someone who jokes a lot?"

"No," I grumble. "No, you do not."

He extends his hand. "It's important to apply what you've learned in a realistic simulation. It helps cement the movements into your muscles and increases your knowledge on how to effectively use them."

I reluctantly place my hand in his, exhaling a long, loud sigh. Draven pulls me up and escorts me to the fighting circle, where he struts over to the far side, turning to face me with a sly smirk on his face.

And I can't help but notice that, unlike when he sparred with Kiran, he leaves his shirt on.

As if summoned by my thoughts, Kiran appears, stretching his arms far above his head. His lips part as a yawn breaks through. "What'd I miss?" he asks, dropping his arms back down to his sides.

I brace a hand on my hip. "And where have you been all day?"

The corner of his lip tugs up, mischief holding the string. "I found a delightful pool of water to freshen up in, and it was such a beautiful day, I decided to take a nice nap. I feel quite rested, in case you were concerned."

While every muscle in my body screams with exhaustion.

"I'm so happy for you," I mutter with no small amount of sarcasm.

Kiran scans the scene, his eyes lingering on Draven and me in the sparring circle, and then rove to Gray, Marcella, and Griff, who have already gathered around to watch. He cocks his head. "Is this what I think it is?"

"Yup," Griff confirms, jubilant.

Kiran's brows kick up. "Interesting," he murmurs. He studies Draven and me a moment longer before chuckling. "Well, don't stop on my account." He slides his sapphire eyes to me and winks. "Put him on his back for me, would you? I'd love to be avenged by a brave heroine."

Marcella chuckles darkly, and I hear her coo, "Oh, I'm sure Lyra would *love* to put him on his back."

Heat floods my cheeks, and I shoot her a look that could stop even the god of death in his cold, ruthless tracks. She bites down on her grin and shrugs her shoulders, silently saying, *What? It's true.*

Oh, she is definitely getting a laxative in her food later.

When my eyes return forward, I find Draven watching me with a slight curve in his brow, his arms folded over his distractingly defined chest.

And by the gods, I am going to kill Marcella.

I shake out my hands and adjust my stance. "Alright. Let's get this over with."

Draven's mouth tugs up at the corner. "The faster you beat me, the sooner this will be over."

"I thought you never lose?"

He flashes me a quick, cocky grin. "I don't."

"Funny," I reply, setting my feet. "Because neither do—"

Before I can even finish the sentence, Draven advances. I immediately pivot, more reflex than skill. We move in a slow circle, closely watching the other. "No more talking," he says with a bit of challenge spiking his tone. "I want to see you move."

I make a show of pouting. "Shame. I do so thoroughly enjoy our conversations."

His lip curves, and then he takes one small step. But before he can strike, I attempt to make my move quicker.

I go on the offensive and try to get him off-balance, keeping my moves sharp and quick, just like Gray and Marcella taught me. Yet Draven simply side steps, dodging me effortlessly, acting as though I am a field mouse attempting to defeat a wolf.

I grit my teeth, frustrated.

"Try again," he encourages in a low, melodic coo. Though, I'm not sure I would call the tone he used "encouraging".

I feint left—pivot right. And then I attempt to strike again. This time, he at least pretends he has to engage me, catching my wrist before I can land the strike.

He tugs me forward, my body helpless to the sheer strength of his. Suddenly, everything Marcella taught me to balance the scale of strength goes out the window as my chest slams into his. "Not fast enough." His voice is low and thick with...something.

My breathing hitches in my throat.

Suddenly, I became keenly aware of how close we are.

The way Draven's skin feels against mine.

As if Draven knows I'm thinking about his touch, he softly brushes his thumb against the inside of my wrist, his gaze remaining pinned on me as he does.

Something tightens in my stomach.

I quickly tug my wrist away from him and recede, reassuming my fighting stance. "Don't go easy on me," I demand. "It'll taint the taste of my victory."

He cocks his head, watching me with a growing smile. "And yet, somehow I am labeled as the one with the overinflated ego."

I shrug. "All men have overinflated egos." I strike again. Draven dodges, smooth as silk.

"Hey," Griff objects from the side of the circle, my attention flicking to him. "Don't put me in that box. I have a perfectly average ego."

Marcella jabs her elbow into his side and hushes him.

When I return my eyes forward, Draven is no longer in front of me.

I make to turn, but before I can, my wrists are being pinned together behind my back with a large, calloused hand while another lightly grips its fingers around my throat, pressing me into an immovable body, holding me captive.

Draven dips his chin, and his lips brush the tip of my ear as he whispers, "*Never* take your eyes off your opponent. Not even for a second." His fingers tighten around my throat. Not enough to be threatening, but certainly enough to be...distracting. "Especially when that opponent is me."

I fight against the small tremble in my voice, ignoring the acceleration of my pulse. "Never?" I say through hollow confidence, feeling every bit of him pressed against me. "But what if there's something more important to look at?"

He drops his chin even lower, his lips moving away from my ear and toward the base of my neck. With a phantom-like touch, I swear the top of his lip grazes my skin.

It sends a shiver sweeping along my body.

"I assure you," he drawls slowly. "When I'm in front of you, that's not possible."

I swallow, my heart rate pounding to an entirely new rhythm. "No? And how can you be so sure of that?"

"Because," he starts, squeezing my throat a little tighter. His thumb traces circles against my erratic pulse. "When you enter this circle, *I* am all that matters. There is no one else. Only me." He loosens his hold on my throat, and his hand slowly grazes up toward my jaw. "And those distracting eyes of yours?" He grips my jaw, sliding his thumb along the curve of it. "They better not look away from me again."

Heat coils in my stomach, licking around my spine and up every nerve ending I have.

And did he say...*distracting?*

"Right," I reply as coolly as I possibly can. "But you don't have an overinflated ego or anything."

Forcing myself to wake up from whatever spell I was just under, I kick Draven's shin as hard as I can. The moment he loosens his grip, I twist out of it, bringing my elbow down on his arm.

Once safely a few paces away—my body a disheveled mess of different feelings—I blow out a breath and reset. "Now, let's try this again."

"Alright," he says with a new wave of amusement. "But try not to get distracted this time." His lip kicks up with a wry grin, and something about the way he says it tells me he wasn't referencing the moment I looked at Griff.

And if I wasn't already committed to bringing him to the ground, I certainly am now. I will win using whatever means necessary. If that means I need to play a little dirty? Well then, so be it. I've done a lot worse for a lot less. And conveniently, I've picked up on a particular thing about Draven when he moves. I just have to distract him, if only for a moment.

I lunge forward, engaging him. I strike, and when he effortlessly dodges, I allow my shoulders to hunch slightly, as if I am bordering on giving up. I pivot back to the left, and when I feint, I make it obvious. Draven catches my punch again, and this time, I am banking on him clutching me. When he does, I flick my eyes up at him, allowing something a hell of a lot like desire to rest within them, and then I slowly use my free hand to graze along his inner thigh, just past that sensitive part of him.

And I make damn sure to ignore the stir it causes within my own stomach.

Draven hesitates, only for a moment—his breath catching as he flicks his eyes to my lips. Slowly, he shifts his weight onto his other foot, preparing for his next move.

The exact moment I'm waiting for.

Right as his balance shifts, I hook my foot behind his knee, sweeping hard against his legs, taking his feet out beneath him.

Draven's eyes widen for a fraction of a second, and then he plummets toward the ground, his back landing with a satisfying *thud*.

The unexpected sound echoes through the stunned silence.

Gray swears under his breath. Marcella chokes on a noise somewhere between shock and delight. Griff outright screams with praise. Kiran claps.

And Draven—

Draven looks up at me, his eyes rounding into an expression he's never gazed at me with before.

He blows out a quiet laugh, shaking his head. "Some would call that a dirty move," he informs me, humor punctuating his words.

I lift a lazy hand and shrug. "I've never been one to play by the rules. I'll win however I can."

He tilts his head. "And who says you've won?" Quicker than a blink, he hooks one hand around my waist and the other around my wrist. Then he yanks me toward the ground—toward *him*.

I let out a startled gasp as the world tilts. I fall—

And laid right on top of Draven.

The impact knocks the air from my lungs, and I find myself half-sprawled on top of him, hands braced against the ground on either side of his head, my braid slipping over my shoulder.

He leans forward, sitting up slightly, and my body heightens with awareness as he shifts beneath me. "Never claim victory prematurely," he says, his voice low in this throat.

I freeze.

He doesn't.

With impressive ease, Draven reverses our positions, rolling me underneath him. He pins both my shoulders to the ground, the action pressing his hips against somewhere I'd rather not imagine them being. And the fires coursing through me as a result are spreading faster than I can quench them.

"I told you," he says, eyes bright. "I never lose." The thick rasp in his voice sends a chill down my skin—and not from fear.

"You almost did," I point out, a slight quiver in my words.

His lip kicks up. "Not the same thing."

"Well aware," I mutter. "But thanks for the reminder. Now, will you let me go?"

His smirk curves a little more. "Say please," he drawls.

I mock a smile.

Then, without warning, I twist sharply, ungracefully wiggling free from his hold.

He releases me, chuckling under his breath as he does, and I roll away in one fluid movement—an action that results in twigs getting intertwined with my hair. When I glance down, I also realize I now have grass stains pressed into my clothes and dirt smudged across my cheek.

Draven, propped upright on his knees, watches me with a curious expression on his face.

Kiran approaches from behind, crouching down next to me, offering me his hand. "You performed admirably," he praises, genuine pride caressing his words. "I've never seen a single person put Draven on his back before. Ever."

"I still lost in the end," I mutter through a pout. I swipe mud from my cheek and huff a sigh. My eyes slide back to Draven, whose attention remains fixed on me.

The curves of his mouth deepen, spreading until a full-fledged smile consumes his lips. Then, quite unexpectedly, he laughs—the sound low and deep, pulling from his throat. Until, in rhythm with the tilt of my head and the confusion pinching my features, that laugh migrates to pulling from deep in his stomach. And as Draven shifts to sit back on his outstretched arms, he practically doubles over from laughing so hard.

And gods help me, something about it makes my breath catch.

"He's laughing..." Kiran breathes, a poignant bow tied delicately around his words. "Draven's actually laughing again."

I glance at Kiran, a notch in my brow. "Is he really such a stoic ass that it's *that* surprising?"

Yet, despite what I've said, something deep in my gut tells me it *is* that surprising. That, for one reason or another, Draven isn't afforded many moments where he may laugh freely, without restraint. And I understand that sort of feeling more than I wish I did.

Suddenly, Marcella's words ring in my head.

Because those stitched from the same threads will always recognize each other.

Is that what this growing feeling toward Draven is? A recognition? Is it possible—despite how implausible it seems, with him undoubtedly being a highborn noble—that we are somehow stitched from similar threads?

Kiran doesn't respond right away, but instead watches Draven with conflicted eyes that seem to grapple with dueling emotions, deciding if they wish to fill with relieved happiness or pensive sadness. Finally, he murmurs through an attempted smile, "Something like that."

I study Kiran closely. There is something there, hiding in the shadows of his words. But before I can ask what it is he meant, Gray,

Marcella, and Griff shuffle over, whooping and hollering for my—almost—victory.

Marcella tackles me back to the ground and presses a wet, sloppy kiss to my cheek. "That was *badass.*"

Griff, following Marcella's lead, plops himself on top of her, thus on top of me. "*So* badass," he echoes with a humorous amount of enthusiasm. "You dropped a gods-damn *captain.*"

Gray chuckles, folding his arms over his chest at the display. "Damn right she did," he beams.

Kiran rises with not some wry smirk, but a warm, authentic smile pulling at his lips. He walks over to Draven, who watches contentedly as Griff and Marcella squirm on top of me, making whooping noises of praise, showering me with compliments. He has a leg propped comfortably into the air, and he rests his cheek in his palm, placing his weight on his propped elbow.

And I've never seen him look so...at ease. Happy, even.

I'm surprised by how breathtaking of a sight it is.

The sun grazes the horizon, and the sky is cast in such a magnificent red-golden light, my breathing hitches. My heart swells, and the sensation squeezes behind my breastbone before migrating to my chest, as if my heart doesn't know what to do with such astounding feelings of happiness. Between Draven's laugh, Kiran's unforgettable smiles, Gray's loyalty, Marcella's constant support—even Griff's goofy, yet disarming presence—I'm not sure I know how to process something so...good.

And a thought crosses my mind—

Maybe it's moments like this one that are meant to be buried deep beneath my skin. That perhaps I should attempt to be built on memories featuring the warm glow of sunsets instead of the damning glow of flames. Maybe the past isn't meant to be carried around forever—perhaps the past is meant to be nothing more than a fleeting thing. To pass through me like warm wind through open hands. I don't have to forget it, but I don't have to bear the weight of it forever, either.

If I did, there wouldn't be any room for memories like this one.

And I think I want more memories like this.

CHAPTER THIRTY-SIX

The following day of training, I have no special visitors waiting for me when I meet Draven.

The day proceeds normally, and I attempt all of my usual tasks. The good news is I'm definitely getting closer to completing them. But the unfortunate news is that I still did not finish a single one of my assignments. Though, I did make it eleven steps farther when balancing blindfolded across the tree before I slipped on a wide patch of lichen—an unusually exciting thing since I've never reached that particular patch before.

And even though my muscles ache and scream at me every single day, I can also feel them strengthening. I also notice my lungs can push themselves just a little further before burning. Not to mention how sharpened my senses are becoming.

Yet, in spite of all that progress, as I lay awake in bed after another exhausting day—my mind spinning with thoughts of what tomorrow's test will entail—I keep going back to how Draven was today.

Despite yesterday's events, he seemed...off. And for the life of me, I can't figure out why. He still corrected my form like usual, and his touches still lingered for a moment, so I don't think he was trying to be distant. It's more like his every movement, his every word was cradled by a muted sadness.

He didn't even ask me a single question today.

When I inquired about why, he simply shrugged and attempted to offer me a smile that didn't reach his eyes. "No questions today," was all he had replied in a soft murmur.

And within those three words, a story could have been written about the face of unspoken pain.

But the knot I can't unravel is what shifted for him so quickly between yesterday and today.

Even more perplexing is why I care so much to find the answers.

I shake my head and roll my eyes up to the ceiling. After exhaling a long sigh, I quietly throw the blankets from my legs. My fingers stretch beneath my pillow, and I pull Casimir Vivaldri's journal free.

If I'm going to be awake, thinking, I might as well do something productive with my active thoughts.

Making sure not to wake Marcella, I creep out of the room and tip-toe up to the rooftop balcony. I squeak the door open, prepared to be met with the breathtaking view of a silver moon glowing against a sparkling sky, but instead...

I'm met with the sight of Draven sitting propped up on the balcony's ledge, the silver moon casting him in an ethereal mix of shadow and light. His back is leaned up against a stone wall, and there is a wine jug resting limply between his fingers. He stares out toward the starlit hills and waterfalls. And he looks...

Beautiful.

When he finally turns to look at me, his normally bright eyes are dim, as if all the light was stolen like a snuffed out candle wick. It threads a quiet sadness through my heart, seeing his eyes boast their usual color, but without any life in them at all.

"Lyra," he says with a slur. "Welcome." He drops his head back and rests it against the stone. He slides his knee toward his chest, and he takes a swig from the jug.

I approach him tentatively—how one would approach a bird they don't want to fly away. "What are you doing out here?" I ask, making sure to keep my voice soft. "It's the middle of the night."

He slides his gaze to me. "I could say the same to you. You have a big test tomorrow morning, you know."

I laugh. "Yes, I'm aware." I hoist myself up onto the balcony's railing, near Draven's feet.

He watches me quietly.

I nod toward the wine jug in his hand. "Do you want to talk about it?"

He drapes his arm over his propped knee, the wine jug now hovering to the side. Draven tilts his head. "Talk about what, exactly?"

I shrug, making sure to keep the gesture casual. "Whatever has you drinking alone on a balcony in the middle of the night."

He huffs a dry laugh and drops his eyes to the wine, swirling it around. "No," he murmurs, glancing back up at me after. "But maybe someday."

I lean toward him, wearing an understanding smile. "I look forward to that day."

The corner of his lip twitches—a micro gesture. "Me too." He pauses, blowing out a breath. "Want a drink?" Draven lifts off the wall, holding out the jug for me to take.

I stare at it, considering. "Why not?"

When I reach for the jug, my fingers graze against his, and the tiny touch sends electrical currents rippling beneath my skin. I exhale a shuddering breath and press my lips to the tip of the jug, pulling a large gulp of wine. It's warm, but the flavor is woodsy and rich.

"Not bad," I say, handing it back to him.

A pleasant warmth instantly floods my body, coating me like a blanket.

So, not just commoner's wine. Noted.

There is a brief passing silence before Draven nods toward my back. "Were you planning on reading that journal of yours out here again?"

I blink. How could he have possibly known that? It's tucked into my waistband, hidden beneath my shirt.

My brow curves, and I glance at him sidelong. "Maybe," I grumble.

His low chuckle is his only response.

I eye him pointedly before letting my gaze drift to the golden lanterns enclosing the sprawling gardens and walkways below, resting peacefully beneath the glow of a star-covered night. When I finally look away, I find Draven watching me with a small crease between his brows.

"What?"

He doesn't respond right away. "It's just..." he trails off, his voice softening. "Sometimes you remind me of someone I used to know."

I study him carefully. "And is that a good thing or a bad thing?"

"A good thing," he assures me gently. "Definitely a good thing."

For some reason, his answer makes me smile. "You're different when you drink," I point out, a tinge of humor coating my words.

He huffs a laugh. "Aren't we all?"

"Yes," I agree. "But not always for the better. You?" I pause, considering my words. "You're softer. Kinder, even."

He hums, taking another swig of wine. "And what are you like?"

"Me?" A slow grin spreads across my face. "I have two different versions of myself that I can become."

"And they are?"

A wry smile sweeps across my lips. "Perhaps one day you'll see them for yourself."

He leans forward, a knowing expression in his eyes. "I look forward to that day. In fact," he pauses, a smirk on his lips, "I'd find it a privilege."

The words warm my cheeks. I suck in a breath and pull my eyes away from Draven's, unable to hold his gaze any longer. Because when I look at him, something aches inside of me, begging to be released—to be felt.

And I do not wish to feel.

The air between us is silent for a long time. Until finally, Draven takes another swig of wine and speaks again. "I love the nights where I can watch the stars."

"Really?"

A flicker of something—something fragile—quivers at the corner of his lips, as if trying to form a smile but forgetting how. "Mhm," he answers. "My mother..." He stops, his throat seeming to work around something heavy. "My mother," he tries again, voice steadier now. "She loved the stars. Always said they filled her with a sense of possibility."

"A beautiful sentiment," I comment.

"It was," he confirms. "She was a beautiful woman." His voice has the reverent tenderness reserved only for the deepest of affections.

But the word choice is not lost on me.

She *was.*

Draven exhales softly. "When I was a boy, she would take me outside under her favorite tree, spread out a blanket, and we'd lay there all night, pointing out constellations. For a long while, I thought she was a witch because I would always fall asleep with my head in her lap, but when I awoke the next morning, I was always in my bed." He chuckles, the sound heartachingly wistful.

Draven releases a loaded breath, looks up at the bright, silver moon, and takes a long, long pull from the wine jug.

And it's a strange thing—to imagine Draven as a small, curious child, tracing the stars with wide eyes. Until the exhaustion finally bests his trying eyelids, and they fall closed as he curls up in his mother's lap. He feels so far removed from that boy now. Like they couldn't have possibly been the same person. In some twisted way, it makes me want to claw at whoever stole that away from him. Whoever marred his heart with spoiled paint and careless brushstrokes, crushing such a fragile thing beneath the weight of hands that never learned how to handle something delicate and pure.

Draven continues, still staring at the moon. "She would always find the brightest star in the sky, point at it, and say to me, 'Do you see that star, Draven? It's just like you. It doesn't let the darkness swallow its shine; it burns brighter *because* of it.'" He pauses, finding that bright star in the sky and pointing at it, dropping his hand back into his lap after. His eyes go distant, swimming in memory.

And something about the story makes my heart squeeze.

A muscle in Draven's jaw flickers. "I don't talk about her enough," he whispers. "She deserves to be talked about more—to be remembered by someone." His voice is the ghost of a melancholy song, played on the strings of a broken heart.

A weight sinks in my own stomach, guilt throwing the anchor.

When was the last time I openly spoke of my mother? Allowed myself to remember her, fully and unabashedly?

I'm not sure if I ever have since the night she was stolen from me. The night that changed everything.

Draven exhales, tilting his head toward the stars as if searching for her—as if somewhere in that glittering expanse, she is waiting, watching. "Rivara's skies were actually her favorite," he tells me, his tone elevating. "She loved the colored stars more than anything else."

"I can relate to the feeling," I say with a fond smile. But then I blink, surprised. "Wait...have you been to Rivara?"

He nods. "Many times."

"To the king's court in Keziah?"

"Yup."

A slight frown pulls at my lips as I attempt to remember all the faces I encountered there. I draw short on recalling ever seeing Draven—I know that if I did, I would have remembered. A face like Draven's is impossible to miss. Even more impossible to forget.

As if reading my thoughts, the corner of his mouth quirks up, amusement flickering in his gaze. "Don't worry," he assures me. "You never saw me."

But...

Does that mean you saw me?

Draven studies me. His gaze is quiet. And for the first time, unguarded. "She would have really liked you."

The weight of his words crashes into me, rattling through my ribs, stealing the air from my lungs. I swallow. "I'm certain I would have really liked her." The words escape on a whisper, my voice barely my own.

A crease forms between his brows again—like there's more he wants to say, but doesn't. Instead, he turns back to the stars, and I let the silence stretch between us, thick with something I won't let myself acknowledge.

Finally, after the stars have sung and the moon has danced abundantly across the glassy waters, Draven takes his last swig from the wine jug and rises. I swivel on the balcony, putting the hills and waterfalls to my back. I watch Draven as he stands still for a long moment, as if contemplating something.

Eventually, he turns back around to face me, approaching with slow, fluid steps, stopping only when we are knee-to-knee, and I am tilting my chin up to meet the breathtaking green coloring his eyes. His brows furrow slightly as he searches my gaze for something. And then, as if finding his answer, a small curve sweeps his lips into a soft smile, and he lifts his hand to my face, gently spreading his fingers across my skin as he cups my cheek. His thumb moves idly, tracing just below my cheekbone, and the tender gesture forces a knot to rise in my throat—results in something expanding in my chest that scares me more than any monster ever could.

And then slowly, with a featherlight touch, his thumb roves lower, gliding gently across my skin, until the tip of his finger reaches my lips. Draven pauses, still watching me with achingly soft eyes. His brows twitch before he traces the slope of my top lip, down until he grazes his thumb over the sensitive skin of my bottom lip, tugging it with him as he moves.

His touch sends an intoxicating hum down every inch of my skin, the feeling both cold and warm simultaneously.

Suddenly, my pulse kicks into an erratic rhythm as I wonder if Draven—with his low-lidded gaze and contemplative expression—is going to kiss me. As I become aware that I might not move away if he does.

Those peculiar, hypnotic eyes never leave mine as he grips my chin between his thumb and index finger and lifts gently. His eyes crinkle softly, and he smiles at me—different than all the other times before. "Thank you," he murmurs. "For tonight. For listening." And then he does a final sweep over my face, dropping his hand and retreating backwards after. "Good luck tomorrow," he says, turning away from me. "Use your comrades if you need to. Just...stay safe."

Then, without another word, he walks away.

I don't even have time to tell him that he didn't need to thank me—that I didn't do anything worth receiving gratitude over—before he recedes into the shadows, leaving me alone on the balcony.

And it's strange, the way the moon suddenly seems duller—the way the stars don't appear to boast as loudly—in his absence.

So incomprehensibly odd, the way there is a small ache in my chest as I watch him go, feeling like something has suddenly gone missing.

The fact that I have the desire for it to come back.

CHAPTER THIRTY-SEVEN

The energy filling the air is different than how it was during the first test.

There are less excited whispers. Less buzzing noises from ongoing conversations between different groups. Instead, everyone stands around, shifting on their feet, waiting to hear what the next test entails.

Luckily, they don't wait long.

Marcella braces a hand on her hip from beside me. "Here we go," she whispers.

The five captains emerge on the mezzanine and shuffle to their banners. My eyes immediately find Draven, as if on instinct. All signs of the boy I saw on the balcony are gone as any softness has been scrubbed from his face, leaving only a cold indifference behind.

Finlay steps forward and speaks. "Welcome to the second test. The Keeper extends his apologies for not being able to address you all personally this morning. However, he has matters he must attend to." He flicks his eyes to Nuha, who dips her chin before stepping forward.

"For your second test," she declares to the room, "you will be grouped into teams of five that have been pre-selected by us captains. Given the number of remaining examinees, one team will be composed of four. As a group, you will be assigned a creature currently posing a threat to different areas within the Three Kingdoms. It will be your job to both track and dispose of the creature, returning to Bathara with its head in tow. Each team will be assigned an aether-wielder, who will transport your group to its designated starting point, and then back to Bathara once your objective has been achieved...or failed." Her eyes slowly hover across the room. "All wielders will be third-years, and they are not permitted to help you in any capacity. Any team that attempts to receive aid from them will be disqualified immediately. And yes," she says, her eyes narrowing. "We will know." She glances back at the threshold leading into the mezzanine. "Master Cahlmon."

A man with salt-and-pepper hair and stubble coating his jaw emerges. I recognize him instantly as the disgruntled man I overheard discussing the Nightenjoy's state of titles during King Alastair's party in Keziah.

All five captains dip their chins as he struts to the railing and wraps his hands around it. Rolling his shoulders back, he takes in the examinees, and I notice the way his eyes linger on Gray. Then me.

"I am Master Cahlmon," he says in a voice that booms far louder than one would expect given his smaller frame. "I typically teach wielding techniques and magic theory here at Bathara, but for the purposes of the entrance exam, you can think of me as a proctor."

Soft murmurs and whispers fill the air, and a small smile forms on Cahlmon's lips.

"I apologize that I was unable to attend the introductions and properly introduce myself before the exams began, but allow me to now demonstrate my role in these tests."

He moves his hands in a fluid motion, and the anthrine embedded into our bracelets starts glowing faintly, humming. Above our heads, square projections blink open one after the other, each one showcasing a different viewpoint from a different examinee, lagging slightly.

It's...strange, to put it one way.

"As you may have now deduced, I am a Caster. During this test, to help provide the captains with the information they will need to judge you, I will be casting each of your memories for them to watch." He lowers his hands and the projections disappear. "So be wise, and act accordingly. Your every action—every decision—will be not only observed, but scrutinized." And with that, he inclines his head to the captains and walks off the mezzanine.

The room erupts in a flurry of buzzing murmurs.

Arden silences them.

"You will be given five days to complete your task. If any team does not arrive with the head of their assigned creature before the fifth sun dips below the horizon, they are eliminated without further consideration."

Kiran scans the crowd. "There is only one rule governing the second test outside of your ability to be punctual." His smirk turns pointed. "And that is, there are no rules."

Draven lets Kiran's words settle before lifting a piece of parchment and waving it in the air.

And gods help me, for whatever reason, my stomach does a somersault the moment the sound of his voice enters the room.

"I'm only going to read off your team assignments this one time, so pay attention. Don't worry about finding your aether-wielder. They already know who they've been assigned to and will find you themselves. Once they do, you are free to depart."

He begins calling out names, assigning people to their teams.

Not surprisingly, Gray, Marcella, and I are announced last, and we are all paired together. Not that I'm complaining, but I imagine Finlay Fjolla had something to do with that.

Our fourth member is a girl named Nuri—the only other wielder to advance to the next test from our "line of commoners".

We are the only team of four.

"Well would you look at that," Marcella drawls. "All non-nobles paired into a team." She feigns surprise, placing a hand on her chest. "I, for one, am *shocked*."

I laugh and shake my head. "I bet Finlay was involved in that decision."

"Prick," Marcella mumbles, folding her arms over chest.

From the other side of me, Gray huffs a laugh. "At least we all get to stay together," he offers.

I nod in agreement.

Nuri approaches us, and Marcella greets her with a wave. "Hi," she chirps. "Welcome to the team of second-rate citizens."

Nuri laughs. "That is what they'd have us think, isn't it?"

Nuri is beautiful—stunning, even. Her blackberry hair against her warm-brown skin and sharp green eyes could bring anyone to their knees. Her lips are full and feminine, and the twists of her braids pull back enough hair to reveal gold piercings lining her ears and a sun pendant sitting at her throat.

And something about her seems oddly familiar, even if I can't put my finger on what it is.

Marcella makes a sweeping gesture. "Meet Gray and Lyra, your lowborn teammates. Lyra is a flora-wielder like me, and also the daughter of a Gardner. Important to know, because she talks about it a lot."

I arch a pointed brow at the introduction; Marcella shrugs and continues.

"Gray wields illusionary magic and is supposedly the son of a Gardner as well, but he talks about it less."

Nuri's eyes bounce between us, amusement resting within them. "I remember both of you from the first judgement. You left quite the impression on the captains."

Gray exhales a clipped laugh. "If I recall, you left them rather floored yourself. You're a healer, right? Your essence flower was Goldenlight—a flower that typically blooms only for descendants from powerful bloodlines."

"You listen well," she comments. Her accent is thick, unmistakably from the Anatolé Kingdom.

The corner of his lip kicks up, and he cocks his head, folding his arms across his chest. "Yet you said you're the daughter of a merchant," he points out, his tone almost accusatory. "What was your family line again?"

"Calhart," she answers quickly. "My father comes from Lydith, specializing in mineral trades."

"Yup," Marcella chirps, inspecting her nails. "That makes sense. Rich city. Full of merchants."

I glance at Gray, a heavy curve in my brow. "Not that it matters," I mutter, wondering what the hell he is getting at.

"Of course it doesn't," he agrees, finally snapping his gaze away from her and toward me, a tight-lipped smile now on his lips.

I catch Nuri's eyes lingering on Gray a moment longer before she turns to Marcella. "You know Lydith?"

Marcella nods. "I'm from Rolfbear, and my brothers work a lot of trade routes." She shrugs. "They bring gossip from all over the Three Kingdoms."

"I see," Nuri responds.

Before the conversation can carry further, Kiran approaches us, his usual smirk gracing his lips.

"Hello, wielders," he coos.

Nuri dips her chin. "Captain."

Kiran waves a lazy hand at her. "Please, call me Kiran. I've already had enough titles thrown my way to last a lifetime."

Marcella mocks sympathy. "Must be tough growing up wealthy in one of the Great Houses, living with the highest titles one can possess beyond a king."

Kiran smiles wickedly and cocks his head at Marcella. "Oh see, I rather really like you." He leans in closer to her. "And not just because the color of your hair."

Marcella rolls her eyes; Kiran winks.

And by the Mother it is difficult to reconcile that Kiran really *does* belong to House Sulien. That he is an Archblood—basically royalty. I always imagined that Archbloods would act more…well, more like Finlay.

Kiran holds up a small scroll wrapped in twine. "Your creature assignment." He places it in my hand, and his eyes soften as something inscrutable washes over his features. Kiran looks as though he wants to say something else, but thinks better of it. Instead, he simply glances at us all a final time and offers a tight lipped smile. "Good luck." Then he disappears back into the crowd.

"His demeanor is unnerving," Marcella grumbles with a curved brow.

Nuri chuckles, tilting her head with consideration as she stares off in the direction Kiran went. "I find it rather refreshing to see someone of his status act so..."

"Flippant?" Marcella finishes for her.

She smiles, sliding her emerald eyes to Marcella. "I was going to say carefree."

Marcella snorts, and they prattle on about the peculiarities surrounding Kiran's demeanor.

Gray approaches me, pointing at the rolled scroll in my hand. "May I?"

"Oh, right," I say, as if just realizing Kiran handed it to me.

I pass the scroll off to Gray, and he tugs at the twine and unrolls the parchment. His eyes narrow as he reads its contents.

"Well?" Marcella asks.

Gray rolls the scroll back up before meeting everyone's gaze. "Anyone afraid of snakes?"

Chapter Thirty-Eight

"That prick," Marcella sneers. "That stupid, pretentious, stuffy-ass, Fjolla *prick*."

We walk through the eastern woodlands located within Anatolé's borders, the day already fleeting. Soon, we'll need to stop and set up our camp for the night.

"Look on the bright side," Griff chirps. "At least Kiran managed to get me assigned as your aether-wielder." He wears a cropped, white fighter's jacket trimmed in gold with matching pants. The uniform of the Castaria aggregate, I've learned.

Which would explain why he told Gray and me to choose Castaria the day we arrived at Bathara. It's because he's a part of the aggregate, and *Kiran* is its captain.

Marcella clenches her fists at her sides and whirls around on Griff. She jabs her finger into his chest. "A bright side coming from someone who *doesn't* have to wrangle and behead a Blue-Horned Adder doesn't go very far."

Ever since learning of our assignment, Marcella has been rather...on edge.

Griff makes a show of lowering Marcella's finger from his chest, pushing it away slowly with his palm. "News flash, fiery one—I had to complete the same test."

"Oh, and what creature did *you* track and eliminate, then? Hm?"

He lifts his chin. "A troll."

She barks a humorless laugh and crosses her arms. "I rest my case."

Griff's face pinches together. "For the record, trolls are *incredibly* difficult to manage."

"No, they're not," she fires back. "They're ignorant barbarians who are easily ensnared."

Griff leans toward her, leaving little space. "Yes, they are."

She humphs triumphantly. "Great. So you agree with me, then?"

Griff's brown eyes crinkle with confusion as he shakes his head. "No. I meant, yes, they are difficult to manage. Not yes to what you said. Stop twisting my words."

Nuri leans over to me. "Should we separate them?"

I glance between the two of them—their faces frozen with challenge—and laugh. "They'll be fine. Let her use him to blow off some steam—it'll be better for all of us."

The moment we arrived at the outermost edge of the woodlands—Marcella already fuming—we strategized the most logical route through the area. Based on the captains' instructions written on the scroll, we figured the Blue-Horned Adder must be somewhere near the southeastern border, causing issues near one of the outlying villages. So after a long conversation weighing our options, we all agreed the best approach was to travel east, looking for any signs of the creature as we go.

Marcella's frustration seems to have only increased since then.

Griff and Marcella somehow manage to bicker for the rest of the day, only stopping when we set up camp under the cover of dense trees, near a large collection of jagged, lichen-covered rocks. Nuri and I scour for firewood to last us through the night while Gray clears the grounds and pitches tents. Marcella and Griff each decide they're the superior hunter, and they set off on separate journeys to compete over who can catch the better meal.

Within an hour, right as darkness formally sweeps the light away, Griff returns with two squirrels.

Marcella returns with three rabbits, a pouch of fresh berries, a quail, and a very, very large smirk.

Griff doesn't attempt to compete with Marcella again.

"Is it true nobody has ever seen the princess of this kingdom?" Griff asks with a mouth full of food, biting into the squirrel meat he hunted.

The fire crackles and pops as we spin more meat slowly over the flames. Griff and Gray sit on one side, Marcella happily wedged between the two, and Nuri and I sit on the other.

Marcella snorts at the question. "People exaggerate."

"Well, have *you* seen her?" Griff presses.

She clicks her tongue. "Please. I'm from Rolfbear. Of course I haven't seen the princess."

"So has anybody?" Griff raises his eyebrows for emphasis and looks around the circle. "How do we know she actually even *exists*?"

Nuri pops a fresh berry in her mouth. "When the princess was a little girl, it is said she made many appearances. But you're not entirely mistaken. My father was in the capital city recently, and the gossip about the princess was as thick as ever. They say her last public appearance was at the Ardoris Festival many, many years ago."

She hands off the jug of commoner's wine Marcella smuggled in her pack.

A smile tugs at the corner of my lip. "When I was a little girl," I confess, "for years I used to wish upon a violet star every night that, someday, I could witness the Ardoris Festival." I huff a laugh, and I jerk my chin toward Gray. "I read about it in one of his books, and there was even an illustration on the page. It seemed magical."

Nuri listens with soft eyes. "It is," she confirms. "The Ardoris Festival is a wondrous event, and one I hope everyone can experience at least once in their lifetime."

The wine jug reaches Marcella, and she takes a long pull from it, wiping her mouth with the back of her hand after. "My brothers took me when I was thirteen. We started making more money, so they could afford to bring me along that year." Her cobalt eyes come alive as a happy memory dances through them. "In all my life, I still don't think I've ever experienced something as remarkable."

Griff snatches the wine jug from Marcella and takes a swig. "Clearly, you need a good lay then."

Marcella rolls her eyes and scoffs at Griff. "Right, and are *you* going to be the one to give it to me?"

He leans toward her, waggling his brows. "I could be. At least, I am more than happy to oblige, if that's what you mean."

Shameless flirt, indeed.

Marcella clicks her tongue and shoves him off the tree stump they've been sharing. After, she swipes the wine jug away from Griff—who grumbles as he rises from the ground—and takes another drink before passing it on. Her face softens, and she leans forward, bracing her elbows on her thighs, resting her chin in her palm and staring at the fire like it encases distant memories. "You know what I would kill for right now?"

Griff opens his mouth to speak, but thinks better of it as Marcella shoots him a razor-sharp glare. He hunches over and also places his chin in his palm.

She swivels her eyes back to the flames. "I'd kill for music. In my hometown, there was always music."

"Gray plays the double-flute," I offer. "He's quite talented, too. Had he not been gifted with magic, I'm convinced he would have been a musician."

"Historian, actually," he corrects with a soft smile.

Marcella nudges Gray in his side. "Why didn't you tell me sooner? You could have ended my suffering ages ago."

He glances at her through the sides of his eyes. "It hasn't exactly been a relevant topic of conversation."

She huffs, eyeing the satchel on the ground beside him before jerking her chin toward it. "It's in there, isn't it?"

The flick of his eyes and the thinning of his lips are the only answers she needs.

"Oh, it's in there alright." She leans over Gray and grabs the satchel, plopping it in his lap after and arching an expectant brow.

He sighs. But ultimately, he flips the leather open and pulls out a dark-wooden instrument adorned with carvings and thin strips of beige and white leather twine.

Marcella lets out a low whistle. "Fancy."

Gray chuckles. "Well, any requests?"

She pinches her chin. "You don't happen to know any Anatolian folk songs originating from the south, do you?"

He considers before shaking his head. "Not by memory, unfortunately."

"How about "The Boy and the Wolf"?" Nuri suggests. "It's an old folk song that sounds haunting on the double-flute."

Gray nods, wearing a tilted smile. "I know it."

And I have to bite down on my growing grin.

Gray doesn't just know it—it's his favorite song to play. The song that made him want to learn the instrument, after my mother sang it to us one night. It's also his best song, stirring the heart with the sort of filling emotion only music can bring.

Gray wets his lips, puts the wooden mouthpiece up to them, and plays.

As soon as the notes flutter into the air, I am transported to another place. To another time. I am here, but I am nowhere. I am ensconced in a sphere of sound, living multiple lives, multiple moments, through the breaths of these notes.

Within a few beats, Nuri opens her mouth and sings, her warm alto piercing through the air, sending the hairs on my arms rising. I didn't expect her to sing, but I'm glad she does.

"*A wolf that lurks in the blackest of nights, his glowing eyes are a stream. Alone, he wanders lost in this life, awaiting sweet release.*

"*A child, a child, he finds deep in the trees, washed in mud and weeds. A child, a child, a knife deep in his skin, awaiting sweet release.*"

Chills rise and fall along my skin. The moon freezes time while the trees hold their breath. Even the fire rests its bow against its vermillion strings, straining to hear the sounds of Gray's playing and Nuri's voice. Only the wind moves—its sole purpose to sweep the tune to the stars, perhaps even to the gods themselves.

"*The voices, they crow, in the moonlight. Until the child believes. The wolf*

320

will keep him locked in this life, awaiting sweet release. The moon, it shines through the frost light, and now, the child it sees. Fading to ash, the stars, they cried. No longer needing to be."

Nuri's voice softens, her final notes a shade above a whisper.

"A wolf that lurks in the blackest of nights, his glowing eyes are a stream. Alone, he wandered lost in this life, until he was released. But not until he exchanged his eyes for a child that no longer breathes.

"For now, he remains lost in this life, unable to be released."

🌿 🌱

It takes us two more days to make it to the far-east end of the woodlands.

Marcella, being every bit the skilled tracker she claimed to be, found deep, winding tracks in the ground that led us farther south. From there, we began spotting broken rocks and trails of waste filled with bones and half-digested animal prey.

I didn't look to see if the bones were human.

We know we're getting close when the air shifts from damp soil and rich woody notes to slithering decay. Even the birds disappear, taking their pleasant tunes with them.

It's as if this part of the woodlands is...frozen, almost.

Marcella and Gray lead while Griff takes up the rear. We reach a trickling stream where the line of trees thins and gives way to a rocky path leading to a cave opening. Marcella halts, crouching down and placing her palms flat against the soil. Small roots sprout and twist from the soil, zipping quietly across the ground and into the cave. After a few seconds, the roots recede back into the dirt, and Marcella rises.

"The Blue-Horned Adder is in there. Presently, it sleeps."

"That..." Griff starts, his chin between his fingers. "Was really cool."

I arch a brow at him before looking back to Marcella. "That's good, right? We can catch it off guard. Attack it while it sleeps."

Marcella and Gray exchange wary glances.

"What do you remember learning about the Blue-Horned Adder?" Gray's question comes out bleak, and it causes a knot to form in my stomach.

321

"Only that their venom causes hallucinations, and that they abhor Mugwort." And as the words tumble from my mouth, all I can think is: *Great. More venom.*

Marcella slides her eyes to Gray, who nods with some silent confirmation. She blows out a breath. "Blue-Horn Adders have extremely keeled dorsal scales that make their skin as impenetrable as Arellian steel. They are cunning, vile, ruthless creatures that relish in trapping their prey. It's been ages since one has been spotted, and frankly, I'm shocked they sent examinees to dispose of it instead of actual Jurafen." She pinches the bridge of her nose and sighs. "Then again, I'm not surprised at all considering they assigned *us*. I'm sure Finlay is hoping the creature wipes us all out."

Gray watches her, understanding resting within his eyes. "Trying to kill it in its own territory would be a suicide mission," he elaborates. "It knows the cave better than any of us, can see within the darkness, and we'd risk trapping ourselves between the Adder and a wall." He pauses, thinking. "We need multiple, open routes to escape its teeth, horn, and tail."

"Painfully excellent odds," I mutter.

Nuri's brows are pinched with thought. "Its horn is its weakness, correct?"

"It is," Gray confirms. "But it is incredibly difficult to access the horn. The Adder is very aware of its weakness, and it does all that it can to protect itself against it."

"Be that as it may," Nuri begins. "Perhaps it would be best to form a plan that works to exploit its weakness. There are four of us, and the three of you have rather rare magics. If we use that to our advantage, I think we stand a good chance of winning."

I resist the urge to slump, deciding it's best not to sprinkle more pessimism onto an already bleak situation by telling Nuri I still barely know how to use my magic. That I'm only now learning how to fight.

"We do need a plan," Marcella agrees. "And we need one fast. Blue-Horned Adders are nocturnal, but we can't be sure whether or not it'll leave its cave to hunt when the moon rises. We don't have the luxury of time to sit around and find out, so…"

"We need to lure it out," I finish.

She nods. "As soon as the moon peaks, we need to lure that Adder from the cave. Then, we strike before it can realize what's happening."

"Agreed," Gray says. "We just need to figure out a plausible way to do that."

Everyone grows quiet as they float deep into their minds, attempting to find a solution. Griff watches us all silently, sitting a few feet away from us on a large, flat rock.

I begin pacing, determined to find a solution. I know I won't be much help when it comes to taking the creature's head, so I'll be damned if I don't help them at least come up with a way to lure the creature out. But what would entice a Blue-Horned Adder? What would guarantee that it leaves its shelter?

A stray sunbeam hits me in the eye, and I wince, blinking at the golden horizon. It's hard to believe sunset is already approaching. The days are growing shorter, I realize.

Which means we're losing time.

But then that realization smacks me in the face with another one.

I whirl around to face everyone, excited. "The Autumnal Equinox is approaching."

Marcella's features pinch together with confusion. Gray's brows furrow. And Nuri watches me closely with sharp eyes.

"And that matters because…?" Marcella drawls.

My eyes slide to Gray. "Do you remember helping your mother the morning after you told me you were leaving for Bathara? More specifically, *what* you were making?"

Gray's brows wrinkle with thought as he visibly rakes through his memory—until his eyes round with realization.

"The Autumnal Equinox is approaching," I repeat again, my grin wide and unflinching. "And I have a plan."

CHAPTER THIRTY-NINE

We work quickly, not wasting a single fleeting ray of sunlight. After I told everyone my plan, Marcella took three long strides toward me, planted a sloppy kiss on my cheek, and declared me a genius.

I didn't have the heart to say I don't want to be a genius—I just want to be right.

Griff creeps into the center of our preparations, whistling merrily as he walks around with his hands clasped behind his back, observing what we're doing. Once he finishes, he strides to the other side of our work area and waves goodbye. "Well, I'll see you guys later," he chirps. "Good luck with your plan. I'm rather impressed by it, honestly."

"And where do you think you're going?" Marcella demands, rising from the ground and wiping dirt on her pants, approaching him.

"Back to Bathara. Can't help you guys, remember? And, no offense, but I don't particularly want to watch from a bush just in case anything goes a little...off the rails." Griff smirks at her and twirls the tip of her braid around his finger. "But don't worry. I'll still be watching you."

She slaps his hand away. "Bite me."

"Would love to," he coos.

Marcella sneers at him, which makes Griff chuckle under his breath. He turns around and opens a portal, the silver appearing to have an extra glint to it. "I'll be back to get everyone soon." He flicks his gaze over his shoulder, and there is a completely different message resting within the creases of it—one that doesn't match the carelessness of his tone.

None of you better die.

And then he disappears, swallowed by the swirling black and silver. The portal blinks out of existence shortly after.

"Prick," Marcella mumbles under her breath after he's gone.

I chuckle as I approach her. "Ready?" Using a makeshift bowl composed of mud and twigs, I dip my fingers into the sticky, smooth contents, and hold it up for Marcella to see.

She inhales deeply through her nose. "Smack it on me."

I smear the mud across her face, covering her artistic display of freckles, and twine leaves and twigs into her braid. Once I'm finished, she raises her chin and waggles her brows— her bright cobalt eyes a stark contrast against the darkness of the mud.

"How do I look?"

My lips curve with a far-too amused grin given what's about to happen. "Like shit."

She snorts a laugh.

Gray and Nuri join us, their faces already smudged in mud and hair embedded with twigs and leaves.

"I think we look more frightening than the Adder," Nuri comments, doing a sweep of everyone.

"Just think of us like the lost warrior tribe—fearsome, formidable, and focused." Marcella puffs out her chest and lifts her chin.

"You left out forgotten," Gray says with an arched brow.

Marcella clicks her tongue and wrinkles her nose at him. A gesture that has Gray shaking his head and laughing quietly as he watches her a moment longer.

Eventually, he reorients his focus to me. "Is the powder ready?"

I hold up the pouch containing our hopes and dreams, eyeing it before flicking my eyes back to him. "Crushed, dried, and ready to go."

Gray nods, blowing out a weighted sigh. "Well, then," he begins, locking eyes with each of us. "Shall we awaken the stars tonight?"

⚜ ⚜

The moon spills silver across the land, its light fractured by the jagged rock formations and tangled limbs of towering trees.

Nuri and I crouch low behind a towering stone, the cold bite of the night seeping through my clothes.

Or perhaps the coldness comes from the dread working itself up my spine.

Gray is tucked in the shadows of a sprawling tree, and Marcella lingers somewhere in the darkness, waiting.

But she doesn't have to wait much longer.

A low, wet-sounding hiss slithers through the night, and a spike of adrenaline rushes through me as my body goes into high alert. A rustling noise fills the air as leaves crunch and twigs snap under the weight of something massive moving through the underbrush.

I glance at Nuri. "How good of a healer are you, exactly?"

Her eyes remain locked on the cave ahead. "Good enough."

Well that's...comforting.

A shadow unfurls across the grass, vast and sinuous, moving with a grace no creature its size should possess. And then something terrifying emerges.

The Blue-Horned Adder.

Its forked tongue flicks into the night air, tasting it like a fine wine. Twin golden eyes gleam bright against the shadowy night, and its massive coils move like a wave, effortless as an ebbing tide.

Above our heads, a small comet streaks across the sky, its glittering tail soaring in an arc over the trees.

I exhale a loaded breath and glance at Nuri. "Well, that's my cue."

"You've got this," she whispers. "May Saffi be with you."

Saffi. The goddess of cunning. Not Algol, the god of trickery and deception.

Noted.

I dip my chin. Then, on silent feet, I climb the rock formation. Sweat beads across my forehead, slipping down my temple, melting the mud into falling trails against my heated skin. I swipe at it before any can fall into my eyes, and then reach for the pouch strapped to my thigh.

As soon as the plan was set, Gray and I gave Marcella a list of ingredients to forge from the land—we figured she was better suited to grow them in a pinch with magic. Mandrake root, yohimbe bark, goat weed, sage—the basics. Next, using the healer supplies Nuri brought, Nuri ground the ingredients and seeped them using the commoner's wine. Then, using sage paired with heat from a quick, makeshift fire provided by Gray, I dried the concoction into a brittle substance and ground it into a fine powder.

There was some debate about what to do from there. But ultimately, we decided to split half the powder in a pouch, and the other half would be used to mold an incense stick. Presently, that incense is lit at the cave's entrance, burning off an intoxicating aroma.

So, in other words, we concocted a powerful aphrodisiac to use on a Blue-Horned Adder while in the peak of its mating season. If everything works correctly, it should force the creature into a frenzied state where its judgement is tainted by clouded senses, preventing it from thinking clearly.

And hopefully, in turn, diluting its ability to kill us.

A low vibration rumbles through the ground as the Adder shifts, its monstrous head rising, tongue flicking to taste the air once more.

I hold steady, willing my erratic pulse to slow.

I know Gray cast an illusion to cloak us—blending our bodies into the landscape—and that the mud and leaves help mask our scent. But my heart won't stop pounding with the uncertainty of how all of this is going to play out. You can plan and plan, but it doesn't mean shit the moment things fall apart. And if I miss my chance—if I mess up or make a single mistake here—we all die.

Without thinking, I puff out my cheeks, exhaling a nervous breath. The powdered aphrodisiac stirs and swirls in the air, rising into my nostrils from the gust of wind, tickling my skin. It's the fight of a lifetime as I battle against the forming sneeze, the powder rising higher into my nose.

Shit.

I stretch my arm away from my face, distancing myself from the powder, and rub aggressive circles against the tip of my nose.

But it's too late.

I swallow the sneeze and immediately feel the effects of the aphrodisiac enter into my bloodstream, my body growing warm and tingly as heat floods through me.

Fuck.

Not good. *Not. Good.*

The Adder swivels its head in my direction, its small slits for nostrils fully exposed to me. I bite on my lip and shake my head.

Focus.

I lift the powder directly in front of my lips and—with a forceful bout of air that would make even Theora, the goddess of air, proud—I blow it into the Adder's nose.

Its head jerks slightly as it flicks its tongue. The Adder's scaled body starts to undulate, coiling into tight loops. Then, it jerks its yellow-glowing eyes to something in the distance.

A Red-Snout Adder.

Only, it's not a Red-Snout Adder at all.

The Blue-Horn slithers toward the Red-Snout, keeping its head held high.

"Come on, come on," I mutter under my breath. "Work."

This next part was always going to be the real challenge. When Gray said he's been working on evoking visceral responses with his illusionary magic, he informed us that it's a far-cry from reliable yet.

"However," he had said with a tinge of steady confidence, "I think I can make the Blue-Horn believe he's scenting a Red-Snout for at least a few seconds."

And, by the gods, I could shed tears of joy the moment The Blue-Horn's body shudders and hums, rumbling the very ground beneath us with its intense vibrations. It flicks its forked-tongue in a rapid pattern, and the Adder rears itself back, coiling tightly, before striking forward in a lunge toward the illusion of the Red-Snout.

Then, with an amount of force that has me wincing, the Blue-Horn slams into the trunk of a towering tree.

Which means onto phase two.

Leaping down from her hiding spot, Marcella screams a war cry into the night-wind, her sword raised over her copper braid. The moonlight glints off the blue-tipped hilt, and she looks like a warrior goddess as she soars toward the Adder with her blade in hand.

She thrusts the sword into the creature's horn, the force of the collision echoing through the woods as the impenetrable scales of the Adder greet the steel. For a heartbeat, the air stills as time's strings are temporarily held in shaking hands. Until a sharp, agonizing crack splits the air—splitting hope with it.

Marcella's sword splinters under the pressure of the impact, and the blade shatters into fragments, shards of metal glinting like fallen stars as they scatter to the ground. She balances on a knee, gaping at the jagged stump in her hands.

"Shit," I breathe.

The Adder—now in a state of frenzy *and* rage—lurches its head back, sending Marcella flying through the air and soaring through the trees once more. Only, they do not catch her.

She lands with a dull *thud* near the cave, her body twisted at strange angles. My eyes bulge, and ice overtakes my skin, coating my body with a terrifying chill at the sight. And there are a thousand thoughts racing through my mind as I glimpse Nuri creeping through the trees, trying to remain hidden within the shadows to reach her.

The Adder tilts its head, locking in on the moving shadows, and the movement is nothing short of predatory. Its blue-scaled, colossal tail winds back, back, back, until it has nowhere else to go, and then slingshots forward, slamming directly into Nuri, sending her flying backwards through the woodlands.

I lose sight of her almost immediately.

A blur of movement catches my eye next. I whip my gaze toward it and find Gray sprinting toward the momentarily distracted Adder. He charges forward, up its wide, scaly body, plunging daggers into the creature's armor when the incline is too steep to run. He does not stop until he reaches the very top of its head.

Gray digs his heels in, assuming a wide stance after he sheaths his daggers. Slowly, he pulls the long sword from his back scabbard, staring at the creature's horn with a terrifying determination. And as the moon casts shadows across his face, I swear I glimpse another flicker of gold in his eyes.

Gray shouts, the cry coming from deep within his gut, and then he slams the sword down into the horn of the Adder.

A sharp noise splits the air, and the Adder shrieks, writhing under the impact of the blade. Its neck swings around with wild movements, and Gray quickly drops to his knees, clutching onto the hilt of the sword as it remains lodged deep into the Blue-Horn's scales.

Still, the creature does not fall.

Which means we still have not won.

Suddenly, the Adder whips its head toward Marcella, its eyes dilating. I follow its line of sight, and find a rich pool of crimson blood seeping into the ground. My heart rate spikes in my chest before feeling like it dies altogether.

Without another thought, I leap from the rock and down to the ground, a jolt of electricity surging through my ankle from the impact. I grit my teeth against the pain, but I do not let myself feel it—process it. Instead, with a small limp, I sprint for Marcella.

"Lyra!" Gray's voice echoes through the sky, imbues itself into the very fabrics composing this world. "Watch—"

Before he can finish the sentence, a razor-sharp fang slices into my shoulder and down the entire length of my arm.

The impact sends me rolling.

My face hits a twisted network of roots, and dirt stuffs its gritty contents into my mouth. But when I try to rise, my muscles don't respond—don't move.

A panic lances through my every nerve ending when I try again, shouting at myself, *Get up! Get up! GET UP!*

My body does no such thing.

And then realization clamors through me like a death sentence.

The Blue-Horned Adder's bite is lethally venomous.

At this strange angle my neck is paralyzed into, I can still see Marcella. See her parted lips, looking as crimson as the blood pooling around her. In my mind, I am reaching a hand out to her, trying to touch her, even if just for a final time.

Someone so filled with life can not possibly look so dead.

Desolate thoughts destroy me.

Why am I so useless? Why can I never do anything to help? Why did I ever think I could do this; I can't do this.

Why must people always leave me...

I hear Gray screaming. I hear the clattering sounds of steel against scales. I hear the Adder moving. I hear trees groaning, winds howling—lives fleeting.

My vision fogs over, and my chest suddenly feels lassoed by an invisible master, tugging for breath only when it decides it wants to.

And as this world fades away, a final thought lingers, clinging to this body a moment longer—

I have lost.

CHAPTER FORTY

I open my eyes and am shocked to recognize this realm of the afterlife. I sit up from a ground that is water-like, yet is not water at all. Everything is black, yet...not. I am ensconced in a colorless void that is endless, formless. The familiar fog hovers over the rippling floor at my feet, beckoning me closer to the veil of mist where colors talk.

Where a poison-induced version of myself teetered between life and death as the Mirefiends threatened to clip the strings of my life.

I know Bathara's entrance exams are known to be lethal, but nobody said anything about venomous creatures lurking at every corner, waiting to pump toxins into you.

A burst of color materializes in the hovering mist, catching my eye. With slow steps, I approach, never taking my eyes off the deep pink and rich purple as it swirls and shifts. A voice soon follows.

"You're back," it says, low and deep. A voice of ages. A voice that is worn and beaten and tired.

"And you're real," I reply. With a cocked head, I take another step, peering into the veil as far as I can see—which isn't very far given how dense the mixture of mist and fog is.

"I am."

"Can you show yourself?"

"If you come to me."

I frown. "And how do I do that?"

A bright white light appears, flaring brilliantly. *"Step through the mist."*

My brows pull together as I observe the light carefully. "You said you have much to tell me—that there is much I should know."

"There is, and I do."

I fold my arms across my chest and set my features. "So tell me, then."

"No," the voice declares, leaving no room for negotiation. *"Not here. It requires too much of me."*

I glance around the place of beginnings and ends. "And where is here, exactly?"

"The Veil," he answers. *"You have the gift. Just like your mother."*

The shock washes over me in two parts. The first layer is composed of denial, rich and hot. That what this hauntingly smooth voice is saying isn't possible—I am hallucinating.

Yes, that must be it. I am hallucinating from the venom, just as I probably hallucinated when under the Mirefiend's poison.

But clearly my mind wants to play Merikh's advocate, because as soon as the thought crosses, it's instantly countered with one simple fact...

Veilreaders sip from a potent elixir typically featuring some form of a hallucinogenic or mind-altering substance. It's the only way they can enter the Veil. So, the poison, the venom—it's the reason why *I've* been able to enter the Veil.

But...

I can't be a Veilreader. It's just not possible...right? I mean, I know nothing about it. Not in any way that counts. My mother...she never said much about her ability. She didn't like to enter the place called the Veil. She only did so out of necessity—which was so, so rare. And she certainly never told me the things she saw or how she managed to interpret them. I wasn't even allowed to see her on the days she entered. I would sleep with Gray in his family's chambers, my mother picking me up in the morning and immediately taking me to her favorite greenhouse, after.

The second layer of shock comes in the form of questions and anger. I'm angry because I don't understand. I'm angry because there is so much about myself—about my *mother*—I clearly know nothing about. Because this...person, thing—whatever the hell lingers behind the misty fog, the *Veil*—knows enough of my mother to reference her ability.

An ability she told very few about.

A cold fire burns my skin. "How did you know my mother was a Veilreader?"

"*I told you,*" the voice answers, the colors shifting in the mist with it. "*There is much that I know. And much that you should, too.*" That white light brightens, pulsing. "*Now, come.*"

"Why did you heal me that time? *How* did you heal me? Who even *are* you, and what the hell do you want from me?"

The final question strikes me like a blade.

"*So many questions. Step through, and I will tell you anything you want to know.*"

As if I conjured the memory, the light floating within the fog charges with a series of bright, vivid colors. A scene forms, and I see an Abdite standing over me—though it's not the Abdites from the valley. There are flames burning behind the gnarled-looking wielder, whose eyes are blackened shards of burning coal. It speaks two words, sharp and clear: *A gift.*

"*The Veil responds to you.*" That sultry, male voice almost sounds impressed. "*Please. We are wasting time. Come to me. I will show you how magnificent you truly are.*"

I shake my head and back away.

The memories ravage me. The Abdites. Meiji. Their lunatic ravings. The dark voices whispering as something sinister entered the air. I still hear it in my nightmares. *Erhé akta maht.*

And of course, the explanation I've never understood.

You are the key. And the one hunting you will stop at nothing until you are his. That's why we were sent. To recover the key.

"You...you sent them, didn't you?" My voice is a harsh whisper. "Those Abdites in the valley. You are the one they call Master."

A long pause.

And then—

"*I am.*"

It's like a blow to the gut. "Someone *died* because of you." My voice is a low, broken rasp. "Because of me." I flick my eyes back up to the shrouded vapor. "What could you *possibly* want with me?"

But before he can answer, I feel a small tug, and then a forceful yank, and I am being pulled backwards, away from the Veil. Away from the swirling mist and fog—the floating colors.

I hear his final words like a softened parting. *"Fine. If you will not come to me, then I guess I will have to come to you."*

It takes a moment for everything to come into focus.

For Nuri's face, her dark brows pinched together with concentration over me, to fuse together into a cohesive image.

"It's almost out," I think I hear her say.

I pry my tongue from the roof of my mouth and try to speak.

Nuri shoots me a sharp look. "Don't try to speak or move. I'm erasing the venom from your bloodstream, and I don't want to lose its trail."

My head throbs, and I gasp for air. I stare up at a canopy of leaves washed in hazy light, and I blink as I attempt to make sense of the last...

Wait, how much time *has* passed? Where is Gray? And Marcella? What of the Adder?

"Calm down," Nuri says in a soothing voice from above. "Just keep breathing. I'm almost finished."

I force myself to do as she asks and keep breathing. Deep and thorough. I command my lungs to expand and retract, trading fear for hope. I try to focus on the twinkling night sky instead of the raging thoughts in my head, but...it doesn't work.

I can enter the Veil. Which makes me a Veilreader, just like my mother was.

That hadn't been a dream or a hallucination. It was real. The *voice* is real. It belongs to the person who sent the Abdites after me. To the one they call Master. The one they claim won't stop until I am his—whatever that means.

And I haven't the slightest clue what to make of all that. Where I should even begin to do something with that information. Because it feels like, somehow, I know even less than I did before.

I certainly have more questions than I did before.

"There," Nuri says, leaning back into a crouch on her heels. "All finished."

Tentatively, I blow out a breath and sit up. My head reels, my vision swimming with fuzzy dots. But eventually, the sensation washes away, and I flex my fingers and wiggle my toes, relieved to find everything working as it did before.

I immediately scan the terrain once I'm capable of doing so, looking for Marcella and Gray. My eyes find that crimson pool of blood almost instantly. Only, Marcella isn't lying in it. No one is.

I crane my neck as far back as I can, and when I catch a glimpse of blue scales, I whirl around completely, scurrying backwards on my hands and knees.

Nuri grabs me, stilling my movements. "Don't make too much noise."

"What is going on?" I ask her, my eyes roving across the massive length of the Blue-Horn's frozen body.

"Your friend, Gray, has the Adder locked in an illusion. It thinks it's frozen in a block of ice or something." She flicks her eyes over toward the east, near a line of staggered trees, and I follow her gaze.

Gray stands in front of the Adder, unmoving. Like he, himself, is frozen by a block of ice. His arms are adorned with golden veins, and his pushed-up sleeves reveal his wielder's mark glowing brilliantly in the night.

But not as brightly as the gold awakened in his eyes, like gilded suns.

For a moment, I'm too stunned to speak. Because that is Gray, the boy I have known and loved all my life, but that looks nothing like Gray.

"I healed my wounds as quickly as I could," Nuri explains in a hushed voice. "And when I returned, I found him like that. He seems...transfixed. I don't think he can move so long as he keeps the Adder under the illusion. I could barely get him to utter the words, *ice block*." She blows out a quiet sigh. "I was only able to piece it together because I touched the Blue-Horn's scales, and they are as cold as a frozen river."

I whip my gaze back to her. "So that means he is creating a visceral response?"

She dips her chin. "He must be. It's probably why it's taking so much of his magic and concentration."

I look back at him, my lips parted slightly. "And Marcella? Where's Marcella?"

"Unconscious, but alright. I've healed her most concerning wounds and moved her to a safer location. All she needs to do now is wake up."

I could cry from the relief washing through me at those words.

"What should we do?" I ask Nuri, swiveling my gaze between her and Gray. "How do we help him?"

"Truthfully," she begins slowly, "I've been wondering that same question. I am quite skilled at close-range combat, daggers being my speciality, but I don't have the strength to decapitate a Blue-Horned Adder. And if Gray and Marcella couldn't get their swords through the horn, I worry about our ability to do so as well."

"Which means we need a new approach," I offer.

She nods. "An approach I have yet to identify."

I drag a hand down my face, blowing out a long sigh.

What can we do? How can I help? Think—I need to *think*.

I'm not sure how much longer Gray's magic can hold out, and once it gives, I know Gray is going to be drained. He probably won't even be able to wield his sword, having lost so much strength, leaving him entirely defenseless against an enraged mammoth-sized snake.

Like hell I am going to let that happen.

With a newfound focus, I scan the scene. Absorb all the details I can, consolidating them into small possibilities.

It seems at some point, Gray dislodged his sword from the Adder's horn. It lays discarded beside him, coated in dried blue blood. I flick my eyes back to the Adder, a thought taking shape. We couldn't pierce the horn from the outside, but what if somehow we were able to do so from the inside?

I glance at Nuri. "I think I have an idea," I say slowly, knowing there's no way in hell I look confident.

She arches a surprised brow. "Is it a good one?"

I shake my head. "Absolutely not. But it may be the only option we have."

"What do you need me to do?"

I exhale all the air from my lungs. "To heal me before I die if it all goes to shit."

"What are you goin—"

Before she can finish her question, I take off on a sprint, reaching for Gray's sword and plucking it from the ground. My feet carry me to the Blue-Horn's tail next, and I crouch down before phase two of my terribly concocted plan can begin. I throw my hands out, visualize the plant in my head, and pray to the gods that my magic will show up.

A strangled gasp escapes my throat when it does.

I grab as much of the silvery-green leaves as I can, and I stuff the herb into different parts of my clothing to store it until I'm ready. Then, with a trembling, uncertain breath, I sprint up the Adder's long, sloped body, just as Gray had done. Luckily for me, Gray has the Adder frozen mid-lunge, so I don't have to use daggers to scale its body like he did. Unluckily for me, however, the incline is still incredibly steep, and I am nowhere near as strong as Gray.

With my calves screaming and my thighs burning, I reach the very top of the Adder. But I walk past the horn, striding to the furthest tip of its flat head, where its fangs rest directly beneath.

My heart hammers in my chest, and every instinct in my body is screaming at me that this is a terrible idea.

But it's the only one I have, so...

Here goes nothing.

I lower myself into a stabilized crouch—doing my best not to pay attention to how high up from the ground I am—and find a hold on some of the Adder's armour-like scales.

"Gray!" I shout, cupping my free hand around my mouth. "Gray! Drop the illusion! I have a plan."

It takes a moment, but eventually, the gold in Gray's eyes flickers before fading altogether. He snaps into focus, and he locks eyes with me.

His expression can only be described as pure horror when he sees where I'm standing, having no idea what I intend to do.

Within seconds, the Blue-Horn regains control of itself, and it finishes its attack at Gray. But the movements are lethargic—sluggish. Because since Gray created a visceral cold response in the Adder, that means the creature is in brumation, making him not as sharp and quick.

Which may just allow me to pull this off.

Gray dodges, having to roll to the side to evade, before getting up immediately and tracking the creature's movements.

I steady my racing heart, preparing for the next part. But my body locks, not wanting to move or cooperate. Though I can't say I blame it, considering how reckless this is. But I need to be brave—or at least emulate someone brave, someone strong and capable.

Who can I channel, if only for a moment? Who is someone that could do this without question? Who can I be like in this moment that would give me strength?

For some reason, Draven's face is the one that enters my mind.

And so I allow it to stay there. What would he do?

He would charge forward with a quiet arrogance, knowing that he would win. And he would never look back.

I never lose.

Fuck it.

Without another thought, I reach down and jab my fist into the Adder's nostril, immediately enraging the giant creature. It lets out a sharp *hiss*. Knowing what happened to Marcella when she angered the Adder, I brace myself for it, bending my knees, making sure my sword is gripped tightly in one hand, and the herbs are secured in the other.

Then, I blow out the breath that could very well be my last.

The Blue-Horn lurches its head back, but I am prepared for the motion. The moment I feel the creature coil, ready to fling me, I gather all the strength I can possibly muster into my already screaming legs and grip the herbs. And when it rears its body backwards, I propel myself upright, jumping as high as I possibly can from the ledge of its flat head—which, even when paired with the boost of momentum from the Adder, is not really that impressive.

I'm sent soaring, weightless, and the Adder tracks me immediately. It unhinges its terrifying jaws, exposing its cavernous pink throat.

Onto phase three.

As I begin descending from the sky, I clutch onto the tightly bundled herbs in my hand, wind my arm back, and hurl them toward the back of the creature's throat. They strike true, and the Blue-Horn lets out a wet, choking gag before it slams its jaws shut, locking me inside in a blanket of darkness.

I land hard against slick flesh—my breath heaving, the scent of musk and decay clogging my throat. I reach for something as the creature swallows—for *anything*—but my fingers grasp only air.

I slide backward.

I kick out, clawing, but gravity drags me toward the abyss of its stomach. And I am seconds away from being consumed whole—

But then the Adder's body seizes, and its jaw snaps open with a violent retch. The creature shudders as it starts to gag and heave.

Blue-Horned Adders abhor Mugwort more than anything else, and I just sent bundles of it flying down its throat.

I cling to the shifting flesh beneath me, steadying myself as the creature writhes, unable to shut its locked jaw. Between its slowed movements from brumation and the uncontrollable gagging, it is completely vulnerable.

And I am exactly where it never expected me to be—a place where there are no armor-like scales. Where it can't just fling me through the air.

But the Adder thrashes wildly, and I can't find my balance. Until suddenly—

It halts.

As if something has leashed it, anchoring it in place.

I whip my head to the side, and my chest tightens at what I see.

Marcella stands below, arms outstretched and green-veined, palms open, eyes burning with iron resolve as a cold rage lines her still-bloodied face. Vines and branches whip from the ground and weave around the

Adder's massive body, locking around it, holding it in place and containing its movements.

She slides her gaze to me and nods. Once, but steady.

And that is all I need.

I inhale, centering myself as I reach for that last bout of strength. My fingers curl around the hilt of Gray's longsword and squeeze.

With a defiant scream—a cry that rises from my gut, tearing through my lungs—and all the strength my beaten body can muster, I plunge the blade into the roof of the Adder's mouth, straight through the center of its horn.

The creature stills.

And I hold my breath.

Until a violent tremor rips through its massive frame, and its body gives out—crumpling in on itself, collapsing toward the ground, bringing me crashing down with it.

The ground quakes beneath the impact, a resounding boom echoing into the night as dust and debris explode outward, curling into the charcoal sky like a passing ghost.

And then there's silence.

Utter, ringing silence.

Until something moves, crawling from the ashes.

But the movement does not come from the Adder. Instead, it is the shadow of my own tattered body dragging itself free.

Because the creature is dead.

And I am still standing.

CHAPTER FORTY-ONE

"Well, by Raffir's fortune, you guys didn't die after all."
I squint my eyes open and see Griff standing over all of us, his arms folded across his chest and a proud smile pulling at his lips.

The fire from last night still clings to burnt embers, and the morning sun has arced into the sky, painting the world in warm, golden hues.

Next to me, Marcella grumbles something under her breath, finds a rock, and chucks it at Griff's head. He swoops his fingers, and a tiny portal blinks open and swallows the stone, ejecting it back toward Marcella, pelting her in the temple.

Nuri giggles, now also awake, and despite only getting a few, short hours of precious sleep, I have to swallow the laugh bubbling in my throat. But Marcella...

Oh, that is the promise of death if I've ever seen it.

"It's not nice to throw rocks at people," Griff scolds in a taunting tone. "Especially when that person is here to transport you back to the academy."

From across the makeshift fire pit, Gray rises and stretches his arms over his head, yawning. His hair is bedraggled and clinging to his skin.

"You'll be proud to know your team is the first to achieve their objective," Griff continues. "My captain is quite proud of you."

His captain. The captain of Castaria. Kiran.

Griff folds his arms and lifts his chin. "You guys made me proud as well. You know, as your third-year supervisor and all."

Laying back down, Marcella drapes her arm over her eyes. "You aren't our supervisor; you're our mode of transportation. More like a mule than anything else."

Griff shoots her wicked look. "Is that your way of telling me that you'd like to ride me?"

She peeks at him from beneath the crook of her elbow and clicks her tongue. "Please. You couldn't handle me."

His smirk turns sharp. "Wanna bet?"

I clear my throat, glancing at Marcella with a subtle curve in my brow before back at Griff. "You said something about taking us back to the academy?"

His gaze lingers on Marcella a moment longer before he finally drags it away and onto me. "Yes. The illustrious captains have requested I bring you back for judgment."

Nuri's face scrunches. "We are to be judged now?"

Griff nods. "Yup."

"But what about the other examinees?" I ask. "I thought you said we were the first ones finished."

"You are. But since you found your creature and decapitated it within three days, I've been instructed to bring you back." He shrugs. "The captains see no point in keeping you out here for the remaining days of the test, and they also see no merit in making you wait to receive judgment." He pulls at a hangnail on his index finger. "Plus, if you ask me, I think it's good you're getting judged early. It'd be shit having a bunch of creature heads gathered in one place."

"So, when do we leave?" Gray asks, smoothing his hair back into a tight bun.

"Well, now I guess," answers Griff.

We all glance around at each other, uncertain and exhausted.

We left the Blue-Horn and its now removed head where it had fallen. It had taken hours, but using Marcella's magic and Gray's strength, we made it happen.

After the shock of the night's events drifted away, Gray inspected

Marcella and me while Nuri lectured him, saying that she is perfectly capable of making sure that we are mended correctly. Marcella still had a gnarly gash in the back of her head that Nuri needed to finish healing, and I had a twisted ankle and wrist from my fall. I squeezed Marcella's hand the whole time Nuri attended to us, still reeling from thinking I had lost her.

After we could be sure that everyone was fine, we went as far away from the pungent smell of blood and death as our exhausted bodies would take us before giving out. With our eyes basically closed, we scraped together a makeshift camp and then simply collapsed into sleep around the fire right as the sky was starting to brighten.

And now the sun hasn't even peaked, and we are up again, heading for judgement.

"What about the head?" Marcella lifts her back from the ground, braces her weight on her knees, and rises. She swipes dirt off her pants and tunic. "And what of our appearances? Look at us—we're *disgusting.*"

Now that she mentioned it...

I glance around to see just how right Marcella is. We all look terrible. Our clothes are dirty. Our hair is disheveled. We are coated in crusty blue blood mixed with hardened mud, and we are as battered and bruised as discarded fruit.

"They know what you look like," Griff offers. "And I'll throw a portal at the head, forcing it through. You guys won't have to do anything."

"You can throw your portal at things?" Gray questions, impressed. He rolls his sleeves up to his elbows, and I find myself staring a few seconds too long at his strong forearms, feeling a slight stir.

That's weird.

A smile finds its way to Griff's lips. "I can," he answers with a proud dip of his chin. "Though, not all aether-wielders can say the same. It's not a common thing."

Gray tilts his head, and the sun falls perfectly onto his beautifully formed face. "Interesting."

Nuri stands, readjusting her clothing, and pulls her braided hair over her shoulder.

344

She really is quite beautiful.

"Have they been watching us?"

Griff nods, running a hand through his unruly brown hair. An action that flexes his bicep—though it's not nearly as impressive as Gray's muscles. Or Draven's.

Thinking of Draven's arms sends a wave of scorching heat through me. I cough at the unexpected intensity of it.

What in god's veins is going on with me?

Marcella flicks her eyes at me and raises a questioning brow. Eventually, she looks back to Griff and sighs. "Well, let's get this over with."

The judgment is surprisingly seamless.

Smooth, easy, quick—something I'm not expecting considering the tension and drama of the first one.

The captains are all in their chairs, waiting for us when we arrive. They take a few minutes to examine the head of the Blue-Horn, ask some members from the Philator aggregate to take it to their wing for further examination, and then, for all intents and purposes, basically give us a pat on the back and tell us our whole team passes.

It's all rather…underwhelming. Almost unnervingly so.

Though I guess there is one thing that keeps the judgement interesting—for me at least.

The effects of the aphrodisiac are still in my system.

I finally realized it the moment we stepped through the portal, and, as if on instinct, my eyes found Draven's—his eyes already on me. The eye contact sent a warm pulse flooding my every nerve-ending. And yes, I've been affected by Draven's striking looks before, but…never like that.

I should have realized it sooner. Like when I started feeling stirs in my stomach from looking at Gray and Griff. My guess is that I haven't noticed the effects until now because the venom and adrenaline were overpowering it. And then once the venom was out and the adrenaline finally faded, I was asleep. Normally, a good night's rest is enough to let the effects of an aphrodisiac pass, but in my case, the powder I inhaled was strong enough to affect a colossal beast. And that was only a few measly hours ago—even though it already feels like days ago.

So for the whole judgement, I have to make sure not to look at Draven—to not meet his beautiful and peculiar mismatched eyes. In my current state, I *physically* can't handle it.

Which also means I have to endure strange, unfounded feelings toward Kiran, Finlay, and Nuha the whole judgement—I don't dare even look at Arden. She's too close to Draven.

After it's all over and we're dismissed, I scurry from the arena as quickly as I possibly can without being considered suspicious. I am disgusting, and I want to bathe myself more than anything in this world—well, perhaps second to one other thing at the moment. But I can't risk bathing in the communal bathing chambers. It's too risky given my...condition.

Like a trained assassin, I creep around the back of the guest wing and swipe some freshly washed clothes drying on a line—not bothering to check the sizes—along with a lone bar of soap.

Then I sprint for the sparkling pools resting between the hills.

🌿 🪶

I dunk my head deep beneath the turquoise waters.

Despite the days just now shifting from warm to cool, the water still bites with a prickly chill—a feature I decide is a blessing considering my present affliction. But after a few minutes submerged in its embrace, the chill fades, leaving nothing but a pleasant bath coupled with tranquil sounds of humming waterfalls and chirping birds.

I swim a few laps around the basin once I'm finally scrubbed clean. The water is fed by a small channel stemming from the tiered waterfalls, and being within its grasp awakens my senses in a positive way. Eventually, though, when I'm pruning and my already fatigued muscles are absolutely exhausted, I reluctantly pry myself from the glittering pool of lapping blue.

The clothes I smuggled are—of course—two sizes too big. I throw on the oversized shirt, fitting me like a dress, and forgo the pants entirely. And then I take a deep breath, allowing my eyes to slowly scan the picturesque scene in front of me, finding myself overcome by the oddest urge to simply lay in the fluffy grass and find pictures in the clouds.

And so I do.

All the while, the rays of a golden sun caress my cheeks, and my bare feet tingle with the soft, velvety touch of the ground beneath me. My chest swells with an overwhelming feeling of contentment. It could be the aphrodisiac making me romanticize everything, but...

Everything about this moment feels so simple, so easy—so beautiful. Not because the waters sparkle like a diamond, or the green is so saturated, a painter would have to create a new color just to capture the depth in its hue. Not because of the symphony of sounds filling the wind, or because the waterfalls singing in the background are so achingly comforting.

It's simply because I chose to sit here, staring up at a powdery sky because I wanted to. A bird unbound from its cage at last, free to flap its wings in the direction it desires.

I throw my arms back over my head and smile—wide and unflinching. This moment...it is a captured happiness I intend to hold on to.

"Daydreaming, are we?"

That voice.

Oh, no. Oh no, no, no.

He can't be here right now.

Slowly, reluctantly, I drag myself up from the grass and turn around. Draven stands behind me, corded arms folded across his chest, his head cocked in question, eyes narrowed and sharp. His night-dark hair is tousled messily with waves, and there are smudges of dark beneath his eyes.

I bite my lip.

Fuck—gods help me.

He wears a hemp shirt that sags low and sits loosely across his shoulders, revealing a strip of his chest. I look at his sandy-beige skin, the black ink poking through the fabric, grazing the marred scar along his collarbone. My eyes rove across the exposed pieces of his tattoo, or wielder's mark, or...whatever the hell it actually is...as I imagine him shirtless, the design stretching over his sweat-slicked body. I imagine what that body would feel like if I pressed mine against it. Imagine—

I shake my head.

Snap out of it. I have to *Snap. Out. Of It.*

I suck in a breath. "I think I've earned the right, considering what nightmares we just faced."

Draven observes me a moment longer before approaching me, crouching down in a fluid movement. He rests his forearms on his knees and studies me closely. *Too* closely. "You didn't look at me once during your judgment," he points out, smooth yet sharp. "Why?"

My pulse kicks.

I attempt a casual shrug, but the movement is jerky and unnatural. "No reason. I'm surprised you even noticed that."

"And why wouldn't I notice that?"

I feel every moment of his gaze on my skin as if it were a physical touch. "I—well...I mean, why *would* you?" My voice comes out all wrong, entirely too flustered.

He arches a pointed brow. "Why would I care that someone is avoiding eye contact with me?" An aching pause. "Or why would I specifically notice *you* avoiding eye contact with me?" He leans toward me, his eyes clear and focused. "Both seem like pretty substantial things for me to miss."

My breathing hitches, and...

Did I just *arch* toward him?

At my lack of an answer, Draven chuckles under his breath and shakes his head. "What was that powder you inhaled while fighting the Blue-Horn?"

My face bleeds red. "I—the...powder? What powder?"

The tip of Draven's lip curves. "The powder you blew into the Adder's nose. What was it? I'm curious—indulge me."

A breeze blows my still-wet hair across my face, swaying the grass in a rustling melody. It also blows Draven's scent directly into my line of smell—citrus mingling with sandalwood. I inhale it deeply, and a flood of heat rushes through me as the fragrance sinks into my skin, coiling tight in my chest, curling low in my stomach.

By the Mother, I am so *fucked.*

My breath is shallow in my chest as I try to subtly put distance between Draven and me, not trusting myself to keep my hands where they belong. He truly is the *last* person I should be around right now.

And I'm not even going to begin pondering the reasons for why that is.

My eyes make their way back to his, and his features are set in an inquisitive calm. His gaze does not falter, staying steady on me—waiting.

I sigh.

"It was an aphrodisiac," I confess.

"I know," he replies tauntingly. "I just wanted to hear you admit it since you've told no one else."

My jaw pops open. "You are unbelievabl—"

"—ly perceptive? Yes, I'm aware."

The urge to smack him overtakes the urge to straddle him.

Until I think of straddling him—which results in a distracting ache appearing between my thighs, forcing me to press my knees together.

Draven watches, something glimmering behind his eyes. He looks...amused.

The bastard.

He huffs a laugh before clapping his hands to his thighs and rising. "Alright," he says. "Stand up."

My brows furrow. "Come again?"

"I said stand up. You and I are going to train."

I look around the placid hills, the open fields of grass in between. "What, right here? Right *now?*"

He folds his arms and swivels his head, glancing around. "Unless you prefer to train in the water come nightfall?"

Actually, that...doesn't sound half bad.

But I at least have the wits not to say that out loud.

349

At the confusion still pinching my face, he drops his arms and elaborates. "It'll be an effective way for you to sweat the effects out of your system. And if you get too hot—" an entirely too-knowing smirk tugs at his lips "—you can just jump into the water and cool off."

This is absolutely, most definitely, a very, very bad idea.

"But..." I glance down at my exposed legs. "I'm not wearing any pants."

Draven shrugs, the gesture lazy and indifferent. "I don't mind if you don't."

Chapter Forty-Two

"What you did during the second test was reckless," Draven says while effortlessly dodging my attack. "But...it was also impressive."

"Oh?" I respond through ragged breaths, reorienting my hands to cover my vital spots. "An actual compliment from you. To what do I owe the pleasure?"

Draven huffs, circling me. "I'm capable of compliments—they're just rarely earned."

"Right," I drawl, mirroring his movements.

"But I'd advise you from doing anything as reckless as that again. One wrong step, Lyra, and you would have been dead." I'm caught off-guard by the tightness in his voice.

I shrug. "There are worse things."

He stops, frowning. "Than *dying*?"

"Oh, yes." My brows furrow at his expression. "What? Don't tell me you haven't heard the age-old adage: dying is easy, it's living that's the harder task."

His brow arches with a deep curve. "Yes," he says tentatively. "But I've never had someone actually *use* it against me before."

My shoulders rise and fall once more. "You have now."

Draven studies me. But then without warning, he moves—faster than a blink. He twists my arms and pins them behind my back, tugging me back into his bare chest. His breath caresses the skin on my neck, and my stomach turns molten—my pulse immediately skipping a beat as it starts working overtime.

"Your life is not so worthless that you should be willing to throw it away that easily."

I tilt my chin up to meet his eyes in defiance, bringing our lips way too close. And I swear I catch Draven flicking his eyes at my mouth, his lips tightening. "Careful," I warn, my voice tangled with a teasing tone. "Say anymore, and I'll think you're starting to care about me."

His grip on me tightens. "And who said I don't?"

It's the same conversation we had on the roof the night he caught me reading Casimir's journal. With coals burning in my stomach and an ache throbbing between my thighs, I continue playing it through, somehow managing to hold his gaze despite the intensity resting within it.

"Do you?" I challenge, breathless from him touching me—from being so close to him.

Something shifts in his expression, and the corner of his mouth kicks up. Yet instead of answering, he releases his grip on me. I immediately whirl around on him, ready to strike. But he moves before I get the chance, swiping my legs out from beneath me.

I land on my back, and the air rushes from my lungs.

"Gods," I say through a cough. "Kiran wasn't being dramatic. You really *do* love doing that."

Draven offers me his hand, a far too smug smile on his face.

I click my tongue. "Again," I demand, placing my hand in his as he helps me up. As soon as I'm upright, I retract my hand as fast as I can. His touch is too...explosive.

He dips his chin and slides his feet into his stance, a smirk playing at his lips. He flicks two fingers, beckoning me. "If you think you can handle it, then come for me."

Oh.

Oh.

Why did his choice of words feel distinctly...intentional?

My breathing hitches, and I have to shut my eyes against the immense heat rushing through me—the overwhelming ache threatening to split me. When I reopen them, Draven has the sharpest, most amused smirk I've ever seen resting on his lips.

I narrow my eyes. "Could you at least put your shirt back on?"

"Why?" he croons, tilting his head. "Is it distracting you?"

I bite down on my irritation. "I'm under the influence of an aphrodisiac. *Obviously* it's distracting me."

He folds his arms over his chest, and every muscle on him ripples from the movement. My breathing stutters with desire.

And then the bastard chuckles. He actually *chuckles.*

"Just consider it another lesson on control."

I pinch the bridge of my nose. "Your ability to accommodate others is truly a marvel."

He shrugs. "Never was very popular in the sandbox."

I tilt my head and mock sympathy. "Gee, can't imagine why."

His lips curve up. Again, he motions for me to attack. "No more talking."

"But I enjoy our conversations so thoroughly."

He shoots me a look. "Last chance."

"I —"

Draven charges at me, throwing a punch I know is not with his full force nor with his full speed. I block it with a bent arm, and parry when he swings with his other.

He smiles. "Good."

His leg swipes at me, attempting to knock me over again. But I dodge easily this time and counter with my own attack, landing a blow on his quickly moving forearms, swinging together to form a protective wall over his face.

He drops his arms and smirks wider. "I think the aphrodisiac makes you move better."

Then, with zero warning, he rolls his neck slowly before charging at me, tackling me to the ground.

He leans back and draws his arm like one would when drawing a bowstring. But before his punch can make contact, I kick at his shoulder, stopping the force of the blow and jarring him back. I buck at him, just like he showed me, and seize upon his momentary unsteadiness.

Draven's mouth curves with approval, but unlike during our previous training, he does not fall off me.

Instead, he stacks his fists as if holding an imaginary dagger over his head, ready to plunge it into my chest. We've trained for what to do in this position many times, and it's like he's testing me.

He thrusts his imaginary dagger down to strike its intangible tip into my chest, but I turn my elbow out and brace one arm horizontally, stopping the make-believe dagger in its tracks. Then, in one, swift motion, I brace my feet against the ground, bridge my hips forcefully, and step over when his body inevitably tilts.

Now, it is him who is pinned underneath me.

Feeling bold in my triumph, I lean down, my lips grazing his ear, and whisper, "How does it feel being the one put on their back for once?"

I pull back just enough to meet his eyes. He lifts a surprised brow—something indiscernible passing through his features—before he effortlessly breaks free of my hold, reverses our positions, and pins both my wrists above my head with only one hand.

His answering smirk is sharp. "You were saying?"

I can't even answer. My body is sent into an incoherent frenzy the moment I feel his hips pressed against me. My skin is buzzing—*humming*—from his touch. And it screams at me, loud and demanding. *More. More. More.*

Draven's brows rise with amusement as he cocks his head, studying me with a wry smile. "Your face is as red as Kiran's hair." A cruel pause. "Tell me, is it really just from the powder, or..." He lifts his hand and, with a torturously soft touch, glides a finger from one side of my cheek, over the slope of my nose, down to the other side of my face, tracing the red stain mottling my skin. "Is it me who makes you blush?"

The ache between my legs becomes almost unbearable as my skin erupts in flames.

But I set my features in a mask of cool indifference, huffing a hollowly arrogant laugh. "Anyone could make me blush right now," I counter. "Even Finlay Fjolla, and I loathe him."

Draven's eyes darken, and I swear I feel him stiffen. His grip on my wrists tighten, and he shifts his weight back onto his heels, allowing me to feel even more of him pressed against me.

Oh gods—*yes*.

His mouth tightens. "You know, I've never cared for hearing another man's name on a woman's tongue when I'm on top of her."

I'm not sure where my reply comes from—if it's the effects of the powder, or my pulsing need, or something else. "Would you prefer to hear your name on my tongue instead?"

I watch Draven's throat bob as he swallows, his jaw flexing after. It sends a wave of satisfaction coursing through me, seeing him react.

So I press it further.

"I wonder which would have the better taste—your name, or Finlay's? I guess I haven't said yours yet, but Finlay, his—"

Draven curls his fingers around my jaw, gripping it lightly. He lowers his lips until he is mere inches from my face. "Say his name again while I'm touching you, and I'll see to it that you forget every other name but my own." Lazily, he lifts his hand, exposing only one finger. "Because this?" he challenges. "This is all I need to make you forget about every other name."

Holy gods.

Something coils in my stomach, desperate for release. My body is a vessel composed of licking flames setting my every nerve-ending on fire.

I release a trembling breath. "And is that a promise, or a threat?"

His eyes flare with challenge. His breath caresses the sensitive skin of my mouth, and despite myself, I bite down on my lower lip. My body pulses with an overwhelming, incomprehensible need that only Draven can fill.

"It is a fact." Draven flicks his gradient eyes to my lips, something burning in the rich color of them. "Because it *is* a fact, Lyra, that my finger is all it would take to have my name tattooed on your tongue."

I melt.

"Right," I breathe, hearing the shakiness in my voice. "But you don't have an ego problem or anything."

He leans closer, and the movement presses his hips deeper into mine. And Draven is either naturally blessed, or he is beginning to harden. Because his bulge presses against his pants and thus against me, nothing more than this oversized shirt keeping me from him. Without thinking, I grind against him. And something as trivial and friction-filled should not feel so unbelievably divine.

"I assure you," Draven murmurs, his voice rough-edged and thick. "Ego has nothing to do with how I would make your body sing."

Something white-hot coils in my stomach, and my willpower is seconds away from snapping completely.

Draven, breathing deeply, watches me for a moment longer, something sharp still simmering in his gaze as he tucks his bottom lip between his teeth. But eventually that sharp intensity dulls into something soft, and the hand containing both my wrists tightens its grip before releasing me altogether.

He blows out a long sigh and rises. Then, without a word, he scoops me up into his arms with astonishing ease, cradling me to his chest, and walks toward the water.

The feeling of his touch on my bare thighs sets me on fire, and I am burning, burning, burning. Aphrodisiac be damned, I want him to take me right here. I *need* him. I—

In a fell swoop, he lowers his arms and tosses me into the sparkling pool. The cold is a shock to my system, but I take a few seconds and sit beneath the surface. A newfound clarity washes over me, and *oh gods...*

What the hell had I been *thinking?*

Did I really *grind* against him?

Pulsing desire is replaced with absolute mortification.

I stay beneath the water for as long as my lungs can manage. When I resurface, I swipe the moisture from my eyes and find Draven standing off to the side of the pool, his arms crossed and...laughing. He is *actually* laughing.

His smile is breathtaking.

It's like glimpsing a perfectly preserved snowflake. It's impossible not to inspect it—to savor and cherish the beautifully delicate details of it, knowing how fragile a thing it truly is.

"You needed to cool off," Draven supplies with open palms.

The humor leaking from his words makes me grit my teeth and glower at him. I push back the wet hair from my face and challenge, "And what about you? I have the aphrodisiac as my excuse. What's yours?"

He chuckles under his breath, shaking his head. "I don't need one."

I arch a brow. "So you just...what? Like toying with people who can't control themselves?"

"Only you," he replies, still smiling.

I cross my arms in the water and huff a breath. "Lucky me."

Draven studies me, a soft curve on his lips. "Funny," he says gently after a passing moment. "I was just thinking the same thing."

Chapter Forty-Three

F our days have passed since the end of the second test.

Of the eleven teams—not counting our own—only six completed the test and returned with the head of their assigned creature. Of those six teams, three examinees failed and were asked to leave Bathara—for what reasons, I don't know.

That leaves thirty-one examinees left to take the third and final test in three days; the test that, according to Marcella, has the lowest passing rate of them all.

An incredibly comforting fact, I might add.

After the day in the hills, things with Draven have felt...different. Though, I'm not sure how that's possible considering I've been trying to keep my distance as much as one person can when seeing someone morning, noon, and night.

We've officially incorporated magic into my training, working on it after all my daily tasks have been completed—or rather, once I've attempted them and answered a million questions afterwards, when I fail to complete them successfully. But I am getting *very* close in my defense. Still, despite Draven's admirable magical instruction, I haven't been able to successfully wield magic under his guidance once. Not even so much as a tiny weed sprouting from the ground.

And my frustration with that is growing hotter day by day—as well as my self-doubts.

But, as Draven reminds me, at least I'm trying. He says it probably has something to do with my unmanifested wielder's mark, and I shouldn't take it as a reflection of my capabilities.

Which always leaves me wondering—

Why the hell *hasn't* my wielder's mark manifested yet, and when is it planning on appearing?

I heave a sigh, rounding the corner of one of Bathara's many walking paths in their expansive and elegant gardens.

Draven cut our training short this morning—though I have no clue why—and so I've been walking around Bathara, exploring ever since. So far, I've found four new gardens I didn't know existed, a stunning greenhouse that I plan on visiting later—once healers aren't within the glass panes attending to their herbs—and scattered marble statues of different gods and influential people from Solaya's history.

Notably, three of the statues I discovered were the founders of the remaining Archblood lines—the first descendents of the gods, according to some legends. Though, I've never been one to believe receiving magic from the gods made them descendants of them.

Declan Sulien's statue was carved from fire quartz, featuring a shimmering base filled with fiery red, vibrant orange, and molten amber streaking throughout the stone. Resting on its platform is a golden plaque, labeled "Declan Sulien: Son of the Sun".

Then there was Elwin Fjolla's statue, carved from a stunningly pure block of winter crystal. His statue featured a plaque forged from beautiful turquoise with the writings, "Elwin Fjolla: The Frosted Prince".

And lastly, there was Kyros Dalmar's statue. Created using the glittering, onyx anthracite mined in the Endymion Mountains, his statue sparkled in the sun like a starry night. His violet-colored plaque read, "Kyros Dalmar: Ruler of Night".

For some reason, of all the statues, it is the Dalmar one that I find to be equally the most beautiful and unnerving.

I find another statue tucked deep into a neglected garden filled with weeds, catching my interest. It is crafted from a beautiful, yet eroding, purple agate stone. The arms have crumbled, leaving nothing but legs and a feminine shaped torso, and the face has eroded into a flat surface. Still, the bronze-colored plaque is semi-legible, showing at least the deteriorating woman's name. "Lucillia Izavarda, Daughter of—".

I can't make out the final part, with the words being too rusted and weathered.

I continue with my stroll, my mind fixated on the name. Why does it sound so familiar? I don't recognize it from any history lessons with Sterling—at least I think—but instead from something more recent.

It hits me right when I turn a corner, finding a large fountain with stone outlines of small creatures I don't recognize spewing water from their mouths opposite of each other.

Casimir Vivaldri's journal.

I remember him mentioning the Izavarda name. But why? What was the reason again?

I sit against the edge of the pouring fountain and pinch my chin as I think. My brows knit firmly together, and I stare at the stone pathway underneath my feet. He sought out someone with the name for...*something*.

I'm so lost in my thoughts, I don't hear the footsteps approaching.

"Oh? What's this? A lapdog free of its leash?"

Ice crawls down my skin, sending the hairs on my arms rising. I jerk upright, my eyes immediately finding the sound of the voice.

Smooth face. Neat, slicked-back, ebony hair that is a few shades darker than his inky eyes. A slimy smirk curling his entitled lips.

Eri Valenwood.

The right hand to the Supreme Commander, Tynan Dalmar.

What in god's veins is he doing here?

I tilt my head and mock a frown at him. "Strange—all I see before me is a slithering snake."

Eri's lip curls with a sneer. "Your insolence will have you hanged some day."

"A far better fate than spending three more seconds near you," I croon.

I make to strut past him, but he curls his fingers aggressively around my bicep and yanks me back toward him.

"I should have you whipped," he seethes quietly.

"And I should break your nose for touching me." I shrug at him—lazy and indifferent. "But it appears neither of us will be getting what we want." I attempt to wrench my arm from his grip, but Eri doesn't let go. "Let *go* of me," I hiss through clenched teeth.

He cocks his head, pretending to think. "No," he replies with a false softness. "No, I don't think I will. Because you see, *pet*, I am the one who gives the orders, and you—" his grip on my arm tightens "—are the one who *takes* them."

"Not. Anymore," I grit out.

Eri feigns sympathy. "Oh, my dear. You don't actually think you'll ever have a place here, do you? That you could ever belong in our world?" He digs his fingers deeper into my skin, and at this point, I am sure it'll leave a bruise.

I will not cower. I will not yield. I will not falter.

Yet despite seeking strength in those words, my lips thin, and I don't have a reply for Eri.

It makes him grin like a victorious predator who has successfully entrapped its prey. "Let me spell this out for you so clearly, even a lowblooded servant girl like you can understand: I don't know how you managed to convince King Alastair to let you come here and compete, but a girl like you—a whore only good for a night's fuck—has no place in the world of nobility. You are scum. Trash. *Worthless.*"

The hammer that won't seem to go away begins tapping at the wall in my chest again, creating another small fissure.

I clench my jaw against it and lift my chin. "Forgive me if I don't value the opinion of an oily worm."

Eri's eyes flare with rage before his face falls into a strange calm. He tugs me closer into him, and I have never found the smell of rosemary to be so repulsive. "You have such defiant eyes," he sings. "And they are so sharp—so unique with their coloring." He chuckles, the low sound not a happy thing at all. "I remember seeing you that night in King Alastair's hall with an amethyst jewel resting on your head. I was so...enticed." He licks his bottom lip, and his eyes slowly scan my body.

I jerk against his hold, but he does not let go.

He presses his lips against my ear. "Do not think I have forgotten what you owe me." The words are a greasy whisper.

"I *owe* you nothing," I seethe back.

"Fine," Eri says, pushing me backwards toward the fountain's edge. "If you will not give me what you owe, I'll just take it instead."

Fucking *men.*

The moment his lips brush my neck, a boiling heat consumes my blood, and I simply...react—doing what I so desperately wanted to do that night during The Founding celebration. My free arm draws back, and I punch him straight across the face.

He tips over, clutching his angry jaw. "You *fucking* whore."

I click my tongue. "Truly, men must learn to get more creative with their insults." My shoulder shrugs lazily. "If the worst thing I am is a person who enjoys fucking, then so be it. I'd much rather be that than a cowardly man who thinks just because he has a cock between his legs means he owns the world."

Now, I concede provoking him further may not have been the best move...

But it felt damn good saying it.

Until Eri charges at me, pins my arms to my sides, and rams me against the fountain. His following punch is like a shock to my system, rattling my cheekbone and my senses.

I gasp for air, shaking my head against the stars blurring my vision.

Eri yanks my hair and spins me around. I hear him working on the belt supporting his trousers, each *clink* and *clatter* like a death sentence. I pull my bottom lip between my teeth to keep it from quivering—I won't give Eri the satisfaction—and attempt to count my breaths.

It's the only way to survive something like this with a semblance of sanity.

But before Eri can finish the work on his belt, I feel him being yanked off of me by something—*someone.*

When I turn around, Draven has Eri pinned to the ground on his back, a jet-black dagger at his throat. And the look screaming in his eyes is a rage that burns hotter than a flame.

"What the *fuck* are you doing?" Eri seethes from below him, his teeth stained in crimson, his lip split down the middle.

I don't think that's a result of my punch.

"Trying very hard not to kill you right here and now," Draven growls, his voice sharp as the dagger at Eri's throat.

"Have you lost your gods-damn *mind?*" Eri looks at Draven, incredulous. "She's a *whore*, Draven. It's her fucking *duty.*"

I blink, confused why Eri speaks to Draven like he knows him.

Actually...

He must know him—he said his name.

Draven presses the tip of his blade deeper into Eri's skin, drawing blood. "Call her a whore one more time," he warns. "And I will slice your neck without so much as batting an eyelash."

"It's what she *is!*" Eri shouts, like he can't believe he's having to explain this.

Draven cocks his head. "That's close enough." He moves, prepared to slide the dagger along Eri's throat, when a voice calls out, stopping him.

"My, my," the voice says, smooth as silk. "What do we have here?"

I track the sound, finding a man standing before us with a slightly cocked head who is mid-aged, strikingly handsome, and possesses eyes that glisten like the sea. His hair is tied neatly back and is as dark as a starless sky. His nose is prominent, his jaw sharp.

I can't really put my finger on it, but he almost looks familiar, in a way.

"Your insubordinate, infuriatingly difficult—"

Draven cuts Eri off by pushing the dagger's tip even deeper into his skin.

"Hm," the man hums. "I see." He clasps his hands behind his back and strides toward me. "And who are you?"

I clear my throat, feeling slightly unnerved by this man's presence. "Lyra," I say, steadying the tremor threatening to crack my words the best I can. "Lyra Izacalli."

"Izacalli?" the man questions. "I've never heard of such a surname."

"It belonged to my mother."

He tilts his head, watching with me quiet interest.

Another gesture that looks oddly familiar.

"I see," he muses softly. "That may do it, then. It's not very often a woman passes on a surname." He turns his back to me, studying Draven and Eri. "Would you be so kind as to remove yourself from my lieutenant commander?"

Draven does no such thing. "If your lieutenant commander could be so decent as to keep his filthy hands to himself."

The man grunts his agreement. "Forgive him. Although, if my ears did not deceive me, I overheard him yelling that the girl was a night attendant for King Alastair. Being from Erandor Kingdom yourself, and from Talderine no less, you understand first hand our customs with our own courtesans." The man flicks his gaze over his shoulder and looks at me. "We don't call them night attendants in Erandor Kingdom," he elaborates. "Only courtesans."

I barely register his words.

Draven is from Talderine? Erandor's capital city—wealthy, pompous, and overflowing with nobility. He truly *must* be a purebred highborn to be from there.

Keeping his dagger securely wedged in the crook of Eri's neck, Draven slides his gaze to the man. "You know, I don't understand what a woman's past profession has to do with a man's entitlement in claiming her against her will. Not to mention, we're not in Erandor, and she is a student of these exams, making your point irrelevant."

Cooly, the man just listens. "It seems your time away from home has made you bold."

Time away from...*home?*

Why do I feel like I'm playing catch up right now...

"And your time spent dawdling with your king has made you forgetful." Draven's cold face is a quiet, raging storm. "Make no mistake, I am a captain on these grounds. And as such, I am well within my right to apprehend any person I find disrupting the peace."

"Ah, yes, but see, apprehending and maiming are two very different things." The man claps his hands in front of him and swoons his voice. "I tell you what—you let him go, and I promise to personally see to a just punishment for this indiscretion. Sound fair?"

At Draven's lack of an immediate reply, the man adds, "Consider it a favor to me. I would be most grateful. Perhaps even…indebted."

Draven bites down on his scowl. Then, he leans down and glares into the very fabrics of Eri's soul. "I swear by Merikh," he begins in a rough whisper. "I will inspect every inch of her skin, and for every mark you left on her body, I will ensure to pay it back tenfold." He glances at me, and my body reacts before my mind, covering my cheek with my hand, afraid that the skin will already be discolored with red and purple splotches.

His expression tightens as his lips thin into a straight line.

Draven fixes his gaze back on Eri. "Starting now." Without another word, Draven twirls the dagger in his hand, shifting the hilt's position, and drags the blade across Eri's cheek.

A long gash oozes crimson down Eri's pale skin, and he screams—though whether from pain or anger, I can't tell.

The man tsks at Draven as he rises from atop of Eri. "Now, was that truly necessary?"

"It was," is Draven's only reply.

The man glances between Draven and me, his brows high on his head. "My, my," he drawls, the undercurrent in his voice reminding me of the quiet steps of a predator before it pounces. Those sea-colored eyes slide to me, where they remain. "It seems, for one reason or another, my son feels very protective over you, Lyra Izacalli."

His—*what*?

This is Draven's *father*?

My eyes bounce between the two of them, and suddenly it makes sense. Why the man and some of his mannerisms appeared oddly familiar. It's because he looks like *Draven*. Or well, I guess Draven looks like him.

Now that I look more closely, their similarities are striking. The only differences are Draven's skin has a golden undertone, whereas his father's skin is paler—more peachy—and Draven's eyes are more green, where his father's eyes are more rich in their blue. Oddly, and poorly timed, it makes me wonder what Draven's mother looked like.

Draven's father watches me with a slight frown on his lips, as if waiting for an answer.

"Sorry?" I say, attempting to not let my brows pull together.

"I asked if you happen to know why Draven is so protective over you?"

I swallow against the sudden dryness overtaking my throat and shake my head. "No," I answer truthfully. "I don't."

A small curve forms at the corner of his mouth. "Ah, well, I have a few guesses myself, but best not to speak on conjecture." He glides his eyes to Draven, then at Eri—who finally rises from the ground—and there is this eager look resting within them.

And seeing it, I still can't shake this feeling that I'm missing something. Something that's right under my nose...

Eri approaches Draven, a line of blood dripping down his marred cheek. "You may be the Supreme Commander's son and heir to your house, but I still outrank you. You'd do well to remember that."

Draven folds his arms over his chest. "In martial rank only." He shoots him a sharp, lethal look. "Something that matters little in Erandor. You'd be wise to remember *that*."

And there it is.

Holy *gods*.

This man isn't just Draven's father. He is Tynan Dalmar, the Supreme Commander in Erandor Kingdom. The Master Strategist. The man known for delighting in bestial acts due to his insatiable curiosity with human nature. The head of a Great House and an Archblood.

And Draven is his son—his *heir*.

Draven is a Dalmar.

Memories of all the rumors I've heard surrounding House Dalmar and its heir crash into me like a lethal blow.

He abused his son to turn him into an emotionless weapon.

Chained him to a wall to teach him how to survive without food or drink.

Had him beaten within inches of his life to teach him how to recover from a lost battle.

Locked him in a pitch-black dungeon for a month so he could learn to hone his other senses.

His mother was murdered in front of his very eyes.

The memory of the last rumor sends a shockwave through me as I think of Draven on the roof that night, drunk, talking about his mother.

I don't talk about her enough. She deserves to be talked about more—to be remembered by someone.

Nausea rolls in my stomach.

Tynan watches me, then presses his palm to his forehead—the movement slow and precise. "Ah, where are my manners? Allow me to formally introduce myself." He takes a few fluid steps toward me and outstretches his hand, bending slightly at the waist to better lock eyes. "I am Tynan Dalmar, and I am very pleased to make your acquaintance."

My body moves on muscle memory alone as it clasps his hand.

Sterling's warning rings loudly in my head.

I've heard Erandor Kingdom's Supreme Commander often frequents Bathara. I hear he offers stratagem advice to the council at times. I would like to warn you to avoid him at all costs, but I fear that is not entirely feasible. So instead, I'd advise that, should you ever cross paths with him, mind your words, and remember that everything is a game of wits with that man.

And suddenly, everything about this conversation has changed.

Tynan studies me, that small curve permanently wedged in the corner of his lips. "I must say, judging by your shock at hearing my title *after* learning I am Draven's father, I'm almost inclined to believe he never told you about his rather...prestigious heritage." He turns, sliding his sharp gaze to Draven. "Would I be correct in that deduction?" he asks him.

Draven simply glares at him silently.

An action that has Tynan curling his lips with satisfaction.

"I can't say I blame him entirely," he continues, fixing his bright gaze back on me. "It can be hard to escape the politics associated with such a title—why with strategic marriage proposals flooding in daily. People are always looking for something." He cocks his head, that diplomatic smile returning. "Tell me, my girl, what is it you're searching for with my son?"

I ignore the obvious bait and hold his gaze, thinking.

Should you ever cross paths with him, mind your words, and remember that everything is a game of wits with that man.

He may think I'm just some lowborn night attendant for King Alastair, but I was raised by Sterling Nightenjoy—a man who could go toe-to-toe with Tynan Dalmar in a battle of words and wit.

And I intend to make him proud.

"I think the better question is what was your son searching for with me?" I shrug, taking care to keep slight rigidity in the gesture to make it seem more authentic—like I'm intimidated by him. "I never knew he was a Dalmar, after all. Let alone your Great House's heir."

Tynan chuckles, his grin widening to reveal his perfect teeth. "That is an excellent point you make." He turns around, keeping one arm folded neatly behind his back, and flicks his gaze to Eri. "You may go."

Eri clamps down on his anger and inclines his head, strutting off in the opposite direction after, shooting Draven a murderous look as he goes.

Tynan rubs at his jaw with his free hand. "Would it be too bold of me to presume affections are involved?"

"Presumptions are yours to believe," I supply.

He hums, observing me from head-to-toe. "Would it be too bold of me to state them aloud, then?"

"Yes," I answer without hesitation. "It would."

His brows do a little jump before he resets his expression, clasping his hands together behind his back. "Well then, forgive me for my brashness. You see, it's just..." He trails off, glancing at Draven—who remains insouciant as ever—with an unreadable expression. "Draven has formed *questionable* attachments before, and I just had to be sure."

I'd be lying if I said the words didn't squeeze at some forgotten corner in my heart.

Tynan Dalmar squares his shoulders to me and exhales deeply. "Well, Miss Izacalli, it's been a real pleasure. I do hope we'll see more of each other in the future. In fact... I look forward to it."

"Of course," I reply with a courteous sweetness. "If I hope to be a commendable Jurafen for the Three Kingdoms one day, I imagine our encounters will grow rather frequent."

"Precisely," he says through a hollow smile. He walks over to Draven, who stands still as a statue, and rests a gentle hand on his shoulder, observing him a moment longer. Then, in tune with a sharp draw of breath, he drops his hand and strides off, humming to himself as he goes, hands again clasped behind his back.

I release a sigh and allow my shoulders to sag when he's gone. "Your father is…charming," I mutter with sarcasm, feeling suddenly exhausted.

Draven remains silent.

I steal a glance at him, a deep curve wedged in my brow.

Ghosts dance in Draven's dulling eyes, haunting him from somewhere unseen. A visual that has me blowing out a weighted breath before approaching him with slow steps. I reach for his hand, and he jerks at the touch. But his eyes soften when they glance down, seeing me.

Until he gently sweeps his thumb over the already-sensitive bruise forming on my cheek. Then his eyes go cold as ice.

"It's okay," I whisper. "I'm okay. I'm…used to it." I hate how tiny my voice sounds.

Now his expression looks pained for an entirely new reason. "Give me a list," he murmurs, "and I will make every single person whose harmed you pay with their life."

I huff an empty laugh. "That'd be quite the long list."

His hand remains on my cheek, cupping it with a tender touch. "I have plenty of time."

I open my mouth, so many questions forming on my tongue, but before I can ask a single one, another voice interrupts us. One that I do recognize this time.

And I'm starting to realize these "secluded" gardens aren't all that secluded.

"Lyra?"

I turn, surprised at who I see. "Klytis?" My brows furrow. "What are you doing here?"

He approaches us, his eyes flicking between Draven and me with curiosity. "Transporting a few Rivarian diplomats on King Alastair's orders."

"To Bathara?" My features twist with confusion. "What in god's veins are Rivarian *diplomats* doing here in the borderless region?"

Klytis shrugs, his shoulder-length auburn hair shifting from the gesture. "Couldn't tell you. But Erandor has sent some, too."

"So I've seen," I grumble, folding my arms over my chest.

Still the fact remains, representatives are here from Erandor and Rivara, but not Anatolé. I wonder if that is an active choice by King Yarum, or something else.

Klytis watches me, amusement singing in his pale-blue eyes. "I've missed that endearing spunk of yours."

Draven folds his arms over his chest and cocks his head, staring at Klytis—who meets his intense stare. And I swear Draven suddenly seems a little bit...taller? Am I imagining that?

When Klytis returns his eyes to me, there is a notch wedged deeply in his brow.

"Anywho," he drawls slowly, "I've been looking for you since I arrived. I have a missive from the king I've been instructed to deliver directly to you."

The blood leeches from my face.

Klytis sighs, sensing the shift in my demeanor. "I wish I knew what it says," he tells me, dropping his voice. "But it's sealed with the king's crest."

I swallow down my fear and stick out my hand, glancing at Draven side-long for only a moment. "Let's just get this over with."

Klytis offers me a sympathetic look before reaching into his satchel and pulling out a rolled up scroll tied with twine and sealed with red wax, the king's crest pressed into the center. Gently, he places it in my outstretched hand.

And it takes every ounce of willpower I have not to curl my fingers around it and crumple it into nothing.

I inhale a jagged breath and break the seal, unrolling the parchment. The missive is short, scribed with intricately drawn letters.

Pet,

I hear congratulations are in order. That you have passed not only the first test, but the second test as well. I concede that you have already bested my expectations, but I must warn you, this streak of yours is about to meet a swift and brutal end. You will not win against the third test, though I wish I could be there to watch you try.

I do so look forward to your return to Keziah. I am more than ready to finally receive my heir, and my guests are ready to have their favorite night attendant return to their beds.

Signed,

Your King

My chest rises and falls with heavy breaths while anger corrupts my veins. I wrap my fingers around the parchment and squeeze, attempting to steady my breathing, not wanting to let the king get to me. If he does, he wins power over me, and I will do everything I can to ensure that doesn't happen.

Fuck him.

I shove the parchment against Klytis's chest. "Burn it."

He dips his chin, but shifts on his feet.

My brows furrow. "What is it? What aren't you telling me?"

He rubs at the back of his neck. "What do you mean?"

I shoot him a pointed look. "I've known you since I was fourteen, Klytis. I can tell when you're hiding something."

Klytis drags a hand down his face and heaves a sigh. "I really didn't want to be the one to tell you this, Lyra...not like this."

My stomach drops. "Tell me what?" I ask, each word enunciated slowly.

Draven steps forward and places a comforting hand on the small of my back. I glance up at him before back at Klytis—whose brows are lowered and heavily wrinkled at the sight of Draven touching me.

"I'm sorry, but—" he points at Draven "—is that not the Dalmar heir?"

Well, he certainly figured that out sooner than I did. Though, I guess it makes sense, seeing as Klytis frequently transports emissaries and diplomats for King Alastair all around the Three Kingdoms.

I wave him off. "Yes, but irrelevant. Tell me what you're keeping from me."

Klytis stares at Draven a moment longer, seeming a bit dumbfounded. Eventually, he drags his gaze back to me, his eyes turning downward. "It's about Delroy," he murmurs.

The stablemaster.

The kind, simple man who was always as good to me as he was his horses—which was finer treatment than most in my position see in their lifetimes.

A knot twists in my chest. "What about Delroy?"

Klytis rakes a hand through his auburn hair and braces his other hand on his hip. Suddenly, he won't meet my eyes.

And the fear overtaking me becomes almost debilitating.

Finally, he exhales a long sigh and explains. "King Alastair caught wind of someone passing out some sort of tonic to his night attendants that allowed them to get out of performing their...duties. He ordered every servant who lives on the estate to have their place of residence and workspace searched. When the guards reached the stables, they found a ton of Gardner supplies and ingredients matching the description of what was in the tonics. And the king...he did not take kindly to that."

Needles appear in my closing throat, making each intake of air a painful struggle. "Delroy had nothing to do with that," I stammer. "It was me. All of it. I gave him the supplies. I made those tonics. *Not* Delroy."

Klytis looks at me with sad, sympathetic eyes. "I know that," he confirms softly. "As did Delroy, naturally. But...he confessed to the crimes, saying that he, and he alone, was the culprit."

The world tilts, threatening to knock me over with its sudden shift.

I shake my head. "No. *No.* I'll go back to Rivara myself and confess to King Alastair. You—you can take me back with you. Delroy...he had *nothing* to do with it. The king would be punishing an innocent man. It should be me—not him."

A thought stabs me in the chest.

Not again.

Klytis's features crumble—his expression turning pained. "It's already done," he murmurs. "They hung him, Lyra. Delroy is gone."

I start backing away, my heart decaying with every step. I shake my head. "No. That—that can't be true. He...*no*."

Klytis reaches for me. "It isn't your fault, Lyra. Delroy made his choice. He—"

I don't hear the rest of the sentence.

I turn and sprint, needing to get away. Needing to go someplace to wither—to evaporate into the frigid nothingness I feel threatening to shatter me.

And there is only one place that feels acceptable to fracture into oblivion.

CHAPTER FORTY-FOUR

I throw the doors to the greenhouse open and scramble inside.

I'm greeted by a flurry of smells—mint, a perfume-like floral aroma, spicy notes that carry a rich, earthy undertone. It is all achingly familiar.

I walk through the aisles, past the cascading vines descending from the high glass ceilings, thick with purple, pink, and silver blossoms. I ignore the softly-glowing lanterns strung across the rafter beams and columns, and the beds of soil hosting a spectrum of colors. I don't even marvel at the crystal-like windows enclosing the entire structure, the fading sunlight filtering through like a soft prism.

No—I just find a spot in the very back and drop to my knees, clutching at my chest.

My attempts to draw in a steady breath are pathetic—are as weak and shaky as my trembling body.

It should have been me.

My fault.

How can it all be happening again, so similar yet so different?

Pain wails in my chest, beating against my sternum, demanding I let it out. But I don't want to. I don't want to feel it.

Pain makes things real.

And *gods* I don't want this to be real.

My breathing comes out shallow and uneven—strained. So painfully strained, despite my attempts to control it. My fingers grip at the ice necklace still resting at the base of my throat.

A mistake.

Did Thestis see? Did he have to watch Delroy's body swinging limply, suspended in air by a condemning noose?

What if he did, and it ruins him? That would be my fault, too...

"Lyra?"

The sound of Draven's voice has me jerking upright. I whip around and swallow, trying even harder now to master my erratic breaths. But those angry words continue screaming at me in a place only I can hear, tearing through me like a blade.

My fault. My fault. My fault.

It should have been me.

"Draven?" I ask, my voice trembling. "Why are you here?"

He watches me with tender eyes, but keeps his distance. "Because I know it hurts," he murmurs.

The words threaten to shatter me. But I do not let my stitches tear apart—do not give the hammer rapping at my chest the momentum to cleave me open.

I shake my head, pressing my teeth into my bottom lip. "No, it's okay. I'll be okay."

"What happened is not okay, Lyra. And you have the right to feel upset over it."

I inhale a trembling breath. "It's okay."

He shakes his head gently, taking one step forward. "It's not," he murmurs.

"No, really. It's fine. I'm fine," I repeat, lifting my chin and setting my features. "I am. I'm okay."

"You're not." Draven takes another step toward me.

"Yes, I am. I'm okay."

Another step. "You're not." His voice is gentle.

My bottom lip starts to quiver as the ache that has been wailing quietly inside my chest for so long swells, eager to finally be heard. "I'm okay," I repeat, my voice breaking. The sound is like the first cracks of splintering ice. "Really." I try to fake a smile, and somehow, the lie in the action surfaces more pain.

He shakes his head, keeping his eyes glued to me, dropping his voice another soft octave. "No, you're not. And you don't have to be. Not right now."

I swish my lips side-to-side as something hot claws at my chest, screaming—*demanding*—I let it out. "I'm okay." I say it more to myself now than him. "I have to be okay. Because if I'm not okay, then that means they've all won—that they hurt me. And if I let them hurt me, then everything is real, and I have lost, and see...I can't accept that." I drop my voice into a harsh whisper. "I *can't*."

Draven's gaze holds onto me steadily, refusing to let go. "Feeling what's hurt you is not letting them win, but refusing yourself the opportunity to heal *because* of them is." He takes another step. "Pretending to be whole does not mean you are, just as pretending the pain does not exist won't make it go away."

My lips shake, and I feel suffocated—constricted by all the pressure building in my chest. It's like I'm being buried alive brick by brick, encased in a grave of serrated what-ifs and treacherous numbness that masked the rot needing to be pruned from my body long ago.

Denial is a degenerative disease that robs you of all your senses. Every last one of them.

My lungs stutter. My throat constricts. My heart is squeezed by invisible, rough hands.

"You don't understand," I murmur, the sound encased in a jar of broken hearts and stolen dreams. "I have to be okay. I *have to*." My voice rattles, strained at its attempts to keep the sob at bay.

"No," he counters, his voice achingly tender. "You don't." He stands directly in front of me now, and he reaches his hand out, lightly cupping my face and swiping his thumb along my cheek.

It is the final stone to shatter the glass foundation I've been built upon.

The hammer finally crashes through, cleaving me apart piece by crumbling piece. My chest rips open, and I drown beneath the raging sea.

Draven shifts into a distorted image, going fuzzy and blurry as something wet and hot swells in my eyes, clouding my vision. A cold chill sweeps down the length of my body, and the hairs on my arms rise as my knees buckle, no longer able to withstand the immense pressure that has been begging to be released—to be felt—for so many years.

But I do not wish to feel. It terrifies me. Because what is a person if not their feelings, and then what am I if all my feelings are outlined by sadness? By guilt and regret. By Pain. So much pain. Ignorance is bliss, and I've been willing to turn a blind eye because it allows me to live under the illusion that I'm okay. But...

I'm not okay.

And I haven't been for quite some time.

"Oh, gods," I breathe, crumbling into myself and dropping to my knees, squeezing at my chest. "It...hurts." Hiccups expand behind my ribcage. "Why does it hurt so much?"

It all hits me. Violent. Angry. Merciless. All the things I've been running from. All the pain I've suppressed. All the sadness, the hurt, the anger. It surfaces like driftwood washing to a forgotten shore.

How what happened with my mother left me shattered—riddled with sorrow, regret, and so many questions about the ways of this life. How humiliated and repulsed I've been made to feel with myself by what King Alastair has made me do. How upset with myself I am that I never truly mourned. How infuriated I am to realize I've spent years running from her memory instead of celebrating who she was. Instead of talking about her.

And I feel guilty. I feel so gods-damn guilty. It lingers in the hollow spaces where happiness once resided. A happiness stolen along with my mother; with the pieces of a girl who never truly got to learn who she could be. I am guilty because I've allowed her memory to be forgotten. Because I am responsible for her death. Am the reason she burned.

I am the reason Meiji suffered such a cruel end. The reason Nuha sleeps in a cold bed with no warm body to roll into, just needing to feel her lover's touch.

I am the reason a noose snapped the air from living lungs, eroding a good person into a lifeless shell. Someone who was only ever warm and kind to others. The only mistake Delroy ever made was having a soft spot for me—I was his damnation.

I am everyone's damnation.

A dull yet entirely sharp ache pounds against my chest, and I squeeze at the skin wrapped over my breastbone, desperate to grab what aches beneath the surface and rip it out.

But I can't.

Because even though they have more impact on the world than arguably anything else, feelings don't exist in any tangible sense.

So I sit scratching at an invisible ache that throbs in my chest while hot tears pour down my cheeks like a busted spout, helpless to the overwhelming weight forcefully pushing against my sternum.

"Please," I whisper through my cries. "Make it stop."

Draven kneels down before me.

Trembling, I lift my swollen eyes from my blurry knees and look up at him. "I...I...the king, he..." I trip on a breath caught between sobs. "And Delroy...and my mom..." The sobs tear through me, violent and unrelenting, and my body crumples. I drop my head back into my knees and pull my legs even tighter against my chest, folding myself inward like a collapsing star.

He brushes strands of stray hair behind my ear and watches me patiently with quiet eyes.

I try again. "I...gave him...and it's...it's *my* fault. All of it. My mother. Delroy. Meiji." My body quakes with grief—so unfamiliar with feeling the heaviness of it. "And it hurts. I'd forgotten. I...I..." I grasp for more words through hiccuped breaths.

But I don't feel like I can breathe anymore.

"Shh," Draven soothes as he positions himself behind me, leaning his back against the glass window. "It's okay. You don't need to explain." He pauses. "Is it alright if I touch you?"

My chest stutters, and breathing is so *hard*. My throat feels constricted, like it's closing in on itself just as I am. Still, I nod.

He wraps his arms around me and pulls me into his chest, squeezing just enough to put pressure against my sternum. He does not let go of me.

"You're having a panic attack," he murmurs, his voice like a cradle woven in warmth, meant to hold rather than break. "I'm going to put some pressure on your chest. It should help calm your heart rate, but I need you to help me by attempting to take slow, steady breaths. Okay? Breathe in slowly through your nose, out slowly through your mouth. Think you can do that?"

Through ragged breaths, I again nod my head.

"Good," he says. I attempt to draw in slower, steadier breaths, and Draven gently guides me to lean back against him, wordlessly encouraging me to rest my full weight on him. Then, he holds me just a little tighter. "Now, your muscles are really locked up. Do you think you can begin relaxing them? Try flexing them, then letting them go slack." I try, but the action is met with weight pressing down on my chest, and my breathing shudders. "I'm right here with you," Draven soothes, gliding his fingers reassuringly down my arm. "I've got you. Keep going if you can."

Through the sullen sounds of gasps for air and lingering hiccups, I begin loosening my muscles, releasing them from their captivity. A small relief hits my body.

"There you go," Draven encourages gently. "That's my girl. Now, can you tell me five plants that are in this greenhouse?"

I swivel my head against Draven's chest—my breathing still shaky, straggling tears still pouring from their ducts—and my raw eyes scan the room. As I attempt to identify the plants within the window panes, the world sharpens from a blurry blob of hazy gray into a clear image sprinkled with color. My voice trembles when I speak. "There is...peppermint. Lavender." Another fractured inhale, but one my chest starts to feel like it can handle. "Collytails. Silver leaves." As I search for the final plant to name, a debilitating wave of fatigue hits me. Suddenly, the battle is no longer to locate air, but to remain awake. My voice grows thick with exhaustion. "And...and..."

Draven leaves one arm securely wrapped around my torso and traces soothing lines down my arm with the other, his calming touch nothing short of reverent. "It's okay to sleep," he murmurs, as if sensing my weariness. "I won't go anywhere. I promise."

I want to respond, but my body feels plundered—emptied by thieves who took everything and left nothing—and I cannot part my lips nor lift my tongue. It all feels too heavy. I feel too heavy—too drained.

But right as my eyelids are about to give in to the weight forcing them down, I glimpse the final plant I want to name.

"Bonaria," I whisper.

Then, as my eyes fall shut—no longer capable of withstanding the weight of consciousness—I do not fight it, drifting into sleep not better, but perhaps with a new capacity to become just a bit lighter.

※ ⚘

When I wake up—a faint burn lingering in my eyes, the raw evidence from too many tears, too many spilled emotions—I find Draven's arms still wrapped around me and the moon high in the sky, silver bleeding through the windows.

I blink, but don't dare move. Based on the steady rhythm of his chest and the looseness in his arms, I think Draven is asleep. One hand remains on my waist, the other slack against my arm, as if, even in sleep, he refuses to let me go.

My fingertips twitch with the urge to clutch onto his forearm—to intertwine my skin with his skin. And though I feel perhaps as empty as I ever have, it doesn't feel like an endless void anymore. An abyss of nothingness. Instead, it feels like an emptiness that can perhaps be filled, piece by piece, one small feeling at a time.

So, I don't deny myself the urge. I don't ignore it. I allow my fingers to trace Draven's skin with a tenderness, with a type of touch I have not let myself use before.

He stirs, and his grip on my waist tightens, his fingers pressing deeper into the fabrics of my shirt.

So he's awake, after all.

My fingers continue tracing mindless drawings across his skin. "Draven?"

"Hm?" he hums, the sound rough-edged and low, tangled with drowsiness.

"Can I ask you something?"

He does not answer right away. "Alright."

"Where did you learn to do that? To help someone through a panic attack."

Another pause, this one longer than the last. "My mother suffered from them frequently. She never wanted my father to know, or any of his watchful shadows, so she would come into my chambers." He stops, as if momentarily drifting back into the memory. "Eventually, she told someone else about them, and he sought out a local healer, asking how he could help her through them. I only did the things he taught me to do to help my mother."

I stop grazing his skin and instead press my palm against it, my fingers curling gently around his arm. "Will you tell me about her, your mother?"

He lifts the hand that was slack against my arm and gently glides a knuckle down my cheek. "Will you tell me about yours?"

Though the initial reaction to flinch is still there—something built over years doesn't simply disappear after one cathartic cry—it doesn't bring the same fearful ache it did before. Instead, I attempt to see the pain differently—as a good thing. As a reminder of my love for her.

It hurts because it matters. Because *she* mattered.

And the world deserves to remember such a beautiful light. I deserve to remember, too.

I glide my thumb over Draven's arm. "I will."

He inhales a deep breath, and the rise and fall of his chest pushes against my back. I relish in the warmth of the touch.

"My mother," he begins, his voice tender and full of devotion, "was the strongest, bravest, and kindest woman I have ever known. She was quiet, but fierce in her opinions, and incredibly sharp-witted. In fact, I think it was her wit that drew my father to her in the first place." He huffs a tiny laugh. "In Talderine...hell, in all of Erandor, really, men are still given more respect over women, and I remember watching my mother and wondering how in god's veins that could be possible."

Draven stops, wrapping his arm around me and holding me closer to his chest—as if he needs to be anchored to say this next part. "And she loved me. *Gods*, she loved me so much when she had every reason not to. She was every good thing in this world. And despite what forgettable flaws she may have had, she was perfect. Absolutely perfect."

Though I can't imagine why she would ever have a reason to not love Draven, I place my hand over his as it rests against my torso, a quiet reassurance that I'm here. He flexes his fingers, reaching for mine—and slowly, like estranged stars finally aligning, our fingers intertwine.

He leans down, pressing his cheek against the side of my head. "What was your mother like?"

A rush of memories sweeps my lips into a wistful smile. "My mother was strong-headed, loud, and an absolute force of nature. She was raucous, full of life, and had a laugh that could draw the attention of every eye in the room." An echo of her unmistakable laugh plays in my head like a faint song played on a favorite instrument. "She loved the art of gardning almost as much as she loved me, and she demanded respect. Her tongue was also sharp as a blade, and she had zero quarrels with wielding it like one."

"Sounds like someone else I know," Draven comments, his breath a warm hug to my cheek.

I smile.

It's nice...remembering who she was.

"She also had the biggest heart of anyone I've ever met," I continue. "She cared for anyone and everyone. A beggar on the street, a struggling mother, a pompous noble—it didn't matter. She treated them all equally. Offered every person dignity and respect. She always said there was life in their bodies, and that was enough for her."

"That also sounds like someone I know." His words are gentle, and I can hear the smile leaking through them.

My lips twitch fondly.

"And your father?" Draven asks. "Was he ever around?"

I blow out a breath, puffing out my cheeks. "No," I answer truthfully. "And my mother never told me anything about him, either. I asked once when I was young, but..." I shake my head, the memory squeezing my heart. "The immediate pain—longing, almost—on her face was so palpable, I swore to myself I would never ask again."

"That must have been hard on you."

I consider his words. "It wasn't, actually. She never made me question it because I never felt like I was missing anything. My mother always provided me with everything I possibly needed."

"She must have been a remarkable woman."

My voice drops into a low whisper. "She was." I pause, chewing on my lip in thought. "Draven?"

"Yes?"

"Why didn't you tell me about your father? About being a Dalmar?" My fingers stop, only for a moment, as the gravity of that revelation rattles through me once more.

And my heart braces for destruction—preparing itself to be told it has something to do with my background as a night attendant, or that he didn't think I needed to know something like that because he and I are nothing more than casual acquaintances. Because he is highborn, and I am lowborn.

I hear him draw in a deep breath. "You really want to know?"

"I do," I murmur.

He does not answer right away, seeming to think the question over. Until finally, he glides his knuckles gently down my cheek, to my neck, down to the base of my shoulder, where they still. "The real reason," he starts, his voice reserved, "is because I grew to love the way you looked at me."

My heart freezes.

"Your eyes are so expressive, Lyra, and I don't think you're the slightest bit aware of it. But gods I am so thankful for that, because it allowed me to see into every bit of you—to know what's going on in that beautiful head of yours." His thumb strokes soothing circles along my shoulder. "And I felt like someone was seeing me for the first time. Not Draven, the Dalmar Heir. Not the son of the greatest strategist, or bearer of the most feared magic in Solaya. No, you just saw...me. And the way you looked at me told me that I—just Draven—was enough."

He drops his voice into a low, raspy whisper. "I've never gotten to experience that before. To feel worthy of my skin without it being attached to my titles. I..." He sighs, dropping his voice even lower. "I just wanted to hold onto that for as long as I could."

The breath is stolen from my chest. "You are so much more than enough," I murmur. "Titles or not."

I hear traces of a weak smile in his voice. "I know...your gaze makes me believe it." His fingers rove higher, tracing my jaw with the most reverent touch. "Someone once told me if I ever find a person who looks at me the way you do, I should never let them go."

Fear swells in my chest as I absorb his words. Yet I make a decision after hearing them, turning myself around in Draven's lap so that we're now face-to-face.

The tenderness waiting for me in his eyes is enough to gut me.

"And?" I whisper.

He tucks stray hair behind my ear, sweeping his thumb along my chin after. "And I think, even if I wanted to, I couldn't let you go if I tried. Not anymore."

The confession is like a shock to my heart, nudging it to beat again.

A momentary pause falls between us, our eyes not breaking from each other's. And as that pause screams louder than words ever could, I reach for something different, something whole.

Slowly, with such careful movements, I lean forward, bringing my lips toward an inevitable shattering—a possible mending. I teeter on the precipice of a great beginning, reminding myself that a beginning's end is far sadder than an end's beginning.

Yet I stop right as my lips are about to graze his—my heart screaming incoherent words as my mind cowers with fear in a corner. "I'm scared something like this will end in flames," I admit in a near-silent whisper, not elaborating on why.

Something sad passes through Draven's gentle eyes, and he takes my face in both his hands, locking his gaze to mine. "Then I will burn, Lyra, so long as it's by your flame."

It's the final confirmation I need, knowing he'll catch me if I stumble.

The moment I press my lips to his, the world is suddenly painted with color, and I realize everything I've been feeling is a dull sensation compared to what my body is actually capable of. His lips are soft and welcoming, and the kiss feels like waking up from a long slumber.

We move in such delicate harmony, finding our perfect rhythm as effortlessly as old dance partners. Draven's hand roves to my neck, and he grips the back of it with a tender touch. My breath catches, overwhelmed by the emotion swelling in my chest from the contact. I pull away, needing to steady myself.

"What is it?" Draven asks, his voice gentle. "Are you okay?"

I release a trembling sigh. "Over these past few years, because of my role with the king, I..." I stop, swallowing against the knot in my throat. "I just never knew a kiss could feel like this, that's all."

Draven inspects me with an expression I finally realize he reserves only for me. Then he kisses me with the sort of emotion poets write about. The sort of kiss that has prompted gods to string stars together in a constellation.

He kisses me, and I kiss him back, bright golden lights shooting off behind my closed eyelids.

Time does not exist here. Not in this pocket of our own reality carved exclusively for us—for this moment. So, I'm not sure exactly when he stops—pulling back and gazing at me in a way that would have made my mother proud.

"That's enough for now," he murmurs. "You should finish resting. I'm sure your body is still exhausted after all it went through."

Now that he mentions it...

"Will you stay with me?"

The ghost of a smile appears on his lips, and his thumb grazes across my cheek before he presses a featherlight kiss to my temple. "In this life, and the next."

I nestle back into Draven's lap, feeling like I've just had so many roots pruned from my heart. He wraps his arms around me, and I nuzzle into him, doing my best to let the emotion singing in my chest hum its natural tune. To absorb the feelings at face value instead of shutting them out.

And right as sleep tiptoes through the door, sweeping me away, I voice the final words lingering in my mind to Draven.

"Thank you—for helping me feel again."

He holds me like I am the most precious thing in existence, resting his cheek on the top of my head. "Thank you for reminding me there are still people worth feeling for."

CHAPTER FORTY-FIVE

"And then what happened?"

I blow out a long sigh, playing with the ends of my braid. "Nothing," I admit. "I fell asleep, and he just let me lay in his arms until morning came."

Marcella sits cross-legged and wide-eyed on her bed. She leans forward, bracing her weight on her propped elbows. "And then you just, what? Parted ways so you can get ready for your training with him soon?"

A helpless, smitten smile tugs at my lips. I try to bite down on it, but it refuses to go anywhere as I nod my head in response.

Marcella blows out a low whistle. "By Amala...look at you, all heart-eyed. And for the Dalmar Heir, no less. Which—" she tilts forward "—is one hell of a surprise by the way." She makes a show of heaving a loud sigh and leans back. "Though, I guess waking up in a man's arms—*especially* arms like Draven's—will do that to you."

Gray clears his throat and lifts his hand from beside Marcella. "Do I really need to be here for this?"

Marcella shoots him a look. "You're the one who said you wanted to stay for the conversation."

Gray lifts a brow at her. "I wanted to stay and make sure Lyra was alright after an old friend of ours was forced to provide her with upsetting news, resulting in her disappearing all night. I wanted to make sure she was *okay.*"

An ache throbs in my heart at the mention of Delroy's death; I allow it to be felt.

When I got back to my room this morning, Gray was waiting for me, leaned against the wall on my bed, talking to Marcella who was laying backwards on her own bed. I guess Klytis had found him immediately after I ran off, informing him of everything that happened.

He's been waiting for me ever since.

Marcella folds her arms over her chest. "You're her best friend—her closest companion—are you not?"

Gray narrows his eyes on her. "I am."

"Great, then shut up and listen to your best friend tell the story of how she fell in love, before *I* assume the role instead."

Both Gray's and my brows lurch up at the same moment.

"What?" Marcella asks, bouncing her gaze between us. "If it looks like a flower and smells like a flower…" She shrugs, allowing us to fill in the rest.

Gray studies her a moment longer, a curve still wedged in his brow. "Be that as it may, I did not sign up to listen to you two drool over some guy's arms."

Marcella knocks her shoulder into Gray's. "Jealous?"

He clicks his tongue. "Please," he grumbles.

Smiling with some unspoken victory, Marcella turns her attention back onto me. She jabs a thumb in Gray's direction. "Your best friend here is not very good at girl talk."

I chuckle, shaking my head and mocking a pout. "Such a shame. He used to be so good at it."

Gray rolls his eyes, helpless, before shooting Marcella a look. But once he returns his gaze to me, his features soften. "Just so we're clear," he begins, his voice gentle. "I *am* happy for you, Lyra. Though the circumstances leading up to what happened in that greenhouse were…less than ideal, since the day your mother passed, your eyes have never been so bright." His lips sweep up into a smile. "And there are no words to express how happy it makes me to see you with life in your eyes again."

A swell of emotion hits me in the chest, and though it is difficult, I try not to shove it away—to brush it aside or dilute it with counter thoughts.

Marcella observes Gray with a softened gaze, then sighs. "Alright," she concedes. "I retract what I said—I guess Gray is pretty decent at girl talk, after all."

"My life's greatest accomplishment," he replies.

She huffs a laugh, and there is a passing silence—until Marcella clears her throat. "While we're on the subject of boys..." A rosy hue tints her pale cheeks, and a lopsided curve pulls at one side of her mouth. "I have some news."

Gray's brows twitch while mine jump with curiosity.

"Do tell," I urge through a smile.

She exhales a deep breath and presses her lips into a thin line, picking at her nails. "Don't judge me, okay?"

"Wouldn't dream of it," I assure her lightheartedly. My eyes flick to Gray, who watches her with a tiny indent wedged between his brows.

Interesting.

Her fingers trip over themselves as she bites down on her bottom lip and squeezes her eyes shut. "I slept with Griff," she blurts out.

My jaw pops open while my brows rise to my hairline. "*Griff*?!"

"I said don't judge me." Marcella opens her eyes and blows out a tiny laugh. "It just kind of...happened. After the second test, we were in a competition to see who had the better shot with a bow, and one thing led to another, and then wine got involved, and then..." She trails off, shrugging her shoulders, laughing softly. "It's probably nothing, but I had to tell someone."

I glance at Gray, who remains uncharacteristically expressionless.

I sigh quietly before sweeping my lips into a smile. "You two would make quite the lively pair, that's for certain."

She swats a hand at me and smiles wickedly. "Please. Nobody can keep up with my boisterous personality. I'm sure it's just a fling."

"Is that what you want it to be?"

Her eyes fall to her open palms, and she does not answer right away. "Am I an ignorant fool if I say I don't know?"

"No," I assure her. "You're not."

Her lips twitch up at that, until they fall into a slight frown when she spots Gray rising from the bed and walking to the door. "And where are you going? We haven't spilled all our juicy secrets yet."

Gray smiles—the line tight and rigid, not fully reaching the corner of his mouth. "I'm supposed to be meeting a friend of mine before he departs back for our home kingdom. I told him I'd see him off."

Marcella huffs, tugging her chin to the side. "Fine. Miss all the fun."

I watch Gray closely. I know him like the back of my hand, and I certainly know when he's lying. Still, I smile at him. "Give Klytis my best."

He nods, the gesture clipped. "I will."

And then he departs, leaving Marcella and me to our own devices once more.

Marcella clicks her tongue at the door. "His loss."

I laugh softly. "Marcella, how long was Gray here before I got in? He mentioned he came right after Klytis told him about his encounter with me, but that was around sunset. I didn't get back until sunrise," I point out.

Marcella inspects her nails. "You've got the timeline correct. He arrived at sunset and was here all night until you got in. He pestered me all night."

I tilt my head, seeing her as if in a new light. The smudge of color under her bright, cobalt eyes, the disheveled hair, the extra bit of rasp in her voice. "Did either of you sleep?"

She looks up from her nails and arches a brow. "No," she answers dryly. "He likes to talk. A lot."

A helpless smile sweeps across my lips, a laugh echoing behind my words. "And what is it you two stayed up all night talking about?"

She shrugs—the gesture suspiciously casual. "You know, a little bit of this, a little bit of that. Nothing crazy. Though, I am now *fully* aware of how much of a history buff he truly is."

I chuckle, shaking my head. "Glad I'm no longer alone in that knowledge."

She narrows her eyes on me a fraction, watching me for a long moment. I simply grin at her, my heart laughing with amusement.

"What?" she asks, her eyes narrowing further.

I shrug my shoulders. "Nothing," I say through my smile. "Nothing at all."

I don't meddle, and I certainly don't plan on starting now.

They'll figure it out themselves.

Her gaze lingers on me a few seconds longer. But eventually, she falls back onto her bed and sighs. "Well, one thing is for sure—he has a lot to learn if he wants to participate in any more of our conversations. I mean really," she drops her voice into a grumble, "leaving mid-conversation is just rude."

"Yes," I agree through a quiet laugh, though for perhaps a different reason entirely. "He has a lot to learn, indeed."

CHAPTER FORTY-SIX

The next morning, I am on my way to meet Draven for training—our final day together before the final test tomorrow—when Kiran stops me in the corridor.

"Good morning, Lyra," he coos. He wears a loose black sweater tucked neatly into his trousers, his ruby hair half-tied back, with the other half brushing his shoulders.

"Kiran," I reply, my tone warm—something that seems to come natural in his presence. "To what do I owe the pleasure?"

He clasps his hands behind his back. "Oh, nothing really. I just wanted to see how your training sessions with Draven were going. Any luck with your magic?"

I shake my head. "Not really," I mumble, feeling a frustrating wave of defeat at the words. "It's like it just doesn't want to come out."

"Hm," he hums. "Well, if there is anyone who can help you figure out why that is, it's Draven." He pauses, his sapphire eyes watching me with crinkles framing them. "Mind if I join you on your morning stroll to meet him?"

My brows twitch slightly, but still I shrug. "Be my guest."

We walk together, the silence only lasting perhaps thirty seconds before Kiran's smooth voice fills the air again. "I heard you learned of Draven's...heritage."

I snort a laugh. "I did. And if someone told me during the summer solstice that I would be receiving training from the Dalmar Heir and walking to said training with the Sulien Heir come the autumnal equinox, I would have laughed in their faces and told them to get off the pipe."

Kiran chuckles, nodding with understanding. "Life is an unpredictable game always throwing twists at us. Typically, when we least expect it."

"You can say that again," I mutter.

Kiran's signature smile widens. "Did he tell you that he and I grew up together?"

I pause my steps, turning to face Kiran with a wrinkle in my brow. "You and Draven? Is that normal for Great House heirs?"

He lifts a shoulder lazily. "It's normal for heirs to be socialized with each other. We have frequent encounters given the nature of our titles. However, the circumstances for Draven, Finlay, and me were a bit...peculiar."

My brows scrunch even more. "Wait, *Finlay*? He was raised with you guys as well?"

We resume walking, and Kiran nods, his smile punctuated by a fondness. "Oh, yes," he confirms. "We were all raised just outside of Talderine, living in the Dalmar family's castle, Tylderon. Believe it or not, those two are the closest thing I have to brothers."

Suddenly it all makes sense. Why Kiran and Draven always speak to each other so intimately. Why Kiran and Finlay seemed outlined by a deep-rooted tension surpassing simple blood rivalry. Why Finlay was so stunned by Draven's offer to train me.

They've known each other all their lives. Are brothers, according to Kiran.

"Are you an only child?"

"No," Kiran answers through a laugh. "I have an older sister. And between you and me, I find she is far scarier and even more formidable than both Finlay and Draven combined."

"That is a terrifying thought." I smirk. "She sounds like my kind of woman."

Kiran chuckles. "I think you two would get along quite well, actually."

My lips tug up at the thought. "So if you and Finlay are practically brothers, why are you two always at each other's throats?"

His eyes flick to me before down at his feet. "You noticed that, huh?"

I arch a brow. "It's kind of hard not to."

He sighs—long and deep—shaking his head. "It's complicated," he murmurs after a long moment. "But let's just say he and I had a disagreement, and we've never fully resolved the remaining feelings from the decision." His eyes haze with the fog of a distant memory.

I soften my voice. "If you don't mind me asking, how is it that all three of you ended up living together at Tylderon?"

"It started with Finlay," he answers. "He and his father had a...falling out, I guess you could say, and Finlay was sent away from his home to live at Tylderon while finishing his education and training." Kiran pauses, his brows scrunching together. "Finlay...he wasn't always like how he is now. The events leading up to his removal from his home changed him—and not for the better. Sadly, since the day he arrived at Tylderon, he's been trying to win back his father's favor." He glances at me. "And if you think Finlay is something to behold..."

I arch a brow.

Kiran huffs a dry laugh.

Still, I wonder what happened between Finlay and his father to cause such turmoil.

"I arrived about six months after him," Kiran continues. "My father heard what House Fjolla was doing with their heir, and he decided House Sulien could benefit from a similar decision."

"I should have guessed you three were trouble since birth," I say, amused.

Kiran's lips twitch. "I confess that I earned the decision to be sent away to Tylderon, but Finlay...his story is a bit more complicated." He sighs. "But I digress. My purpose for telling you all of this has nothing to do with that."

I glance at him, studying him for a moment. "It's not that I'm ungrateful for what you're sharing with me, because I do appreciate knowing, but what is your purpose for telling me, exactly?"

He lifts his chin, looking up at the golden sky. "I am the oldest of the three, and as such, I can be a bit protective of them. Finlay is the sensitive one, always has been, but Draven?" Kiran huffs a quiet breath and drops his chin. "Draven is more breakable than he will ever let on, and he has his heart to thank for that."

I bite down on my lip. "He told me about his mother."

Kiran stops walking. I turn back to face him and find his brows heavily furrowed. "He did?"

I nod.

"What did he say, exactly?"

"Not much," I say, recounting the night on the balcony under the stars and the one laying in his arms in the greenhouse. A fluttering feeling tumbles around in my stomach as I remember them. "He just told me about how they would watch the stars together. About how remarkable she was." My voice drops an octave. "He also told me he doesn't talk about her enough. That..." I swallow against the knot suddenly rising in my throat. "That she deserved to be remembered by someone."

The rumors surrounding House Dalmar swirl in my mind, landing on the sharpest of them all.

His mother was murdered in front of his very eyes.

"Kiran?" My voice is a gentle brush of sound. "The rumors about House Dalmar...are they true?"

His lips thin, and he rubs them together into an even flatter line. He exhales a deep breath. "Let's just say there was the version of Draven that was supposed to exist, and the one that actually existed, and it was not in alignment with the version his father wanted. Growing up, Draven was soft-hearted, incredibly sharp-witted, quiet, and caring—much like his mother was. She..." Kiran stops, considering his words. "She was able to act as a shield between Draven and his father, and when she passed, Draven lost not only a mother, but also his best friend and his shield, and that day..." Ghosts awaken on Kiran's face, and his voice falls into a rough whisper. "It was a very horrific day, to say the least."

The dull ache for what was stolen from Draven threads into the seams of my heart. Because I understand. I understand far more than I wish I did. And if I could take that pain away from him, I would in an instant, combining it with my own and carrying it for the two of us.

I deserve to feel the pain; Draven does not.

Kiran sucks in a sharp breath, banishing the ghosts back into their shadowy recesses, resetting his features. "Though that is Draven's story to tell, not mine."

I nod with understanding.

Kiran regards me, a curve tugging at his lip. "I must say—I'm surprised he talked to you about her at all. I haven't heard him speak of her in years." A pause. "He must really care for you."

I feel my cheeks warm, and my mouth flounders like a fish. Kiran smiles wider at the sight, his eyes crinkling as warmth returns to them.

We reach the path leading to the spot where I'm supposed to meet Draven. Kiran turns to face me the same moment I face him. "Be good to him," he requests gently.

The words catch me off guard, leaving me unsure how to answer.

So, I just blink at Kiran instead, resulting in him shaking his head and chuckling under his breath. "His life isn't easy," he continues, his voice soft yet earnest. "And he has a lot of weight on his shoulders—weight that I fear he will never share. He takes responsibility for everything and everyone he cares about. I need you to understand that—it's important you know."

The words feel like a vague warning in some strange way. I tug at the end of one of my braids, my brows wrinkling with thought. "Why tell me all this?" I ask quietly.

Kiran studies me, ultimately smiling at whatever he sees. "Because you're important to him, and thus important to me. And sometimes, we offer help to those we care about in the ways we can, even when they don't ask for it."

I open my mouth to say something, but before a word can roll from my tongue, Kiran lifts a hand and shakes his head. "Just go to him," he commands gently. "He's waiting for you, and I'd hate to be the reason he's kept waiting any longer."

A soft smile flits across my lips as I watch Kiran, observing him for a long moment.

I'd love to see the day when he and I are truly friends. People like Kiran are rare in this world, and if this conversation has made anything clear, it's that his loyalty is unwavering. Plus, despite the never-ending smirks, he's actually rather pleasant to be around.

"Thank you," I murmur.

Kiran grins, unflinching and beautiful, before he shoves one hand in his pocket and turns around, walking off in the other direction without another word, lifting his other hand lazily over his shoulder as a parting goodbye.

I watch him a few seconds longer. Then, I turn on my heels and go to Draven.

CHAPTER FORTY-SEVEN

"What's your favorite food?"

Draven arches a brow. "You finally complete all your tasks, and that's the first question you choose to ask me?"

I laugh and shove his shoulder. "Don't gripe. Just answer."

Draven and I sit at the base of a small waterfall, eating the dried jerky and nuts I brought for us to snack on. It's a bit salty, but I am on a high and don't care. Because today, I *finally* completed each and every task Draven assigned me. Which means I am the one asking *him* the questions for a change.

"Spiced apple tarts," he admits.

My brows do a little jump.

An action that has Draven bumping his shoulder into mine and mimicking my voice, a smirk tugging at one corner of his mouth. "Don't judge. Just ask."

I scrunch my nose at him. "Fine. Favorite season?"

Draven leans back, popping an almond into his mouth. "That one's easy. Autumn."

"Mine's spring," I confess. "I love to watch all the flowers bloom."

He watches me with a soft smile. "That makes sense."

I take a bite of the jerky. "Hmm, let me think...most cherished possession?"

Draven lifts his eyes to the sky as he thinks. "Back home, I have a pendant made entirely from sea glass, strung on a fine leather cord. It was a gift from my mother." He pulls his gaze from the sky, placing it instead on his open palms. "She said the colors matched my eyes."

"I've had the thought many times that your eyes look like sea glass," I tell him.

Draven turns his chin over his shoulder. "So what I'm hearing is you've thought about me many times?"

I click my tongue at him.

He smirks in response.

I roll my eyes. But then a small crease forms in my brow as I think of my next question. "Do you know why your eyes are the way they are?"

Draven shrugs, staring out at the waterfall. "No clue," he answers. "My father took me to a scholar once who had a particular theory, but that is perhaps a story for another day."

I watch him a moment longer, deciding not to push. I want to know everything about his past—about all the things that have compiled inside of him, shaping him into the work of art he is today. But I want it to be on his time, when he is ready.

I know there are certainly things I still haven't told him—even though he practically knows everything else about me now, thanks to all those previously failed attempts at my tasks.

Draven looks at me, the corner of his mouth curved. "You wear your thoughts like an expression." He leans over and tucks stray hair behind my ear, gliding his knuckles down my check after. "Alright," he says after a moment. "Enough questions for now. It's time for the next part of your training—magic."

"Fantastic," I mutter dryly.

※ ♪※

As the first fragments of sunset appear in the sky, I have to fight the urge to kick and scream with frustration.

"Why can't I summon *anything*? Not a root, not a bud—nothing." I push hair back from my face and clench my fists at my side, the frustration bubbling hot in my chest.

Draven frowns, thinking. "I would say perhaps it's connected to your unmanifested wielder's mark, but you've done those things before, so the action should feel familiar to your lakti."

I groan like a child.

And I don't even care.

Draven watches me. And then, as if deciding on something, he blows out a breath and reaches for my hand, tugging me behind him. "Follow me."

I pull at my brows. "Where are we going?"

"Somewhere that might help clear your head."

He escorts me through the rolling hills, past grand, tiered waterfalls and sparkling pools, and stops only when we reach a small, trickling waterfall covered in ivy.

I glance at him, confused. Not that I don't appreciate all of the wonders of nature, but as far as Bathara goes, this waterfall is rather...nondescript, to say the least.

I glance at him sidelong with a curve in my brow. "And this is supposed to help me clear my head, how, exactly?"

Draven turns his chin over his shoulder and looks down at me, a smile tugging at his lips. "You'll see," he hums, the sound a cryptic melody.

He guides me around the tiny basin, until we reach the base of the waterfall. And then, after a quick glance back at me paired with a smirk, Draven steps through the silvery veil, disappearing behind the cascading stream.

I stare at the spot where he vanished a moment longer before biting down on my lip and exhaling a sigh that puffs out my cheeks.

I follow after him.

And I am entirely unprepared for the sight that greets me once I emerge on the other side.

Sprawling cave walls rise up and up, meeting at an open circle that exposes the dimming sky above. At the very back, another thin waterfall pours into a body of water—the color a glimmering shade of turquoise— stemming from the aperture, appearing as if the sky has cracked open and the stream pours from the very fabrics of it. Along the walls are softly glowing words, scribbled in an almost illegible penmanship, fading from the wears of time.

But it is what surrounds the cave that steals my breath.

Hanging from the walls, dotting the spaces between river stones and twirling around rocks, are bioluminescent flora—the flowers glowing a soft and luminescent blue. And complementing the radiant hue gleaming throughout the cave are moss and water lilies. But my eyes snag on the vine practically swooping down into the water, leading to a bed of deep indigo flowers with star-shaped petals, splashed with white flecks, glimmering under the light's touch like a starry sky.

Nox's Caelum.

My favorite flower.

I'm so lost in the sight of it all, I don't notice Draven sneaking up behind me. Not until he sweeps my two braids over my shoulders and presses his lips to my neck, the kisses soft and reverent.

I shut my eyes against the explosion of feeling his touch ignites.

He traces the slope of my neck, until he reaches the base of my shoulder, where he pauses and breathes onto my skin, "What do you think?"

My eyes do another slow sweep. "I think it's one of the most magical places I've ever seen." I glance back at Draven, my chin turned over my shoulder. "But I don't see how this is going to help me with my magic."

Draven chuckles—the sound low and mischievous. It sends butterflies soaring from the pit of my stomach up into my chest, a trail of heat rising in their wake. "It won't," he answers. At my sharp surprise, he adds darkly, "But it *will* help clear your head, which will help you access your magic."

I arch a brow at him. "Why do I feel like I was lured here under false pretenses?"

He presses his hands to my hips and spins me around so we're face-to-face. "I did no such thing. All I said was I would take you somewhere to clear your head. I didn't specify the whys or hows." The corner of his lip curves with a teasing smile. "However you chose to interpret the information is entirely on you."

The sounds of falling water fill the silence stretching between us as I glare at him with a pointed brow and he smirks at me with satisfaction.

Draven grips my chin lightly with his thumb and index finger, tilting it up toward him. He scans my eyes and murmurs thickly, "Such expressive eyes." He leans forward, hovering his lips just centimeters away from mine. "Tell me, what can I do to make those eyes soften for me?"

I feel my cheeks flush as a wave of heat warms my blood. "I haven't the slightest clue what you mean," I reply with a taunting lilt.

His smirk sharpens along with the hunger simmering in his gaze. "Oh," he counters lowly, "I think you do."

My breathing hitches in my chest as I hold his mesmerizing stare. His eyes practically glow under the soft light of the cave, and my knees weaken with desire.

Gods, when was the last time I felt like this? Have I *ever*?

The way I want him is entirely different than anything I've ever experienced before. It's a pull, a constant magnetism tugging me toward him. But it is more than pulsing heat and desire. It is...is...

It is the giddy exhilaration of falling backwards with outstretched arms, knowing a soft mattress waits to catch me. It is the safety of arms that will never let go, vowing to hold and to shield. It is the disarming scent of home. The comfort of worn pages in an old book, where the ending is known and cherished. It is the struck chords of a favorite song, spoken lines from a dear poem—

A place to go when the world feels like it's folding in on itself.

He is not fire and he does not burn like flames; he is the steadiness and peace of flowing water. And this thing between us? It is like the tide— constant and inevitable.

It makes me want to drown myself in feeling—embedding his voice, the feel of his touch, and that glimmer in his gaze when he looks at me deep into my skin, washing myself in its contents until all the painful numbness is swept away.

"Lyra," Draven drawls, his voice thick. "If you keep looking at me like that, I make no apologies for what happens next."

I pull my bottom lip between my teeth. An action Draven watches, his gaze heavy-lidded. "And is that a promise or a threat?" I question.

"It is whatever you want it to be." His voice is gruff in his throat.

I hum, and his fingers press firmly into my hips. "And if I said I wish it were a promise?"

Draven flicks his eyes to my lips, and he tugs me closer to his chest, wrapping his arms around me. "Then your wish is my command, and I am yours to instruct. I will bring down the stars and string them into jewelry if you wish me to. All you have to do is ask."

I smile, feeling smitten, and press my body firmly against his. I practically melt when I feel him bulging in his pants. "I don't want jewelry."

"No?" he drawls. "What do you want, then?"

I let my silence speak louder than anything else, allowing my gaze to flare with the same desire I feel coursing through my body.

Draven presses his teeth into his bottom lip, and his grip on me tightens. His reply comes low and rough. "Your wish is my command."

He takes a step back from me, and, without looking away, he grips the hem of his shirt and slowly pulls it over his head, revealing his bare chest and all the toned muscle that comes with the sight.

I rake my gaze over him—slightly shocked when I realize I'm licking my bottom lip. A fire ignites in the pit of my stomach, and desire fans its consuming flames throughout every inch of me. Still, I study Draven's tattoos, remembering I still have questions left.

"Did you get the tattoos to purposefully hide your wielder's mark?"

He looks down, inspecting the black lines snaking around his forearm, rising up to his shoulder, reaching the tip of his neck, expanding across his chest. He exhales a deep breath. "Truth?"

"Always," I murmur.

Draven's eyes return to me, and they do not break away again. "It's all my wielder's mark."

Shock courses through me, a slight reprieve from the drunken desire clouding me. "But that would imply..."

He steps forward, lifting my chin with the crook of his finger. "Do you want to talk about some silly magical mark, or..." He jerks his chin to the sparkling turquoise pool filled with glowing flowers and moss-covered river stones. "Do you want to join me for an evening swim?"

I swallow against the dryness appearing in my throat. "A swim sounds nice."

CHAPTER FORTY-EIGHT

The hum of water droplets crashing into the glittering surface is hypnotizing.

But not as hypnotizing as watching Draven plunge beneath the water, emerging like a glistening god as his hair drips wet, tousled and messy, leaving his every muscle outlined by a watery sheen. He swipes water from his face with both hands, and shakes the excess moisture from his sopping hair.

Wearing nothing but my undershirt and undergarments—choosing not to just plunge into the pool naked, Draven doing the same, removing only his shirt, belt, and pants—I walk closer to the waterfall. My hair is unbound, cascading freely down my back, and I hover my hands just above the water as I move, loving the buoyant feel on my palms, relishing in the cool kisses brushing against my fingertips. Luckily, the water rises only to about my ribcage, making it an easy stroll.

I stop once the mist from the downpour of rushing water splashes my skin, and I stare at the network of twisting vines lining the walls, flowers blooming along them like bursts of living color. I glance right and see water lilies. I glance left and catch softly glowing blue light as the bioluminescent flora sways humbly with the breeze. When I look up, I see a smudge of silver in the sky as the moon rises, taking its rightful place in its kingdom of night.

I feel Draven behind me before I hear him. "Beautiful, isn't it?"

I continue staring through the circular opening above us. "Beautiful doesn't begin to describe it."

"I agree entirely." Draven presses a kiss to my temple. And then my cheek. And then my jaw. He nips at my earlobe, and slowly, he begins to trace my neck with his lips, collecting my hair and sweeping it to the other side of my neck.

My eyes flutter closed, and my head tilts, giving every inch of my skin to him. But those intoxicating lips of his still.

"Lyra," he rasps. He drops his voice a scratchy octave. "Tell me these aren't what I think they are."

At first, I don't know what he means. Until his finger traces one of the raised scars, where King Alastair forced me to rub salt into an already bleeding thing.

I clear my throat and lift my chin, refusing to feel shame about them. They are not blemishes signifying damage; they are reminders of survival.

"They are," I answer sternly.

His voice is dangerously low. "Your king did this to you?"

"Yes." I bite down on the acidic taste suddenly coating my tongue. "And he is *not* my king."

Draven responds with a low rattling noise, stemming from deep in his throat. "How long? How many times?"

I swish my lips side-to-side, feeling a weight sink in my chest. "Why does it matter?" I whisper.

"Because I need to know exactly how many hours he should suffer, and how many cuts should be sliced into his skin."

The corner of my lip twitches. My hands dance across the water, and I stare at the ripples branching from the touch. "Sorry," I say. "But he's all mine to claim. If anyone is going to make him suffer, it'll be me."

Draven is silent for a long moment. But then he presses gentle kisses along my scars. "That's my girl," he whispers onto the marks, giving something ugly and mangled the chance to feel beautiful.

The words pull at something in my heart, and I turn, facing him. He meets my gaze with tender eyes, and he lifts a hand, cupping my cheek. Then, he wraps his other arm around my waist and pulls me into him, enveloping me in his citrus scent.

It is dizzying, how much he can make my chest swell with emotion and my heart beat with desire.

He watches me for a few, passing seconds. And then, torturously slow, he brings his lips to mine.

And I am again reminded of how devastatingly explosive a feeling can be.

Stars stream across my shut eyes, and I kiss Draven back with every ounce of feeling, desire, want, emotion—all that I'm capable of. I kiss him with everything I have, all that I am. Broken fragments included.

And gods does he stitch the jagged pieces into something whole as he holds me tightly and threads his fingers into my hair.

I get lost in the kiss—lost in the vibrating abyss swirling inside of myself, far deeper and greater than anything I knew was ever possible. I lose myself to the frenzy—to the want.

I suck on Draven's bottom lip and slowly drag my teeth over it. My fingers plunge into his wet hair, and I tug at the strands.

Draven groans, the sound coming from deep in his throat. His grip on me tightens, and he squeezes the back of my neck as he kisses me deeper. Breathless, he pulls away, gliding his thumb across my swollen bottom lip.

"You are so perfect," he whispers. And then he guides me a few steps forward, until the falling water brushes against my backside. "Close your eyes," Draven instructs, his voice soft.

"What?" I ask, my own voice breathy.

"Close. Your. Eyes."

"Why?"

"Because if I look at them any longer, I *will* lose control. And I have thought about this moment many times, through many nights, and I do not intend to rush it."

Something melts in the pit of my stomach as a fresh wave of heat overtakes me. I do as he says and shut my eyes, and he turns me around, to where my back is again pressed against his chest, and the falling water just knicks my skin.

Then he kisses my neck while pressing both his palms flat against my ribcage. Until one hand moves toward the thin fabric of my undergarment while the other slides upwards, his fingers spreading across my neck and squeezing gently.

A moan rises in my throat.

His fingers rub circles against the soft fabric—against the part of me throbbing from the desire to be touched by him.

"Tell me something, Lyra."

His breath on my jaw sends sparks of electricity skittering along my skin. Well, that and…other things. "Yes?"

"When I touch you, would you like me to tell you about the many times I've touched myself, fantasizing about you? Or do you want me to tell you about how hard seeing you aroused makes me?" His hand slips underneath my undergarments, where his fingers brush against the apex of my thighs, making teasing circles against the bundle of nerves, coiling my stomach into knots. "Or," he says lowly, "would you prefer I say nothing at all, and simply show you all those things through the ways I choose to worship your body?"

Everything inside of me melts into oblivion, replaced instead by sparks of light, heated explosions, and consuming vibrations humming along my skin.

I have never known a touch to feel this good.

And gods do I want more of it.

"I want you to make me feel," I breathe. "Give me everything—shatter me for all I care. But don't hold back."

Draven stills—only for a moment—before he whispers into my ear, "Your wish is my command."

And then he slips a finger inside of me, curling it up with every thrust. His other hand—maintaining a firm pressure—slowly slides up my throat, until those fingers reach my jaw, where they lock into place. He presses a firm kiss to my neck, then sucks my skin against his tongue, biting down.

The resulting sensation sends blasts of radiant color exploding behind my eyelids, and I open my eyes as I gasp for breath.

Only…

I can't see anything.

My fingers rise to my face, expecting to find the blindfold Draven carries around pressed against my eyes. Yet I feel nothing but my bare skin.

"Draven..."

"Yes?"

"Why can't I see anything?"

I can hear the smirk in his voice. "You asked me to make you feel, and I intend to do just that." His finger slides in and out of me with delicious strokes, his movements intentional and precise. A moan slips past my lips, the knot tightening in my stomach.

Without my sight, everything feels so...heightened.

His thumb drags across my jaw before skimming lower, grazing the seam of my lips. "I am selfish," he murmurs thickly. "And I want you focused only on me." His thumb presses against my bottom lip, making it hum as if my skin sings for him. "Just my fingers inside you, and my name inked on your tongue. That way, when you are alone at night, again surrounded by darkness, you will long for the taste of me."

A shiver rushes through me, and, without thinking, I wrap my lips around his thumb and suck, grazing the tips of my front teeth over it.

A low rattling sound rumbles deep in his throat, and a wave of heat curls over my skin, featherlight and electric, leaving behind a slow, aching burn.

And I realize—he is the Dalmar heir.

Which means his magic is dark magic. The strongest magic in all of Solaya.

My voice trembles with desire. "You've blinded me with your magic, haven't you?"

His finger continues gliding in and out of me, sending electrical shocks shooting down my nerves with each thrust. He chuckles under his breath. "Blinded? No, not exactly. It's more like...I've encased you in my darkness." And then Draven's finger slips out of me, and I hear the gentle murmur of moving water—feel the absence of his warmth as his body shifts away from me.

Thankfully, he returns within seconds. His lip grazes the tip of my ear as his hand rests on my hip. "Do you trust me?"

It's strange, the way my heart doesn't even need to think about the answer.

"Yes," I breathe.

His fingers press into my skin, tightening, and then he nudges me forward, through the waterfall, until I feel him turning me around to where my front faces him, pinning my back against a cold surface.

The cave wall, I think.

With measured movements, he grips both my wrists and slowly raises them above my head, pinning them in place with a single hand. And then he kisses my jaw, my cheek, my nose—my lips. Something soft and velvety traces the sensitive skin of my underwrist, trailing down until it reaches my collarbone, sending the hairs on my arms rising as my breasts peak from the overwhelmingly soft yet intoxicating sensation.

I scent a subtle, sweet clove smell. And as the velvety texture glides gently beneath my collarbone, circling my breasts, rising up to my neck, I realize just what, exactly, Draven is using.

The Nox's Caelum.

He lazily traces every inch of my body with the petals of my favorite flower, a torturous tease. My skin is littered with chills, and I am wound as tightly as one can possibly be, reaching the point where I'm ready to beg for more.

In fact, at some point, a breathy plea must blow past my lips, because Draven chuckles and rasps, "Your wish is my command." Suddenly, petals no longer trace my skin, but instead it is Draven's touch now ruffling butterflies in my stomach. He glides his hand down my torso, slips his fingers beneath the thin fabric, and begins rubbing painfully slow circles against my sweet spot.

My body is flooded with a consuming rush of need, and my brain is lost to a frenzy that only understands one word: *more.*

Without my sight, I feel every texture, every tiny detail with shocking clarity. Between my arms being pinned above my head, his lips caressing my neck, and the toying motions of his fingers, triggering my every nerve ending, I am a tightly coiled spring, taut and ready to explode.

And despite myself, a small whimper sneaks past my lips. A sound that sends Draven's fingers slipping back inside of me and his mouth finding my breasts after a soft groan pushes from his tongue. He drops my wrists, and his tongue swirls in circles across my skin, transforming my tiny whimper into a melodic moan as an aching want consumes every part of me.

Acting on nothing but feeling, I reach my hand out and find his shoulders. Then, I glide an idle finger down his chest, over the ridge of his abs, and to the waistband of his trousers. I toy with the fabric, until my hand roves lower, making perfect contact with his considerable bulge. And feeling Draven unrelentingly hard in my palm—even if just through his pants—sends a fresh wave of burning heat coursing through me, warming everything from my cheeks to my toes.

I curl my fingers just enough to put pressure against the swell of him, and then I rub, toying with him like he has been toying with me.

Draven bites down on my shoulder before I feel his head tipping back, groaning. "Fuck, Lyra. You have no idea what you do to me."

My lip tilts with a smirk. "I think I have some idea," I murmur thickly, squeezing just a little tighter for emphasis.

A low rumble sounds in the back of his throat. "Let me worship you," he breathes.

Something swells in my chest. "You already are," I whisper through heavy breaths.

"No," Draven counters. "This is nothing but the opening prayer to a sacred ritual. You asked me to shatter you. And though I have no intentions of ever causing you harm, I will unravel every part of you before taking my time in piecing you back together again."

My voice drops into a loaded whisper. "You have already unraveled every fiber within me, Draven."

I feel his rough palm glide across my skin as he cups my cheek, his thumb moving idly. His voice is soft—different—when he replies, "And you, Lyra, have obliterated all my defenses. You are my undoing. My beginning and my end." He reaches for my hand and guides it to his chest, laying my palm flat against his skin, pressing his hand against the back of mine. "Whatever a heart truly is—whatever substance allows it to feel with such unabated devotion—it is yours, wholly and entirely. I have no need for it without you."

Emotion crawls up my throat, and the rush of feeling flooding my veins is almost too much for me to process.

Thankfully, Draven doesn't wait for me to speak.

He grips my backside, and he lifts me, taking a few steps before setting me down on what I can only assume is a large and flat ledge, where he then slips my undergarments down my legs, removing them.

He places slow, tender kisses on the inside of my left thigh, then my right thigh. I lean back against the cave wall, still unable to see a thing, feeling like all the overwhelming sensations are making me drunk. He grips both my thighs, drawing my knees up, and traces the scars painted across the back of my legs with reverence. Then, he wedges himself strategically between my legs and presses his lips to me, sliding his tongue along my seam, licking the bundle of nerves sitting swollen at the apex of my thighs.

Lightning cracks beneath my skin, igniting me with a staticky fire.

I tip my head back and moan. Loud and unabashedly. I don't even care.

The pressure his tongue places against all the right places sends me spinning. And when he sucks and nips with his teeth, I am spiraling.

But it isn't until he slips two fingers inside me, curling them upward, that I am unraveling.

That knot winds tighter and tighter in my stomach, and the humming pressure it builds inside of me has me breathing Draven's name—the sound rolling effortlessly off my lips.

He hums with pleasure. "Say it again," he demands between strokes of his tongue. "Say my name again."

I do.

"Again," he groans, his voice feral.

I breathe his name like a prayer.

It is his undoing.

One hand grips my thigh tightly while the other makes powerful thrusts inside of me as his mouth devours me. The knot in my stomach coils tighter—seconds away from snapping as the strings of all my nerves pull taut.

I plunge my fingers into Draven's tousled wet hair, close to drunkenly falling off a cliff. Then, I feel something fade—like removing a forgotten thin blanket.

"Open your eyes," Draven instructs.

I listen, officially shattering at what I see.

Inside the small cove behind the waterfall, the water glows aqua as aquatic flowers gleam beneath the surface. Purple petals twirl on forgotten vines along the rocks, bright and saturated. But it is the warm, soft glow of all the dyotana—small, translucent caterpillars—coating the ceiling that stunts the rhythm of my heart. Their glowing blue bodies appear almost crystal-like, shimmering with a glittering light.

And there are perhaps thousands of them twinkling above me, like a foreign, ethereal night sky.

The strings inside of me quiver, preparing to snap and release as Draven continues unraveling me with his fingers, his tongue worshipping me, driving me to insanity.

I stare up, mesmerized by the glow of the ceiling above, for only a moment longer before my gaze returns to Draven—who watches me as if I am something precious, something he'd bring down the stars to protect.

The moment our eyes meet, all the tension beneath my skin explodes in a wave of pleasurable heat, surging and pulsing as an effervescent hum spreads through my limbs in a dizzying rush. My head tips back, and my eyes flutter closed as the waves of pleasure crash through me, shattering all I have ever been, reminding me of all I can be. Draven holds onto me as I explode with pleasure, my moans and squeals oscillating along with my euphoria.

I am left weak and limp when the fluttering dissipates, gasping for breath.

When I reopen my eyes, I find Draven studying me with a softened gaze. His face is a marvel worthy of being strung in the stars—of being among the gods themselves.

"Beautiful," he murmurs gently.

I spend a few seconds catching my breath. Then, I lean forward and kiss him like it's the last kiss this world will ever know.

When I pull back, my eyes trace his body, so unbelievably attracted to every inch of him. But my eyes snag on the small circle of mangled skin hovering just below his collarbone. Gingerly, I reach my fingers out and graze the tips of them across the marring.

Draven sucks in a sharp breath at the contact, and my eyes snap up to him, my brows creasing. "Did that hurt?" I ask, my raspy voice a shade above a whisper.

Draven places an idle hand over my fingertips, stilling me. "Not in the ways you think," he answers softly. His eyes drop to the water.

I study him, sensing a shift. Unsure of what to do, I learn forward and place a kiss on his chest, up his neck, along his jaw, until I again reach his lips, where I offer him something soft and tender.

When I pull back, his eyes remain gentle, though something different now rests behind them. He grips my chin lightly, grazing his thumb over it. "That's enough for now," he murmurs.

"But...you received nothing."

Draven chuckles, the sound soft and airy. "Trust me," he counters with a smile. "I received *plenty*."

CHAPTER FORTY-NINE

Draven and I lay under a starlit sky in a verdant field of lush grass. His arm is bent, tucked behind his head, and I lay nestled against his side, resting on his bicep in his large shirt—my clothes hanging on a tree branch to dry, wet from the cave's ground.

"That one," he says, pointing to a constellation in the sky with his free hand, "is Morwenna's Dance."

I smile as the memory of Gray's story resurfaces in my mind. "I know that one."

"Impressive," Draven coos. "How about..." He searches the sky. "That one." He points up at a collection of glistening stars forming the shape of a lyre.

I squint, thinking. It feels familiar, but ultimately, I don't recognize it. So, I shake my head.

"That one is known is Astralis's Lament," he tells me.

"Lament? What happened to the god of the stars to make him mourn?"

Draven glances at me, a tiny curve in his brow. "Do you not know the story of Astralis and Sitara?"

My face pinches together as I think. Gods, it *feels* so familiar. But I chalk the gnawing feeling up to a forgotten lesson given to me by Sterling.

"Can one still know something if it's simply forgotten?"

Draven laughs. "Depends on the scholar you ask," he answers, looking back to the sky. "Would you like me to tell you the story?"

I bite down on my lip and nod.

"Different kingdoms have different versions. But my mother's favorite to tell was always the Rivarian version."

The corner of my lip tugs up. "We are the kingdom loved by the gods."

Draven hums. "And I'm sure there is a reason for that."

I pause. "Draven?"

"Yes?"

"Your mother...what was her name?"

A passing silence. And then—

"Lealla," he murmurs so tenderly, I realize a heart can break from something soft equally as much as from something rough.

"Lealla," I echo, thinking about how beautiful a name it is. "I wish I could have met her."

"Perhaps someday you will," he offers. "My mother believed we are all descended from fallen stars, and when our time on this plane ends, we return home to them—our souls shining in the mortal sky as a reminder of our time here."

"Do you believe that?"

From the corner of my eye, I catch the twitch of his lips. "I believe I've heard far sillier and much less beautiful theories about where we come from and where we go after." He turns his chin to look at me, his expression soft. "So, I'm not opposed to the idea that the very essence inside of me originates from a fallen star. Perhaps in a way, it's poetic, even. To some capacity, aren't we all fallen stars, anyway?" He brushes his thumb across my cheek.

I turn into his hand and kiss his calloused palm. "I didn't know you were such a skilled philosopher," I joke softly.

He laughs, pressing his lips to my temple. "I am many things. Including an excellent storyteller, so if you're ready..."

I bite down on my grin and nod. "I'm ready."

Draven gazes at me through crinkled eyes, then begins. "In the months leading up to the Great Clamatè War, it is said the gods were divided. Merikh, god of death and war and father to the Canamae, was rumored to be plotting something—which made the Canamae restless. Astralis, being not only the god of the stars but also the god of justice, could frequently be seen—if one chose to watch the horizon close enough—soaring over the ocean as he scanned the skies to ensure their protection.

"But one day, someone discovered a form of magic capable of killing even a god. They imbued that magic into an arrow, shot it through the sky, and pierced Astralis with it. It is said Astralis attempted to call down the stars to save himself, but the arrow had already weakened him, and he could no longer control them. It is also said the stars that slipped from his grasp that day became the seeds that took root in this world, gifting wielders with light magic."

Draven stills, taking a few breaths before continuing on. And I am latched onto every softly-spoken word, already hooked.

He actually is an excellent storyteller. Who knew?

"A woman found Astralis washed up on shore. Thinking he was merely a lost fisherman caught in a storm, the woman, Sitara, took him into her home, where she used her renowned wits to nurse him back to health. And every night as Astralis lay in a haze, barely clinging to his immortality, Sitara sang to him while playing her lyre. This went on for many months, even after the war had started. For without Astralis protecting the skies, much had changed.

"Astralis slowly began regaining his strength. Yet Sitara remained by his side, taking care of him, still entirely unaware of his identity." Draven pauses. "Some say it was Sitara's rumored beauty that made Astralis fall in love; others believe it was her music—her voice—that truly captivated him. But the great poets say they were simply two souls meant to find each other. And once a soul has found its match, it is as binding as the unbreakable oath."

That gnawing feeling returns to my chest, like I'm forgetting something.

What is it about this story that sounds so familiar?

"Their love enraged the gods. But it also enraged another—someone who loved Sitara dearly. He watched in the shadows as Astralis admitted to his identity. Watched as Astralis then strung constellations in the sky and bled color into light for her, crafting the famous colored stars. Watched as Astralis dyed the sky with a sacred spectrum—creating the Great River of Light. And he watched as Astralis gifted her the impossible—the power of the very stars themselves. A power she decided must be used to end the raging war."

As Draven pauses, my mind is spinning.

It's the name...where have I heard her name before?

"But perhaps of all the ways mortals and gods are intertwined, it is their desire to be loved that brings them most closely together; and it is that very desire that tore Sitara and Astralis apart. For the ones who harbored unrequited love formed a pact, vowing to separate them. Astralis was tricked, and he was forced to watch Sitara be taken from his protection, stripped from his love, and cursed to never find him again—not even in the afterlife.

"Astralis created a lyre with the stars in hopes that, one day, Sitara may see it, wherever she is, and return to him—remember him. And in the meantime, Astralis continues searching—both in the realms of the gods and mortals alike—praying he may stumble upon her. For it is said his immortal heart died—stilled from beating ever again—the moment Sitara was stolen from him. And only hearing her sing once more, playing her lyre, will restore it."

Draven looks down at me. "And that," he murmurs slowly, "is the story of Astralis and Sitara."

"Beautiful," I comment, still trying to figure out where I've heard the name. "But depressing."

Draven chuckles under his breath, arching a brow. "The constellation *does* have the word 'lament' in it."

"Fair point," I concede. I steal a glance at him, smiling. "A philosopher and a storyteller," I muse. "Aren't you quite the catch?"

Draven laughs, the sound beautiful. "Perhaps you can write about my talents in that journal of yours." His smile turns sharp. "*All* my talents."

But I freeze, unable to even comment on Draven's taunt.

Holy shit. *Holy. Shit.*

I sit up abruptly.

Draven follows suit, lifting himself from the ground, watching me through lowered brows. "Lyra?" he asks. "What is it?"

I glance at him, an indent wedged between my eyebrows. "I have to go. I...tonight was..." I take a breath and meet his eyes. "Tonight was amazing," I murmur more steadily. "Thank you."

He tilts his head, studying me closely. "And if I asked where you're running off to, I don't suppose you would tell me?"

My lips curve up right before I kiss him goodbye.

"Didn't think so," he mutters under his breath.

I rise from the ground, shove my feet into my combat boots, steal a final glance at Draven, and then I take off in a sprint.

I hear a fragment of Draven's final sentence. "Lyra, you forgot your—"

I am too far gone to hear the rest.

⚔ ⚔

I throw my chamber door open, gulping down air.

And I've never been so thankful for Draven making me run all those miles as I am right now, feeling winded from my sprint here, but not destroyed.

Luckily, Marcella isn't in the room, providing me with full privacy to read Casimir's journal. I lay flat on the ground and reach for the small sack beneath my bed, tugging it out into the light and retrieving the journal from it. In a frenzy to see if I'm right, I leave the sack and sit atop my bed, folding my legs and setting the journal flat in my lap. I thumb through the pages to find where I last left off.

And then I begin to read.

I came back from the battlefield a bloodied wreck.

It seems an infection found me at some point through the ongoing chaos of war, and today, it made its presence known in my body.

In my delusional state, I saw a woman with hair like ash, sparkling. She hummed to me and played an instrument by my bedside. As a fever threatened to clip the strings of my existence, I thought the woman an angel, sent to guide me somewhere to the realms of the afterlife. Frankly, I was ready to depart. Ready to lift my anchor and float away.

But the fever broke, and I came through the fogs of death. It was then I learned that Sitara had been the one at my bedside.

Yes, Sitara. Loved by all and renowned for her beauty. Magaius' and my closest companion. Featuring eyes that ignite your skin like the living blue fire they resemble. Her hair that is a stunning color of ash, both bright and peculiar at once. Her tiny nose that wrinkles when she laughs, and full lips that form the most breathtaking smile.

When I see that smile, all the heaviness in my mind lifts, and I am reminded of my purpose. Reminded that every sacrifice—every action I take—it is all to see that smile appear again. To give it a safe home, where it may shine without fear or worry of death threatening to deconstruct its delicate curves from tugging upwards ever again.

Casimir

A cold chill sweeps along my body as I attempt to process that knowledge.

It was exactly as I thought—Casimir references someone named Sitara in this journal many times. He always speaks of her tenderly, with respect. In a similar way a painter speaks about their art.

With love and admiration.

Draven's words echo in my head.

But perhaps of all the ways mortals and gods are intertwined, it is their desire to be loved that brings them most closely together; and it is that very desire that tore Sitara and Astralis apart. For the ones who harbored unrequited love formed a pact, vowing to separate them.

I've always believed myths were grown from seeds of truth. That perhaps there was a real woman who found a man washed up on a shore and took care of him. But I always figured the stories were embellished—romanticized.

Falsified.

It's a large part of why I never paid attention in my myth and lore studies. Why I never cared much to remember the mortals who walked among gods.

But I know Casimir Vivaldri was a real person. And, for some unidentifiable reason, I believe everything he's written in this journal is true. That this lost version of history actually happened, despite what we've been taught. And he writes of Sitara—of her existence. Plus, that journal entry was in eerie alignment with the story Draven just told me, with mentions of her beauty, her voice, and her playing.

Which leads me to wonder...

Is it possible that Astralis, god of the stars, truly fell in love with a mortal girl? If he did, did he truly give her the power of the stars? Did that affect the outcome of the Great Clamatè War?

Was it Casimir who plotted against her—the person he claimed to be his closest companion, outside of the man he mentions, Magaius.

And then there is perhaps the most unsettling question of all...

What happened to her?

Hoping to learn more, I flip to the next entry and read.

I followed Magaius late in the night.

He went to the Temple of Rhylia, the sacred place where one may commune with the gods, should a god or goddess be willing to speak. I suspect that is where he has been sneaking off to lately.

I plan to go back tomorrow when all have retired to their beds and confront him—to see with my own eyes what it is he has gotten himself into.

Whatever it is, I pray it is redeemable.

I record this knowledge in case I do not return.

Casimir

My brows scrunch together, and I bite down on my thumb with thought.

The Temple of Rhylia...

I don't recognize it by name, but I also don't recall any temples where one could go to actually *commune* with the gods. Casimir was the first Crowned Prince of Rivara, meaning he was probably located around Keziah. And around that area, there's only one temple I can think of that remotely fits such a description.

I could be wrong, but...

I think the Temple of Rhylia is the lost temple within The Ruins. The very temple Gray and I explored before our departure. A temple steeped in stories. And I wonder...

Could any of those stories *actually* be about Casimir?

With my mind reeling, I turn to the next entry—

And am shocked when I realize it is the only one left.

The final passage.

I swallow, feeling strangely nervous. Still, I read.

I have not scribed these pages for a long, long time.
In a way, I suppose I was right to suspect I wouldn't return from that temple.
I never did.
I am—

A knock at the door has me slamming the journal shut and jerking upright. I set it next to me—sliding it both hurriedly and sloppily beneath my pillow—and scurry from my bed.

"Coming," I call out as I go, my voice carrying a strange hitch.

When I pull back the door, I'm surprised to see Griff, his fist mid-knock. He smiles. "Lyra, hi. I—uh, I was looking for Marcella. Is she in?"

My lip tips up with a pointed curve. "Marcella?" I question, acting confused. "What has you searching for her?"

Obviously I know, but watching Griff squirm with a flushed face is too good to pass up.

"Oh, well, uhm..." He stops, clearing his throat. "She and I had uh...plans."

"Plans?" I repeat. "It's starting to get late, and we have our final test tomorrow. What could you two possibly be up to?" My tone drips with playfulness.

He rubs the back of his neck and chuckles, the sound coated with nerves. "I was going to give her a tour of the Castaria wing. After your test, if Kiran Selects her to be a member of our aggregate but other captains do as well, I want to show her why she should pick Castaria." He drops his eyes to the ground, releasing a quiet sigh. "I thought I would pick her up and escort her, but..." He chuckles. "She probably already escorted herself."

"Probably," I confirm through a laugh. I lean my head against the door frame, a soft smile tugging at my lips as I study Griff. "You really like her, don't you?" The question comes out gentle.

He snorts an entirely unconvincing sound, mussing a hand through his hair. "What? Where'd you get that? She and I are just...well, we're just..." Griff stops, blowing out a breath, and slides his gaze back to me. "I don't want to scare her off," he murmurs with a shrug, exposing his palms.

My smile widens. "You should tell her how you feel. You never know what might happen." I pause, tapping a finger against my chin. "Tonight, perhaps?"

His lips twitch as he rubs the back of his neck again. "You really think I should?"

"Yeah," I murmur. "I do."

Griff exhales loudly through his nose, shaking his head. "Great," he mutters jokingly. "Now I'm nervous all of a sudden."

I watch him, chuckling under my breath. "You're nervous because you care."

"Or," he counters with an arch in his brow. "I'm nervous because she's scary."

I snort a laugh. "All of the above?"

He smiles. "All of the above." Griff's eyes crinkle with warmth. "Thank you."

"No thanks necessary," I say through a gentle grin.

He huffs a laugh, then turns to walk away. But he stops suddenly, reorienting himself to face me. "Oh yeah, I almost forgot—Nuha is looking for you. She's requested that you meet her in Philator's library. I think she found something on that weird essence flower of yours."

Clearly unsure of how to react to the information, a weight sinks in my stomach while butterflies awaken in my chest. "When does she want to meet with me?"

He scratches at his temple. "I'm not sure. But I know she's in the library right now. I could open a portal for you, if you want?"

I sigh, weighing the choice. Ultimately, I decide I need to know what my essence flower means perhaps more than I need to know what Casimir Vivaldri's last journal entry says.

At least, I think.

"That'd be great."

Griff slowly scans me, his eyes lingering on my lower half. He clears his throat and points at my legs. "Uh, you may want to put on pants first."

I glance down, suddenly reminded I'm still only in Draven's oversized shirt.

Griff's smirk turns pointed, and he folds his arms over his chest. "Don't think I don't know whose shirt that is."

I make a face at him, willing my burning cheeks to thaw. "I'll only be a minute," I grumble.

CHAPTER FIFTY

The entrance into the library is as elaborate and beautiful as anything I've ever seen.

I push against the bronze, swinging the large doors on their hinges, and the smell of old parchment and wood greets me like a hug. My eyes glide across the room, drinking in the sight, and my jaw unlocks from the beauty of it.

Towering shelves curved in grand arcs—their mahogany spines decorated by glistening gold vines—consume every inch of wall, housing what has to be thousands of books. To reach those books, spiraling staircases twist round and round, their steps illuminated by floating lanterns that cast light along the curved balconies. At the heart of the library, a curling tree rises all the way to the glass-domed roof, and within the branches, hundreds of softly glowing, golden orbs rest.

I shuffle deeper into the large room, entranced.

"What a pleasant surprise."

I snap my head left and find Nuha sitting behind a large oak desk, parchment scattered everywhere on the table along with a few vials of different colored liquids. She braces both hands on the wood and rises, scooting her large chair backwards.

I'm not sure why, but I feel this strange need to courtesy or to do...*something.*

I decide that a simple incline of my head should suffice. "Griff told me you wished to see me?"

"I do," she replies in a warm voice. She steps from around the table, her onyx hair twisted back into a single large braid, wisps framing her oval face, and approaches me.

For some reason, I feel the need to flick my gaze to her finger to know whether or not she has Meiji's ring on.

She doesn't.

And for the life of me, I can't understand why that continues to gnaw at me.

Nuha's arms and shoulders sway loosely as she walks. She halts just a few steps from me and tilts her head, studying me with her emerald eyes. "Do you see this library?" She swivels her gaze around the room.

I follow where she looks, nodding. "It's beautiful," I confirm. "Astounding, even. It rivals that of a king."

Nuha smiles. "I've collected many books throughout my years here, but the majority of the credit goes to my predecessors. They're the backbone of what you currently see."

"Then I extend my gratitude to you all for creating such a wonder."

She smiles wider at that, the curves noticeably delicate yet powerful. "I have searched this entire collection—through all the archives and every book with knowledge or mention of essence flowers—looking for information on yours. Would you like me to tell you what I found?"

I swallow against the sudden dryness in my throat and nod. "Please."

Nuha studies me a few seconds longer. "Nothing."

The blood leeches from my face as my stomach hollows out.

"Until," she amends slowly, the pause cruel. "I stumbled into some scrolls from the First Age. Do you know anything about the Jurafen's history?"

The question makes me wish Gray were by my side right now.

He would.

He would know—would be able to recite it like a fond story.

It makes me realize I really should show him Casimir Vivaldri's journal. I don't know why I've kept it secret for so long—at least, a secret from him. He is a walking well of knowledge, and I'm a fool for not leaning on him to help me understand the contents of that journal—why

Sterling thinks it's going to impact me so severely.

I bite at my lip and shake my head. "No," I confess. "Not really."

She nods, as if expecting that. "The biggest thing to know is that the Jurafen were formed after the Great Clamatè War, as a means to protect the Three Kingdom's divisions of power and maintain the peace without bias. A sort of check and balance, if you will."

A word enters into my head, faster than I can stop it.

Allegedly.

"Bathara has scrolls documenting this history," Nuha continues, "detailing the conception. The original principles and the governing laws a Jurafen should abide by. The academy also kept records of what their agreement was with both the first kings and the Tani. This is all known as the scrolls from the First Age of Kings."

Feeling a tinge confused, I simply blink.

She draws in a measured breath and starts walking. "Follow me."

I do as she says, and Nuha leads me through a tight passage enclosed by cluttered bookshelves, around a corner, and to the very back of the library, where noticeably older shelves, tomes, and scrolls await. Encased by the worn shelves is a small wooden desk, not nearly as ornate and decadent as the one I found Nuha sitting behind.

She pinches her chin, looking around the space. "Now let's see. Where did I... Ah! There it is." Nuha walks to a knee-high shelf and plucks a yellowed, thin book from the very top of it, placing the aged book in my hands after.

I peel back the cover and read the title scribed beautifully in ink on the first page.

We Sang the Dawn.

I flip to the next page and skim the first few lines.

Beginnings promise nothing of their ends, despite what most think.

This beginning was golden.

A glimmer before the dusk. A bloom before the withering. A song worth singing, if only for the dawn.

With a heavy wrinkle in my brow, I glance up at Nuha, who watches me intently. "What is this?"

She shrugs. "The only known record of your essence flower. A story in an old, old book dating back to somewhere around the conception of the Three Kingdoms. As you've probably read, it's called "We Sang the Dawn", and it's about three people and their quest to achieve what they believe is right in a world torn apart by war."

I thumb through the pages. "Did you read it?"

"I did," she informs me. "A rather moving story, it seemed. I wish I could have finished it."

Curious, my eyes snap up to Nuha. "Why couldn't you finish it?"

"The ending pages were ripped out," she supplies. "I don't know who would be so cruel and reckless to do such a thing to a historical artifact, but I never did get to learn how, exactly, the story ends." She points at the book. "May I?"

With a knot beginning to tangle in my stomach, I nod and hand her the book. Quietly, she flips through it, stopping when she finds a faded drawing of an essence flower that indeed looks a hell of a lot like mine.

"It belonged to the one the story calls Prince. Also known as the Wielder of All. In this story, he was bestowed with a great gift to wield all magic from the Mother Goddess herself, after the Commander, known in the story as the Wielder of the Forbidden, received access to forbidden magic without consequence. As the tale goes, Prince's blood actually created essence flowers, after he bled red in a field of white gardenias." She points at the picture resembling my own essence flower. "The flower is evidently known as Threadweaver, for its ability to weave itself together with any magic its match has touched."

A cold chill sweeps across my skin, skittering down my spine, twisting between every crevice of bone.

The voice's words in Foreigner's Valley echo in my head.

Remember this, Threadweaver: love is no lesser force than hate, and a scorned heart does not wither—it burns. And fire does not choose sides.

The voice called me Threadweaver that day in the valley. That can't be a coincidence.

Not to mention...

When my essence flower contacted my hand, the threaded petals glowed with green and gold threads, stitching over themselves.

And the fact that Marcella and Gray, the two people I am most near, possess a wielder's mark that glows green and gold when they wield is not lost on me.

My throat becomes unbearably dry, and it is the fight of my life to keep my voice steady. "And what do you make of that?"

She hums with consideration. "Well, one can't exactly form a factual conclusion based on a work of fiction from over four hundred years ago. Especially when it features grandiose concepts like someone being able to wield all magic and access forbidden magic without consequences." She pauses, biting down on her thumb with thought. "Yet...the fact remains. It feels too distinct to be a mere coincidence that you presented a flower perfectly matching the photo in this story—the only known record of its existence."

My heart is hammering in my chest. "Soo...all that to say?"

She looks at me sympathetically. "All that to say, I haven't the slightest idea what to make of it, or your flower."

A weight sinks in my stomach.

But not because she doesn't have the answer, but because I suddenly realize I think I know who will—or perhaps, *what* will—understanding now why Sterling must have warned me to read until the very end of the journal.

The answers surrounding my essence flower must reside there— within Casimir's last entry.

Sterling's words from that night ring in my mind, a loud bell suddenly awakening every slumbered detail.

I wish I could save you from your fate. But what is chosen by the Cycle cannot be undone. Besides, I fear they already know you've awakened.

What has he known about me all along, and why did I not contemplate those eerie words of his with more scrutiny? I understand I was focused on the exams and how I would pass them, but I should have still questioned him more—realized that Sterling, being who he is, was trying to tell me something.

Because when he said, *they already know you've awakened,* he meant the Abdites, didn't he? Somehow, and for reasons I'm not sure I'll ever know, he knew they would come after me.

And when Sterling said, *what is chosen by the Cycle*, he was trying to tell me something, wasn't he?

The Cycle and fate are referenced so interchangeably, I had brushed it off to mean something more like, *this was always meant to be your fate.* But that isn't what he meant at all. He was *truly* referencing the mystical force known to wielders and scholars alike as the Cycle. The unknowable power that moves, redistributing the energy all magic possesses. Even the oldest of magic cannot truly die. At some point, the energy it carries—its essence tying it to our lakti—is redistributed. Whether at random or by some grand, divine plan depends on the scholar you ask.

Still, what could have made the journal so important that my mother asked Sterling to retrieve it? And just as importantly—why was Sterling so adamant I read it?

There is only one logical answer I can come up with to those questions. And it's that, in some strange and twisted way, the journal must be tied directly to me—hold answers meant only for me.

And how could a journal from over four hundred years ago have anything to do with me, the Cycle, and the Abdites hunting me...

It could only if Casimir Vivaldri and I, somehow, are connected.

On the verge of understanding, I ask Nuha the final question that might just solidify my evolving theory. "You said the story was about three people. One named Prince, who wielded all magic. One named Commander, who wielded forbidden magic without consequence." I pause. "Who was the third?"

A small indent forms between her brows. "The third was named Adored. The one who wielded the power of the stars themselves."

The hairs on my arms prick up, standing at attention as the story Draven just told me swirls in my head.

And he watched as Astralis gifted her the impossible—the power of the very stars themselves. A power she decided must be used to end the raging war.

Holy shit.

The book in Nuha's hands isn't a fictional story at all. It is someone's account of what happened with Casimir, Sitara, and Magaius. The Prince. The Commander. And the Adored.

And the Prince—*Casimir Vivaldri*—somehow was able to wield all magic.

And somehow he and I are connected.

I need to get back to my chambers so I can read his final journal entry.

I turn to face Nuha, doing my very best to look normal. "Thank you," I offer as plainly as I can. "For showing me this."

She offers me a kind smile. "I wanted to show you before I showed it to my fellow captains. That way, whatever they decide based on the information, you don't feel blindsided."

Her words still my racing heart—if only temporarily. "You have my deepest gratitude for that. That is..." I scoff a dry laugh and lift my brows with shock. "That is far kinder than most in your position would ever be to someone like me."

Her gaze softens. "I know about Meiji," she blurts quietly.

I freeze.

She glances down to the worn wood of the desk next to us. "I know about what happened in the valley. That you were the one who offered him peace—who listened to his dying wishes and relayed it to the ones you thought would be better suited to inform me of them." She scratches at the desk, lost in a momentary trance. "Consider this my way of showing you just the smallest bit of gratitude for what you did for him, in the way I'm able to."

A pang appears in my chest, clamoring against my sternum. "You owe me nothing—no displays of gratitude."

Her lips twitch weakly, and she huffs a hollow laugh. "Meiji always used to say something similar." She lifts her eyes from the desk, locking them onto me. "And so I will tell you the same thing I always told him: Sometimes, expressions of gratitude aren't just for you, but for those who feel indebted to you. Refusing them is selfish, and denying them is an act of belittling yourself—shows you refuse to see your worth." The corner of her lip tugs up with the sort of smile that makes me realize she doesn't say this next part to me, but to Meiji, wherever he is. "So, shut up and take the thank you," she whispers.

I study her for a long moment. "Can I ask you something?"

She dips her chin. "You can."

"Why don't you wear his ring?"

Her brows skip up as she openly wears her momentary surprise. But then her expression softens, her mouth again curving weakly. "Have you ever lost someone you love?"

An invisible fist squeezes my heart. "I have," I rasp.

She exhales a long sigh through her nose, and slides her eyes down to her ring finger. "Meiji did not give me that ring because he wanted me to wear it. He gave it to me only as an act of his final promise—to love me even in death, but to wed me first in this life." Nuha stills, continuing to stare at her finger. Her green eyes grow hazy—dimmed suddenly by an obvious pain. "That's why he said he was sorry for being unable to keep his promise. He wasn't able to wed me first, as he had wanted."

I want to comfort Nuha as I glimpse the ghosts haunting her. To tell her she doesn't have to be alone in her pain, as Draven showed me. But I realize suddenly I don't have the slightest clue how to do that—to comfort without minimizing. Falsely promising. To simply be there in a way that counts.

It makes me wonder how—or what—forced Draven to learn.

"I know it's hard to understand," Nuha murmurs. "Seeing as you were given a great emotional burden of his without knowing him for long. But...Meiji wouldn't have wanted me to wear the ring." She huffs a small laugh, shaking her head. "I can hear the choice words he'd have for me if I did."

There is a long, stretching silence as Nuha loses herself momentarily in the haze of her memories.

Eventually, though, she releases a quiet sigh and starts again. "We make promises to those we love and hope to keep them. But breaking a promise to our fallen is not what hurts them most. What truly destroys them is watching us stunt our lives, burying our own dreams beside them—allowing ourselves to hold onto pain so heavy, it dims the light they once loved in us." She pauses, her green eyes sliding to me. "We do not have to forget to heal. But we do have to move forward."

I press my fingertips to my cheek, realizing it is slick with moisture.

I'm not sure when my eyes started to leak.

Nuha reaches for my hand and squeezes. "Meiji is a great part of my story, and there is a chance I won't ever love another. But I'd be doing his memory a great disservice if I didn't try to open my heart and love again, eventually." Her soft smile assumes a mischievous quality. "Besides," she drawls through her smirk. "We always find our own ways to keep them with us." With her thumb, she tugs a golden chain from behind her tunic, revealing Meiji's ring attached to it.

She leans forward, dropping her voice into a whisper. "Between you and me, I think his ring is far better suited next to my heart than it is on my finger." Then, she winks at me, somehow still able to smile.

In a way, seeing her smile, despite what she's lost, inspires me.

And a realization courses through me—

If I truly believe in the Hanging Gardens, where Gardners ascend to live in beauty beneath the Mother Goddess's watchful gaze, then my mother has been watching me all this time.

And I must have made her so sad.

She must have mourned not just my pain, but the loss of the light she so often told me she loved. The way I used to smile. The way I used to dream. In all my grief and attempts to deny its existence, I never stopped to wonder if perhaps she was made to mourn me more than I ever mourned her.

Has she been able to smile in the afterlife since she left me, seeing what I've become?

Maybe, if nothing else, that alone gives me reason to live in a way that ensures she can smile again.

CHAPTER FIFTY-ONE

When I return to my chamber, I'm surprised to find Draven sitting on my bed, Casimir's journal next to him.

His night-dark hair is extra wavy and a tousled mess from the night's events, sending butterflies fluttering in my stomach. A feeling that is inconveniently timed, considering the pivotal point I'm at in discovering so many answers.

"What are you doing here?" I ask, flicking my eyes between him and the journal.

Draven lifts a brow. "Not exactly the warm greeting I was hoping for." He holds up a bundle of my clothes. "You left your clothes hanging on the tree. I thought I'd return them to you."

I huff a laugh and sit down next to him. "Sorry," I murmur. "I..." A sigh escapes my lips. "My mind is being pulled in a lot of directions right now."

He watches me with tender eyes, his brows scrunching. In a comforting gesture, he glides his thumb across my cheek. "Have you been crying?"

I turn into his palm as it cups my face, and I press a kiss to the calloused skin. "Yes, but...it was a good cry. A necessary one, I think."

Draven wraps an arm around me and tucks me into his side, resting his chin on my head. "Was it about your mother?" he asks, the question gentle.

"Sort of," I answer. "I saw Nuha, and we talked about Meiji. But she said something that resonated with me."

"Can I ask what she said?"

Nestled into his side, I inhale a breath filled with citrus and sandalwood, and my lips tug up with a wistful smile. "That healing is not forgetting. That if we forget ourselves in our grief, we may as well bury ourselves besides those we've lost—an act that would bring them far greater sadness than anything else we could ever do."

Draven's hold on me tightens, and he presses a kiss to the top of my head. "A lesson not easily learned," he murmurs.

I pull back from his arms, finding his eyes. "But it's one you've already learned, isn't it?"

From the words he's spoken to me, the way he consoled me that night in the greenhouse... I have no doubts he has experienced great loss and pain, and somehow, found a way to overcome it—to move on from it.

To heal.

His mouth curves with a weak smile. "A story for another day," he whispers, the words becoming increasingly familiar.

Still, I accept his answer.

Though, I do arch a brow and mutter, "Seems one day you will have quite the epic to share."

He chuckles softly. "So it would seem." He tilts his head, studying me. "You said your mind was being pulled in many different directions. What else is tugging at you?"

I turn and glance at the journal. My eyes return to Draven, and I point at the old, worn thing. "You didn't read that, did you?"

His brows lower. "Your journal? Of course not. I mean, don't get me wrong, I'd love to know every thought inside that beautiful head of yours, but I'd never invade your privacy to get it."

I stare at him for a long moment, slightly awed. Then slowly, I press a gentle kiss to his lips, allowing myself to reap every bit of emotion he's sewn in my chest.

"What was that for?" he asks through a lopsided grin.

"Just because." I exhale loudly and pick up the journal from beside me. "I'm going to need you to give me a few minutes while I read the final entry in this thing."

A wrinkle forms between Draven's brows. "The final entry? Is that not your journal?"

I heave a sigh. "I think I'll be far more qualified to answer questions in a few minutes."

His face is scrunched with confusion. "Lyra, what is—"

I cut him off with a lifted hand. "I swear, I'll explain everything to you. Just first...let me read, okay?"

Confusion scribbles itself in Draven's features. Yet still he nods, respecting my request.

I offer him a tight smile, then scooch backwards and prop myself up against the wall. I crack open the spine of the journal, find the final entry once more—my hands shaking slightly as they flip through the pages—and then I read, somehow knowing that in some capacity, I will not be the same once I'm finished.

I have not scribed these pages for a long, long time.

In a way, I suppose I was right to suspect I wouldn't return from that temple.

I never did.

I am...different. Someone who, for a continuum of time, I thought would be better. A man charged with saving my kind and preserving the chances of peace for these Three Kingdoms.

I am no better.

I am no man.

There is no such thing as peace.

And I have never known relief and guilt to merge so painfully into one sensation.

Would you like to finally know the burden I carry? Would you like to hear the words that have haunted me since they were spoken all those years ago? Perhaps if I share them, my shoulders will feel a little lighter. Perhaps the ache of loneliness will dull—if only for a moment—with the knowledge that someone else has finally heard them.

The prophecy once whispered to me went something like this:

"Beneath the gaze of a gripping white moon, where a lone, starry-eyed wolf waits, a raven will be made, forged in the weight of his sins. Cursed by another and rejected by the

435

threads sewn into his withering heart, the raven will no longer be shackled by the weight of time, but rather a servant to the whims of it—destined to forever fly, no matter how many times it clips its wings to fall.

But a promise, I can give: another shall come.

One who is defined by a name both two and one, born from the ashes of what the raven desired most, yet never found. And when they awaken—chosen by the Cycle to harbor the greatest power of all—the ashes of one great war will stir, giving way to another, and the Chosen will decide the fate of kingdoms, just as the raven himself had.

Yet to all who hear these words, I beg—heed my warning. For it was whispered to me by the stars themselves.

Where one begins, the other must end, never meant to live beneath the same sky. For the two cannot wield the same power without breaking the spine of this world, and should the Chosen fall as the raven fell, the Cycle shall not turn again, but instead collapse beneath the weight of its own creation. And if such a fate unfolds, the skies shall fracture, the stars shall flicker and drown, and the gods, for the first time, shall know true fear."

For many hours, I sat with those words. Night after night, my eyes shut, but my mind conjured picture after picture. I tried so hard to decipher their meaning. Yet in every scenario, I saw myself as the hero—someone whose ultimate goal was to instill peace and preserve the sanctity of life through diplomacy.

I never imagined I would be the one who destroyed it.

Do you want to know why your history books lie to you, Chosen One? It is because I—and I alone—committed such a brutal massacre, took so many lives, and robbed the world of so much hope and magic, that in order for Solaya to have even the faintest chance at prosperity—at peace—history had to be rewritten. The tragedy of what I had done had to be forgotten.

And now, the power I wielded to commit those atrocities—the power that could instill fear into even the gods themselves—flows through your veins.

You are a Binder, second of your kind. Heir to my magic. Decider of Fate. A Wielder of All.

You will find, Chosen One, that the power in your veins is as peculiar as it is intoxicating. As boundless as it is constricting. Remember, with it, you are not like them.

Now that you know the truth of what you are, I shall leave you only with this:

My name is Casimir Vivaldri, Crown Prince of Rivara and son to King Isaphus, the first Rivarian King.

And I was denied love. I was denied peace. I was denied civility. I reached, and they turned away. I fractured, and nobody cared, only noticing when I could no longer carry their weight. I was left to bleed on the altar of their indifference, hollowed out, left to rot beneath the mountain of all I was willing to give. They forged me in their flames, yet blamed me for when they burned.

Yet within those bitter ashes, I learned a valuable truth—

We are not creatures of devotion, but of desperation. We know not how to love, but how to survive. We break. We rebuild. We break again. And if that is the root of humanity, tell me—

What is there worth saving?

My chest rises and falls with jagged breaths, my throat constricting around incoherent emotions stuck in my throat. I blink, staring absently at what I just read, my mind spinning with too many thoughts to process.

A considerable amount of time must pass with me like that—frozen, stunned, and locked in a hazy daze that doesn't feel real. Because it isn't until I hear genuine worry in Draven's voice as he repeats my name again and again I snap back into my body.

"What?" I mutter while shaking my head.

His brows are pinched together as he studies me. "Whose journal is that, exactly? And what the hell did you just read? You look like you've just seen a ghost or communed with a god."

In some twisted way, it almost feels like I have.

I swipe a hand down my face, trying to stabilize my dizzy mind. "We need to find Gray and Marcella."

CHAPTER FIFTY-TWO

"Holy. Fucking. Shit."

Marcella sits on her bed, wedged between Draven and Gray. Her cobalt eyes are round, and her brows are so high on her head, it looks painful.

Finding Gray had been easy. He was in his chambers, reading. Finding Marcella had been a bit more difficult, but made possible through utilizing Draven's peculiar magical abilities. Thankfully, she and Griff at least had half their clothes on when we found them, and Griff was kind enough to open a portal for us back to my chambers.

What's been truly difficult is explaining the four-hundred-year-old journal I've kept hidden from all of them. Watching Gray's face fall—if only slightly—with hurt as I recite the words his father spoke to me the night my magic awakened—as he learns of the knowledge I've withheld. As I explain my mother's role, her request. I tell them everything I know, down to the finest of details I can recall.

The most difficult of which is explaining Casimir Vivaldri's final entry. What it means. All that it implies.

What it states I am.

A Binder, as he called it. Second of my kind.

Draven and Gray take the overload of information with surprising grace. Marcella, on the other hand, has not stopped gaping at me as the journal is passed around and everyone takes their turn reading the last entry, dissecting Casimir's final words and eerie prophecy. She's only been able to utter one sentence.

"Holy. Fucking. Shit," Marcella breathes again.

Yup—that's the one.

I blow out a sigh, puffing out my cheeks. "I don't even know what I should be doing with all this information," I murmur. "Should I tell someone important? Go to Bathara's council?"

"No," Draven and Gray answer at the same time. They exchange looks, Draven's stare lingering a few seconds longer than Gray's.

"Until we have a better idea of what's going on, we don't say a word to anyone." Gray holds the journal in his hands, flipping through the pages. He looks up at me, his mossy eyes lined with a quiet disappointment. "You could have told me," he whispers in such a gentle way, I know the words are meant only for my ears.

I drop my eyes to the ground, biting at my cheek. "I know," is all I have to offer him in response.

"It's understandable why you said nothing." Draven cuts Gray a sidelong look, his tone leaving no room for objection. "If this type of information got into the wrong hands—"

"—You mean like your father' alls?" Gray interjects, his tone like a sharpened blade.

Draven swivels his steely gaze to Gray. "Yes," he replies firmly. "*Exactly* the type of wrong hands I mean." He runs fingers through his tousled hair and blows out a breath, as if checking himself. "If someone like my father got a hold of this knowledge, Lyra would be subjected to all kinds of..." Shadows awaken in his eyes, and it's like he can't make himself finish the sentence—imagine the thought of it. "Anyway," he breathes, shaking his head, his eyes returning to me. "I understand why you did what you did."

Marcella bounces her stare between the two of them, an arch in her brow. "Perhaps our time would be better spent figuring out if what the journal says about Lyra is true," she says, shooting each of them a look.

Draven nods. "Agreed. We need to first figure out how your magic works—why you haven't been able to use it."

Gray clears his throat, lifting his fingers. "I have a theory about that, actually." He glances at me, then back down to the journal. "Assuming Lyra *is* the one referenced in the journal, he called her a Binder, implying she *binds* to things. And if Lyra is right and the story Nuha showed her is true, then her essence flower represents any magic she's *touched.* Meaning, connected to." He pauses, pinching his chin as he thinks. "I think, somehow, Lyra's magic is that her laktî binds to other laktî. In theory, it *would* allow her to wield all magic."

Draven glides a hand along his jaw. "That would make sense, even if it defies any present understanding we have of laktî. It would at least explain why she's been unable to conjure anything alone. In fact..." He tilts his head. "Lyra, when you've wielded, has Marcella always been near you?"

"No," I answer. "The first time I wielded, it was only Gray, his father, the King, and a few of his personal guards."

"Where a network of vines and roots appeared out of nowhere, scaling the throne room, leaving no trace of damage," Gray whispers. He snaps his gaze up and at me, his eyes rounding. "You didn't wield flora magic that night like you thought; you wielded an illusion of it, pulling at the thing that's always comforted you most. You used *my* magic to do it." His features wash with both shock and understanding simultaneously. "It explains what I felt that night. I just thought it was a result of the whipping—of the loss of adrenaline mixing with the exhaustion from the pain. But...it wasn't." His voice drops into a whisper. "It was the fatigue from losing so much of my magic's resources at once."

Marcella watches Gray through lowered brows. "Whipping?" she asks, the question quiet. "Aren't you a Nightenjoy? Why in god's veins would you be whipped?"

My voice is just a shade above a whisper. "Because he took the lashings in my place." A heavy ache squeezes in my chest, as if I'm just feeling the full weight of that night for the first time.

I guess in a way, I am.

Gray does not meet Marcella's downturned gaze. "It all makes so much more sense now. Why my father sealed your magic away, never to speak of it again. He knew what your magic was. I'm not sure how, but my guess is it has to do with whatever your mother told him she saw in the Veil." Gray's brows are wrinkled as he leans forward, peaking his fingers and pressing them to his lips. "And then after he found the journal, he must have read it and pieced everything together. That's why he collapsed in front of the king when your magic appeared—until the very end, he tried to keep it sealed. To prevent you from revealing yourself. There's no other explanation."

A long silence stretches across the room.

"Whatever information he did or didn't know," Draven begins, his tone low and rough-edged, despite his gentle words. "The fact remains that your father's choices very well saved Lyra's life."

Spoken aloud, the realization rushes through me like a storm, rattling my bones and flooding my heart.

Sterling knew better than anyone about my position with the king. He knew King Alastair's cruel tendencies. Knew how capricious and whimsically foolish he could be—how bloodthirsty. And he must have realized one small slip on my end, whether I knew what I was or not, and it would have put a terrible target on my back, larger than the one I already wore.

And the gods only know how King Alastair would have abused a power like that. The things he would have made me do...

Guilt sprouts suddenly in the pit of my stomach.

The night Sterling confessed to me what he'd done, he looked as if he had been carrying such remorse for his actions—for the path he had chosen. He appeared to clutch tightly onto regret for taking such a pivotal thing away from me for so long.

But I owe him for all the breath that got to live in my lungs; for all the rhythms my heart has been allowed to dance to.

I owe him everything.

And I have not done nearly enough to show him my gratitude for that.

I watch Marcella study Gray, a crease between her brows, then blow out a sigh. "Since you thought you were a flora-wielder to begin with, and seeing as I'm right here, why don't we test this theory and have you try to conjure something."

Nerves creep into my veins at the request, yet still I nod.

I close my eyes, but I do not give the flash of the white soporis plant the room to take shape in my mind. Instead, I allow the image of petals splattered with stars to form. And when my veins hum, I flick my wrist.

A vine of Nox's Caelum appears, stretching along the wall—resulting in Draven's lips tugging up with a soft, knowing smile as he glances down at the floor.

"Pretty," Marcella comments, observing the sparkling petals, oblivious to the way Draven had used the flower on me a few, short hours ago. "When you did that, I definitely felt...something. I think Gray is right, and you pull on our direct resources. Remember the first test, when you wielded in front of me?"

I nod.

I do remember. I wielded, and Marcella suddenly became light-headed.

She dips her chin, not needing to elaborate. "Now try to conjure an illusion."

My brows pinch together as I think, wondering what in god's veins I should create. Until, all at once, it becomes glaringly obvious.

I close my eyes, and I try to feel for something...different. To connect to Gray, the person so familiar to me. I'm shocked when my lakti answers, and my veins hum a different tune—when I realize, if I pay attention to it, I can recognize the difference.

I flick my wrists and reopen my eyes, unprepared to actually be met with the sight of a glittering comet soaring above our heads, lost in its own orbit and system of stars. When I glance at Gray, I find his eyes filled with something wistful and delicate.

"Well," Marcella murmurs, staring up at the illusion. "That settles that." She slides her gaze to Gray. "Did you feel anything?"

He nods, the gesture soft. "I did."

Marcella hums, folding her arms over her chest. "Everything lines up, then. Makes sense."

"It does," Draven agrees. "Without your wielder's mark, your lakti probably hasn't been able to pick up on the frequencies of all the laktî around you yet. My guess is your magic has basically been a drugged captive in your veins, stifled and diluted—which would also explain why you've been mostly unaware of its true potential."

"And," Marcella continues, drawing on his line of thought, "if you were always reaching for flora magic, then you were unintentionally closing yourself off to everything else, too."

My head is spinning from everything moving too quickly. "So, all that to say…"

Gray huffs a laugh. "All that to say, once your wielder's mark manifests—whatever it may be—the Dalmar over there will no longer possess the strongest magic on the continent." A pause. "You will."

A cold chill dances down my skin, sending the hair on my arms rising. I shake my head. "But I don't want that," I answer truthfully. "I don't want any of this." My arms make a sweeping gesture.

And I hate the sympathy that suddenly appears in all of their eyes.

Well, all except Draven.

"Then don't accept it," he states, plainly. "Say the word, and we forget everything we've just learned. I will find you someplace where you can live safely, away from all of this."

Both Marcella and Gray whip their heads toward him. "If that prophecy rings true," Gray warns in a low voice, "then Lyra's magic could decide the fate of kingdoms." He glances at me, his expression apologetic, before back at Draven. "I'm sorry, but she no longer has the privilege of just walking away."

Draven does not balk. "She has the privilege of doing whatever the fuck she wants, with me standing by her decision. I will not ask anything of her that she doesn't want to do. I think she's bled enough for kings already."

"So you'd let kingdoms fall?" Gray counters. "Let hundreds, *thousands* of people die in a potential war Lyra might be able to stop?"

Marcella looks conflicted as she weighs the questions herself.

But Draven doesn't.

"Yes," he answers without a shred of thought. "And it's a damn shame you don't feel the same, considering how much she loves you—considering even I know, without a doubt, *she'd* do anything to protect *you*, right or wrong."

The words send Gray's jaw snapping shut. He drops his head, his shoulders hunching forward with the action, as if they've suddenly become too heavy to carry.

Marcella glances between the two of them and sighs. But not before she places a comforting hand on Gray's back—without even realizing she's done it, I think. "Perhaps for now we can all agree that everyone needs to sleep. I know tomorrow's test takes place later in the day, but we'll all be useless at this point if we don't shut our eyes for a few hours."

I suck in a breath, feeling all at once hollow and overflowing. "Agreed."

CHAPTER FIFTY-THREE

The sun has just surpassed its peak, beginning the slow process of descending into the horizon.

After last night, we only discussed the journal and the truth behind my magic one more time, and it was only to agree that we wouldn't discuss it again until after the exams. Draven, though unable to go into specifics, believes I'll be fine during the third test without fully understanding my magic. And so it was decided—get through the final test, worry about everything else after.

Still, I've been unable to shake the subtle worry I glimpsed resting within Draven's eyes when we parted ways—him going to meet with his fellow captains, and me falling in line as examinees prepare for their last challenge. It left me with this gnawing feeling that, whatever the test is, it won't be kind to me.

Yet I force myself to focus on Josiah as he stands on the balcony, preparing to address the room. And it is a will of control not to look to the mezzanine beside him and find Draven. Something I cannot allow myself to do. Not right now.

For right now, the arena is filled with an audience—students and diplomats alike—who watch, eager to see the third test unfold. And sitting on his very own balcony, perched contentedly with an inscrutable, keen gaze, is Tynan Dalmar.

"Examinees," Josiah bellows, his voice steady and clear. "You have been tested on your ability to detect the essence of your magic, your ability to work in a team to fulfill a mission, and now today, the remaining thirty-one of you will be tested on your ability to overcome *yourselves.*" Slowly, his eyes glide across the room. "What will you do in the face of your greatest fears? How will you handle yourself? Who will you become?"

Dread piles beneath my skin, pooling deep in my stomach. Shadows, hazy and dark, dance merrily in the back of my mind.

A voice. A command. A death.

My fault.

It should have been me.

No—I'm not ready. I've only just started my path to healing, to attempt to bloom after withering for so long. It's too soon to ask me to face what lies in the dark places—I need more time to secure my stitches.

"I will explain the third test to you carefully," Josiah continues. "And it is important you listen closely. If you do not heed my words, you may enter the test, but you will not emerge from it."

As if sensing my rising panic, Marcella—standing next to me—reaches for my hand and squeezes. Gray, standing to the other side of me and glimpsing the gesture, does the same.

And the panic eases, just a bit.

"In a moment, you will be given a tonic that opens the darkest recesses of your mind and compels you to confront what lies within its shadows. Then, using your magic and the instructions I will soon give you, you will open something called a Feargate. Two things will become apparent to us once your gate opens. The first is the depths of your individual laktî, based on the size of the gate you conjure. The second is, once you enter it, we will learn who you are, down to the very fabrics of your soul."

A buzz of whispers swirl in the air. When I glance around, I see examinees now shifting on their feet. Gray's cousin, Huxley, included. But not Nuri, who I glimpse standing in a group of nobles, her chin lifted and spine straight. She looks completely undaunted.

"To call open the gate, you must offer the sky your blood and summon its power through an incantation. After you've bled in sacrifice, say the following words, and your gate will appear: *en vuhltum tamoris mei venio meisum.*" Josiah pauses, studying the examinees with a sharp eye. "Since I know most of you are probably wondering, it means, *I find myself in the face of my fear.*"

Josiah takes a long pause, and he quickly steals a glance in the direction of where Tynan Dalmar sits. As I trace his gaze, a sharp cold spikes down my spine.

Tynan's eyes are glued to me, as if he's been watching me the whole time.

He tips his head to me, a soft curve tugging on his lips. I incline my head in response, refusing to back down. Then I turn my eyes forward, not sparing him another glance.

"Once inside the Feargate, you will face nothing but yourself. Every sight, every sound, every shadow—all of it will come from you. A labyrinth of illusions, each one drawn from your deepest fears, shaped by the things you do not wish to see—to confront.

"You must endure them. Unravel them. Dig through their wreckage to find whatever may be buried beneath. And then—if you can—let them go." Josiah clasps his hands behind his back, his gaze steady. "This is a test of courage. Of resilience. Of whether you can hold onto yourself when the world around you demands that you break. Cahlmon will be casting each of your journeys, so please know, all of us here will be watching. As Jurafen, we must know each other—our faults, our fears, our weaknesses."

Four healers emerge suddenly from an unmarked corridor carrying trays of small vials.

"You are about to be handed a vial. Drink every drop of it, and then the test will begin." Josiah inclines his head to us, something strange resting in his expression. "Pledge your lives. Dedicate your souls. Offer your magic." A pause. "May the gods be with you." Then without another word, Josiah turns, retreating back into the shadows.

A healer with frosty hair approaches me and extends her tray. "Please, take only one."

I do as instructed, plucking a vial from the tray. Swirling the clear liquid, I lift it to my nose, but smell nothing. No scent, no familiar trace of herbs or minerals. It's as if the tonic's scent has been masked—or this is all a cruel prank and the vials are actually water.

An option I know isn't true, but hey...a girl can dream.

By the time I'm done studying the vial, Gray and Marcella have theirs in hand. Marcella raises hers like a goblet of fine wine, her lips pressed into a thin, weary line.

"Bottoms up," she says.

Gray huffs a quiet laugh, but ultimately, we all clink our vials together and throw them back. The liquid slides down my throat like chilled tea, smooth and cool, yet it is tasteless.

No bitterness, no sweetness—nothing.

Odd.

We set our empty vials back onto the tray and the healer moves on to another group of examinees. A beat of silence lingers between us before we exchange curious glances, each of us waiting for something—anything—to happen.

"Does anyone feel anything?" I ask, my hands folding over themselves with nerves.

Gray shakes his head. "Nothing."

"Nope," Marcella chimes. She pauses, her demeanor shifting dramatically. "You want to know what I *do* feel, though? I feel like asking us to confront our deepest fears while a crowd of strangers watch isn't a test—it's sadistic and humiliating." Her face reddens as she braces her hands on her hips. "Not to mention, these assholes have the—"

The ground at our feet begins to rumble and shake, cutting Marcella off. A low hum echoes through the air as the glass dome roof groans open, sliding apart as the panes shift away from each other, revealing an unobstructed view of the sky above us. Streaked in soft lavender, pale pink, and a deepening midnight blue, the sky looks stilled, cemented even, at the perfect twilight.

The familiar sight has fire flashing behind my eyes, raging within the walls of my mind.

A body. Eyes that don't see. An instruction.

I love you.

Another violent tremble almost knocks me down, dragging me from my daze. The ground creaks and grumbles, and raw stone juts up, rising in a column of reddish-brown rock. Then without further warning, I'm soaring through the air, going up, up, up as the pedestal of stone at my feet rises into the twilight sky.

Until it stops.

Stunned and disoriented, I scan my new surroundings.

Without a trace of another person in sight, I crawl to the edge of the column and peek out over the jagged side. All I see are swirling clouds and fractured light, as if I'm suspended somewhere between the heavens.

I exhale a shaky breath and sit back on my heels, staring absently at the rock face for a long passing moment, fear and anxiety and anticipatory pain already clamoring through me, beating against my chest. But...

I can do this.

I *have* to do this.

For my mother, so she can smile again.

For myself, so I can heal.

For Thestis, so he can dream.

For Meiji and Delroy, so that their lives were not forfeited in vain.

For Gray and Marcella, so we can all move forward, together.

And for Draven, so perhaps I can one day love him in the ways he deserves to be loved.

For us all, I will do this.

From the small pack strapped to my hip, I retrieve the dagger Marcella slipped me after she and I trained together in the hills, and I use it to slice my palm. Positioning myself over the edge of the rock face once more, I tip my hand over and drip crimson into the sky.

I lift my chin, steady my voice, and say the given words. *"En vuhltum tamoris mei venio meisum."*

I find myself in the face of my fear.

And I think...

I'm finally ready to be found.

Chapter Fifty-Four

It blinks into the sky with a soft hum, and I gape at it.

An ornately carved marble archway—overflowing with vines, flowers and intertwined with tree bark—towers before me. A small golden loom rests at the tip of the archway's intricately woven peak, crystalline looking threads spilling from the bottom of it, weaving and twirling over themselves all the way down the threshold. Inside the creamy marble frame is a sea of glowing teals and arctic blues, mingling in a veil of mist and smoke around clouds of indigo and periwinkle. They move like a wave in the ocean, roaming in circles around themselves as if enclosed by some invisible force. Right at the peak of the golden loom, the smoky water glows a deep and vibrant burnt amber.

I take a step toward it. Then another. On my third step, I reach the threshold of the gate, and a splashing noise echoes beneath my feet. I glance down and realize I am now standing in a shallow body of still water—impossibly calm and eerily blue, like the bottom of the ocean. The sky shifts from pastels to midnight black, and innumerable colored stars line the inky expanse of an endless sky, circling around me like a falling wave.

It's hard not to just stand there and gape. To simply be still and marvel at the new world I've been sucked into, seemingly independent of the one I was just in.

A voice begins to sing, the tune sweeping on a gentle wind. It's a voice I recognize with the utmost intimacy.

My own.

"*Come in,*" my younger self sings. "*Come and find me.*"

And so I do.

I am floating—no, walking—through a maelstrom of darkness and shadow that writhes and twists around me like serpents on a branch. The shadows hiss and whisper taunts.

Worthless whore. Lowly servant. Naive fool. Hopeless. Inadequate. Breaker of all things.

We see what you do not wish us to see.

The darkness falls in on itself, squishing me—suffocating me. I open my mouth to scream, but I have no voice.

In and in the darkness pervades. Solid, unbreakable.

It swallows me whole.

I am falling, falling, falling and land with a *thump* inside curling gilded bars. A hanging lantern sways rhythmically in the center, squeaking. Back and forth, back and forth. Yellow, luminous light falls down, caressing my face, and I blink at it.

Realizing I'm trapped within a cage, I rise. "Hello," I call out. "Is anyone out there?" I wrap my fingers around the golden bars, and they begin to glint as if a sun is shining on them. "Let me out of this cage," I demand, my voice trembling despite my best efforts.

Sounds of snickering fill the air.

"*You'll never be free,*" King Alastair's voice echoes, coming from nowhere but everywhere. "*You will be my little birdie forever, bound to your cage. My pet. My puppet. My toy.*"

"No," I whisper.

A cacophony of voices ricochet off the darkness.

Dance, little monkey. Fly for me, little birdie. Sing us a song, little pet.

"Please..." I swallow against the tightness in my throat. "I only want to be free. *Please.* Do not lock me in this cage."

The sound of a cracking whip harmonizes with agonizing screams. Mine. Gray's. My mother's. They echo and swirl in the air, playing the notes of bitter pain and acidic sorrow as if reading from a parchment of sheet music.

My stitches start to unravel, fighting with everything they have not to split apart.

Flashes of images form in the mist.

Gray's bloodied, mangled back. His horrified face as he watches the whip break my own skin.

A memory I haven't thought of in so, so long.

Suddenly, the gilded cage melts, and I am toppling over onto the floor. When I gather myself, horror strikes me like a physical blow as I realize I am now reliving that forgotten memory. One where a guard pins me to a wall, his hand forcefully plunging into my pants. I bite his other hand as it attempts to muffle my screams.

Red splatters across my face.

And then comes the whip. Just an average leather one, thankfully not laced with metal or glass. But he snaps it down on me. Again. Again. Again. Gashes form, and crimson oozes from me like my dignity, pooling on the white marble floor. But my blood is tainting its purity, ruining its beauty.

That's why I'm forced to clean it up, soaking it into a rag. My commonblood is not worth staining such an expensive floor. At least, that's what the guard tells me as he continues bringing the whip down on me.

The weak, mumbled words I had whispered sing in the mist. But instead of the plea for aid they once were, they are twisted into a cruel taunt meant to mock.

"Please...someone, anyone, please help me. Please..."

A tinging noise—like fracturing ice—splits the floor. It opens wide, and the entirety of the scene shifts as the floor becomes the ceiling and the ceiling becomes the floor.

My world has literally turned upside down.

When I look up, I glimpse grayish-blue feet hanging idly, swaying like a forgotten branch above me. The sound of damnation hums as the noose creaks, gliding back and forth, back and forth.

And then another pair of feet appear. And another. And another.

I drop my head and grit my teeth as my body screams at me to turn away—to shut my eyes and refuse it exists. But…

I don't want to be that girl anymore.

Because I've finally learned turning away from unpleasant things does not make them go away—it merely delays the inevitable confrontation of them. The truths that define us do not disappear; they wait.

I lift my head, steeling my trembling bones with the resolve to survive. To be a whole version of myself. To live again.

My fingers tighten around the dagger at my side, and an outline of what appears to be shadowy crates catches my attention. Without thinking, I move toward them, using them to climb higher, stopping only when I reach the top of the creaking ropes. I cut through the thick twine, the strands splitting apart as each set of floating feet drop from the weeping sky.

The moment the last pair falls into oblivion, the darkness whooshes, and I am falling with them, dropping—plummeting—down, down, down until I crash against something soft and plush. My fingers feel the fluffy sensation of fur and the delightful touch of silk. My eyes survey the area, and I find that I am in a room I've never seen before.

A fire roars in a hearth as two goblets sit on a table in front of me. Next to them are my Gardner supplies and the soporis plant. A voice that sends icy chills down my spine carries into the room.

"Alone at last," he says.

I look left and see Eri standing at the edge of the bed, shirtless and with his pants unbuttoned. I glance down at my body and see my exposed legs, nothing but a sheer nightgown covering my middle half.

No. No. No. No.

Eri crawls onto the bed and tucks a strand of hair behind my ear. "So beautiful. Such a prized toy." He kisses my neck, my collarbone and shoulders.

Nausea roils through me.

"Be a good girl and lay down." He pushes me back against the sheets with a firm hand. "Good, good," he soothes while slowly gliding his fingers along my exposed thigh. "Now, spread your legs."

Bile burns my throat.

I glance at the goblets on the table. I can smell the hints of soporis on his lips. It should have kicked in by now. He should be fast asleep. Which means...

It didn't work this time.

His lips find my mouth, and he kisses me with savage hunger. The kiss is hard and aggressive. Empty, hollow, cold—so different from what Draven showed me a kiss should be.

Using his knee, he kicks my thighs apart, spreading them open and settling between me.

Horror heats my skin as the room plunges into darkness. The fire in the hearth dies, the walls around us fade, and something in the shadows catches my attention. A sort of flicker.

Words fall into my mind.

You are not defenseless any longer. Fight him off. Fight.

Fight.

I can fight.

I shove Eri from my body and knee him in the groin. I jump up from the bed, slide my foot back, and I assume my fighting stance. "Never. Again," I growl.

The scene shatters, and I again find myself plummeting through a rush of wind as I freefall. I squeeze my eyes shut against the dizzying sensation. When I reopen them, I am in a beautiful garden stretching as far as the eye can see. The sky is powdery-blue, and the sunshine kisses my cheeks in greeting. Birds sing as they fly across candied clouds and insects chirp with cheer. I take it all in, confused.

Am I out? Did I complete the Feargate?

I see Marcella and Gray talking. See parents that aren't my parents, but also are. A tsunami of relief washes over me at the sight of them. "Azalea! Sterling!" I rush over to greet them. "You're here!"

But right as I'm about to reach them, ready to pull them in for an embrace, my muscles fill with lead. And as I try to push through the heaviness, my feet become cemented in mud. I glance down and watch as my body becomes tangled in a web of vines and weeds.

What is—what's going on?

Slowly, everyone swivels their gaze toward me. Their eyes are black and empty. So I squeeze mine shut, thinking I'm imagining things. But when I reopen them, their depthless stares remain.

And my heart falls into my stomach.

I am still in the Feargate.

Azalea pouts her bottom lip. "Oh, Lyra." The voice sounds like Azalea—she *looks* like Azalea—but I know with utter certainty that could never be her.

Sterling shakes his head at me. "You damned us all."

"It's your fault," Marcella sneers.

"What is?" My heart skips in my chest as panic presses into me, sharp as thorns.

"You've as good as killed us yourself," Gray responds in a venomous whisper. "Our blood is on your hands, Coward."

A sob forms in the back of my throat. "No...I'm not a coward. I just—just..."

Their black eyes pin me. "*Coward*," they hiss in unison.

One-by-one, down the line, they all cock their heads and frown. "It should have been you," Azalea drones.

"It should have been you," Sterling says next.

"It should have been you," Marcella sneers.

Gray's black eyes stab me like a blade. "It should have been you. It was your fault, after all. It always is. Always will be."

The conversation repeats on a loop, seeping into the fabrics of the wind.

You damned us all. It's your fault. You've as good as killed us yourself. Our blood is on your hands. It should have been you. Damned us all. Your fault. Killed us. On your hands. Should have been you. Damned. Fault. Killed. Hands. YOU!

The last word booms in the air like a crackling thunderclap, making me crouch in fear. "Please," I whimper. "Stop."

Yet something inside tells me to get up. To not let these voices win.

And though it takes me a moment, I remember myself. "I only want to save you. *Help* you."

A wicked cackle splits the air.

"*Help us?*" Azalea coos. "Darling, you are our damnation."

I shake my head. "No, that isn't true."

"Isn't it?" Sterling counters. "Look around."

I do, and all the flowers suddenly bleed red, pooling into a puddle of crimson at my feet.

"It's your fault," Marcella repeats. "All those lives lost—both past and present. You are responsible for every single one."

"Do you remember who you first made bleed?" Gray asks.

My breath catches in my throat. "Stop. Don't go there."

This isn't real. This isn't real. This isn't real.

But it feels, looks, and hurts as if it is. So what does it matter if it's an illusion or some variant of reality? The damage still cuts the same.

They all cock their heads in synchrony, their black eyes lighting like a wick catching flame. "She's waiting for you," they sing, stepping forward.

Knots twist in my stomach.

They circle me, creeping closer and closer, stretching their tainted hands, reaching for me.

But I lift my chin and leave my arms at my sides. "No matter what you do, I won't hurt you."

The words send them crumbling to ash.

But not before Azalea sings a final time, her song a fading lullaby. "*She's waiting for you.*"

Everything shakes and groans as the scene crumbles away. It all tilts and shatters, leaving behind a blinding white light. When the light recedes and my eyes readjust, I find that I am in King Alastair's throne room.

She's waiting for you.

As I stare at the room—at the still picture of what I know is about to unfold—there is a moment where I think I would rather die than face it. That I'd rather be whipped or beaten than relive it—to acknowledge what it's done to me. All the ways it's obliterated me.

But then I remember Draven's words. They wrap around my skin, holding me steady.

Pretending to be whole does not mean you are, just as pretending the pain does not exist won't make it go away.

I'm ready to stop pretending.

I'm ready to move on.

I'm ready to face this.

"She's waiting for you," voices hum once more.

I guess I shouldn't keep my mother waiting any longer.

Chapter Fifty-Five

"Let's start from the beginning," a sinister voice hisses in my ear.

Why? I want to ask. I already know how the story goes.

It starts with me in chains.

It ends with her being burned alive at the stake.

"Lyra, come here," my mother calls to me.

I move, but a buzzing child with long, frosted lilac hair runs past me.

"Coming mother!" she sings. The child with eyes like amethyst wraps her tiny arms around her mother's waist and squeezes.

My mother embraces her with such warmth. "Where have you been, my sweet flower?"

The girl beams, boasting missing teeth. "Gray and I were playing hide-and-seek. I hid in a cabinet inside an abandoned chamber. He had to give up because he couldn't find me."

My mother chuckles and strokes the girl's hair. "You must be careful where you venture."

"Yes, mother."

The scene blurs and shifts.

Tears pool in my eyes.

"Gray, we're getting too old for these games," a version of me whose body is maturing says through laughter.

"Come on," he urges, his voice sounding squeaky yet deep all at the same time. "It's raining outside, and I'm bored."

"Then attend to your studies."

He arches a brow. "Have *you* completed Sterling's assignment?"

He got me. "Hide-and-seek it is."

Another shift in the scene, and I see myself running through a corridor, glancing over my shoulder, giggling. I veer left, then right. I run until I reach a dimly lit corridor with a large, beautiful wooden door sitting at the foot of it.

I reach my fingertips toward my younger self. "No," I whisper. "Don't go in there. *Please.*"

But she can't hear me, and I can't change this scene.

There is a large male body grunting in a bed, sweat dripping down his back. I can't see his face, and his hair is tied back in a bland way. Beneath the body, I catch a glimpse of silvery-violet hair and unseeing mauve eyes.

My mother's face looks distant, lifeless. On the floor is a spilled tonic, her Gardner supplies scattered across the ground. I note the rip in the hem of her dress, see the split in her bloodied lip.

A frenzied rage overtakes my child self.

I watch in terror as the young version of me reaches for the first thing she sees—an ornately forged silver candlestick. It's sturdy—heavy. Enough to knock someone unconscious.

Before I realize, I am reaching for that girl—trying to hold her back. Prevent her from what she's about to do. "Don't do it," I plead. "You're going to be filled with so many regrets because of this mistake."

But my hands grasp nothing but mist and smoke, and regardless of my pleas, I'm forced to watch the girl raise the candlestick high above her head and smash it down onto the head of the unidentified man.

He collapses with a dull *thud.*

My mother blinks, as if just now coming back into her body. Her watery eyes take in the scene. "Oh, Lyra," my mother breathes. "What have you done?"

The scene crumples away, and I sink down to my knees, shaking—convulsing. Everything around me merges and blurs in a collage of shadow, mist, and smoke. A blinding light flashes, a scream pierces my ears—everything stills.

My eyes flutter, adjusting to the new scene. I am back in the throne room, but this time I am not looking at a past version of me—I myself am bound in chains, kneeling at the throne of the king.

"Foolish, insolent girl," he hisses.

I blink at his face, finding it to be strangely warped—half-rotted, almost. A dark aura pours from his skin.

My mother kneels unbound beside me. "Please, My King. Please forgive my daughter. She did not know it was you in that room. She was just a scared girl fearing for her mother. She is young, and does not yet understand the nature of such relationships."

King Alastair scoffs, disgusted. "Please," he spits. "There are courtesans already training at her age." He tilts his head, and his face is so, so cold as he addresses me. "Did you know if a healer had not been nearby, I would have died from the trauma to my head?"

My eyes bulge with terror.

"Sterling?" The king calls out to his advisor.

"Yes, Your Highness?"

"What is the usual punishment for an attempted murder of a king?"

Sterling's throat bobs, the only reaction he'll allow. "Death, Your Majesty."

"And what sort of death?" he coos, ice punctuating each word.

Sterling's features are strained, so filled with grief. "Whichever death His Majesty finds most fitting."

King Alastair clicks his tongue. "Ah, yes." His dark eyes slide to me. "And do you know why that is, child?"

I want to kill him right here and now. Yet I can't move—can't speak. All I can do is mirror the past.

My head glides back and forth.

"It is because *I* am the *king*. I am of the highest birth. My word is the word of the heavens themselves. And you—with your worthless, dirty blood—bludgeoned me." He releases a sigh and slumps down in his throne, resting his cheek upon his closed fist. "She is to be executed at dawn tomorrow. I choose…death by flogging."

Terror stains my cheeks while my stomach hollows out, horror flashing in and out of my eyes. Regret, pain—so much pain and anger—flood through me. Not at his order. Not at the decree. No—there are days I *wish* for that to be what happened.

It is the knowingness of what happens next that mutilates me.

I hang my head and begin to cry. Tears stream down my face, and my body shakes. "Please," I murmur. "Please. Stop this now. Don't make me watch it again."

"*What will you give us?*"

"Anything," I breathe. "Anything. But don't—please don't make me relive this."

"*Stay,*" the slithering voice of one yet many replies. "*Stay with us. Become us. Then we'll stop. Then we'll make it all go away.*"

I open my mouth to accept their terms—

But a voice that could rattle the stars stops me.

"*NO.*" It comes from the essence of darkness itself.

I blink.

No.

That's right.

I have to face this. There is more for me to live for now—people that need me.

Thestis's sweet face appears in my mind, and I can almost feel him squeezing me, nestling into the crook of my neck. *My 'Ma said if you make it—if you actually get accepted into Bathara—that maybe there will be hope for me after all. She's going to allow me to train with a real tutor if you're admitted. Said that it'll be the start of a new future.*

Make them see us.

I glare at the king, reawakened defiance burning in my gaze. His face morphs under my stare—his eyes going wholly black, his face sinking in and hollowing out in the cheeks. I look over to my mother, who still stands next to me; she shines with a bright luminescence.

Her eyes are practically glowing as she lifts her chin and calmly says, "I invoke Samsara."

King Alastair's warped face twists. "Don't be ridiculous. I will not lose the brightest, most accomplished Gardner seen in centuries to such nonsense."

My mother does not balk, her eyes a combatting light in the darkness. "You don't have a choice."

The king whips his head to Sterling, whose face is already beginning to fade away. "She's right," Sterling murmurs. "Samsara is as old and unbreakable as Tani Law. If you do not honor it, the gods will curse our lands and take revenge by claiming the life of your future children and your own."

King Alastair swivels his attention back to my mother, gaping. "You would invoke Samsara for some worthless, groveling child?"

She raises her chin. "My daughter's life is worth more than you could ever imagine."

Everything shatters and breaks inside of me. Burning, freezing, crumpling—like trampled petals trapped in burning ice.

My fault. My fault. My fault.

It should have been me.

This world of mist and smoke and darkness pulses and blurs as the scene shifts again for the final time. The last moments where my heart remained alive and unbroken—my canvas still fresh and unblemished, ready to become a work of art instead of a thing of nightmares.

The king watches as two guards finish binding my mother's wrists above her head and drench her in oil, departing back down the hill once finished. "Let's get this over with."

Sterling clears his throat and unrolls a scroll. He reads from the parchment. "Samsara exists so that a parent may pay a life debt in the place of their child. A soul for a soul, sanctioned by the gods. But only fire can wash away the stain of what the child has done. So, as Samsara is invoked, a parent must burn by their child's flame. And as the smoke reaches the heavens, may the debt wash away, and the charred blood serve as penitence." He refolds the scroll and looks at me with impossibly sad eyes.

A burning wick appears in my hand. I glance down at it, then up at my mother.

I have spent every day since this moment trying to forget—forcing the scream out of my head and pushing the smell from my memory.

Running and running and running and running from it.

I can run no longer—only resign to the brutal, debilitating pain of it.

With slow, rigid movements, I approach the post binding my mother. Her face still looks how I remember. Calm, peaceful—incomprehensibly serene. She watches me closely. As if she wants to memorize every pore on my face to take with her to the Hanging Gardens.

Tears slide uncontrollably down my cheeks. "It should be me," I whisper. "I'm so sorry, mother. This is all my fault."

She catches my eyes with a gentle dip of her chin. "No, it isn't," she whispers back. "It never was."

I blink at her unblemished face.

It's strange, seeing her so clearly. I'd forgotten the way one brow sat slightly higher than the other. That she had a small cowlick near the back of her head, making her braid rest funny.

I'd forgotten so many small details.

My mother's face slowly fades. Yet even as it goes, her eyes hold mine, as if she can see something I can't. "You remember," she says sternly, "this is *not* your fault. You do not let this break you. You do not let them win." Despite everything, she brims with strength. "You do not cower. You do not yield. You do not falter. Say it."

My lips tremble. "I will not cower. I will not yield. I will not falter."

Despite the nightmare, hope blooms across her lips. "That's my sweet flower."

Against my own volition—despite my attempts to fight back and hold steady—my arm extends and my fingers uncurl, releasing the burning wick.

"I love you," she whispers as the wick falls to the spilled oil in slow motion.

My mother disappears behind an eruption of hungry flames.

I fall to my knees, screaming, cursing—sobbing uncontrollably. My fists pound at the ground. Again. Again. Again. Until they are a bloodied, ravaged mess, chunky skin peeling away from my knuckles.

A cacophony of voices sing in my ear. *"She is waiting for you. She is coming. Finally, she comes."*

The fire dims to a dull glow, revealing an incinerated corpse. The horrifying thing creaks its neck and pins me with a molten stare, charred skin reaching toward me. "This is *your fault*." The body once belonging to my mother pries itself from the wooden post, making strange popping noises that make my blood run cold. "Look what you've done to me. *Look.*"

Limping toward me, my mother's black, crumbling fingers grip my chin, and she forces me to look at her.

I shatter completely.

"I'm so sorry," I rasp with utter brokenness. "I am so, so sorry."

A horrid cackle breaks from her lips. "And what am I supposed to do with apologies now? Do you see this burnt skin? Do you *know* what it feels like to be burned alive?"

"No," I squeak.

"Want me to show you?"

I lift my head and stare into the abyss of her eyes. "Yes," I breathe. *Finally, what I deserve.*

"Say it," the voice hisses. "Say you want me to make you *burn.*"

I choke back my sob. "I want you to make me burn."

She grins, her chapped lips splitting open to reveal rotted teeth.

Suddenly, her burnt body morphs, and black and brown, thorn-coated vines twirl around her torso, twisting and knotting across her arms, rising up into her neck, covering her scalp. Beneath the vines, a fiery glow—resembling charcoaled embers after suffocating flames from wood—intensifies, making her burn a shade of vermillion. Her black eyes become ringed with that same glowing fire, and at the center of her forehead a mark appears—one I don't recognize.

And it's like I suddenly can't look away. My eyes are drawn to that strange, glowing ring of fire circling her depthless eyes.

Voices whisper in a frenzy, different from the ones before, just barely audible. *Erhè akta maht. Erhè akta maht. Erhè akta maht.*

That's when I realize—with no small amount of horror—this is an Abdite.

My whole body explodes with a sharp, searing pain. It's like a hot iron is being shoved against every crevice of my skin. Panic sweeps through me as I grit my teeth against the baffling sensation. Needle-pricks, being stabbed—throbbing, pulsing, *burning*. It *hurts*.

I scream and collapse, my body shuddering and thrashing against what's too immense to even fully process.

The Abdite kneels down next to me. It glides a strangely cold hand along my cheek. "It hurts, doesn't it?"

I can't speak; the pain is too great. I whimper instead.

The Abdite leans forward and brushes its chapped lips against my ear. "Want me to tell you a secret?" she whispers. "It doesn't hurt forever. Not if you give in to it."

I claw at my throat, edging madness. It feels like I've swallowed molten lava, blisters replacing saliva.

The Abdite chuckles, watching me with delighted interest. "The throat hurts, but not as bad as the eyes." She points to her own as if for emphasis. "Let the fire ravage you. Once it does, you will have power far greater than you can imagine."

I gasp in wet-sounding breaths and begin choking on ash.

The Abite strokes my hair and hums. Then, as if hearing something, she whips her head toward something in the distance. When she returns her attention to me, her expression is entirely changed. "A gift before I go, Master's Precious."

She presses her finger against my forehead, and a blast of searing heat sizzles against my skin. A choked, gurgling gasp of pain is the only sound capable of leaving my lips.

"Goodbye for now. I'll be seeing you again very soon."

A wave of total darkness crashes onto the Abdite, shattering it into oblivion like an ice sculpture cleaved by a hammer. Branches whip and extend from the charcoal sea, bringing everything around me toppling. The unfurled darkness lassos around the sky and sends it plummeting. Forces the ground to crumple.

A small tendril extends to me and whispers something in my ear. It feels familiar and warm and good. *"It isn't your fault,"* the darkness whispers. *"It should not have been you."*

Confused, I blink—still clutching at my burning throat, pain creating flurried snowflakes in my vision.

"It isn't your fault," it repeats. *"It should not have been you. Say it. You must say it aloud."*

Maybe it's because of the delirium I feel setting in or the sheer amount of pain warping my senses, but I do as it asks while everything crashes and crumbles into dust around me.

"It isn't my fault," I croak. "It should not have been me."

Everything fades to black.

CHAPTER FIFTY-SIX

A voice hums while hair the shade of ash falls into my eyes. She sings a song while gliding gentle fingers along my skin. Her voice is so beautiful—so haunting. I want to capture it in a jar so that it will last forever.

Another pair of small hands caresses my face. One I recognize—that I long to hold me each and every day I breathe.

My mother joins in on the girl's song.

Two voices become one, and I wish I could make out what they are singing. But the words are inaudible, and I am drifting away—falling away from their beauty.

But not before a loom begins spinning glimmering threads around me, wrapping me in a warm light that sends a rush of heat through me.

Their voices crescendo, and then they disappear altogether.

I am gasping for air, my hands still clawing at my throat.

Coppery flames fall into my eyes. "It's okay. It's okay. Breathe. *Breathe.*" Marcella grips my wrists and pins them down. She looks up from me and off to the side, seeming worried. "Nuri!"

I hear hurried footsteps before I see Nuri kneeling down next to me. "I'm here." Her hands hover over me, and warm golden light seeps into me. It feels nice.

A wall of glittering darkness rises and swirls in a circle, cocooning me in. When I glance around, my head slumping to the slide, I realize I'm not alone, but instead surrounded by all the captains, Josiah standing in the center. All except Draven.

A small panic spikes my heartrate, but then I hear his familiar voice sounding from behind me, quenching the ember before it can spark into a flame. "I've got you," he murmurs, sounding calm yet deeply pained. I only realize my head is in his lap when he moves my hair to the side.

A familiar set of hands reaches for mine and cups it between their fingers. My head swivels to the other side of me, and my eyes prick with tears, somehow feeling better yet worse the moment I see Gray.

How much had he seen? Will he think less of me, knowing what I've done?

Will they all think less of me?

Kneeling next to Marcella, Gray clutches my hand, his eyes red-rimmed and wary. I open my mouth, but he silences me.

"Don't speak," he instructs, his voice weak. "Let Nuri repair your throat first."

It's as if mentioning my throat gives it permission to scream at me, its skin anguished and ravaged. A searing pain burns my windpipe, feeling like a white-hot blade is pressed against it. As if on reflex, I bring my hand to my throat, and my fingertips graze across scattered gash marks.

Marcella immediately reaches for my free hand and pins it back down. "Don't move, okay? Just...let Nuri work."

Finlay steps forward. "What have you been hiding from us, Draven? Why was an Abdite in her Feargate?" His voice is low and accusatory. "You've known something about her all along, haven't you? It's why you wanted to train her."

Josiah steps forward and rests a quieting hand on Finlay's shoulder. "There will be time for questions later. For now, we have an arena full of people who just saw an Abdite attempt to recruit this girl."

Recruit?!

"Which means," Josiah continues, his voice remaining admirably soft. "The girl has something they want. Which in turn means Lyra has something those men out there will want as well."

I glance up, tilting my neck just a hair to glimpse Draven. His eyes are downturned and tender, still only looking at me.

Josiah sighs. "I am going out there to buy us some time. Nuha and Arden, please join me. Kiran and Finlay, remain with Draven. Do not come out until she is fully healed."

A small opening splits the wall of darkness, and Josiah, Nuha, and Arden step through. As soon as they pass, the black slams back together before even a stray beam of light can pass through, leaving just the seven of us.

"Draven, you better start talking," Finlay demands.

Draven says nothing. Instead, he continues stroking my hair, watching me with quiet eyes.

I glance at Gray and Marcella, who exchange looks, probably thinking the same thing I am. I squeeze Gray's hand to get his attention. When he looks down at me—his eyes still glassy from either spilled or unspilled tears—I give him a brisk nod, attempting to bring the words I can't speak to my stare.

Tell them.

I trust Kiran in a similar way I trust Draven, and though Finlay has been nothing short of a pompous ass to whom I disagree with entirely regarding his methods to achieve his objectives, he attempts to keep the Three Kingdoms safe—wishes to protect them with everything he has.

Plus, they are Draven's brothers. I can't ask him to keep this from them. I'm not sure why I feel that way, I just...do.

Gray watches me closely, making sure he reads the words in my eyes correctly. Once he's sure he has, he heaves a drawn out sigh and rakes a hand through his hair. Then, as Nuri mends my destroyed throat, Gray tells them everything, beginning to end. The throne room. The Abdites in the valley. What happened during the tests. Casimir Vivaldri's journal, and the prophecy within it. The truth of what I really am—

A Binder, as Casimir said.

Hearing it spoken aloud still sounds so odd.

When he finishes, Kiran is stunned into a momentary silence, and

Finlay looks oddly...hurt.

Kiran pinches his chin between his fingers, his face scrunching with thought. "It's strange to think this journal you speak of exists. According to historical records, both Prince Casimir and King Isaphus died in a fire that consumed their wing of the castle. And yet, somehow, a personal artifact—something as fragile as a journal—survived. Rather interesting, don't you think?"

Gray's expression sharpens with realization. "You're right," he murmurs. "I hadn't even considered that yet."

Finlay, not deigning to discuss Kiran's point, flexes his jaw and slides his turquoise eyes to Kiran. "Why didn't you tell me about the valley," he whispers in a harsh voice.

Kiran glances at him sidelong. "We were instructed not to," he answers simply. "And that hardly seems like an important question at the moment."

Finlay ignores the last part. "Instructed by *whom?*"

But before he can answer, my skin howls with agony, feeling like it's been electrocuted and erupting with a heated pain so thick, I'm convinced I'm being flayed alive.

I scream and grunt, the sound coming out choked and raspy.

"Lyra," Draven's voice remains calm, but not calm enough to mask the panic hiding behind the words. "Tell me what hurts."

But I can't speak—can't *think.*

My skin is living fire, and it *burns.*

Of all those around me, I'm surprised when it's Finlay who speaks first. "It's her mark," he mutters. "It's awakening." He pauses, and I catch the confused tilt of his head. "But it's...wrong. Premature and...tainted, almost?"

All eyes swing back to me.

"You need to remove her shirt," Nuri says to no one in particular, her face looking strained. "I need to see what's happening."

"I'll do it," Gray says through a pained sigh.

"Like hell you will," Draven bites, his words like death swept on a wind.

But Gray is in no mood to entertain death, seemingly willing to blow it back in the direction from which it came. "Lyra has been in my life far longer than she has yours. *I* will do it."

Draven opens his mouth, but Marcella shoots them both a silencing look. "Both of you will shut the hell up and quit this ignorant bickering while *I* do it."

Nobody challenges her.

Her fingers tug gingerly at my shirt and undergarment, stripping my chest bare for yet another time in front of an unwelcome audience.

"Can you turn her to her side?" Nuri asks with an authority that isn't overpowering, but seems practiced.

Marcella flicks her gaze to Draven—as if out of courtesy. Whatever gesture he gives has her looking at Gray next and nodding. Draven stabilizes my neck, making sure not to harm the blistered skin, and they turn me on my side—hissing at what they see, the sound a fused harmony of shock, awe, and fear.

I try to speak, to demand what the hell is on my back, but my voice comes out like a rasp of smoke and dust, and I am met with a symphony of shushing noises. Yet I am ready to protest, prepared to make whatever grunting noises necessary—until I glimpse the thread-like markings twining down my entire right arm, and my voice dies in my throat.

Nestled between the coiling threads are flower buds. Small, delicate, and sleeping—as if the curled petals remain shut, waiting for something.

Gently, I'm lowered onto my back, and I grit my teeth against the jolt of pain.

Until it all just...stops.

Like a fire finally burning through its last ember, whatever was scorching my skin vanishes. And somehow, I know what's left behind in the ashes is permanent.

Nuri exhales, pulling her hands back. She rocks onto her heels, breath unsteady, sweat beading along her brow. "There," she says, sounding fatigued. "Her throat is mended."

I sit up—covering my exposed chest with my forearm—and immediately turn to glimpse my back. But of course—because even with my so-called magic, not even I can defy human anatomy—I can't see anything but a small arc near the top of my shoulder blade.

"What is on me?" I ask, my voice rough like sandpaper.

Draven is the one who answers. "Your wielder's mark."

But the tone of his voice...

"What's wrong with it?" My question comes out far weaker than I wish it did, barely rising above a whisper.

But before Draven can respond, sirens howl through Bathara, their oscillating screams swelling—cresting—tearing through the sky in relentless, ear-splitting waves.

"What the hell is that?" Marcella demands, voice taut with unease.

"Bathara's alarms," Finlay answers, his features drawn tight, his voice lined with a quiet, simmering rage.

"What do they mean?" Gray asks. "Why are they going off?"

Draven doesn't answer right away. Instead, he stills. The kind of stillness preceding a predator's attack. The quiet before a storm breaks. And when he finally speaks, his voice is razor-edged, stripped of any warmth.

"It means Bathara's wards have been breached."

The words strike me like a physical blow to the gut.

"Breached?" Nuri echoes, her brows drawing tight. "How? By who?"

My stomach hollows as ice fills my veins, circulating to my heart, stilling its beats.

A gift before I go, Master's Precious.

I'll see you again very soon.

Realization bludgeons me like a club upside the head.

The gift was awakening my wielder's mark—something I didn't even know was possible. And the words were a warning. Or perhaps, a taunt.

The Abdites are coming—are *here.*

And they're here for me.

Before I can voice the realization, the ground beneath us convulses, and a thunderous boom splits the earth—sending tremors through stone and bone alike. The walls groan. Distant shouts pierce the air, and our eyes dart frantically, searching for the source of the commotion.

But while housed within these black walls, we remain blind to whatever is happening beyond them.

Kiran's gaze snaps upward, his body going rigid—as if he senses something none of us can. And when his eyes find us again, there's no hesitation.

Only certainty.

"We're under attack."

Chapter Fifty-Seven

"By *who?*" Nuri asks again, growing more impatient.

Yet instead of Draven, Finlay, or Kiran answering—who rise in unison, their hands moving with quiet precision, checking the weapons strapped to their bodies, preparing for battle—I do.

"Abdites," I rasp.

Gray, Marcella, and Nuri snap their heads toward me.

"How the fuck did Abdites get past Bathara's wards?" Marcella's words are edged with a quiet rage.

"That is the million-dollar question, isn't it?" Finlay replies, dry as the Arid Wastelands.

Marcella clicks her tongue at him before rising, unsheathing her daggers in a fluid motion. "Well, whatever the reason," she mutters, voice tight, "they won't be walking out of here with their lives."

"No," Kiran agrees while rolling back his sleeves, revealing his wielder's mark that looks like scarred flames. The white, coiling tendrils start glowing red, like a river bed coming alive as a molten stream flows through them. He flexes his fingers, rolling his neck with a slow, deliberate ease. "No, they will not."

Finlay straightens, nodding once at Draven. "We're ready when you are."

But Draven doesn't move. Instead, he looks back at me. "Just a moment."

Finlay starts to protest, but Kiran's hand lands firm on his shoulder, and the small, almost imperceptible shake of Kiran's head has him snapping his mouth shut, his lips thinning with impatience.

Draven strides toward me, taking my hand as if it's the most precious relic. He lifts it to his lips, pressing a kiss to my palm, and his eyes are scrunched in a way that makes him appear as if he's wrestling with something. "I hate to ask this of you, Lyra. Please know that. If there were any other way, I wouldn't. But..."

"You want me to stay inside your walls," I finish for him, surmising the rest.

His expression looks pained, but still he nods. "I can ensure your safety if you stay within them." His fingers tighten around mine. Then another kiss, softer than the first. "We know what the Abdites are after— *who* they want. And I couldn't live with myself if I let anything happen to you." His gaze drops to the ground, and the ghosts I now recognize—the ones lingering in his eyes far too often—rise to the surface.

Everything inside me screams to fight. Every bone, every muscle, every furious, burning piece of me demands vengeance.

But what good am I against the Abdites?

I've trained, yes. I've bled. I've learned so much since leaving Rivara. But what is a handful of weeks compared to those who have spent years feeding on forbidden magic? Even wielders as strong as Kiran and Draven struggle against the Abdites—I witnessed that firsthand in Foreigner's Valley.

I am not ready. Not yet.

Someday, I know I will be. Someday, I will stand—I will fight alongside someone as strong and formidable as Draven as an equal.

But that day is not today.

And what good is dying for the sake of pride?

I squeeze Draven's hand. "Alright," I murmur. "I understand."

Draven's eyes shudder with relief, and he throws his arms around me, tugging me into his chest, pressing a kiss to the side of my head. He holds me in the same way I imagine the night sky holds its stars.

When we pull apart, I'm surprised to find Marcella stepping next to me. "I'm going to stay with her."

I whip my eyes to her, my brows rising to my hairline. "You don't want to fight?"

She clicks her tongue, like I've just asked the most ignorant question in the world. "Of course I do. But..." Her expression softens. "I wish to remain by your side more."

Something in my chest tightens as emotion blooms. But it's not in the sharp, suffocating way I used to expect, nor the fragile, unsteady thing I've recently nurtured.

This is different. Softer, almost—freer.

And for the first time in so, so long, it feels like there is space for it to truly grow into something more. Which, despite the situation—the raging chaos and disturbingly uncertain future—I imagine the progress makes my mother smile.

Which then makes the swell in my chest evolve, morphing into a feeling of pride. For the brave actions of my mother. For the resilience I've found in myself. For the fact that I confronted my darkest fears— looked them in the face and unveiled their shadows—and even in the deepest depths of them, I survived.

Draven's words in the greenhouse suddenly glow as if under a new, gilded sun.

Feeling what's hurt you is not letting them win, but refusing yourself the opportunity to heal because of them is.

That persistent, tumultuous sea within me finally calms into a smooth tide. Because finally—*finally*—I truly feel like I've won.

That I did not let them win.

Because I've started to heal—*despite* their cruelty. They wanted me to shatter and bend, yet instead I mended and stood.

And it feels *damn* good.

I part my lips to speak, feeling awakened, but before I can, a sharp, splintering crack shatters the air—like glass splintering beneath a forceful blow. The walls around us groan as magic pounds against them.

"They've located Lyra." Gray ties his hair back with steady hands, the motion slow and measured. He unsheathes the sword at his back after, the steel flashing. He slides his stony gaze to Draven, assuming a demeanor

476

that makes him almost unrecognizable to me. "Can your walls hold?"

Draven grits his teeth, and a muscle flexes in his jaw. "They can. But since they're attacking the walls, I'm unable to keep them intact while creating an opening to let some of us out." He exhales sharply, seeming conflicted.

Nuri tilts her head. "Can those outside handle the threat on their own?"

Finlay scoffs. "We don't even know how many Abdites we're facing. Bathara has powerful wielders, yes, but the three strongest are standing right here, when they are needed out there." He jerks his chin for emphasis.

"Four," Draven corrects, softly. "The four strongest." And despite everything, Draven winks at me, a small curve tugging at his mouth.

Finlay sighs, dragging his eyes skyward. "Forgive me for not counting the one who's barely learned to stand."

"Careful," Draven warns, his quiet voice lethal.

Kiran steps between them, shooting them both a silencing look. "The only option is to drop the barrier. *All* of it." Kiran holds Draven's gaze sternly.

A muscle again twitches in Draven's jaw, and he curses under his breath. When he returns his gaze to me, all I can hear are my mother's words.

I will not cower. I will not yield. I will not falter.

Despite the traces of fear coiling around my spine, I square my shoulders and lift my chin. "Drop it."

But Draven doesn't move—not right away.

He only watches me. And I watch him back, caught in the strange, weightless pull of something we still haven't truly named. Something worth bleeding for. Something I would claw my way through fire to protect.

And I think he sees the promise resting in my eyes.

That the kings and their gods, the Abdites, his father, the classist world that shaped us—hell, even fate itself—

They can all be damned.

Because I choose him.

And the way he looks at me right now tells me everything I need—

He chooses me, too.

Draven clutches his sword by the hilt and offers me a final glance. One filled with a promise, an apology, a silent request...

There are so many words overflowing in that one, simple look. Perhaps even three words that terrify me more than any Abdite ever will.

But before I can consider that further—

Draven drops the barrier.

※ ♪

We couldn't have been inside those walls for more than a few minutes after Bathara's alarms sounded and the battle began. And yet...

Bodies are littered like bleeding flowers throughout the colosseum, and half of the Arena's walls have been toppled, crumbling to ash, entirely destroyed.

My breath catches in my throat, as if it is too scared to force itself out. I scan the scene with hurried eyes, trying to calm my racing heart.

So many.

There are *so many* Abdites.

And one is charging right at me, its burgundy cloak covering its face.

"I have found you!" the female Abdite shrieks with delight. "Master will reward me. Master will *choose* me. Come! Come!" She twists her palm, and an invisible force tugs at me, yanking me toward her.

But before my heels scrape more than an inch into the dirt, the female Abdite is confined by a case of slithering vines and roots that wrap around her. Marcella, with a cold fury dancing in her eyes, squeezes her hand into a fist, and the roots tighten, pushing the hood from the Abdite's face.

I tilt my head and blink.

She looks...normal.

Until her face turns blue, and her eyes bulge in her skull as Marcella quite literally squeezes the life from her.

Gray, appearing as if out of nowhere, glides his steel blade through the Abdite's neck, sending her head toppling to the ground. After, Marcella opens her fist, and the roots recoil, slithering back into the soil, releasing their hold. The lifeless body drops like an unwanted anchor, hitting the ground with a dull *thud*.

Gray, already somehow covered in dirt and black blood, dips his chin at me, then slides his gaze to Marcella, where it lingers for a moment. But then the moment passes, and Gray disappears into the background, charging into the disarray.

Marcella and I glance at each other, blowing air through our puffed cheeks.

"Come on." She tugs me forward, her gaze sweeping the dust-filled chaos, searching for a place we can lay low and offer aid from the shadows.

But then, portals blink into existence, one after the other.

Marcella jerks to a halt, her head snapping toward the swirling colors—black and silver twisting like ink spilled over the sky. Her eyes sharpen then dim with sudden worry.

"Griff," she murmurs. "He—he isn't a fighter."

I swivel my gaze and realize the aether-wielders have assumed posts at each corner of the Arena, opening portals to funnel out everyone they can. As I assess the scene, my eyes rove up to the balcony where Tynan Dalmar had resided.

Only, I am floored when I find him still sitting there, watching the scene unfold with an entirely too calm curiosity. And when his wandering eyes land on me, his lips tilt in tune to the incline of his head. At the almost-challenging look, something inside of me catches fire, a feeling of defiance boiling in my stomach. But then he slides his gaze to the center of the chaos, and I feel compelled to follow his lead.

A line of third-years stands with a handful of diplomats in a tight formation, guarding the aether-wielders, trying—*failing*—to keep the Abdites at bay. They fall one-by-one, crushed like trampled blades of grass, no match for corrupted magic.

For the whipping licks of black, inverted flames.

For spun air that shatters like glass.

For the molten balls of glowing ash.

For veins of light that pulse with something so *wrong*.

They are horribly outmatched by the magic that bends where it should break. That breathes when it should burn. That takes what should never be taken.

Chills rise and fall along my body as those ancient words slither into the air, temporarily transporting me back to the valley.

Erhè akta maht. Erhè akta maht. Erhè akta maht.

Whatever is on my back tingles and pulses, a warm sensation stemming down the thread-like marks now twining around my arm—a new feature of mine I still haven't had time to inspect or attempt to understand.

Erhè akta maht. Erhè akta maht. Erhè akta maht.

The words start to sound different in my head, morphing from unintelligible ramblings to something more akin to breathy mumbling, too low for me to interpret.

I'm so focused on deciphering the words, I almost miss the four Abdites now charging at Marcella and me.

"Shit," she and I both whisper at the same moment.

The leafy vines composing her wielder's mark come alive with green, and I...I can *feel* it. Feel her magic. Feel it calling to me, asking me to touch it. The sensation is almost tangible, electric. I can taste the rich, musky scent, thick with fresh herbs and damp soil.

It wants me.

And so I do the one thing instinct demands: I reach back.

Marcella moves first, tugging vines from the ground and wielding them like living whips. The moment I connect to her magic, she exhales sharply, glancing at me quickly. But she clenches her teeth and forges ahead.

Her magic surges through my veins, the sensation sweet.

Why does it feel so different than all the other times before? Is it because my wielder's mark has manifested? Does having one truly make *this* much of a difference?

Is this what having true power at your fingertips feels like?

One Abdite remains in front of me, watching. He giggles with delight. "You understand. Master was right to suspect you'd join our family." The Abdite spins on his heels, clapping his hands together. "All you needed was a little...push."

"Push? What does that mean?"

He stops spinning, and though I can't see his face, I swear I see a sinister fire burning in his eyes through the shadows of his hood. "Up the cliff we go, to plunge below. If you hadn't jumped, you'd never find water. But if you'd stayed, perhaps you'd have found a god."

I shake my head, fighting the urge to pinch the bridge of my nose. There is no point in trying to talk with them—they are lunatics, after all.

So I guess, no more talking.

I tug at the humming magic in my veins, the feeling like a swell of pleasure under my skin. The ground cracks open, and thick, gnarled roots explode upward, ripping through stone, bursting through the battlefield like wild, flailing limbs. They lash out, serpentine and relentless, tearing through the air, spearing straight for the Abdite's heart.

But the Abdite counters with a coursing stream of water running red, as if composed entirely of blood. Actually, for all I know, it may *be* a river of blood.

The blood water burns through the roots and vines, disintegrating them into nothing more than charred flakes of ash.

"Why does the key wish to hurt me?" The cloak's hood shifts, as though he's tilted his head. "Do you not wish to serve your purpose?"

I quickly look for Marcella, needing to know she's okay. I find her with a snarl on her lips, twisting her hand and sending a cluster of thick, snake-like roots shooting forward. They wrap around three of the Abdites' torsos, slamming them into an already crumbling wall.

So, more than okay—noted.

I return my attention to the Abdite. "I would ask you what that purpose is, exactly, but I fear you'd be unable to give me an answer."

"What is a key without their lock? And what is a lock without their key? What is the purpose of our existence if not to serve, but what is the purpose of an existence if all we're meant to do is serve?"

"Yup," I grumble. "That's about what I expected." I roll my neck, and I unsheath the dagger from my hip. "Alright," I say, feeling like I've had enough. "Let's do this."

Through the cloak, I again see the Abdite tilting his head. But this time, I don't wait for him to speak—I move.

Still connected to Marcella's magic, I throw spear after winding spear of twisted roots at the Abdite.

As if giddy, the Abdite twirls its wrist and swallows them all with its blood water. "You are lucky I cannot hurt you, Master's Chosen. My blood is thirsty. *I* am thirsty. We wish to drink. To collect your magic in our stream."

I don't bother unpacking that. Instead, I conjure a vine of thorns—long and gnarled like monster teeth—and crack it through the air like a whip, slicing deep into his skin.

He squeals, but this time, there's no delight in it. He inspects his wounds, and I seize on his momentary distraction.

The small roots I've been weaving all this time—crawling up his legs, his torso, his spine—tighten all at once, locking his limbs in place. He jerks, but it's too late.

I conjure another vine, this one thinner—sharper—and wrap it around his wrists, letting the thorns press into his skin, biting with every jagged inch.

And then, with the twist of my hand, I make them sink deeper.

His scream rakes through the air—blood-curdling and desperate.

Still, I don't stop.

The thorns spin, twisting, tearing—unraveling tendon and ligament alike. Another vine slithers forward, curling into the wounds like it was always meant to burrow beneath his skin.

And then I tighten my hold, pulling.

Until his hands are no longer his own.

Until they fall to the ground in a similar ruin that he and his kind have brought to Bathara.

Feeling slightly drunk on power—like a version of me I never knew existed—I stride toward him. "There is only one person who can call me their chosen, and it sure as hell isn't your master."

Then I use my dagger's blade to saw through its neck, the head a jagged mess of skin as it tumbles to the ground.

I swipe the dirt and blood from my eyes, immediately turning to look for Marcella.

She makes her way back to me, three headless Abdites scattered behind her. She flicks her eyes to the decapitated Abdite beside me then back up at me. "Nice work."

"You too," I say. "How do you feel?"

"A lot more fatigued than usual, but I'm alright." Her gaze roves toward the portals, searching for the owner of each one.

I rest my hand on her arm. "Go," I say softly. "Like you said, he isn't a fighter. He could use you."

Marcella's cobalt eyes bounce between the portals and me. "Will you be okay?"

"I'll be fine."

And for the first time, I mean it—*believe* it.

She dips her chin and extends her arm. I clap my hand to her forearm and she does the same. We lower our foreheads, bringing them together, and I shut my eyes against the swell in my chest.

When we pull apart, she looks at me with a steel-lined gaze. "No goodbyes," she says, stern and ironclad.

"No goodbyes," I agree.

Without another word, Marcella charges into the raging chaos.

I watch her go, but an explosion of fire mixed with a burst of ice has me tearing my gaze away and turning toward the on-going slaughter in the center of the Arena. It's hard to see through the clouds of dust, smoke, and ash clotting the air, but I'm just able to make out Finlay and Kiran as they battle an entire horde of Abdites, protecting the aether-wielders as they continue to hold their portals, still evacuating those they can.

My knees buckle when I realize the entire line previously protecting them has fallen, and Kiran and Finlay are there to replace the entirety of their defenses.

My eyes scan the scene wildly, looking for Draven. I'm unable to find him.

Brilliant, bright flames pour from Kiran's palms, spiraling outward in an inferno of power, clashing against the black, inverted flames being speared toward them from the Abdites' fingertips.

But Kiran's fire shifts from vermillion and gold to a flame burning blue and green. The fire seems angry, licking at broken stone and bone alike, as if its flames are ravenous, and devouring the world is the only thing capable of sating its hunger.

Kiran redirects the black flames with the grace of a dancer, and he counters with the destruction of a god—arcs of fire unfurling from his fingertips, blazing into spears before impaling Abdite after Abdite straight through the heart. As they fall to their knees, hunched forward, clutching at their chests, an unseen force moving quick as lightning streaks through the world, decapitating them.

Gray.

I know it with every ounce of my being.

He is casting an illusion, hiding his presence, and beheading the Abdites as they fall.

The teamwork appears so seamless, I can't help but wonder if it's the same strategy they used in Foreigner's Valley.

Finlay moves next.

He sweeps his arms forward, and the air bends to his will—moisture crystallizing, ice surging up from the ground, as jagged and merciless as his personality. He covers the battlefield in frost, freezing the stone beneath their feet, locking the remaining Abdite's in a prison of solid ice.

But the corrupted wielders cock their cloaked heads, and though there is no way for me to actually know, I swear I can feel them...smiling.

The words hum in the air, and that feeling of wrongness plunges the world in a bone-chattering chill.

Erhè akta maht. Erhè akta maht. Erhè akta maht.

Kiran sees it before it happens.

"Finlay—*move!*"

Molten ash funnels from all the trapped Abdites' palms, and it crawls over the ice, swallowing it like an eclipse swallows the sun.

A chorus of giggling sweeps along the wind, and the hairs on my arms rise as it sounds like the echoes of ghosts. They extend their palms and unleash a flurry of condensed balls of burning ash straight for Finlay and Kiran.

And the attack would have destroyed them—devastated their skin and devoured them with the wrongness of its molten touch.

But then Draven is there.

He moves like the darkness itself, an extension of shadow, and throws up an impenetrable black wall that makes the burning ash ricochet back to the ground like small pebbles bouncing off an unbreakable window. Then Draven charges without thought.

He is terrifying—death given form.

He is beautiful—my heart given shape.

Draven, running at full speed, erects two panthers from the shadows, and they rush forward at his side, swallowing the bursts of magic with their terrifying jaws, roaring into the rising night.

I blink.

I know dark magic can do things most magic can't—one of the many reasons it's so feared and labeled as an enigma—but…

I didn't know it could do *that*.

Draven reaches the remaining Abdites, and his blade sings as it cuts through skin. The inky panthers at his side sink their black-coated teeth into necks, ripping heads from falling bodies.

And for a brief, heart-stirring moment, it seems like the tide of battle is turning.

Until a low horn sounds, and more Abdites file through the cracks in the colosseum walls, bringing more corrupted magic with them.

Bringing more wrongness.

Erhè akta maht. Erhè akta maht. Erhè akta maht.

The words sing louder.

Kiran sends out a scorching arc of fire, slicing through the dust-thick air, incinerating two unsuspecting Abdites. Finlay sweeps his arm out and razor-sharp spears of ice impale another mid-step. Draven is a blur of blade and shadow, his sword cleaving through the chaos, his magic spreading like ink while his panthers act as his personal guards.

The world is fire and frost and ruin and shadow. The sky is split with magic, the ground trembling with death, dripping in red and black blood alike.

But then another horn cuts through the air—this one rich and regal, screaming of importance.

Every Abdite halts. Their heads snap toward the sound, as if the very marrow in their bones tells them to. In eerie unison, they kneel, bowing their heads as they fold their arms over their bent knees.

And everyone seems so stunned, no one attacks.

Instead, all eyes seem to wander to the figure emerging through the swirling haze of dust and smoke, moving with a sort of authority no person could ever fake.

The cloudy silhouette of a man strides through the battlefield as if it's nothing more than a garden filled with crimson and onyx flowers. His hands are clasped behind his back, and he moves with a slow purpose. Eventually, he stops, and I glimpse him surveying what lies before him.

And then, with a shift in the wind, the smoke around him clears, revealing his face.

I blink—

Entirely unprepared for what I see.

CHAPTER FIFTY-EIGHT

The man wears a regal black tunic and pants trimmed in rich gold stitching.

On his black head of hair—a black deeper and more depth-less than any lump of coal or mountain of anthracite—rests a crown woven from raven feathers. At its center, resting between his impossibly black brows, is a large, luminous stone the color of honey or aged amber. It matches his eyes.

It reminds me of the way King Alastair made me wear an amethyst jewel between my own eyes, always saying it pleased him to see the two paired together.

The rising moon casts a faint silver shadow on his already gray-tinted skin, and as he turns his gaze—finding me in the sea of battle effortlessly—I realize he is…is…

Equal parts beautiful and terrifying.

A person shouldn't look so angelic while looking so full of demons.

And when he speaks, his voice is silk.

"Fight, my brothers and sisters. Fight." The words carry on the wind, as if he commands its very laws and movements.

At once, the Abdites rise, and like suffocated embers breathing oxygen again, they resurge and catch aflame, attacking with newfound vigor.

An uneasiness fills my chest, something telling me to run.

But there is also something telling me I should stay. A giddy pull in my veins that squeals eagerly, as if sensing a reunion on the horizon.

I don't understand the sensation at all.

Within a blink—no, *faster* than a blink—the man leaves his place on the battlefield behind and appears right in front of me, standing only a few paces away.

Being this close to him, I can make out the details of his eyes, and...

By the Mother, I have never seen eyes like his before.

They are bright and radiant, glowing softly like they possess some secret source of light. They appear gilded; the golden hues glittering like the incarnate of living stars. Against the contrast of his pale-gray skin, they burn with a hypnotic quality, beckoning me to look deeper.

In a way, he feels oddly familiar. Like I know him, and he knows me. But that's impossible because I've never seen him before.

The man tilts his head and smiles at me. The gesture is twisted, sincere, haunting, and beautiful—

Which makes it the most terrifying thing I've ever seen.

"Hello," he says. His low voice is filled with age and youth simultaneously—a feat I also don't understand at all.

I arch a brow, gripping my dagger and assuming my fighting stance.

He frowns, lifting a steady hand. "There's no need for that. I'm not here to hurt you."

I squeeze the hilt of my dagger, still not entirely sure how to use the weapon skillfully. But I am fully familiar with the concept of stabbing—and bluffing. "Then what are you here for, exactly?"

His frown deepens. "I told you," he begins, his voice soft and calm. "If you didn't come to me, I would come to you."

It takes a minute before the realization slams into me like a forceful blow.

I know his voice—have heard it before.

He is the voice from the Veil. The one the Abdites call *Master*.

So many thoughts spill through my overflowing mind, tumbling down my head and rolling to my tongue, begging to be released.

I focus on the most pressing question first. "What the hell do you want with me?"

"To show you how magnificent you are."

My breath evaporates in my throat. I shake my head. "You don't even know me," I grit out.

"Oh," he coos hypnotically. "But I do. You are Lyra Izacalli, daughter to Railiana Izacalli, a Gardner who was in service to King Alastair until she met a brutal, unjust end. You have been blood-sworn to King Alastair ever since, serving in his court as a night attendant." He draws back half of his inky locks, gliding his hands along his head, smoothing out the hair as if preparing for something. "You made a blood wager with your king on your ability to be accepted into this academy in an attempt to regain your freedom—to regain control of your life. And then, in a remarkable twist of fate, you were given a journal and learned within those veins of yours, an old, powerful magic lurks." A small curve tugs at the corner of his mouth. "How'd I do?"

My heart pounds in my chest, and my breathing grows shallow—erratic. "How could you possibly know all that?"

"I keep close tabs on those I care about."

I recede a step, fear prickling at my neck as warning bells ring inside me. "And why would you care about me?"

"Because you and I are the same. Perhaps the only ones who could ever truly understand each other. A true gift in this world, I've come to learn."

I take another retreating step, shaking my head. "You say we are the same, yet I don't even know who you are."

He tilts his head. "Don't you?"

My lungs stutter. "Who even *are* you?" The trembling question comes out breathy, fear outlining its seams.

Not because I fear the answer, but because I'm terrified I already know it.

The pieces fall together too perfectly to be anything but the truth, no matter how impossible—how utterly unbelievable—it may seem.

His tilted head cocks further, his beautiful smile growing. "Based on the way you're looking at me, I think you've already figured out the answer to your question."

I fight against the quiver threatening to rattle my words. "No, see, I can't be right. Because the person I'm thinking of has been dead for over four hundred years"

His smile sharpens. "Stranger things have happened in this world of magic."

"No," I counter. "Not stranger than something like that."

He hums, as if amused.

Fear, uncertainty, confusion—so many different feelings crawl up my throat and sink their teeth into me. "Tell me who you are. Tell me your *name*."

"Very well," he coos. His eyes brighten, crinkling with the fully-formed smile now splitting his lips. He inclines his head to me. "My name is Casimir Vivaldri, and I am here to take you back with me—to bring you home."

A chill twirls down my spine as the words slam into me, fuzzy and nonsensical. My mind reels as it tries to make sense of this...*impossibility.*

Because Casimir Vivaldri is dead.

Casimir Vivaldri lived over *four hundred* years ago.

I shouldn't believe a single word falling from this stranger's mouth because what he claims cannot possibly be true—*shouldn't* be true.

Yet something deep in my bones tells me it is.

Or if nothing else, the way my magic hums for him—as if begging to be released to connect to him—forces me to believe it.

Casimir Vivaldri watches me quietly, his eyes oddly gentle, as if letting me process the revelation in peace.

Which makes me realize how peaceful this conversation has been. As if the roar of battle has been suddenly snuffed out like a dying flame from a wick.

Did he use his magic to do that?

The magic he and I share...

Everything suddenly tilts as my world falls off-kilter. "This should be impossible," I whisper.

"Impossible is a human word, and human words have no meaning when it comes to the dealings of the gods."

The words sound familiar...

Where have I heard them before?

I shake the question away, deciding I can't take my focus off Casimir—not even for a second.

"Was that really your journal?"

He nods. "It was."

"And was it true? Your account of history, the things you said, the..." I swallow against the dryness overtaking my throat. "The prophecy."

"Every word written, everything I said—it was all true, down to the barest sentence."

My chest tightens while my heart flounders in my chest, feeling unable to keep up.

"But what you said in your final journal entry about humanity..." I shake my head, both terror and sorrow crawling up my throat. "About the things you've done. The things you feel..."

Casimir Vivaldri dips his chin. "All true. Remain true, even now."

I again shake my head, trying to understand. "But you once had such faith in the world. Advocated for diplomacy and peace. What—what changed?" For some reason, I feel like I need him to explain it to me so I can make sense of it.

"The world." He pauses, considering. "Or perhaps it's better to say my perception of it."

"What about Sitara?" I murmur.

He stiffens. "What about Sitara?" His voice is clipped—different.

"She was your friend," I murmur. "She was someone you loved, and you—you did such wrong by her." I think of the story of Astralis and Sitara. Think of his final journal entry.

We are not creatures of devotion, but of desperation. We know not how to love, but how to survive. We break. We rebuild. We break again. And if that is the root of humanity, tell me—

What is there worth saving?

My lip curls, and I take another retreating step. "After all I know, what makes you think I would ever willingly go with you?"

Casimir Vivaldri frowns. "Am I so wrong in my thinking?"

"*Yes.*"

"Why?"

"Because... because..." I press my palm to my forehead, my nerves stretched taut. "Just because someone doesn't love you doesn't mean you have the right to sabotage their love for another. Just because you do not agree with humanity's choices does not make you its savior. Yes, we are flawed. But we are also resilient, capable of great good. And no one—no *single* person—should ever believe they have the right to choose for humanity."

"And if someone claims they do?"

"Then I would say that person is more a threat to this world than any evil they claim to fight against."

Casimir heaves a drawn out sigh, gliding a hand through his hair. "What is good but love that was returned? What is evil but love that went unanswered? And what is humanity, if not the ghosts of the love we could never hold?"

Unease pools in my stomach. "What are you even saying?"

"That the root of humanity stems from the ceaseless search to be wanted—to be loved. We burn for it. We break for it. We tear ourselves open, carve ourselves hollow, and still, we reach. Still, we beg." He pauses. "Still, we hope. It's a terribly cruel fate."

His glowing amber eyes pierce me at my very soul, unrelenting. Feeling slightly dizzy, I manage to get the question off my tongue. "And what is it you hope to accomplish by being here? By doing all of this?"

"I hope to bring you back with me," he answers simply. "I hope to teach you the nature of our magic. I hope to provide you with a home and a family—with my own family a home." He inhales a slow and deep breath, exhaling it loudly through his nose. "But most of all, I hope to die."

And there is something in the way he says it...

No—I'm not even going to tread down that path.

I straighten my spine and steel my gaze. "I won't go with you."

"And if I said I'll make you?"

"Then I'll take my own life before you can."

Casimir nods, as if expecting that. "Unfortunately, I believe you.

Which means, to motivate you, I will instead have to threaten to take the lives of everyone you care about after you're gone." He steps forward and reaches for me.

I pull away and slap his hand.

He clicks his tongue before frowning. "I guess I'll have to show you my threats aren't hollow." Casimir turns, dropping whatever sound barrier he created. The jarring noises of magic clattering and blades clashing funnel into my ears like a jolt to my senses. "Let me see," he hums under his breath. "Ah, there she is."

Within an instant, Casimir opens a small portal and steps through, transporting to...

Oh gods.

He appears behind Marcella, who is fighting off two Abdites while Griff continues to evacuate students.

"Marcella! *MARCELLA!*"

But it's no use. She can't hear me over the roar of battle.

Casimir slides his eyes to me before returning them to the girl with coppery flames for hair and cobalt eyes, so full of life and personality. He unsheathes the blade from his hip, and he draws it back slowly, as if moving at an intentional pace to make me suffer.

Yet as the blade plunges through the air and into a heart, it is not Marcella's heart that is pierced through its beating seams.

It is Griff's, who saw what was happening and pushed Marcella out of the way.

He falls to the ground clutching his chest, crimson seeping through his fingers as blood pools around his lips.

I drop to my knees—agony tearing through me—angry with myself that I'm already wishing my heart away after it just started beating again.

How could it already be broken?

Casimir's words hum softly in my head. *We break. We rebuild. We break again.*

Using some twisted feature of his magic, Casimir twirls a hand and cruelly makes it to where I can hear Marcella as she whirls around, realizing what happened—the sacrifice Griff just made.

The fact that the blade was meant for her and not him.

A small rectangular projection blinks into existence directly in front of me, revealing intimately what happens next.

"No…. *NO!*" She stares at Griff—who clings to the thinnest strings of mortality—sinking down to her hands and knees beside him, putting pressure on the wound. "Stay with me. *Please*. Don't go." She snaps her head up, looking around the battlefield. "Healer! I need a healer!"

The cracks in her voice gut me.

"No," she whimpers again when she looks back down at him, her tears spilling over her eyes, streaming down her cheeks. "Stay with me. Hey—*hey!*" She taps his cheek. "Don't close your eyes."

Griff groans, his eyelids fluttering. "Hey, Marcella?" His voice is so weak. So removed from the bounciness it usually carries.

"Yes?" The word breaks like glass in her throat.

"No tears, okay?"

But Marcella's eyes won't listen—tears stream anyway. Still, she nods. "Okay."

Griff swallows, the movement appearing strained. He reaches his hand up to touch her cheek, but falls short. Marcella catches his fingers and presses them to her face.

Griff smiles, as if content. "Guess what?" he says through wheezes.

She attempts to smile and lighten her voice. "What?"

"I finally beat you." He pauses, drawing in wet-sounding breaths. Somehow, his lip still manages to curve, despite the crimson encasing it. "I made it to the afterlife first."

Marcella chokes a laugh through her tears and presses a kiss to his fingers. "You finally beat me," she concedes.

His eyes sharpen, his expression growing solemn. "Be happy, Marcella. Promise me."

Her bottom lip quivers. Still, another nod. "I promise."

"Good," he breathes. "That's good…"

Griff gurgles a few, final rattling breaths, and then the light—the beautiful light that shone so brightly within him—fades from his eyes.

A fallen star returning home, assuming its rightful place in the night sky.

Marcella bows her head onto his chest and cries.

Until she just…stops.

When she lifts her head, her eyes are free of tears, sadness instead replaced with a hollow rage—lifeless and cold. Slowly, she rises and walks to the center of the battlefield. Her arm pulses with a green so bright, it looks like an emerald sparkling in sunlight. The magic funnels up her arm, into her neck veins, where it turns her eyes from a rich cobalt blue to a portrait of sparkling green.

She throws her hand out and destruction follows.

And that is all I am afforded to see as Casimir returns, the projection blinking from existence in tune with the closing portal snapping shut behind him.

He approaches me, and I don't even realize I'm crying until he attempts to swipe the tears from my cheeks, kneeling down next to me.

"They are not worth your tears," he murmurs. "This is the fate of humanity. The curse of our existence. You love? You hurt. You do not love? You still hurt."

I pull away from his touch, flinching. "You're a monster," I seethe.

Casimir hums, the sound deep in this throat. "Whether true or untrue, you are the only one who could ever stop me, Lyra. Your magic is made from my own. We *are* the same, you and I."

"I am nothing like you," I growl through clenched teeth.

He studies me with sympathetic eyes. "Regardless, you can die in your quest for stubbornness, dragging all those you love to the afterlife with you, or you can live and spare them." He frowns. "To be quite truthful, the better option seems glaringly obvious to me."

I spit on the ground at his feet. "Go. To. Hell."

"Unfortunately," he counters calmly. "I've already been living there for quite some time." He rises—swift and quick—and scans the dust-shrouded chaos around us. "But fine," he sighs. "Let's see how far you're willing to push me."

A sharp warning shoots down every nerve-ending in my body. "What are you doing?" I ask, my unsure voice low and rough.

He glances back at me and shrugs. "Testing you—proving that you and I are not so different, despite what you claim."

"What does th—"

Before I can finish, he coos, "Ah, there he is."

Ice slices my veins while venom floods the chambers of my heart, stilling its movements and clotting my breaths.

He offers me a final glance over his shoulder. "Would it be cruel if I asked you not to hold what comes next against me?" Without waiting for my answer, he swivels his gaze in another direction. "I suppose it might be."

The wrinkle that's been permanently wedged between my brows deepens, and I trace his line of sight. Whatever shred of warmth I possibly have left bleeds from me the moment I see who he's staring at.

Gray.

He appears suddenly, as if stripped of his invisible cloak. But he doesn't seem to notice.

Can only I see him?

I open my mouth, ready to agree to anything—*anything* at all. But Casimir moves, disappearing into the swirling dust, swallowed by the chaos.

Panic, fear, horror—it all slams into me, sharp and breathless. I lurch to my feet and stretch my hands out, as if I can rip this image by the seams and tear it away, crumpling it into fiction.

Everything slows.

Reality freezes into a nightmare moving moment by moment.

And I watch as the world twists into something unrecognizable.

I shout his name. Scream it with every bit of raw power my vocal chords are capable of mustering. Yet they buckle and crack, unable to carry the weight of my desperate screams.

Just like Marcella, he doesn't hear me. It seems like *nobody* can hear me.

Gray plunges his sword directly into the heart of an Abdite, slicing its head from its body after. When he steadies his blade, his eyes rove toward me in the distance, as if hearing me—finding me.

He always finds me.

His face pinches together, and he cocks his head, as if he's attempting to decipher something.

And I realize my mistake a second too late.

I've distracted him.

There is an odd warp, and then Casimir appears directly behind Gray, unsheathing the sword attached at his hip once more and positioning the hilt easily in his palms.

The world stutters, then stops, and I am clawing at gravel before I even realize I've fallen flat on my chest. The battle fades to a quiet, buzzing hum—the clattering of swords and clashes of magic dimming into near-silent whispers.

Strangely, I think of Astralis, wondering if this is what it is to live while carrying something dead in your chest.

I fooled myself into thinking my heart had died once before.

It is only now, in this moment, I feel what death truly is.

A scream of sheer agony rips into the world, and I haven't the slightest clue if it comes from me or not.

All I know is, one moment, I am looking at Gray, the person who has always loved me selflessly—who gave me his best shirts and held me during my worst nightmares—alive and breathing.

Then the next moment, I am watching Casimir tear his blade through Gray's neck, the metal singing eagerly as it eats skin.

Gray's head falls to the ground with a gentle thud.

CHAPTER FIFTY-NINE

I t starts slow.

The realization. My ability to process it—to make *any* sort of sense of what my eyes just witnessed.

Gray is dead.

Casimir Vivaldri *killed* him.

That is—is actually Gray's body lying awkwardly on the cold ground, headless. Those are his eyes, still mossy and gold, yet...not. His blood seeping into the dirt.

Casimir's words creep into my head, unwelcomed. Yet they persevere in the swirling climate of my mind, nestling comfortably in the toppling walls of all that I am.

This is the fate of humanity. The curse of our existence. You love? You hurt. You do not love? You still hurt.

I grit my teeth, biting down so hard, I think they might shatter and crack beneath the pressure, just like me.

Fuck—*FUCK!*

I think I scream, or cry, or vomit. Whatever I do, it ignites a physical pain—matching my invisible torment—and my veins burn, feeling like glass shards stream through them, slicing muscle and tissue alike.

Voices echo in my head. The mark on my back pulses and flares, and my miserable skin cries as living flames awaken and trace the markings of my wielder's mark. The thread-like design twining down my arm comes alive as silver winds itself through the fibers, as if the mark is blinking its glowing eyes open for the first time.

My body heats at an alarming pace, and the words singing in the air grow louder—sharper.

Erhè akta maht. Erhè akta maht. Erhè akta maht.

A lasso tightens around my lungs, and my fingertips tingle as my head builds with an enormous pressure. I feel dizzy—out of control.

Enraged.

The voices no longer sing; they scream.

ERHÈ AKTA MAHT! ERHÈ AKTA MAHT! ERHÈ AKTA MAHT!

I clutch at the ground, resting my forehead against the dirt, gritting my teeth against the feelings raging and bucking in my chest—the wrongness of them.

A silky voice swirls around me. *"Let go of your control. Listen to the words in your head. Give in to your anger, and watch what you can do. "*

A scream rips from my throat, and my skin feels like it's unraveling at its seams, ready to melt straight from bone. I gasp in a breath, anger pelting me, rage calling out to me like a lover needing to be touched.

There's so much of it.

I have so much anger. So much rage. So much pain and hurt needing an outlet.

Maybe I should give into it.

Those voices calm into a soothing lullaby, hypnotic and enchanting, demanding with a gentle hiss. The words morph from hysteric ramblings into something clear and concise—something I can understand.

An action.

A command.

Erhè akta maht. Erhè akta maht. Erhè akta maht.

Hate take harm. Hate take harm. Hate take harm.

Harm.

Harm.

Harm.

The hissing whispers coil through the air, threading into my skull, and my vision pulses red. The pressure crashes against me like a hammer striking an anvil, over and over, unyielding. The mark at my back sizzles and sears, and I need a release.

For my anger. For my magic. For my jagged emotions, broken and sharp.

The image of Gray's head sliding from his body replays in my mind, as if planted there cruelly, and whatever leash that was tethering me to...something...snaps. Because the image makes me feel as though I have lost.

And I refuse to lose any longer.

So, I do not break. I do not lay down and just let cruelty win.

I erupt.

With nothing more than a thought, I become living fire. Then ice. I am shadow, flora, light. A conglomeration of everything and nothing, splintered and whole at once.

The world blurs and images grow hazy—dreamlike, smearing into colors that don't belong together—as power courses through me that shouldn't exist. That shouldn't be real.

Fire does not mix with ice. Light does not conjoin with water, whipping and burning in a glowing hurricane. The wind does not mix with molten ash, blowing funnels of burning destruction.

These things simply don't happen.

My body tires—fades—as if life bleeds from it like sadness bleeds from my torn heart.

Wait...

Perhaps I am dreaming. Maybe that's all this is. Another one of my nightmares.

It would explain how Casimir Vivaldri lives. How magics that do not belong together clash, using me as a medium. How Gray could be stolen from this world so soon.

Yes, that must be it. And when I wake, Gray will be there, laying in bed next to me, ready to hold me if I ask.

The words hum in my mind softly like a wall of protection.

A dream, a dream, a dream.

None of this has been real. I don't have magic. Gray isn't gone. I never left for Bathara. I remain in Keziah with the king.

But then a sudden sadness floats through me, weighing heavy on my bones. Because if none of this is real, then that means I never met Marcella.

Never met Draven.

Draven.

As if summoned by thought, his scent fills my lungs—warm and familiar and *real*. Too real. I swear I can feel him—his arms wrapped around me, his breath curling against my burning skin. His voice follows—the sound a soothing melody—as if he's right next to me, whispering into my ear, clutching me like I might slip through his fingers.

I can feel it in his touch—he doesn't want to let go of me.

Life feels easier when he's near. More possible. It makes me want to not be a thing of rage and anger, but of grace and acceptance. To not be filled with power, but with love.

Casimir said, *You love? You hurt.*

And maybe—maybe that's okay. Because Draven? He is worth hurting for.

Because Draven said—

Then I will burn, Lyra, so long as its by your flame.

And he meant it.

At the calming thought, a blurry image of his face forms in my vision. Even in distortion, he is beautiful.

Wait...

Is he speaking? What's he saying? More than that, why does he look like he's in pain?

"It's that you live, Lyra. You must live. And if you don't, then I'm coming with you, because I don't want to be in a world where I can't wake up and find you."

Why is he saying that?

I think there's more he tries to tell me, but my grip on whatever I was clutching at weakens, and a wave of debilitating fatigue washes over me. And as I feel words take shape on my tongue, desperate to find Draven, they aren't able to leave my lips. They remain trapped behind them, stuck, as if my mouth is incapable of moving.

I drift backward, falling into myself. As if the anchor dragging me beneath the roaring waves has finally been released. But instead of sinking—

I float.

A calm, buoyant sea catches me, cradling me as it hums, lulling me to sleep. I slip into the abyss of it, not drowning, just... drifting. Consciousness slips from my grasp, but not before a heaviness settles in my stomach, making me wonder...

Why do I feel like I've just done something terrible?

CHAPTER SIXTY

The moment Draven feels Lyra's magic disappear, he knows
something is wrong.

He spins, slashing his blade through one neck, and then another.
Once the two Abdites fall, he sprints across the Arena, looking for Lyra in
the last place he sensed her. But a burning wall of black flames stretches
across the ground like a demarcation line, halting his sprint.

Like fucking hell that will stop him.

He calls for his shadow panthers, and they lick the flames away,
swallowing them into their shadowy bellies. The magic enters Draven's
bloodstream like venom, scorching his veins.

But he doesn't give it a second thought. He charges ahead, searching.

He spots her all the way across the Arena, encased in a sound barrier,
the faint yellow edges giving it away. She is on her knees, sobbing,
clutching her stomach like she might vomit.

It's a sight that burns him far greater than the forbidden magic he's
absorbed into his skin.

He draws a bout of oxygen, preparing to break the barrier, when
Lyra rises absently—as if her body moves on the commands of another
mind. She strolls forward, shuffling toward the brute of battle.

He runs for her, desperate to reach her. To hold her—even if just for
a moment—to make sure she's okay.

But he stops when he glimpses the silver awakening beneath her
skin, trailing the seams of her wielder's mark stretching down her arm.

The silver glides along her mark, sparkling as it comes alive. It reaches up and up, until it mingles with the whites of her eyes, shifting the beautiful amethyst hue of them into something silvery-white.

Then she erupts with a colorful burst of magic.

She pulls fire first. It swirls along her arm and rises up her shoulder, stopping at the crook of her neck, burning brilliantly in the night. Then she finds ice next, the glistening substance crystallizing along her other arm, forming a barrier as it mimics the route of the flames.

And when she brings her hands together, fire raging in one palm while ice sings in the other, she explodes in a remarkable display of power, twirling the contrasting elements into a helix as she sends them roaring across the battlefield, not discriminating as it claims life after life.

To Draven's dismay, she attempts to pull at his dark magic next. And though he would offer any part of himself to Lyra willingly, he does not allow her to take from him, knowing it would destroy her if she tried to wield his magic too soon.

But that doesn't prevent her from pulling at other magics as she trudges ahead to the center of the chaos.

And Draven can't help but wonder—

What happened to make her explode with such rage-coated ferocity?

He turns to take a quick inventory of the battlefield. Yet he stops short when he realizes everyone has stilled—if only temporarily—to watch Lyra, stunned to be witnessing what most believe to be an impossible display of power. Even Finlay and Kiran watch slack-jawed and wide-eyed, stunned into an uncharacteristic stillness at what they see.

She pulls at light, water, wind—wielding them as carelessly as foolish men wield their words. But she can't keep going at her current rate. If she does, she will burn out, eviscerating her body and magic alike. Draven doesn't have the slightest clue how deep her magical resources go—though he has his guesses—but he still knows, based on what he's witnessing, she can't last much longer like this.

"Let go, Lyra," he whispers under his breath, his brows creasing. "You have to let go."

She does no such thing.

Instead—in a feat that, under any other circumstance, would both impress and attract Draven—she conjures a hurricane of water and light, fusing the two together in a blinding wind, unleashing it upon the bloody battlefield.

But it isn't until she fuses molten ash into her raging storm that the damage goes from horrific to cataclysmic.

She destroys everything in her wake, taking the lives of Abdites and students alike.

That's when he realizes she's losing herself, succumbing to the magic, letting it control her instead of the other way around.

Reaching deep into his resources, he conjures a shield as he and his panthers sprint for Lyra. Once within about thirty paces of her, however, he slows, gritting his teeth against the swell of magic radiating from her. It's like attempting to touch the sun.

He pushes all his weight into his shield of darkness and pushes forward, taking step after painful step. He only makes it about ten marks until he has to relinquish his hold on his shadow panthers. He can't keep them going and maintain his protection at the same time—he doesn't have the strength. His magic can't withstand the force of Lyra's.

As he nears her, his bones rattle and his skin pricks with heat from all the magic swirling around her—*too* much magic. It burns his skin and yells at him to turn away.

He never was one for listening.

Reaching her is like entering the eye of a storm. She has funneled herself in a cocoon of wind laced with fire, ice, flora, and water—the core elements. Light flashes in and out, like bolts of sizzling energy breaking behind a cloudy sky. Yet she remains oddly still at the center, her hair flapping wildly as her eyes glow silvery-white and silver trails glimmer along her skin.

And despite what's happening, Draven still can't help but to admire her.

She is magnificent—destruction unleashed. She is the terrifying beauty of purple lightning streaking across a midnight sky. The haunting echoes of a howling wind as it whips between mountains, bending rock to its will. She is the ferocious waves of a raging sea, the force of a magnetic moon, the fiery path of a falling star.

She is the girl to wake Draven up—with her defiant eyes, resilient will, and strong heart. He knows she would describe her heart as cold and broken, but he always saw it differently. Lyra's expressive gaze didn't just give her emotions away, but it revealed the composition of her soul—if a person believes in such a thing. Her eyes betrayed the tenderness stitched into the seams of her heart. The care she has for others. The passion she has for life, whether she's fully realized it yet or not.

The world rejected her, turned its back on her, and still she laughed. Still she fought.

Still she won.

But the girl who holds his heart is lost in her magic—*consumed* by it, killing herself and everyone around her. Draven hears the resulting screams oscillating in the wind, agony coating their voices as her magic tears through red and black blood alike.

He curses under his breath, realizing the decision he has to make.

He cannot save them all. Not while stopping her.

So he must choose.

Feeling pinned against difficult decisions, Draven ultimately does what he must. Because at the end of the day, he's never claimed to be a hero nor someone who does good.

Draven shuts his eyes and searches for the laktî he's most familiar with. His brothers come to him the most easily, and he shelters them in a dome of his darkness the second he locates them. It takes him a moment longer to sense Lyra's fiery friend, Marcella, but he does the same for her when he finds her—her magic weak and barely hanging on. He finds Gray Nightenjoy next, his magic surprisingly well-stocked.

He doesn't let himself dwell on the fact that he can't locate Griff anywhere, not sensing even a drop of his laktî.

Draven then senses all the healers he can locate, knowing Lyra will need mending once he snaps her from this daze—because he *will* get through to her. No matter the cost.

Once he's sheltered everyone he can, extending his magic to its farthest reaches, he approaches Lyra, the heat emitting from her making it feel like he's walking into a furnace.

"Lyra." He grips her shoulders, and the touch burns his palms. Still, Draven searches her glowing eyes for any signs of her, but... She seems lost. His precious girl seems so, so far away, detached from reality, floating in a dream of consuming power instead.

He isn't sure how to reach her. How to get through to her.

So Draven does the only thing he can think of. He wraps his arms around her, holds her, and reminds her she isn't alone. That he is here, and he is with her. And all he can do is hope the touch is enough to bring her back to him.

Despite his efforts, a gut-wrenching scream rips from his throat as the magic chews at his skin, tearing through his flesh in an instant. It feels like being stabbed and burned simultaneously. Still, he does not let go of her. If nothing else, he tightens his grip on her.

"Lyra," Draven tries again, biting back the agony in his voice. "You have to let go of your magic. I understand how consuming it can be, but it's killing you. Please...*please*, let go."

He glances at her cracking face—the skin peeling from bone as it burns—and blinks when he realizes there is a constant flow of silver-tinted tears streaming down her glowing eyes.

It hits him, then.

She isn't letting go because she doesn't want to. Whatever she witnessed, it snapped her will to exist.

And all Draven can think is—

If she can no longer breathe, then he will act as her lungs and give her all the oxygen his body has. If her heart will not beat, then he will give her his. If her body insists on remaining cold, then he will hold her until he has transferred all the heat within his bones. And if whatever wound causing this refuses to heal, then Draven will slice his skin and bleed alongside her for as long as she needs.

No matter what, he will not give up on her—even if it kills him.

Through gritted teeth, Draven clings to Lyra with every bit of strength he has. "I'm calling in my price. Naming what you owe me for training you." He fights against a surge of unbearable pain ripping through his muscles. "It's that you live, Lyra. You must live. And if you don't, then I'm coming with you, because I don't want to be in a world where I can't wake up and find you."

Her eyes flicker, shifting from that silvery-white to their normal color, and he can feel her body slacken, if only just a little.

So, he presses on, hoping his words will reach her. Praying to whatever god will listen that they are enough to convince her to let go of all the magic destroying her body.

"I told you I would burn, so long as it was by your flame. And I meant it. I will hold you until my skin melts from my bones if I have to. Because I'm not letting go, Lyra. If you walk into the afterlife, then I'll be right there behind you, happy I wasn't left in a world without you in it." Draven swallows, the action painful from the burns now coating his throat. "So that's the bargain: either you live, or you take me with you. Because where you go, I follow. Even if it leads me straight to the gates of Merikh's realm."

The howling winds quiet, and the tongues of fire retreat back into her fingertips as ice falls from the sky like glittering stones. The hurricane dissipates, and all the magic she was wielding disappears. Lyra turns to look at him, her eyes slowly saturating into his favorite color. Her lips part, like she wants to say something to him. But when her skin dims, she collapses in Draven's arms, going fully limp as consciousness leaves her.

The pain of catching her is so great against his burnt body, specks of red flood his vision. It is the best pain he has ever felt.

Yet the sound of wet, rattling breaths has Draven's eyes snapping down.

Holy *gods*...

Her skin.

He has never seen anything like it.

Her body is like a desiccated shell, charred in some places and simply nonexistent in others. Angry, swollen tissue and ligaments seep out from her, and clean ivory bone peeks out randomly. Her hair is fried, sprouting on her head like crisp, withered weeds, and her skin is a mangled mess of burnt deformities.

Slowly, Draven lowers himself to his knees, holding her delicately against his aching chest. Once she's propped gingerly on his thighs, his eyes rove across the Arena, looking for the healers as he releases his magic.

A terrifying cold Draven hasn't felt in a long, long time runs through him as he realizes the battlefield has been cleared, leaving only burnt corpses sprinkled across the ground.

Past those he protected, he can only spot a handful of other survivors, crawling out from a ditch hidden underneath a large slab of rock and from the shell of protection Nuha and Arden provided.

Lyra obliterated everyone else, Abdites and fellow wielders alike.

He glances down at her, his heart squeezing painfully in his chest.

A slow applause echoes in the distance. Draven snaps his gaze up, finding the man crowned with raven feathers striding toward him. The Abdites' Master, he's decided.

"I must say," the man croons. "I've heard a lot of speeches in my many years, but yours?" He lets out a low whistle, shaking his head. "Before I became what I am, it probably would have moved me to tears. Love is a remarkably powerful force, isn't it?"

Before I became what I am.

Keeping Lyra secured in his arms, Draven focuses on the man in front of him, attempting to sense his magic. To his surprise, it feels like Lyra's. But where hers is like tasting something sweet and scenting crushed sage, his is like tasting blood tainted by venom, corrupted and bitter.

And Draven realizes, despite how impossible it may seem, the man in front of him is without a doubt Casimir Vivaldri.

A troubling equation he will have to work out later.

Draven narrows his eyes on the former prince, who appears to be frozen in his mid-twenties somehow. "What did you do to her?"

Casimir clasps his hands behind his back, watching Lyra with a sort of gaze that sends Draven's blood boiling. "I do concede I played a part in unleashing her. I was proving a point, and I fear I got last in my objective."

"Lost *how?*" Draven growls.

Casimir studies Draven, as if deciding something. "I cast an illusion on her," he confesses. "One I knew would push her to her limits. She needed to see what she's truly capable of. Understand the power coursing in her veins. But having her hate me would be no good, so I simply needed her to *believe* she lost someone who's a pillar in her world. What's his name..." He pinches his chin with thought, snapping his fingers once he remembers. "The Nightenjoy boy. Gray, I believe his name is."

Draven glances down at Lyra briefly, sadness echoing in his chest. The devastation she must have felt thinking she lost Gray would have destroyed her. It is a sadness Draven is familiar with, and it brings him no joy to consider the lethal effects it can have once it sinks its teeth into you.

It makes sense now, why she exploded. How she lost control. She thought she watched her whole world turn upside down.

A terrifying quiet settles in Draven. "Give me one good reason why I shouldn't rip your heart from your chest."

The corner of Casimir's lip kicks up. "I'll give you two. The first being that would do nothing to stop me. The second being, Lyra needs me." He shrugs. "It's why I've come for her. To bring her back with me—to take her home."

A wildfire unleashes itself beneath Draven's skin. "Like. Fucking. Hell."

Casimir sighs. "Please don't make this more difficult than it needs to be. Too many have died already. Let's not have any more casualties."

Through the sides of his eyes, he sees Kiran and Finlay unite with Gray and Marcella in the distance, their tentative eyes watching Casimir and Draven.

It goes against his instincts not to press Lyra against his chest. But doing so would crumble her already ruined body. So instead, he glances down at her briefly, gliding a painfully gentle touch down her marred cheek, before reorienting the full weight of his stare onto the former Crowned Prince of Rivara. Draven rises, laying Lyra delicately on the ground, and faces the man—*thing*—with cold, ruthless eyes.

"You will not touch her. You will not be taking her *anywhere*. And you sure as hell will not be walking out of here with your life."

Casimir clicks his tongue repeatedly. "Such empty promises," he murmurs, as if more to himself than Draven. "At this point, I am the only one who can save her." Casimir Vivaldri takes a step forward. "And make no mistake, I *will* be saving her before such a gift is lost to this world." Casimir's eyes harden. "She is dying. I know you must be aware of that."

The words almost bring Draven to his knees.

Casimir sighs, long and deep. His voice softens. "If it's any consolation, I didn't know she'd be able to draw so much magic at once. Her mark only just awakened, and so I thought she'd have more limitations." A pause. "I regret causing her such harm."

The sincerity in his voice perhaps angers Draven more than anything else.

"Yet, the fact remains," Casimir continues. "I am not leaving here without her. And there is little you can do to stop that."

Draven brings every ounce of magic he possesses to the surface. "I'm not only going to prevent that from happening, but I'm also going to make you suffer every ounce of pain that she—" Draven points at Lyra "—was made to suffer because of *your* actions. And only when your body has burnt up its every nerve ending with pain and you have become numb to its suffering, only when your skin is as burnt and mangled as hers— only then will I kill you."

Casimir does not blink. "Oh, how I wish that were possible. But..." he trails off, his voice filled with an odd sincerity. "I'm afraid it's not."

Casimir Vivaldri and Draven remain at a standoff, their expressions equally as determined yet vastly different. The wind dies, and even the sky pulls clouds over its eyes, too terrified to watch what happens next.

Black veins crawl beneath Draven's skin, spreading like ink in water, twisting around his forearms, coiling up his biceps, threading through his chest and neck. He knows the whites of his eyes will soon fade to black as the magic consumes him from the inside out.

Casimir studies Draven. "I truly am sorry," he offers, his voice surprisingly soft. "I can see how much you care for her, but...you don't want to do this."

Rage ignites in Draven—not a spark, not an ember, but an all-consuming fury.

"You know," Draven drawls, his cold voice terrifying. "I've never been one to appreciate being told what I do or do not want."

Draven lifts his hand, but before he can strike, Casimir attacks with a spear of fire and ice erupting from his palm, spiraling toward Draven in a blur of vermillion and white.

Draven—not having used the full potential of his magic in so, so long—conjures his black panthers from the darkness, and they lunge at the spear of magic, swallowing the attack whole.

A river of glistening shadow falls from Draven's palms and surges across the battlefield, roaring toward Casimir's feet. But Casimir, with a smirk tipping his lips, flicks his wrist and commands the wind. The black tide twists midair, reversing, hurtling back in the opposite direction. And then Casimir attacks with a rapid succession of fire, light, and water, one after the other.

But Draven is quick.

He slams a wall of darkness into place and absorbs the blows, the impact rattling the ground. Shards of obsidian magic split from the wall like fractured glass—a clinking noise filling the air as they detach—and the pieces soar toward Casimir's chest.

Casimir merely side steps the attack. "Really," he says as if disappointed. "Is this truly the best the continent has to offer these days?" He walks forward, as if Draven is no threat to him whatsoever.

Draven watches as Casimir's eyes then shift to Lyra, where his gaze sharpens.

And something inside Draven snaps.

The final bits of magic he's kept restrained—the part he always keeps caged, terrified of its true prowess—bursts free.

The air around him warps as darkness spills from his pores, surging into the air. It envelopes him, swallowing his form, consuming him whole. His body is nothing but a silhouette against the void—a living nightmare, a god of darkness given form.

"There's a reason it's called dark magic, you know." Draven's voice is different now—thick with something no human voice should carry. "And I spent a long time wondering why having it made me the most feared wielder in Solaya. Why men cowered in front of me when I was no more than a child."

Casimir watches Draven with interest. "Oh?"

Draven keeps his anger on a leash a moment longer. "I figured out the answer eventually."

"Please, do share."

Draven feels the magic bubbling into his throat. "It's because, as long as I can drain it of light, nothing is beyond my magic's reach. I can inject darkness anywhere, in anything. And all those shadows you see without realizing? Every cover of black or patch of night? It all answers to me."

The sky splinters with black streaks of lightning. Ebony flames ignite along Draven's arms, coiling around his skin, as the remaining bit of light vanishes from his eyes, leaving nothing but a pit of darkness in their wake.

His fingers twitch. Darkness obeys.

An army of shadow panthers rise from the ground, their eyes burning with violet fire.

Casimir simply watches. "Oh, to think what you could become," he muses quietly. Then he exposes his palms—facing them skyward—and the air sharpens as a surge of magic awakens, collecting in his hands in a warping ball of amber light.

And Draven is prepared to die—to set this whole world on fire to keep this creature of a man from taking Lyra.

But then the last person Draven ever expected to see strides between them, hands clasped behind his back. And yet, Draven also should have expected nothing less.

Tynan Dalmar appears through the haze of dust. "That is enough."

Draven's magic flickers.

Fuck—why him.

His father glares at him. "You will let him take her."

"I will do no such thing," Draven bites out.

"Then you're a selfish, foolish child who should have never been given a rank. Look around you." Tynan sweeps his arms across the crumbling arena. When Draven doesn't move, Tynan shouts, "*Look!*"

The shadow forms evaporate in the air like mist, and Draven can feel the flames dying along his skin. Draven does as his father commands and looks at the broken scraps of what remains. Who remains.

They all glance between Draven and Casimir with terror in their eyes. Even Arden and Nuha look at him as though they have never seen him before.

Everyone cowers.

Everyone except his brothers, Gray Nightenjoy, and Marcella Lynderby.

Tynan does not relent. "You would have them all die for her? For a crumbling body that is probably lost to this world already? Haven't we lost *enough?*"

Gods-damn him. Despite his rage, hearing him speak of Lyra's critical condition guts him.

She can't be gone. She *can't* be.

Draven wouldn't survive it. Wouldn't want to survive it.

"Yes. I would." Draven spits the truth in Tynan Dalmar's face, dragging his steel-lined gaze to the man who was never worthy of the title *father*. "I would burn them all myself if it meant she survived."

The resulting murmurs do not go unnoticed by him.

Fury twists Tynan's features, but he quickly resets. "Well then, allow me to give you perspective. There is another I don't think you'd be so quick to throw in the flames. Isn't that right, Draven?"

Fuck him. *Fuck him.*

Draven clenches his hands and inhales a breath that feels like shards of glass in his lungs. He glances over his shoulder at Lyra's brutally deformed body, and something that feels a hell of a lot like a sob pounds in his chest.

This—*this* is what Draven has always feared. Why he has always remained so guarded and distant from the world. So careful with his every action.

But he never stood a chance with her. He was doomed the moment he saw Lyra, with those defiant eyes and that fighter's heart. And after the night of his mother's birthday, when he sat drunk on the edge of a rooftop, his demons clawing free—when she simply sat beside him and let him remember, unaware of how badly he longed to feel warmth—only then did he realize.

He had already fallen.

Gods help him, he is so lost on what to do. How he can possibly protect them both now.

"If you do not let him take her," Tynan continues, his voice as cold as the ice creeping into Draven's heart. "Then I will see to it personally that the...*other one*...is met with as violent an end as you'll be giving everyone here." He pauses, letting his words settle. "And you and I both know how creative I can be."

A silent scream tears through Draven's whole body, raging in his head. Blurry images of red-stained memories ravage him, and he runs his hands through his hair repeatedly.

Draven shakes his head, fear and panic seizing in his chest. "No. *No*. I won't let her go."

It feels like all he can say.

There has to be a way—he just needs to think. He can come up with a way out of this.

"It's your choice," Tynan says.

Draven's eyes slide to Casimir, who has been standing quietly, watching the exchange with interest. A fist squeezes around his heart, and his lungs feel suffocated—deprived of oxygen.

He can't...there isn't...

No.

He will—

A sharp crack against his skull sends pain rippling through him. His vision flickers with crimson snowflakes before the world tilts.

Everything goes black.

CHAPTER SIXTY-ONE

"He is not capable of making this decision, so I will make it for him."

Finlay Fjolla stands behind Draven, his pale face and snowy hair caked in blood and dirt.

Tynan looks at him with approval in his eyes. "You always have been the more sensible one."

Finlay bites down, flexing his jaw, before he drops his eyes to the thick ice club resting in his hand—the weapon he used to knock Draven unconscious. "He won't forgive me for this," Finlay starts, eyes rippling. "But he would never forgive himself for whatever he decided today, either."

After a remorse-coated moment, Finlay remembers himself and sets his features with icy indifference, stepping to the side and looking at the one he's surmised to be Casimir Vivaldri, just as he's sure his brother had.

"Take her," Finlay demands. "Before he wakes up."

Casimir inclines his head. "Thank you." He reaches her in three strides, kneeling beside her and tracing the destruction carved into Lyra's body. He drops his head. "Why must it always come to this?" he whispers.

Finlay is surprised by how soft and caring the words sound.

Casimir glances over his shoulder at Tynan, then at Finlay. "Give me just a moment, and we'll be on our way." Then he lifts his hand into the air, and rippling branches of golden light appear, ripping through the sky like a glowing scar, streaming into his palm.

One-by-one, wielders collapse. Finlay surveys the scene, realizing Casimir is reaching for every remaining healer's magic, sending their eyes rolling to the back of their heads as they fall.

The golden light gets brighter; the translucent orb in his palm gets larger.

Until he slams the golden beam into Lyra's chest, an explosion of glittering light ricocheting like living sparks.

A warm, humming glow swallows her, and within a handful of seconds, Lyra's body is restitched with new skin. And even if that skin is still raw, blistered, and painful to even look at, it is a considerable upgrade from the charred ruin obliterating her body before.

Casimir cradles her in his arms and rises.

Lyra's limp body hangs like a lifeless doll.

He strokes the crisp sprouts of hair she has left and observes her with tender eyes. "I will save you," he promises in such a low voice, Finlay almost misses the words.

Casimir turns his back to everyone. He turns his chin over his shoulder, and his eyes trace the remains of every fallen Abdite as he strides past—as if acknowledging each one.

Someone runs past Finlay in a blur, making for Casimir Vivaldri.

He is stunned when he realizes it is Gray Nightenjoy.

When Gray reaches him, he is panting in ragged breaths. Casimir turns slowly to face him, keeping Lyra close to his chest.

"I hate you for what you're doing," Gray says, voice quivering. "But please—" he pulls his tattered shirt over his head and gently covers Lyra's bare chest with it "—allow me to give her this. Let her keep it with her, no matter where you take her."

Casimir watches Gray silently for a long moment. "Alright," he finally murmurs. "I promise that I will."

And then he turns again, walking away.

"We will find her," Gray calls out. "No matter where you go. No matter where you take her. We will find her, and we will bring her home."

Casimir only spares him a glance over his shoulder. With Lyra still clutched in his arms, he flicks his wrist, and a portal composed of swirling silver, white, and blue blinks open.

And as Finlay watches Casimir step through, taking Lyra with him, all he can do is replay the power he watched the girl wield. It lingers with him like an unattractive scar. Because she, a night attendant with commonblood, possesses arguably the most powerful magic ever seen in the history of the Three Kingdoms.

Just wait until his father finds out.

Oh, how he will laugh.

He will take the knowledge and stab Finlay in the chest with it, twisting the handle deeper and deeper as he stares into Finlay's eyes, reciting like a fond poem all the reasons why Finlay is inadequate—is unsuited to be the Fjolla heir.

Not deigning to consider all that further, Finlay slides his gaze to Draven, who remains slumped on the ground, still unconscious.

When he wakes up…

Gods, when Draven wakes, Merikh's realm of death will seem like a paradise compared to the hell he will wreak on this continent to get her back—*if* he can get her back without sacrificing the only other person he has ever known Draven to love. A person Finlay is almost positive he did not tell Lyra about.

Finlay drops his head and presses a hand to his forehead. When he finally looks up, he catches a glimpse of Casimir and Lyra vanishing into the portal, just before it winks out of existence.

And then they are gone.

CHAPTER SIXTY-TWO

Kiran watches patiently as Draven tears everything apart—ripping curtains from walls, shredding pillows, throwing vases, and shattering every glass piece in sight.

A week has already passed—a brutal set of days not for the faint of heart as so many mourn and grapple with all the devastating loss. Tonight, Bathara holds a requiem for all the fallen stars, and attendance is mandatory for every captain. For Draven, it will be his first time facing the world since Lyra was taken, not leaving his bedchamber after Finlay and Kiran scraped him off the ground—all the fight leaving his body once he learned what happened.

It seems the thought of not only leaving his room, but having to make a public appearance, has sent Draven spiraling.

Though it probably doesn't help Draven's father is also forcing him to attend—to save face— leveraging the card he has always used to make Draven bend to his will.

Gods, Kiran hates that man. Hates all that he's had to watch Draven endure because of him.

Draven continues destroying everything within his reach, sparing only the spread of maps he's been poring over—littered with pins as he attempts to trace Lyra's most likely location—and the official missive he drafted, informing King Alastair he has Selected Lyra to join his aggregate.

Kiran sighs and shakes his head, wondering how the hell he's going to get his brother into the bathing chambers and clean-shaven. Their spare time is dwindling, and it won't be long until Kiran is forced to intervene. Still, in spite of that, Kiran watches Draven with only a single thought—

May the gods help anyone who gets in Draven's way as he fights to get Lyra back.

And may the gods help them all until he does.

EPILOGUE

Dappled sunlight filters through my fluttering eyelids. The sun is piercing—bright and warm and entirely different than how I've ever experienced it before. It's like a hammer to my skull, making my head throb.

I sit up, rubbing at my forehead and scanning my surroundings.

My jaw falls open when I find myself resting in a beautiful garden oasis so elaborate, for a moment, I think I've reached the Hanging Gardens.

But the sight of Casimir Vivaldri stepping into view, slowly kneeling in front of me, handing me a white and lilac-speckled flower—one I do not recognize—assures me I haven't.

I glance at the flower, looking up at him after. "Where am I?"

He smiles, the gesture oddly sincere. "Exactly where you should be."

ACKNOWLEDGMENTS

I've always wondered if I would someday get far enough to write one of these; what the moment would feel like as my fingertips tapped against my keyboard, expressing all the gratitude for those who've helped me along the way.

It feels damn good.

First, I have to give a symphony of thank-yous to Tabatha. Your eye for detail, plot, and character development is unmatched. Neither this story nor its characters would be what it is today without your devotion and love for *A Requiem for Fallen Stars*. From my semi-crazed phone calls to the sporadic, "I'm changing it," moments, you rode the storm with me the whole way—and you did not relent for a single second. So thank you, my editor-in-chief.

To Sharilyn, my fellow anime girlie and lover of all things nerd-culture—thank you for being the best copy editor around. In another life, I'm convinced you were an English teacher who taught grammar for 50+ years.

Milleniah, my vibes girlie, my professional reader, my all-things-trending guru—you are the best professional reader a girl could hope to find. Thank you.

To my fiancè: I love you. Crazy that the next time I write one of these (because now that I have, I never plan to stop), you'll be my husband. Thank you for being there through the highs and lows of my writing. When my self-confidence is shot, you're the one stitching it back together. When I'm buzzing with ideas and practically bouncing off the walls because I'm so sure they're good, you're right there watching me fly. Thank you for spending hours with me discussing names, magic types, systems—there's no other person I could ever imagine walking this path of life with. So, thank you.

To my family, who have no idea I'm doing this but will be damned proud once they find out I am—I love you all. Thank you for keeping my life saturated with humor, sprinkled with sarcasm, and filled with dinners. I know you'll always keep me humble. (But can we at least agree that me being a book nerd is cool now?)

To my sweet, sweet great-grandma Linda—thank you for always encouraging me to write, for making me feel like I was good at it.

And then to you, dearest reader. Thank you for giving *A Requiem for Fallen Stars* a chance. Thank you for giving me a chance. Thank you for giving Lyra and all the other boisterous characters in this story a chance—for letting them into your heart. (I hope they can stay.)

This story would be nothing without you.

And to the version of me, cradled in a tree somewhere, flipping through pages with an enamored heart—knowing your dream was to write your own story someday, but believing you weren't capable of it:

You did it. So be proud.

Don't over-obsess or over-analyze. Don't let your perfectionism blur the lines of the accomplishment. You worked your ass off, and you did it—

Which is enough.

Lastly, to my bookish besties, Milleniah, Sharilyn, and Tabatha. Because it started with the encouragement and support of each of you, and it ended with your cheers of triumph.

Thank you.

ABOUT THE AUTHOR

Hazel is simply a lover of words and stories, overflowing with made-up worlds, scenarios, and characters. Ever since she was just a small girl, climbing out of her bedroom window to read on the roof under the stars with her trusted book light (sorry, Mom), she has been enchanted by stories and the art of storytelling. Though her path diverged from the dreams she once weaved with wide-eyes and scribbled about in fluffy purple journals, she has found her way back to the first thing to ever hold her heart: the beauty of make-believe.

Hazel lives in Texas with her equally nerdy fiancé, her fluffy dog-child (who's named after a character from the novel that first truly revealed the beauty in crafting words to her), and the two sweetest cats a pet mom could hope for. Aside from writing, she enjoys playing and coaching sports, watching anime, spending time with her family, and discussing books with her bookish besties.
A Requiem for Fallen Stars is her debut novel.

www.hazelwilkes.com
instagram.com/hazelwilkesauthor